THE POTTER'S THUMB

THE POTTER'S THUMB

A NOVEL

FLORA ANNIE STEEL

GYAN

Published by

GYAN

Gyan Publishing House
5, Ansari Road
Daryaganj, New Delhi-110002
Phone: 011-47034999, 9811692060
E-mail: books@gyanbooks.com

Distribution Network
gyanbooks.com
India, USA, Canada, UK, Australia, France

ISBN : 978-81-212-9180-4 (PB)
First Published, 1894

2nd Impression 2023

Printed at: Gyan Press, Delhi.

THE POTTER'S THUMB
Author: FLORA ANNIE STEEL

THE POTTER'S THUMB

A Novel

BY

FLORA ANNIE STEEL

NEW YORK
HARPER & BROTHERS PUBLISHERS
1894

THE POTTER'S THUMB

CHAPTER I

"'Tis only the potter's thumb, *huzoor*."

As she raised the parti-colored rag covering the child's body the noonday sun streamed down upon a pitiful sight. Yet her eyes, despite the motherhood which lay in them, accepted it as the sun did—calmly; emotion, such as it was, being reserved for the couple of Englishmen who stood by; and even there curiosity and repulsion froze the surface of pity, especially in the younger of the two faces.

In good sooth not a pleasant sight for mankind, to whom sickness does not as a rule bring that quick interest born of a desire to aid which it does to most women. The brown skin was fair with the pallor of disease, and the fine, sparse, black hair showed the contour of the skull. The unnatural hollows of the temples emphasized the unnatural prominence of the closed eyelids, round whose ragged margin of clogged lashes the flies settled in clusters. Below this death's-head an over-large body, where, despite its full curves, each rib stood sharply defined, and whence the thin limbs angled themselves in spidery fashion.

"The potter's thumb?" echoed Dan Fitzgerald, interrogatively. He was a tall man, broad in the shoulder, lean in the flank, and extraordinarily handsome; yet the most noticeable quality in the face which was looking down at the very ordinary woman squatting upon a very ordinary dust-heap was not its beauty, but its vitality. "Is that a disease?" he added, almost sharply.

She gave the native cluck of emphatic denial. "No, *huzoor!* The child dies because it does not drink milk properly; yet it is the potter's thumb in the beginning. Lo! many are born so in this place. The doctor *sahib* who put the *tikka* on the arms for small-pox said Hodinuggar was too old for birth—that it was a graveyard. I know not. Only this is true: many are born with it; many die of it."

"Die of the potter's thumb? What potter?"

Her broad face broadened still more into a smile. "The *huzoor* doth not understand. Lo! when the potter works on the clay his hand sometimes slips in the moulding. It leaves a furrow, so"—her brown fingers, set with tarnished silver rings, traced a girdle round the baby's naked breast. "Then in the firing the pot cracks—cracks like these"—here the finger pointed to the shards among which she sat; "so when children are born as this one, we say 'tis the potter's thumb. Sometimes there is a mark"—again the finger softly followed the line it had traced before; "this one had it clear when he came; sometimes none can see it, but 'tis there all the same—all the same. The potter's thumb had slipped; the pot will crack in the firing."

Her voice took a cadence, as if accustomed to the words.

"What *is* she saying?" interrupted George Keene, impatiently. He was a middle-sized lad of twenty or thereabouts, powerfully made, with gleaming gray eyes and white teeth, set in an aquiline, sunburnt face.

"Something ghastly," replied Dan. "It always is so, you'll find, my dear boy, when you dip below the indifferent calm of these people. It's like deciphering a tombstone. But come on; we are due already at the World, the Flesh, and the Devil's." Then he paused, gave a short laugh, and flung out his hands in an impulsive gesture. "By the powers!" he went on, his face seeming to kindle with the fuel of his own fancy; "its grewsome entirely, this heap of dust they call Hodinuggar, as they call thousands of such human ant-hills all over India. Wherever, when you dig, bricks grow bigger and bigger, until, hocus-pocus! they vanish in the dust from which God made man—that is Hodinuggar. The old city, it means. What city? Who knows? Then in the corner of this particular one a survival"—his eager hand pointed to the pile of buildings before them—" not of those old days—for no Mogul in India dates beyond Timoor, and these people are Moguls — but of that Mahomedan civilization which overwhelmed the older one, just as we in our turn are overwhelming the Mogul, who in the meantime bullies the people by virtue of an Englishman's signature."

"But I suppose we found the dewan in possession when we arrived," began George, stolidly.

Dan scorned the interruption and the common-sense. "Ah! 'tis queer, looked at any way. A mound of shards and dust higher than the gateway of the palace. I'll go bail that reed hut yonder on the top is higher than old Zubr-ul-zamân's tower. He lives up there winter and summer, does the old dewan, looking out over his world and the strength of it—that's what his name means, you know. His son, Khushâl Beg, lives in the next story — a Jack Falstaff of a man; that's why I call him the Flesh. Then Dalel, the Devil, roams about below that again, seeking whom he may devour."

"A charming trio; and what part have I to play in the drama?" asked George, with a laugh.

"St. George, of course."

The lad laughed louder. "So I am, in baptism. George for short. Born on the saint's day — father a parson. Fire away, old chap; don't let me pull Pegasus."

"Sure, my dear boy; and aren't you sent to fight them all—sent into this wilderness of a place to be tempted?"

"Oh, don't talk rot, Fitzgerald! I suppose you mean about the sluice-gate; but it's sheer folly."

"Is it? My two last subordinates didn't find it so. Perhaps the potter's thumb had slipped over their honesty. So the authorities gave me you—a real white man. They said it was my last chance. Think of that now, my boy, and be careful."

George Keene frowned perceptibly.

"That's a fine old gateway," he said, to change the subject.

As they approached it a flock of iridescent pigeons rocketed from the dark niches, to circle and flash against the sky. It was a great square block of a building, cut through by one high arch of shadow, showing the length of the tunnel in the smallness of the sunlit arch beyond. On the worn brick causeway as they entered, half in the sunshine, half in the shade, were the scattered petals of a pomegranate blossom, which some passer-by had flung aside.

"By Jove, what a color!" said Fitzgerald; "like drops of blood."

George Keene frowned again. "If I had your diseased imagination, I'd engage lodgings in Bedlam. Seriously I mean it. Fellows as you are get rid of it in words — all froth and fuss; but if that sort of thing ever gets a real grip on me— Hullo! what's that?" He flushed through his tan, in sheer vexation at his own start. From the deep recesses which on either side of the causeway lost themselves in shadow came a clash of silver bells, and among the arches something showed white yet shadowy — something of exceeding grace salaaming to the *sahib logue;* something sending the scent of jasmine flowers into the hot air.

"That is Chândni," said Dan, passing on, regardless; "she generally sits here."

George, imitating his companion, felt the thrill still in his veins. "Chândni," he echoed; "that means 'silvery,' doesn't it?"

"Moonshine also. They call her Chândni-rât, or Moonlit Night, as a rule. If tales be true, a good deal of the night is about her. She and Dalel— But here he comes, innocently, from a side door. The Devil loves moonshiny nights."

The figure approaching them was not outwardly of diabolic mould; it was altogether too insignificant. The oval face was barely shadowed by a thin beard, curling in an oiled tuft on either side of the retreating chin, and the only Mephistophelian feature being the narrow line of mustache waxed upward towards the eyes. The dress was nondescript to absurdity. The biretta-shaped Mogul cap, heavy with church embroidery, sat jauntily on the long, greasy hair; the blue velvet shooting-coat, cut in Western fashion, was worn over baggy white cotton drawers, these again being tucked into sportsmanlike leather gaiters, ending in striped socks and patent-leather highlows. Such was Mirza Dalel Beg, the dewan's grandson. Behind him came lesser bloods of the same type; one with a falcon on his wrist, all with curious eyes for George Keene, the new-comer.

"Hullo Dalel *sahib!*" cried Dan, in English. "Keene! let me introduce you in form to his highness." The mirza thrust out a small, cold, clammy hand; but thereafter relapsed into such absolute inaction that George found no little difficulty in finishing the ceremony.

"Aha, I see!" said his highness, jerkily, in a voice many tones too low for his chest measurement. "Glad to see you, Keene. You shoot, I lend you gun or rifle; you hawk, we go hawk together; you hunt, you use my crocks. Come, see my stable."

Dan's eyebrows went up expressively. "Don't tempt him to-day, mirza *sahib*," he interrupted, gravely, "we are already due at the state-audience with your grandfather. Aren't you to be there, as heir-presumptive?"

Dalel crackled with a high-toned laugh which did not match his voice. "Bosh! My gov'ner is there in swagger dress. He likes, I am different. Good-bye, Keene! You must come often, and we will go shoot, hunt, polo, billiards, and be jolly. Ta, ta! I go to stables."

The two Englishmen walked on in silence for a while, then George Keene looked at his companion with a queer smile.

"So that's the devil—that—that heterogeneous bounder!"

"Heterogeneous bounder is good—parlous good," replied Dan, still gravely; "but here is our reception-party, so for Heaven's sake look dignified and don't shake hands, mind, unless they offer to do so. They know their own rank, you see; you don't know yours—as yet."

The lad as he obeyed orders felt that he knew very little of anything in this strange world, the fact being evident in the surprise with which he noted the squalid appearance of everything he saw; even of the state-room, where on a cane-bottomed chair, set on a filthy striped carpet, a mountain of flesh awaited them. It did not need his companion's whisper to make him understand that it must be the heir-apparent, Khushâl Beg, who came forward to the appointed stripe of carpet, thus far and no farther—and held out his hand.

"The *huzoor* is young," he wheezed, in a stately, dignified voice; "but youth is a great gift; with it even the desert need not be dull. 'Tis only as we grow older"—he paused, and crossed his hands over his fat stomach with a sigh, as if to him the only consolation for age lay there. Dan shot one of his almost articulate looks at his companion as they passed on to a stone stair so narrow that there was barely room for single-file order up the steep steps. Up and up they went, seemingly in the thickness of the wall, with little loop-holes sending a faint light at the turns; up and up, breathlessly, till the party emerged on the roof of the dewan's tower, where in a pavilion set round with arched arcades they found the old man himself, backed by a semicircle of shabby retainers, whose gay clothes showed tawdry in the pitiless sunlight. Yet Dan's whisper of "the world" provoked no smile in his companion.

There was nothing to smile at in Zubr-ul-zamân, old and shrunken as he was—so old that those steep stairs cut him off from his kind; so old that his chin lay upon his breast, his palms upon his knees, as though both head and hands were weary of the world. What his heart thought of the ninety and odd years of life none knew. None could even guess, for the simple reason that Zubr-ul-zamân had never showed that he possessed a heart. Of brains and skill, no lack even now; but pity, love, tenderness? This much was certain—he had never sought them even in others. Yet the English boy had eyes only for that wrinkled, indifferent face, while Dan Fitzgerald, seated in one of the two cane-bottomed chairs set opposite the dewan's red velvet one, explained in set terms why George came to be seated in the other. Not a pleasant tale altogether, even when told, as it was, with official baldness of expression.

Briefly, the sluice-gate of the canal had been opened too often, and the government did not intend it to occur again.

When he ceased, the dewan raised his head slowly, and George felt an odd thrill at his first sight of those luminous dark eyes; a thrill which continued, as, at a sign from the old man, the court-rhetorician, standing surcharged with eloquence at the dewan's right hand, burst into a stream of polished Persian periods which,-hitting the key-note of the empty pavilion, roused a murmurous echo in its arcades.

It reminded George of the general confession in his father's church on a week day, when the choir was absent. One certain note followed by faint efforts after repentance. The fancy, indeed, clung closer to facts than his ignorance of the language allowed him to perceive, as the speech dealt chiefly in regrets for the untoward events in the part which had made it incumbent on "*Gee uff Keene sahib bahâdur*" to languish in the wilderness of Hodinuggar, though doubtless the presence of the said "*Gee uff Keene sahib bahâdur*" would cause that desert to blossom like a rose—despite the want of water. These reiterations of his own name made George feel a sense of unknown responsibility, as a baby might at its own christening. He looked anxiously at Dan, his sponsor; but the latter was now conversing with the dewan in explosive sentences followed by the decorous silences due to mutual dignity, while the attendants brought forward divers round brass trays covered with Manchester pocket-handkerchiefs and laid them at the visitors' feet. George's share consisted of three: one containing dried fruits and sugar; one of various rich cloths topped by a coarse white muslin *puggree;* the third conglomerate. A French clock with Venus Anadyomene in alabaster, some pantomime jewelry, a green glass tumbler; a tin of preserved beet-root, a lacquered tray with the motto "For a good boy," and various other odds and ends. Among them a small blue earthen-ware pot. Was it blue after all, or did a gold shimmer suggest a pattern beneath the glaze? A queer, quaint shape, dumpy, yet graceful. That broad, straight ring around it should have marred its curves, but failed to do so; strange!

how these people had the knack of running counter to recognized rules, and yet—here George was recalled to the present by Dan whispering,

"Take it man! Take it!"

Looking round he saw the latter removing something from a tray, and his own head being full of the blue pot his hand naturally went out towards it.

"No, no!" continued Dan, in the same voice, "the *puggree.*"

"But I've got one already!"

The instinctive greed of the reply made his companion smile even while he explained that the *puggree* was put there on purpose. But as he spoke the dewan signed to an attendant, who, stepping forward, transferred the blue pot to the tray of dried fruits.

"It is nothing," came the courteous voice, setting aside all disclaimers; "our potter makes them."

"I did not know they could put such a good glaze on nowadays," remarked Fitzgerald, yielding the point. "A first-rate piece of work indeed. Does the man live here?"

Khushâl Beg turned to the speaker, breathlessly.

"He is crazy, *huzoor.* The Lord destroyed his reason by an accident. The old wall fell on his house one night and killed his daughter. Since then he lives away, where nought can fall; like the crazy one he is."

The stress and hurry of the speech were evident, but the fat man was still suffering from the stairs.

"Thank the Lord! that's over," said Dan, piously, when the last diminishing tail of escort left them with but one orderly to carry the spoil. "I ought to have warned you about the *puggree*—but there, you might have done worse—the French clock for instance. Come, let's strike home across the mound. I want to show you a dodge of mine in the canal-cut."

He plunged headlong, after his wont, into professional matters, till even George, fresh from college technicalities, could scarcely follow him, and found himself wondering why a man of such vast capacity should have succeeded so indifferently;

for Dan Fitzgerald was not a *persona grâta* at headquarters. To be that a subordinate often has to conceal his own talents, and this man could not even conceal his faults. Some folk are so self-contained that a burden of blame finds no balance on their shoulders; others so hospitable that they serve as hold-alls both for friends and foes. And there was plenty of room for both praise and blame in Dan Fitzgerald's excitable nature.

"What's that?" cried George, suddenly. With the best intentions his attention had wandered; for everything in that circle of dun-colored horizon domed with blue was new to him. Dan paused, listening. An odd rhythmic hum came from the highest hut, which was separated from the others by palisades of plaited tiger-grass which, in the afternoon light, shone like a diaper of gold.

"The potter's wheel!" he cried, his face changing indescribably in an instant. "Come on, Keene, let us see the man who made your first bribe."

He gave no time for reply, but turning at right angles through a gap threaded his way past piles of pots and shards until he ran the sound to earth—to a circle of the solid earth spinning dizzily in front of a man buried to his waist. At least so it seemed, at first, to George Keene's ignorance of potters and their wheels. A circle dazzling at its outer edge, clearer at the centre where something beneath the steady, curved hand shot up, and bulged, then as the whirr slackened, sank into a bomb of clay.

"*Salaam alaikoom!*" came a pleasant voice, as the worker sat back in his seat-hole so as to ease his feet from the treadles. A mild-faced old gentleman with nothing remarkable about him save a pair of shifty eyes; the light hazel eyes seen so rarely in a native's face.

"*Salaam alaikoom,*" returned Dan. "The little *sahib* has never seen a wheel worked. Will you show him?"

"Wherefore not, *huzoor!* The *sahib* could come to none better, seeing we have spun the wheel of life for years—for ages and ages and ages."

The words blended with the rising cadence of the wheel as he leaned forward to the task again—faster and faster, with a swaying motion. Only one thing: the potter's hand, poised motionless above the whirring clay, which showed, as the children say, like a top asleep. Then suddenly the turn of the potter's thumb, bringing a strange, weird life with it. One curve after another, swelling, sucking, shifting, falling. The eye could scarcely follow their swift birth and death until the potter, sitting back once more, the slackening wheel disclosed the hollows and bosses.

"The clay is good," he said, as if deprecating his own skill, "and it fires well."

"When the thumb does not slip," put in Dan, quietly. The potter turned to him in sudden interest.

"The *huzoor* knows the sayings of the people—that is well; it is not often so. Yea! it slips—thus." The wheel still spun slowly, he shifted his hand almost imperceptibly, and a deep furrow scored itself upon the biggest boss. "So little does it," he went on, "a grit clinging to the skin—a wandering thought. It is Fate. Fuzl Elâhi, the potter, cannot help it."

"Fuzl Elâhi?—then you are a Mahomedan?"

He shook his head. "I am as my fathers were. The Moguls call me so, the Hindoos otherwise; but it means the same—the grace of God. By the grace of God, potter of Hodinuggar, since time began. Lo! my fathers and my children are in the clay! I dug a grave in the dust for the boy; the girl dug hers for herself. It was deep, *huzoor*. I search for it always in vain, in vain." The wheel set up its rhythmic hum once more, but the hands lay idle.

"Poor old chap," said Dan, aside. "I suppose he is thinking of the accident; but by the powers, Keene! it is a situation. Seated on a pinnacle—a crazy, irresponsible creator—"

"Ask him if he made the pot, please," interrupted George, brutally. "If I could get a pair I'd send them to the *mater*. Those things are always in pairs, you know."

"Pairs!—you intolerable Philistine! A potter's vessel trying to be matched before it's broken in pieces. Think of the tragedy—the humor of it."

"Will you ask, or shall I?"

Fitzgerald grinned maliciously. "You, I like to hear you stuttering."

George smiled, rose, and taking the blue pot from the attendant's tray, laid it on the potter's wheel.

"Did you make that?" he asked, in English. His meaning was palpable.

"No, *huzoor*."

"If you did not, who did?" he continued, his triumph mixed with anxiety for the future; but the old man's thoughts did duty for an answer.

"Without doubt my fathers made it, since it is an Ayôdhya pot."

"Ayôdhya!" broke in Dan, "that means old, Keene. You'll have to send it back. I half suspected it was valuable from that old ox's look. But he said it was made here—the sinner! Can you make pots like that, O Fuzl Elâhi?"

The old man smiled. "None can give the glaze, *huzoor*—there is a pattern on it, but none can catch the design. Even I know it not; that is the secret of Ayôdhya."

"What *is* he saying? What *is* Ayôdhya," asked George, irritably.

"Same as Hodi—old. The half forgotten heroic age. Well, as you can't get a pair, we had best be moving. *Salaam!* potter—*ji*, and don't let your thumb slip too often in the future."

"Godsend it hath not slipped too often in the past," he replied, half to himself.

An hour afterwards the two Englishmen sat on the low parapet of the canal bridge looking out over a world-circle of dusty plain; treeless, featureless save for the shadowy mound of Hodinuggar on one side, on the other a red brick house dotted causelessly upon the sand. A world-circle split into halves by the Great Canal; eastward, towards the invisible hills, a bar of silver; westward, towards the invisible sea, a flash of gold at whose end the last beams of the setting sun hung like the star on a magician's wand.

"*Water, water everywhere, and not a drop to drink!*" murmured Dan Fitzgerald, discontentedly. "Upon my soul it must be rough on them watching it all day long, and knowing that if they could only get *you* to open the sluice *they* would get rupees on rupees from the rajah. That's how it stands, you see. It isn't so much for their own bit of land, but for the bribe. I sometimes wish the overflow cut had been higher up, or lower down; but we had to protect the big embankment against abnormal floods. Confound the thing! what business has it to put hydraulic pressure on us all."

"Don't feel it much as yet," said George, cheerfully, with his eyes on the palace, which was gaining an unreal beauty from the dust of ages. For the village cattle were returning to the thorn-set folds, and the cloud from their leisurely feet lay in a golden mist between the shadowy plain and the shadowy mound rising against the golden sky. A lingering shaft of light showed the white fretwork of the dewan's tower clear against the pale purple of the potter's thatch beyond.

"Perhaps not; you will, though. The wilderness plays the dickens with civilization sometimes."

"Does it. I don't believe it will with mine. Not that sort; I haven't your imagination, your sensitiveness, your poetical—"

"Pull up," said Dan, laughing, "you'll come to my vices soon, and as I've pet names for most of them, I object to have them scientifically classified. But I wish I hadn't to leave you there," he pointed distastefully to the red parallelogram with the initials of the Public Works Department stamped on each brick, like the broad-arrow on a convict; "it isn't fit for a youngster like you. But as it can't be helped, there's the key. For my sake, don't let the world, the flesh, or the devil wheedle it out of you."

"All right," replied the boy, pocketing the Chubb key. "If you are engaged to be married, go and do it right off. Promotion in due course guaranteed."

Dan Fitzgerald looking down at the sliding water was silent for a minute. "You've hit the right nail on the head," he said, at last. "That's why I'm anxious; but by the powers! your work is cut out for you if you are to keep me from getting into hot water!"

"It isn't the water that does it," muttered George, as they strolled off to dinner; "it's the spirits."

That was the truth in more senses than one. George had been living with his superior officer for two months at head-quarters; and his cool, clear head had noted the fascination which stimulants of all kinds had for Dan's excitable nature. But he had said nothing, after the manner of men. Therefore it came as a surprise, even to himself, when that evening something made him put in, hurriedly:

"Better not, Fitzgerald; you've a long ride before you."

Dan, his hand on the whiskey-bottle, paused, surprised in his turn; but George seemed to feel that key in his pocket outline itself against the thumping of his heart.

"Are you afraid I won't leave you enough?" asked the elder, quickly. "I'll send you a bottle by post, if that's it. Come! hands off, youngster; don't be a fool! That's enough."

The angry red was not on his cheek only. It had spread to the boy's, as he stood back in a sudden flare of utterly unexpected dignity.

"Quite enough, Mr. Fitzgerald. I've been your guest for two months, I know; but you are mine now. This is my house, and that's my bottle. I'll trouble you to put it down."

For an instant it seemed on its way to the speaker's head; then it was pushed aside scornfully; the next Dan held out his hand.

"Thanks! No one has taken that trouble for years. What made you do it?"

The Englishman's shame at his own impulsiveness was on George, and he laughed uneasily. "I—I believe it was that confounded key," he began.

Dan's smile was transfiguring.

"God bless the boy!" he cried, with the ring of tears and laughter in his rich brogue. "So you're the Keeper of the King's Conscience, are you? The saints protect you! for, see, your sort don't know mine. We leave off the effort after virtue where you begin, and I spend more solid holiness in refusing a glass of sherry than you do in keeping all the Ten Commandments. Sure, the sun's got into my head, and I must be off to the water-cure."

He was out of the room, the house, standing on the bridge abutment and stripping as for dear life, before George caught him up breathlessly and asked if he were quite mad.

"Not yet!" came the joyous voice. "I'm going to swim up stream till I'm beat, and come down with the current—an epitome of my life."

The rapid Indian twilight had fallen into night, but the moon had risen, and the air was warm with the first touch of spring, which, in northern India, treads close on the heels of the new year. Fitzgerald, pausing for a second, showed like a white statue on the buttress; then his curved body shot into the shadow with the cry, "I come, mother of all!"

Tristram's cry, when he sprang to "the sea's breast as to a mother's, where his head might rest," thought George, watching the stream with the vague anxiety inseparable from the disappearance of life beneath the water. Ah, there he was, safe!

"Don't wait, please. Tell the *syce* to have the mare ready for me in half an hour."

Yet George did wait—waited and watched the arrowy ripple cleaving the steel-gray path leading straight to the steel-gray sky, where the stars hung sparkling. If they were reflected in the still water ahead as they were in the still water below the bridge, Dan must feel as if he were swimming in the ether!

Decidedly imagination was catching. George Keene was reminded of the fact again as he stood looking over to the mound of Hodinuggar, and listening to the last echo of the horse's hoofs carrying Dan away from the wilderness. There was a light in the dewan's tower, another in the potter's hut; he wondered vaguely which was really the highest. Then to check such idle thoughts, began the first duty of youth in a foreign land—home letters.

"Dear father," he wrote, fluently, "I arrived at Hodinuggar, my headquarters, to-day. It is—" Half an hour afterwards he tore up the sheet angrily, and went to bed.

CHAPTER II

Band night in the public gardens; mail-night also—a combination of dancing and picture-papers, insuring a large attendance in the big hall which had been built, gravely, as a memorial to some statesman. English girls in twos and threes hurried through the dim corridors to the ladies' dressing-room, intent on changing tennis-shoes for dancing-slippers; English women took possession of the comfortable nooks between the pillars, where there was room for two; English boys lounged about the vestibule, finishing their cigars and waiting for the band to strike up; English men drifted to billiards and whist, or to their own special corner in the reading-room.

A weird-looking place even at noon was the big hall, set round with paste-and-paper mementos of historical festivals held beneath its big roof—a shield from the Prince of Wales's ball, a flag from the imperial installation, a trophy from the welcome given to British soldiers after an arduous campaign. But seen now by the few lamps lit at one end, it looked positively ghostly—as if it must be haunted by a thousand memories of dead men, women, and children, who had flitted across the kaleidoscope of Rajpore society.

Up in the gallery the native band, after playing "God Save the Queen" to the Aryan brother outside, was tuning up for dance-music. And by-and-by a couple would come waltzing out of the shadows into the bright reflection of the polished floor, and waltz back again. Then three or four couples—perhaps ten or a dozen; not more. Viewed from the other end, where the non-dancers sat in darkness, the scene looked like a dim reflection of something going on in another world.

And outside, under the rising moon, the builders of the hall trooped home to the packed highways and byways of the native city, full, no doubt, of that silent, ever-green wonder at the strange customs of the ruling race which is an integral part of native life; that ruling race which, with all its eccentricities, rules better than even the fabled Vicramiditya himself!

In the far corner of the reading-room a girl about twenty stood looking at the new number of the *Scientific American*, keeping a stern watch the while on the present possessor of the *Saturday Review*. A tennis-bat lay on the table beside her, and her workman-like flannels and tan shoes showed what her occupation had been. For the rest, a well-made, well-balanced girl, looking as if she walked well, rode well, danced well, and took an honest pride in doing so. Her face was chiefly remarkable for a pair of beautifully arched eyebrows, and her best point was undoubtedly the poise of her head, with its closely-plaited coif of hair.

A sort of snore, followed by a thud, told that people were passing in and out through the swing-doors of the outer room. Here, however, as befitted the abode of more serious literature, all was peaceful—almost empty, in fact, its only other female occupant being a medical lady, deep in the *Lancet*.

"Oh, Gordon," called a voice from the outer room, "have you seen my daughter?"

"Miss Tweedie is here, sir," replied the young man addressed. "She has been for the last five minutes trying to make up her mind whether to go and dance or brain Dr. Grenfell for keeping the *Saturday* so long."

"Really, Mr. Gordon!" cried Rose Tweedie, aghast. "No, indeed not, Dr. Grenfell! I didn't, really—I mean I was, of course, but I don't now—oh, it's awfully good of you." Then as the apologetic little doctor moved away, pausing to say a few words to a tall, gray-haired man who was entering, she turned aggressively to the offender. "Why did you say that, Mr. Gordon?"

"Why, Miss Tweedie? Because you insisted yesterday that you women preferred the truth, even when it was rude. And it was true. I suppose, as your father wants you, I have no hope of this dance, and I'm engaged for all the others."

Rose Tweedie's eyebrows went up. "How lucky for you—I mean, of course, how unlucky for me." Then she added, in more conciliatory tones, "I'm not dancing to-night; these shoes won't do." She thrust out her shapely foot with the careless freedom of a child.

"I can see no fault," he replied, artfully putting up his eye-glass. "They appear to me quite perfect."

"Your knowledge of women doesn't apparently extend to their understandings," she retorted, quickly, her voice, as usual when she was irritated, showing a trace of Scotch accent. "Oh, father, if you want me to come home, I'm ready."

Colonel Tweedie hesitated. A single glance at him suggested that the late Mrs. Tweedie must have been a woman of strong individuality, or else that Rose had reverted to some ancestral type.

"Not—not exactly, my dear. I only—wanted to—er—speak to you."

"Good-bye, Miss Tweedie," said Lewis Gordon, taking the hint. "Oh, by-the-way, sir (if your daughter will remember I'm a personal assistant, and excuse shop for an instant), Fitzgerald came back to-day from Hodinuggar."

Rose Tweedie's face lit up. "Did he say how Mr. Keene liked it?" she asked, eagerly.

"I'm afraid not; but he can scarcely be expected to like the desert after—Rajpore. I shouldn't—under the circumstances. That's all, sir, except that he reports all satisfactory, so far."

The colonel gave a little cough; it was his way of starting the official machine inside the social one. "I hope, for Mr. Fitzgerald's sake, it—it—er—may remain so. The past scandals have been a disgrace—er—to the department."

"Not to him, though," broke in Rose, hotly. "I think he is quite one of the nicest people I ever met."

"And, what is more, the ablest man we have in our service," added Lewis Gordon, heartily. The girl's face softened at his tone. If he would only speak like that always, instead of simpering and scraping.

"Well, father, what is it?" she asked. The other readers

had drifted away, and the medical lady looked as if even the last trump would not rouse her from the *post-mortem* she was perusing. To all intents and purposes they were alone. Colonel Tweedie gave another little cough — an usual occurrence in private matters — and she repeated her question with quickened interest.

"I want you, my dear, to go and speak to — to Mrs. Boynton. I've—I've asked her to come into camp with us this time."

"Why?"

Pages full of words would fail to give a better idea of Rose Tweedie's mental outlook than this simple interrogation. Briefly she must have a reason—good, bad, or indifferent—for everything. Her father, being her father, had several ready.

"Dacre's wife isn't strong enough to face the sand. You must have a chaperone — I mean another lady; you never need a chaperone, of course, my dear; but if anything happened— Besides, we shall be very busy, and it will be lonely. I thought it better than leaving you at home. It isn't as if she were quite an outsider. She is Gordon's cousin, and he is my personal—"

"The widow of a cousin, you mean," she interrupted, with emphasis — "a cousin he scarcely knew; and he never even saw her till he returned from furlough last year."

"Didn't he, my dear," said the colonel, feebly. "Still, they are relations—call each other by their Christian names, and—"

This time a laugh interrupted him—rather a hard laugh for a girl.

"What a number of cousins the Rajpore ladies must have," she began.

"Not Mrs. Boynton, Rose—not Mrs. Boynton," protested the colonel, with spirit.

"No, I admit it. She is perfectly lady-like. I don't really dislike her a bit."

"Dislike! My dear Rose, who could dislike so—so—"

"I admit it again, father. She is charming. I catch myself watching her, just as if I were in love with her—like all the nice men."

"Really, my dear Rose—"

"Well, dear, why not. She is perfectly sweet. Then she has such tact. Do you know she never allows an ungentlemanly man to fall in love with her. I often wonder how she manages it. It's awfully clever of her." Rose, standing by the fire, shifted a log with her foot, and the sparks flew upward. "Of course I would rather have had a girl; but I suppose it wouldn't have done. There, don't worry! Go off to your whist. I'll settle it all."

"My dear girl—"

She told him calmly that there was no need for gratitude, and Colonel James Tweedie, R.E., head of a great department, slunk away, abashed, to the card-room. Rose was very fond of her father, though she understood him perfectly, after the manner of modern children, accepting him reasonably, with all his weaknesses, as the parent Providence had assigned to her. And why, if she would have him, should he not marry Mrs. Boynton? The mother who had died when Rose was born had been well remembered; the colonel was still middle-aged, and when his daughter married might have long years of solitude before him. Would it be fair for her to object? It was another of Rose Tweedie's characteristics that this question came uppermost in her dealings with both friends and foes. No! it would not be fair; there was no reason against it. None.

So she walked off calmly to the big hall, waiting to see Gwen Boynton's graceful figure, paired with some worthy partner, of course, come swaying out into the ring of light. But she was disappointed, for the very simple reason that the lady she sought was sitting with Lewis Gordon in the most comfortable corner in the whole building.

"Miss Tweedie," said an eager voice behind her, as she stood instinctively marking the rhythm of the dance with one foot, "have you seen Mrs. Boynton? I can't find her anywhere."

She turned gladly. It was Dan Fitzgerald, representing, as he always did, humanity at its handsomest. "So you're back!

No, Mr. Fitzgerald. She is not dancing, anyway; but as those are the last bars, that is cold comfort. What a pity, when you came down to the hall on purpose."

He flushed up like a girl, and she pointed to the gardenia in his button-hole.

"You don't go in for decoration except on state occasions," she continued, "and then you weren't at tennis. I always keep a lookout for you there; that backhanded return of yours from the line beats me. I've been trying it with the *chuprassie* bowling at me, but it doesn't come off somehow. You must teach me when we are in camp."

"Of course I will," replied Dan, cheerfully. Lewis Gordon would have simpered, and said "Delighted, I'm sure." The remembrance vexed Rose by its very appearance—as if it mattered what Gwen Boynton's cousin said or did. And the vexation accounted for the phrasing of her next words. "Mr. Keene sent me a message, didn't he? No? How stupid of him. It was about his *Nature.* I was to have it, and he was to let me know what he wanted me to do with it."

Dan's face, which had shown perplexity, cleared. "Oh, it's the paper you mean. Sure you puzzled me entirely. It is not Nature you want, Miss Tweedie; though, 'tis true, one can't have too much of a good thing."

A distinct compliment, or meant to be one; but Rose listened to it gayly, and five minutes after, despite her shoes, was whirling in and out of the shadows, full of the keen enjoyment which dancing brings to some people.

Lewis Gordon, lounging lazily in his dark corner, noticed her with certain irritated surprise. It was a more inconsequent, therefore a more womanly, action than he expected in a girl who annoyed him by refusing to take either of the two places he assigned to women folk in his Kosmos. There were those of whom wives and mothers could be made discreetly, safely, and those who would be utterly spoiled by the commonplace process. He turned to his cousin, feeling no such difficulty in regard to her classification. Yet in the dim light nothing could be seen save the outline of a small head, a huge fur boa, and long curves, ending in a bronzed slipper, catching the light beyond the shadow in which they sat.

"Shall we not dance?" he asked. "It is the best waltz of the three. Then I could bring you some coffee, and we could rest—on our laurels."

"No, thanks. I was engaged to Mr. Fitzgerald for the last, and I must give him time to cool down." The voice was sweet, refined, careless.

"I believe you are afraid of Fitzgerald!"

There was a touch of hauteur in the sweetness now.

"It is the second time this evening you have hinted at that, Lewis. I suppose—being a sort of relation—you know something of that boy and girl entanglement before I married your cousin. Is it so?"

Her unexpected and unusual frankness took him aback into faint excuse.

"There is nothing to apologize about, I assure you," she went on, regaining her carelessness. "You may as well know the facts. I was engaged to Mr. Fitzgerald. We were both babies, and my people disapproved. Then your cousin proposed, and good sense came to us; for we were not suited to each other. *Du reste*, Mr. Fitzgerald and I are still friends, and he is the best dancer in Rajpore."

There was a pause before he said, quietly:

"Why not be quite frank, Gwen, and say he is in love with you still. Surely that is palpable."

"Perhaps. But I prefer to leave such questions alone, even with my cousin. Especially, since that cousin has done me the honor of telling me many times that he is devoted to me himself."

He smiled at her deft evasion.

"What is the use of any one being devoted to you, Gwen, if you are going to marry Colonel Tweedie?" he replied, half-jestingly.

"I did not know I was going to marry him, but I am certainly going to look after Miss Rose Tweedie in camp—if she will have me. Do you think I shall want a new riding-habit, Mr. Gordon?"

"I really can't help you on that question, Mrs. Boynton."

She bent towards him, so that he could see the laugh pass from her pretty eyes.

"Don't be foolish, Lewis. You have been too good and kind to me for that. You, who know my affairs as well as I know them myself, must see that I have scarcely any choice between marrying again and going home to live with my mother-in-law, or starving in some horrid, poky lodging. How I should hate either! I can't live without money, Lewis; I don't spend much—but it goes somehow. Then my pension as a civilian's widow is but genteel poverty. Clothes are so expensive, to begin with; yet even your best friends don't care for you unless you are well dressed."

The real regret in her tone made him quote a trite saying about beauty unadorned.

"Rubbish!" she interrupted, sinking into her cushions again. "Beauty is like the blue teapot; you must live up to it. I must marry some one who can afford a well-dressed wife. I must, indeed, in common honesty to my future creditors. Personally I should prefer it to the mother-in-law. Besides, if I went home I should never see you again, Lewis. I should not like that—would you?"

If the words in themselves were a direct challenge, they came from the shadow where she sat so daintily, so airily, that half a dozen replies were possible without trenching on sober affirmation or denial. Yet her hearer hesitated. There must always be a time when a man settles whether or no he shall ask a certain woman to be his wife; and this was not the first time the idea of marrying his cousin had occurred to Lewis Gordon. He was not the head of a department, but he was in a fair way to become one in the future. He had money of his own, and she liked him in a way. As for her, she was perfection as a companion. As a wife?—

"My dear Gwen! I should hate it," he said, fervently, being certain of so much. But when he had said the words they sounded too little, or too much, so he took refuge in jest again. "*Faute de mieux* I should prefer the family party; that is to say, if you could induce your future step-daughter, Miss Rose, to bear with my presence."

The light on the bronze slipper shifted, showing an impatient movement of the pretty foot.

"Impossible, I should say," came the voice, airy as ever. "But as you seem to be imitating the barber's fifth brother to-night, why not settle that she should marry? Girls do, sometimes, especially in India."

As she spoke a couple swooped out of the almost empty circle of polished floor. The waltz, nearing its end, gave them a swinging measure, and those two were dancers indeed. One could not choose but look, until, as the last chord crashed, they stopped, as if petrified, to smile at each other before hurrying away. Lewis Gordon watched them, his hands on his knees, a cynical smile on his face.

"By all means!" he said, languidly. "Suppose we say Dan Fitzgerald, and so get rid of our two *bêtes noires* at once."

Mrs. Boynton started from her cushions and gathered her boa together.

"What nonsense we are talking! Stupid nonsense into the bargain, which is intolerable. I am ashamed of myself. Come, let us have some coffee, and forget our folly."

Her companion rose to accompany her, with a shrug of his shoulders. "I beg your pardon, even though I fail to see the enormity of my offence. Fitzgerald, if he were once settled—"

She interrupted him with a gay laugh. "So you aspire to the barber's office in other ways, and would like to *ranger* your friends. When I am duly installed as chaperone I must consult you on matrimonial questions; but not till then, if you please, Lewis. Ah! there is Mrs. Dacre. I haven't seen her for an age; not since I went to Meerut."

He took his dismissal placidly, as men do in a society where they cannot claim the undivided attention of at least one woman. Besides, Gwen Boynton's chief charm lay in the impossibility of forgetting that—provided she did not wish to do something else—she would be quite as gracious to the person who cut into your place as she had been to you. Furthermore, that he was sure to hold as good a hand, and know the game as well as you did. For Mrs. Boynton, as Rose Tweedie had remarked, admitted no inferior players to her table. Seen now in the full light of the coffee-room, she showed slight and graceful in the soft gray draperies which she wore as half-mourning for the late Mr. Boynton—a perfectly unexceptionable man who, on the verge of retirement, had lost all the savings of a long bachelorhood in one unfortunate venture, and had died of disappointment. Beyond a perfectly lovely mouth, and the faultless curves of chin and throat, there was nothing remarkable in her face; nothing, at least, to account for her remarkable charm. That, however, was undeniable; even Lewis Gordon, sipping his coffee outside the circle which gathered round her quickly, kept his eyes upon her. So he noticed her turn more than once to Dan Fitzgerald, who stood at the table waiting to replace Rose Tweedie's tumbler of lemonade. "She is afraid of him," he thought. "I wonder why? Perhaps she hasn't got over her fancy, either; that is the only thing I can think of likely to create a difficulty." Then he went off to button-hole another secretary about business, and forgot even Gwen Boynton.

Yet if he had by chance wandered into the portion of the gardens devoted to zoölogy half an hour afterwards he would have seen something to confirm his suggestion. For the two figures leaning over the iron rail surrounding the ornamental water were those of Mrs. Boynton and Dan Fitzgerald. The moon shone on the water; the clumps of bamboo and plantains on the central island showed softly dark; masses of feathery ferash-trees and the sweeping curves of a sand-hill or two beyond the garden shut out the world. Otherwise not a suitable spot for sentimental interviews, by reason of the ducks and geese, whose sleepy gabblings and quackings were apt to come in unsympathetic chorus to lovers' talk; while the adjutants, standing in pairs side by side, their heads under their wings, were ever suggestive of Darby and Joan. The conversation between these two, however, was sufficiently sensible to stand the test of their surroundings.

"It is really absurd," she said, in, for her, quite a querulous voice. "I accept a pleasant invitation to make myself useful to the Tweedies, who have always been most kind to me—and my cousin; and why every one should jump to the conclusion that I am going to marry a man almost old enough to be my father I cannot imagine. Really the world is too idiotic!"

"You don't lump me in as the world, do you, Gwen?" he answered, in a lower tone. "Surely you make a difference—surely there's some excuse for me, dear. I haven't seen you for six weeks, Gwen; you've been away, remember. And I hurried so for that promised dance which you forgot. Yes, we'll say you forgot it. Then every one is talking of your going into camp with the Tweedies, wondering at your giving up the pleasures, the society, hinting at some reason—"

"If you can't trust me, Dan, that is an end of everything," she interrupted, sharply. "No, don't—please don't; one never knows who mayn't come this way. Do let us be reasonable, Dan. We are not boy and girl now, to squabble and make it up again. You tell me always that I love you—have always loved you—will never love any one else; and perhaps you are right. Isn't that confidence enough for you?" She tried her utmost to keep an even tone, but something made the unwilling smile on her lips tremulous.

"It is, dear, and it isn't," he said, his face showing soft and kindly in the moonlight. "If I were only as sure of the rest of you as I am that you love me! But it was so, Gwen, in the old days. Yet you threw me over. I knew it then, and it made me go to the devil—more or less. For if I had had the pluck to say 'you sha'n't,' you would have been happier. I spoiled your life as well as my own by my cowardice. And I'm as bad as ever now, Gwen—afraid to make you poor. Why don't I speak up, Gwen, instead of waiting for promotion, and making you more extravagant by paying the bills?"

"You needn't have reminded me of that," she cried, hotly; "I'm not likely to forget it."

He stared at her for an instant in sheer downright incredulity. Then he laid his hand on hers sharply, and with the touch something that was neither dislike nor fear, yet which seemed to alarm her, came to her face.

"Don't say that, Gwen! you don't—you can't mean it; for you know it is all yours—that I'd starve to give you a pleasure. Oh, Gwen, if you would only marry me to-morrow you'd never regret it! Why shouldn't you, dear? There's no fear; look how I have got on since you gave me hope two years ago, when I came to you in your trouble. If I had only had the pluck then to marry you straight away—"

"But it was impossible," she broke in, quickly, as if to lure him from the point. "What would people have said?—it was so soon."

"What do I care? But now there is no reason — no reason at all. I'll get my promotion all right; Keene is there at Hodinuggar, so nothing can go wrong again. Gwen, why shouldn't you marry me to-morrow?"

"To-morrow!" she echoed, faintly, yet for the life of her unable to repress that tremulous smile.

"Yes. Oh, my darling, you don't know what the uncertainty means to a man like I am! You don't know — you don't understand. If I only had you to myself, I would not fear anything. And you wouldn't either, if I had the chance of teaching you what it means to a woman to have some one between her and the world—some one to hold her fast—some one—"

She shrank now from his increasing emotion. "Don't! oh don't! you frighten me! And don't be hurt or angry, dear. I've promised to marry you some time; I have, indeed. Oh, Dan, how foolish you are!"

She laid her delicately gloved hand on his arm as he leaned over the railings, trying to hide the bitter pain her look had given him; but he only shook his head.

"You can't make me different from what I am," she went on, almost pettishly; "you can't, indeed!"

"I could, if I had the chance; that is all I ask."

"And you will have it some day, Dan. Perhaps you are right, and I should be happy; only what is the use of talking about it just now? We have settled so many times that nothing can be done until your promotion comes. That will be next year, won't it, if nothing goes wrong at Hodinuggar? Oh, Dan, do cheer up. I have to go out to dinner, and it's getting late; but I'll drop you at the club, if you like. I didn't mean to hurt your feelings—you know that; but you are so impulsive. Dan, do come; the geese are making such a noise I can scarcely hear myself speak."

It was true. Something had disturbed the peace of the pond, for a confused gabbling and quacking filled the air. Dan tried to fight against it for a minute, then with an inward curse gave up the struggle. As they walked back to the carriage Gwen felt grateful to the birds; they had saved the Capitol. For a very little more of Dan's hurt feelings might have made her promise anything; it was her way when brought face to face with pain. To make up for what he had suffered, she was very gracious to him as they strolled along the winding walks, set with English flowers and barred cages, where big yellow tiger-eyes gleamed out of the shadows — gleamed quite harmlessly, of course.

But when she returned that evening to the rooms in the hotel which she occupied during the winter months, her mood had changed; for Lewis Gordon had been at the dinner. She went over to her writing-table, took out a bundle of receipted bills, and looked at it with a distaste seldom displayed towards such a possession. How foolish, how wrong, how unfair to poor Dan it had been to let him pay, and what a dreadful tie to her; for, of course, if he did not get his promotion, she could not possibly marry him, and then the obligation would be unbearable. Gwen brooded over the situation by the fire until she felt aggrieved. She was one of those women who, paradoxical as it may seem, gain the power of exciting passion by their own absolute lack of comprehension as to its first principles. To say she had no heart would be an unkind calumny. She was really very fond of Dan—more fond of him when he was absent, perhaps, than when he was present; but she had not the remotest conception of what her love meant to him. So as she sat thinking of him in her seamless dress — Gwen's evening dresses always had a seamless look, and the lace about her fair shoulders always seemed pinned on with cunning little diamond brooches glittering and sparkling — she told herself that it all depended on promotion, and that, in its turn, depended largely on a boy she had never seen, who had gone to live in the desert for the sole purpose of forcing her to keep her promise! A queer tie indeed between that branded bungalow set in the sand and her refined little sitting-room.

And at that moment George, pondering over a cigar on the veranda, before turning in, was meditating, not upon the mysterious mound of the Hodinuggar, with the light in the dewan's tower challenging the feeble flicker in the potter's house, but on something far more mysterious than either— his dinner; that dinner of six courses, compounded out of the desert fowl in various stages of existence, to which his factotum, a man whose imaginative faculty outran his creative power, had given such topsy-turvy yet familiar names. Wherefore? Why was it deemed necessary to feed a *sahib* on salt fish concocted out of chicken and anchovy sauce, and then to give dignified support to the fraud by handing round the conventional egg sauce? George gave up the puzzle, and went to bed depressed by the consideration that if Hodinuggar was strange and unkenned to him, he was quite as strange and unkenned to it.

CHAPTER III

Chândni was standing in the cool recesses of shadow at the farther end of the gateway which adjoined the little strip of bazaar leading past the palace, a bazaar but a few yards long, yet retaining in that small space a specimen of all the vices which in past times had made the Moguls of Hodinuggar infamous. A couple of young men with uncovered heads were dicing on a string bed thrust under a patched, dyed awning stretched from balcony to balcony; a group of half a dozen more were quarrelling vilely over a quail fight, beside the liquor-seller's booth, gay in its colored bottles. Two or three of various ages and heavy with drugs were sprawling and nodding in the gutter. Just across the street a *sutâra* player was twanging away, and above him a girl, powdered and painted, leaned over the wooden balcony, flinging snatches of hideous song on the passers-by, and shrieking with coarse laughter at a naked monstrosity, who, as he begged, made capital of his misfortunes. On this girl, with her grease-smirched hair and Brummagem jewellery, Chândni, from her shadows, cast glances of scorn, which she transferred after a time to Dalel Beg, who sat crouched up against a plinth, smoking a rank *hookah* and sipping a râjah's peg of brandy and champagne (?). He had discarded European dress entirely, and that which he wore smelled horribly of musk.

Against the darkness of the arch behind her the woman's tall figure showed like a white shadow; not a scrap of color anywhere save in her stained lips and the pomegranate spray she twirled idly in her hand as she kept time to the thrum of the *sutâra*, with a clash of the silver anklets hidden by her long gauze draperies—for she wore the Delhi dress.

"Yea, Dalel!" she said, mockingly, and the creamy column of her throat vibrated visibly with the smooth, round voice, "'tis over-true what the little *sahib* said of thy coarse attempt. The pack of us are fools. The *sahib logue's* drink, yonder, steals what brains God gave thee; then Meean Khushâl was never aught but a big belly, and the dewan—Heaven keep him for the best of the lot—sits too high. There remains but Chândni the courtesan, and she—"

"Hath failed!" broke in Dalel, with a forced explosion of malicious laughter. "Lo! thou hast not had a civil tongue for others since he flouted thee. Sure, the plant must be trampled in the dust ere it blossoms. Have patience, heart's delight."

He was too weary even in his malice to seek the amusement of watching the rage grow to her face as she stood behind him.

"Whose fault?" she began, hotly; then with a louder clash of the anklets ended in a laugh. "Lo! 'tis past. And what care I? 'Tis nought to me; but if the treasure-chest of Hodinuggar be empty, 'tis good-bye to Chândni. She goes back to Delhi."

"Nay, nay!" whimpered Dalel, with a maudlin shake of the head, as he sought comfort in finishing the tumbler, "we will succeed yet; but the boy hath no youth in his veins. I know not how to take him as others do, yet have we done our best—"

"Best," echoed the woman, scornfully. "Stale old tricks! A gold mohur under his plate at dinner, forsooth! That was soon over in a beating for the servant who should have seen it put there. A dish of oranges stuffed with rupees which the same servant, wise man, kept for himself. A gun he would not take; a dinner he would not eat; a horse he would not ride; even a woman he would not look at! What care I? there be others who will. Stale old tricks indeed! insipid as uncooled water on a summer's day, or that thing yonder" (she pointed to the opposite balcony) "compared to me—think not I did not see thee ere I came out, O Dalel! Not that I care. There be others, and Delhi is but a day's journey."

"Mayhap the tricks are old," he muttered, in sullen discomfiture; "hast new to advise?"

She laughed. "Not to thee; thou hast not the wit for it. And there is nought new. The crazy potter is right when he saith the world is in the dust. Sure, every ploughman knows that, no matter what the surface be, the sand lies under all. Thou hast but to dig deep enough."

She had moved forward to lean against the plinth. In the action her thin draperies clung to the long curves of her limbs from hip to ankle. Her right hand supported the head which was thrown back against it, the arm framing her face. It was the attitude of the Medea in Pompeian frescos; the face of a Medea also, till the downward glance of her eyes met an upward one from the *sutâra* player. Then with a flash and a laugh the pomegranate blossom flew out into the sunlight and fell at the young man's feet. Dalel clutched at her savagely amid a volley of coarse English oaths.

"Let me go, beloved!" she giggled. "Did I not say the sand lay under all? what! art jealous? jealous of Chândni the courtesan? Wouldst have me *Dalilah* since thou art *Dalel?* If that be so I will put thee in good temper again."

She snatched at an old banjo hanging on a nail, sank down amid her draperies like a cobra on its coil, and began recklessly to sing "Ta-ra-ra, boom-de-ay," while Dalel waggled his head, but half mollified.

"Thou canst not dance it, though," he maundered, sleepily, "not as 'twas pictured in the papers at the Jubilee Institute. Thou art no good at all. I will change thee for a half-caste girl. Yet if there be no money in the treasury? Lo! Fate is hard, and I have done my best."

And still the song of civilization went on, full of incongruous, barbaric intervals. The girl in the balcony retreated in a huff before an accomplishment unknown to her; the quail fighters laughed at the noise. Only George Keene, wandering about one of the inner courts of the palace, seeking a good spot whence to sketch a certain blue-tiled mosque, found himself unconsciously whistling a refrain, and paused to listen in sickening suspense. Yes, it was! Fitzgerald was right when he said that the country was being ruined by culture! What an inconceivable, unthinkable contrast to that quiet ruined courtyard, with its blue tiles decorated in endless writing with the attributes of God. At least, how inconceivable it would have been six weeks ago, when he had first seen the mosque with Dan as his companion. For George Keene was becoming accustomed to being, as it were, depolarized. It would have made him very angry had any one told him that Hodinuggar had already altered his outlook on life, but from its very strangeness it could scarcely have failed to do so. To begin with, Dalel Beg's Occidental follies, grafted on to a sound stock of ancestral vices, made him, as he leered over a billiard cue and tried to induce George to bet, quite a startling study. Not so much so, however, as the sober, gentle, inoffensive villagers, with the confession "It is God's will" forever on their patient lips; content to toil and die, smiling over the fact. Surely something ailed the terminology of religion if these were heathen, and certain Western folk in his father's suburban parish were Christians? Then there was the mad potter in whose walled yard George listened to the oddest Old World tales, and the dewan with whom the lad played chess. To tell the truth, he never climbed up for that purpose to the tower without a breathlessness not altogether to be accounted for by the steepness of the stairs. Face to face with the old man, sitting still as a statue before the pieces, George felt himself face to face with something he could not set aside with a sneer; yet he might have been playing with an automaton for all the interest Zubr-ul-zamân displayed, though he on his part was agonizing in anxiety. But once George's hand had left the piece, the old man's would rise from his knee and hover over the board for a second; then swoop down unerringly with the murmur, "my play is played." The move generally disposed of all George's deep-laid plans; for the dewan was a pastmaster in chess. Yet the lad returned again and again for a beating, being dogged in his turn; he was, in fact, on his way from one when Chândni and the banjo started his thoughts along a familiar channel. Certainly they were odd people, and somehow it was difficult to write home letters which should at once reflect the truth and give satisfaction to the British public.

Meanwhile Chândni, desisting with Dalel's first snore, threw the banjo aside and reviewed the position. There was no mist of reserve between her and her profession; she had been born to it, as her forebears had been. Her success in it was rather a matter of pride than shame, her only anxiety being the future. Should she linger on, as she had been doing, in hope that out of sheer conservatism Dalel Beg would attach her to him permanently by some of the many possible marriages; or should she risk the life of a go-between in her old age; return to Delhi and amuse herself? The reappearance of the painted girl in the balcony decided her. She would not give way to such creatures as that until the emptiness of the treasury was indubitable; yet, as she sat rolling the little pellets of opium for her mid-day dose between her soft palms, she looked at her lover distastefully.

He was no good. If the sluice-gates were to be open that year she must bestir herself; she and the dewan. So much was settled before she swallowed the dream-giver, and threw herself full length on the bare string bed set deep in the shadows. Then the silence of noon fell on that sinful slip of bazaar. Even the quails ceased to challenge from their hooded cages, and the *sutâra* player, with the pomegranate blossom stuck in behind his ear, had forgotten the giver in sleep. But out in the fields the peasants were at work on their scanty crops, and George Keene, as he entered the red-brick bungalow, paused to listen to a cry which never failed to engross him—the cry of praise to the Giver with which the villagers drew water from the wells which stood between them and death. Truly, in that wilderness of sand, water was the Mother of all things. What wonder, then, if it became the motive power in life? What wonder that, like the silver sword of the big canal, it cut the world into halves—the people who wanted, and the people who did not want, the sluice-gates opened. With a laugh at his own fancy he went into lunch, wondering what form the desert fowl would take this time. It certainly was the Mother of all food! Hodinuggar might have its serious aspects, but on the whole it was farcical as well as tragical, and "Ta-ra-ra, boom-de-ay!" counterbalanced the cry of thanksgiving.

And that same evening, while he was reading the last number of the *Nineteenth Century* in the veranda, Chândni had an interview with the old dewan on his tower, which, had George been aware of it, would have seemed to him farcical beyond belief, though it was deadly earnest to the actors. She sat at the old man's feet so as to be within earshot of a whisper, since walls, especially in an Indian palace, have ears. That was why the dewan's chair was set out in the open, under the star-gemmed dome of sky paling to its circled setting of plain, which, seen from that great height, seemed in its turn to curve, cuplike, to meet the sky. The decent domino she had worn on her way was cast aside out of sheer coquetry, so that her supple figure, unadorned save for the heavy chaplets of jasmine flowers shrouding the filmy muslin, might stand outlined above the low parapet among the stars. For Chândni was shrewd. The ordinary jewels of her class might arouse memories in the old man, and she wished to impress him with her individuality.

"Nay, daughter," he said, approvingly, "I well believe failure was not thy fault. As for thy plans—speak."

She drew her lips closer to his ear, and laid one hand on his knee as if to hold his attention.

"Father! all men care for something; he cares not for what he has been given, let us try others. If they fail, well and good. Now there is one thing such as he favor—God knows why, but I have seen them myself at the bazaar at Delhi: *sahibs* who have come over the Black Water to buy ragged rugs and battered brass pots. Why? Because, forsooth, they are old! The crazy potter would say it was because they remember them; I know not. But this boy pokes about the old things, questions of the old tales."

Zubr-ul-zamân nodded approval. "True, he favored the Ayôdhya pot; but he returned it."

Chândni's eyes sparkled. "Lo! that is one thing to begin with. Then he is of those who watch flowers grow and birds build their nests; who paint colors on paper for the love of it. Again, when the fowler fails in all else he baits the snare with pity, and sets a decoy bird a-fluttering within the net. This boy gives quinine to the old wives, and fish-oil to the babies who are born with the potter's thumb-mark!" Her laugh crackled joylessly.

"Words—words!" muttered the old man, impatiently. "What wouldst thou do?"

She drew closer, and the movement sent a wave of perfume from the jasmine chaplets into the air.

"Lend me Azîzan for a week, and then thou shalt see." Scent, so people say, is the most powerful stimulant to by-gone memories; perhaps that was the reason why her words brought such a pulse of fierce life to the old face.

"Azîzan! Nay; she is of the house."

"Why not say of the race, father?" retorted Chândni, coolly. "Nay; in such talk as ours truth is best. Thinkest thou I am a fool when I go to dance and sing in the women's quarter? It is not sixteen years since the potter's daughter disappeared on the night of the great storm; and hath not this fifteen-year-old the potter's eyes? Heaven shield us from them!" Her hand went out in the two-fingered gesture used to avert the evil eye in West as well as East.

Zub-ul-zamân scowled at her.

"There be other girls, and plenty; take them," he began. "Besides, she is betrothed. I will not lose the dower."

"Wherefore shouldst lose it? I said a week; and Zainub, the duenna, will see to safety. He will but paint her picture."

The dewan spat piously. "And what good will such accursed idol-making do?" he asked, more calmly.

"It will bring the quarry within reach; he lives too far away now. Give me the girl, my lord, else will I know that the Dewan Zubr-ul-zamân Julâb-i-dowla Mustukkul-i-jung is afraid of the potter's eyes."

"As thou art, daughter of the bazaar," he retorted, fiercely. "Shall I set them on thee and thine?"

Chândni essayed an uneasy laugh. "I will do her no harm," she muttered, sullenly. "I will not even speak to her if thou wilt. Zainub shall do all."

Half an hour afterwards Chândni, wrapped in her white domino, paused on her way home at the door leading to the women's quarter and knocked. After a while an old woman appeared at the latticed shutter. The courtesan whispered a word or two, the door opened, and the two disappeared down a dark passage. "'Tis Chândni, come to dance." The whisper ran through the airless, squalid rooms, causing a flutter among the caged inhabitants. Out of their beds they came, yawning, stretching, to sit squatted in a circle on the bare floor and watch Chândni give a spirited imitation of the way the *mem sahibs* waltzed with the *sahib logue.* It was not an edifying spectacle, but it afforded infinite satisfaction to the audience—an audience which has to take its world at second-hand, and in the process has grown careless as to the abstract truth. The young women tittered, the old ones called Heaven to witness their horror; and then they all sat without winking an eye, while the courtesan sang the songs of her profession.

But little Azîzan's light eyes saw nothing at which to smile or to cry in either performance. She was young for her years, and very sleepy; besides, she was betrothed to an old man whom she had never seen, because, as all the other girls took care to tell her, she really was too ugly to be kept in the family. And that sort of information is apt to take the zest from life.

When the entertainment was over, Chândni sat and talked with Zainub, the duenna, until dawn, with that careless disregard of bedtime which makes it quite impossible to foretell at what hour of the day or night a native of India will be asleep or awake.

But George Keene, over the way in the branded bungalow, though he had much to do with their conversation, was safely tucked up in sheets and blankets, whence nothing short of an earthquake would have roused him—an earthquake, or else a prescience of the hideous caricature Chândni had been making of the *trois-temps* over in the palace.

CHAPTER IV

George Keene was trying to translate the cloth-of-gold sunlight into cadmium yellow, with the result that the blue of the tiles in his sketch grew green and the opal on the pigeons' breasts as they sidled along the cornice was dimmed to dust-color.

The court-yard, with its blind arcades of Saracenic arches surrounding the mosque, lay bare and empty, as it always did, save at the hours of prayer. He looked across it with a dissatisfied expression, noting the intense color of certain tiles which were mixed up with those more modern ones bearing the Arabic lettering. They reminded him of the Ayôdhya pot, and set him wondering if he should ever have an honest chance of procuring one like his first bribe. The old potter, his authority in such matters, had told him they were still to be found, more or less broken, in the digging of graves or the sinking of wells. Hitherto, however, he had failed to hear of one. Yet the possibility remained, since those tiles, which must be centuries older than the *café chântant* sort of proscenium on which they were inlaid, had survived. The latter, he saw clearly, now he came to draw it, had been added on to an older building behind—probably a Hindu temple. So when all was said and done, that figure of a grave and reverend Mahomedan *moulvie*, which he had intended to put in the foreground, might not have so much right to be there as a priest of Baal. It was a confusing country.

When he looked up again from his work he gave a start, for a totally unexpected model was squatting on the flags of his foreground—a mere slip of a village girl; and yet was she of the village? More likely a stranger—perhaps one of the southern tribes of whom the potter told tales, since her dress was odd. It consisted of a reddish-purple drapery, more wool than cotton in texture, with a stitched border in brown and cream, such as the desert-folk embroidered on the camel trappings—an admirable piece of coloring against that blue background, and he began upon it at once, reckless of the averted face. For he was accustomed now to be thus watched furtively from afar, and knew that the least notice would end in instant flight, as of a wild animal. Besides, the faces were apt to be disappointing. This one, however, was not; and his first glimpse of it gave him quite a shock. Without being beautiful, it was most peculiar—a golden-brown face, with a long, straight nose, and a wide, curved mouth; golden-brown hair under the reddish-purple of the veil; golden-brown eyes; the golden-brown arm, circled with big bronze bracelets, stretched out so that the hand rested on— He gave an irrepressible exclamation and half rose to his feet. Down fell his box and brushes, and over went the dirty water, streaming across his hard-won sunshine. He mopped it hastily with his handkerchief—as hastily as he dared; but when he looked up the girl had gone. He sat down and eyed the spot where she had been suspiciously; not because of her disappearance—there had been time for that—but because he was doubtful of his own eyes in thinking that her hand had rested on an Ayôdhya pot. If so, what a rare chance he had lost; if not, he must be going to have fever, and had better go home and take some quinine—go home, however, *via* the potter's house, and ask that inveterate gossip if he knew anything of an odd-looking child with light eyes.

George gave a low whistle as he remembered those of the potter himself, paused in his packing up of paint-boxes, and looked round again to where the girl had squatted. Doubtless she was a relation of some sort, though the old man had always strenuously asserted that he had none living. Perhaps he had meant no male ones; yet strangely enough Fuzl Elâhi did not seem to share that contempt for girls which all the other natives of George's acquaintance professed. He often talked about his dead daughter, and whenever he talked he became excited and restless. Indeed, fear of thus arousing him made George somewhat reticent in his description, which he confined as far as possible to the dress.

"She is not of Hodinuggar, *huzoor*," declared the old man, confidently. "They who wear wool live far to the south. They never leave the hearth-stone where their fathers lie buried. 'Tis the old way, *huzoor*, and we of this place did it long ago." Suddenly his eyes lit up, he let the wheel slacken, and clasped his hands closely over the dome of clay in its centre. It shot up under the pressure like a fountain.

"Perhaps the *huzoor* hath seen one of the old folk. They come and go, they go and come. I see them often—my fathers, and their fathers. But never my daughter; she will not come—she will not come." As his voice died away the cadence of the wheel recommenced, only to stop again with a jar. "*Huzoor*, have *you* seen her—a slip of a girl, with a fawn face tinted like a young gazelle's? Not black, like these people, but sun-color and brown—all sun-color and brown, with little curls on her forehead—"

For the life of him, George could not help acknowledging the thrill that ran through him. The man was mad, of course—hopelessly mad; yet if he had seen the girl, he could scarcely have given a better description. Perhaps he had seen her, knew all about her, and only pretended ignorance to serve his own ends—that overweening desire, for instance, to pose as one apart from commonplace humanity, at which George alternately laughed and frowned.

"Your daughter is dead, potter-*ji*; how can I have seen her?" he said, rather brutally. Yet what else was there to say with that glaring daylight shining down remorselessly on the squalid reality of the scene?—an ordinary potter's yard; no more, no less; the kneaded clay on the one side of the wheel, the unbaked pots lying on the other. In the outer yard a couple of children were playing in the dust, while their mother sought for a satisfactory ring in one of the pile of water *chatties*, ere bringing it with her to haggle over the price. Overhead a kite or two whirling in circles; and down the slope, visible above the palisade, the palace and its inhabitants. Very ordinary examples, also, of impoverished native nobility in its worst aspect. So George Keene meant to be brutal; his commonsense demanded it of him. But that evening, as he sat smoking as usual in the veranda, he saw a light flickering about the ruins. So, despite the young man's reticence, the potter was in one of his restless moods, when he would seek for his daughter all night long, returning at dawn with a handful of dust, which he would knead to clay, and mould upon his wheel into odd little ninepins. Sometimes he would bury these in pairs upon the mound—George had seen him doing it; more often he would give them to the village children as toys. George had seen them, too, with sticks for arms and bits of charcoal for eyes, doing duty as dolls. He had laughed at the oddity of it all, but now in the soft darkness the memory of it sent a thrill through his veins once more. This would never do! He had been too long mooning about Hodinuggar, sketching and playing chess. It was time to ride down the canal, bully the workmen at the brick kiln, and have a day or two at the *obarra* in the desert, between inspection duty. Then and there he called over to the factotum, and gave his orders for breakfast to be ready twenty miles off the next morning. That would settle his nerves.

When he returned, after four days' absence, he set to work rationally to finish his sketch. The cloth-of-gold sunshine was brilliant as ever, the blue tiles glowed, the prismatic pigeons sidled along the cornice. Hodinuggar was not such a bad place, after all, if you refused to allow imagination—

"The *huzoor* gives medicine to the poor," came a voice behind him. "Mother is ill; I want quinine."

It was the girl with the Ayôdhya pot in her hand. George Keene laughed out loud in the satisfaction of his heart at his own wisdom.

"What is the matter with your mother?" he asked, judicially.

"She is sick; I am to get quinine," repeated the girl. "I came once before, but the *huzoor* jumped up; so I became frightened and ran away. Since then I have come often, but the *huzoor* was not here."

George felt vaguely that he, too, had run away before something ridiculously commonplace and simple, and in the effort to bolster up his dignity his tone became pompous and condescending.

"You are not frightened now, I hope?"

The queerest demure look came to her downcast eyes.

"Wherefore should I be afraid? The *huzoor* is my father and mother."

George had heard the saying a hundred times. Even now, incongruous as it was, it pleased him by its flattering recognition of the fact that his benevolence and superiority were undeniable.

"But, unfortunately, I don't carry quinine with me," he began.

"If the *huzoor* were to bring it to-morrow when he comes to put paint on paper, his slave could come and fetch it," she interrupted, readily. He looked at her more sharply, wondering what her age might be.

"Shall I come, *huzoor?*" she asked, with a certain anxiety on her grave face.

"What else?" he answered, quickly. It would suit him admirably, since he could come armed with rupees wherewith to bribe the Ayôdhya pot from her, and with canvas and oil-color more suitable to the portrait which, as he looked at her golden-brown face and reddish-purple draperies, he resolved to have. He would paint her against the dark mound of the river, rising formless and void upon a sunset sky; and he would call it—

"You had better tell me your name," he said, suddenly; "then I shall know to whom I have to send the quinine in case you can't come."

Her white teeth flashed between the long curves of her mouth.

"I am Azîzan, *huzoor.* I am quite sure to come, and I will bring the pot for the medicine."

It was almost as if she had divined his intention, he thought, as he watched her pass out through the gateway behind him. A queer chance altogether, yet the name Azîzan was familiarly commonplace. Briefly, it happened to be that of his factotum's wife. He had, of course, never seen that inestimable female, but he had often heard her addressed in tones of objurgation when delay occurred between the courses. Thus:

"Azîzan! Egg-sarse. Azîzan, salt fish is not without egg-sarse." From which George inferred that she was responsible for the kitchen-maid's portion of the barmecidal feasts. The remembrance made him smile as he packed up his colors, resolving to do no more till he could begin in earnest on that most interesting study. He would have thought it still more interesting if he could have seen it slipping into the white domino which old Zainub, the duenna, held ready at the gate, where she had been warning off possible intrusion by what was indeed the bare truth—that one of her palace ladies was within. For the custom of seclusion renders intrigue absolutely safe, since none dare put the identity of a white-robed figure to the test, or pry into the privacy of a place claimed by a *purdahnishin*.

"Now mind," scolded Zainub, as they shuffled back to the women's apartments, "if thou sayest a word of this to the girls, thou goest not out again; but the old bridegroom comes instead."

"I will go again," said the girl, gravely. "I liked it. But the sun made my eyes ache without the veil. Yes, I will go again, *amma-jân*" (nurse).

To tell the truth, she had small choice. We have all heard of an empire whereon the sun never sets, and where slavery does not exist. Even those who shake their heads over the former statement applaud the latter. But slavery, unfortunately, is as elusive as liberty; and when not a soul, save those interested in making you obey, is even aware of your existence, individual freedom is apt to be a fraud. This was Azîzan's case. Born of an unknown wrong, she might have died of one also, and none been the wiser. The *zenâna* walls which shut her in, shut out the penal-code. If she had chosen to be prudish, the alternative would have been put before her brutally. But she did not choose. Naturally enough, as she confessed, she liked the masquerade even if the sun did make her head ache. So she sat all that afternoon under the lattice-window, whence, if you stood on tiptoe, you could see the flags in front of the mosque, and thought of the morrow; naturally also, since it was a great event to one who had never before set foot beyond the walls of the women's quarters. Yet George had to wait a long time the next day ere she appeared and squatted down before him confidently.

"It was the black man who came with the *huzoor's* things," she explained, quite openly. "Mother would not let me come while he was here. The *huzoors* are quite different; they are our fathers and mothers."

The repetition of the phrase amused George, and tickled his sense of superiority. It scarcely needed stimulus, for, like most of his race, he was inclined to consider the natives as automata—until personal experience in each case made him admit reluctantly that they were not. So he wondered what certain politicians at home would say to this candid distrust of the black man, produced the quinine, and then offered Azîzan five whole rupees if she would let him draw a picture of her, as he had of the mosque.

"Is that the mosque?" she asked, dubiously. George's reply was full of condescension, which it would not have been had he looked on Azîzan in the light of a girl, capable, as girls always are, of mischief; for the sketch was accurate to a degree. It ended in an offer of ten rupees for a finished picture of that odd, attractive, yellow-brown face. It was now resting its pointed chin on the tucked-up knees, round which the thin brown arms were clasped, and the smile which lengthened the already long curves of the mouth George set down to sheer greedy delight at an over-large bribe — which, to tell the truth, he regretted. Half would have been quite sufficient.

"Then the *huzoor* must really think me pretty!" The words might have been bombs, the sigh of satisfaction accompanying them a thunder-clap, from the start they gave to his superiority. So she was nothing more nor less than a girl; rather a pretty girl, too, when she smiled, though not so picturesque as when she was grave.

"I think you will make a pretty picture," he replied, with dignity. "Come! ten rupees is a lot, you know."

"I'll sit if the *huzoor* thinks me pretty," persisted Azîzan, now quite grave. And her gravity, as she sat with the reddish-purple drapery veiling all save the straight column of her throat, and the thin brown hands clasping the Ayôdhya pot, appealed so strongly to George Keene's artistic sense that he would have perjured himself to say she was beautiful as a *houri* twenty times over, if thereby he could have made her sit to him.

She proved an excellent model, perhaps because she had done little else all her life but sit still with that grave, tired look on her face. So still, so lifeless, that he felt aggrieved when, without a word of warning, she rose and salaamed.

"I must go home now, *huzoor*," she said, in answer to his impatient assertion that he had just begun. "I will come to-morrow if the *huzoor* wishes it."

"Of course you must come," he replied, angrily, "if you are to get the ten rupees. Why can't you stay now?"

Azîzan might have said with truth that a hand from the gateway behind the sketcher had beckoned to her, but she only smiled mysteriously. George, left alone in the sunny courtyard, looked at the charcoal smudges on his canvas with mixed feelings. He had the pose; but should he ever succeed in painting the picture which rose before his mind's eye? To most amateurs of real talent, such as he was, there comes some special time when the conviction that here is an opportunity, here an occasion for the best possible work, brings all latent power into action, and makes the effort absorbing. Something of this feeling had already taken possession of George; he began to project a finished picture, and various methods of inducing his sitter to give him more time. Perhaps she had found it dull. Native women, he believed, chattered all day long. So when she came next morning he asked her if she liked stories, and when she nodded, he began straightway on his recollections of Hans Andersen, choosing out all the melancholy and aggressively sentimental subjects, so as to prevent her from smiling. He succeeded very well so far. Azîzan sat gravely in the sunshine, listening; but every day she rose to go with just the same sudden alacrity. Then he told her the tale of "Cinderella" and the necessity for her leaving the prince's ball before twelve o'clock. But even this did not make Azîzan laugh. On the contrary, she looked rather frightened, and asked what the prince had said when he found out.

"He told her that he thought her the most beautiful girl in the world; so they lived happy ever after," replied George, carelessly.

It was two nights after this that old Zainub, the duenna, paid a visit to Chândni in her shadowy recesses.

"What is to come of this foolishness?" she asked, crossly. "'Twas a week at first; now it's ten days. She used to give me no trouble, and now she sits by the lattice in a fever for the next day—that is the plague of girls. Give them but a glimpse outside, and they fret to death. So I warned Meean Khushâl, sixteen years agone, when the mother took refuge with us, during her father's absence, on the night of the storm. But he listened not when he had the excuse of the wall. Yea! that is the truth, O Chândni. 'Tis well thou shouldst know the whole, since thou hast guessed half. Mayhap thou wilt think twice when thou hast heard. *Ai*, my daughter! I seem to hear her now! I would not pass such another year with this one for all the money thou couldst give. Nor is it safe for me, or for thee, Chândni, with those eyes in the child's head. Let be, 'tis no good. Would I had never consented to begin the work. I will do no more."

"True," yawned Chândni, lounging on her bed. "Thou art getting old for the place; it needs a younger woman, I will tell the dewan so." Zainub whimpered.

"If aught were to come of it, 'twould be different; but thou thyself hast but the hope of beguiling him to some unknown snare within the walls."

"An unknown snare is the deadliest," laughed the other, shrilly. "What care I for the girl. 'Tis something to have him meet a screened inmate of the palace day after day. Many things may come of that. If Azîzan pines, tell her the wedding is delayed, tell her anything."

"Tell her," broke in the old woman between the whiffs of the *hookah*, whence she sought to draw comfort, "*Sobhân ul-lah!* There is too much telling as it is. He tells her—God knows what! Not sensible, reasonable things like the "Tales of a Parrot," about real men and women, but upsidedown rigmaroles about beggar-maidens and kings, and sighs without kisses. Lo, she hath them pat! But now, because I bade her hold her tongue from teasing me when I wished to sleep, she flung out her hands so, quite free-like, saying if she might not speak them she would think them, since they were true words he had told her, and the *sahib logue* ever spoke the truth."

Chândni burst into high-pitched laughter. "So! the little Mogulâni learns fast! 'Tis not strange, seeing the blood which runs in her veins. The cross-breed has but given it strength. Lo! if this be as thou sayest, she would not thank thee for stopping her ears with the cotton of decency. Thus, for the eyes' sake, Zainub, thou hadst best let well alone, and give the girl the rein while thou canst."

In good sooth the old dame felt the truth of Chândni's words, and knew herself to be between two stools. Either by interference, or non-interference, she ran the risk of Azîzan's anger, more perhaps by the latter than the former. So the girl in her odd dress continued to steal out in the fresh morning—for March had come with its hot, glaring noons—to sit between George and the mosque, and to steal back again obedient to that beckoning hand from the gate; Zainub's authority remaining sufficient for that, backed as it was by an ill-defined fear on the girl's part that the fate of Cinderella should befall her before the proper time. There was little conversation between the odd couple, chiefly because Azîzan had none, and seemed to know nothing of her neighbors and the village.

Her mother? Ah, yes! she was better for the quinine. She was a *purdah* woman, no more, no less, and lived yonder—this with a wave of the hand palaceward. Yes, she had heard there was a potter, but she had never seen him. Oh no! they were not related. Her dress? It was very old because they were very poor. Her mother had it by her. It was very ugly. She would rather have Manchester stuff, but they—that is to say her mother—would not give it her. The Ayôdhya pot? That was old also. She had asked her mother, and she was willing to sell it. When the *huzoor* had finished the picture, her mother would come, if she were well enough, and settle the price. If not, the *huzoor* might go "yonder" and speak to her mother. The *huzoor* were their fathers and mothers. It was not like a black man.

This much, no more, George gleaned during the morning hours which passed so swiftly for them both: he, in a novel absorption and pride in the success of his own work; she—it is hard to say. She sat listening while the pidgeons sidled and cooed, the blue tiles glowed, and the blind arcades shut out all the world save George and his stories. They were of the simplest, most uncompromising nature; partly because his sense of superiority made him stoop, unnecessarily, to Azîzan's level; partly because his knowledge of the language, though long past the stuttering stage, did not extend to intricacies of emotion. But loving was loving, hating was hating, when all was said and done. Sometimes the crudity of his own words made the lad smile, as by the aid of his complexity he recognized how entirely they dealt in first principles. Then Azîzan would smile too, not from comprehension, but from first principles also; the woman's smile born of the man's. It was different, however, when he laid down his brush with an elated laugh.

"There, that's done! and you have sat like—like anything. Earned your ten rupees, and— Azîzan, my dear little girl, what is the matter?"

First principles with a vengeance, and the sunlight turning tears to diamonds as they rolled down those sun-colored cheeks. He rose, divided between pity and impatience, and stood looking at her incredulously. "Come, don't cry—there's nothing to cry about. Look how pretty you are in the picture; but it wouldn't have been half so pretty if you hadn't sat so still. I owe you more than the ten rupees, Azîzan, and that's a fact. What shall it be? Money or jewels? What would you like best?"

She did not answer, and with the same careless superiority he stooped and turned her downcast face to his. He was used to turning it this way and that at his pleasure. But this was different. Sun-color and brown! Sun-color indeed! He was only one-and-twenty, and the brightness and the glamour which seemed to fall in a moment on everything, as he saw the heart-whole surrender in her eyes, dazed him utterly. Only one-and-twenty! and he had never before seen such a look as this that came to him from the sun-colored face. But brown also! Truth is truth. It was not a sense of duty, it was a sense of color which prevented him from kissing it then and there. So much may be said for him and his morality, that the difference between a brown and a white skin was the outward sign of the vast inward gulf between sentiment and sheer passion. The transition was too abrupt; for a time it shocked his culture, and brought a look to his face before which poor little Azîzan gave a cry, and fled just as she had fled on that day when George had spilled the dirty water over the sunshine.

He had spilled it now with a vengeance. Over the sunshine of her face had come shame—needless shame.

"Azîzan!" he called after her, his pulses bounding and beating, "Azîzan!" Then he paused since she would not. Besides, there was no need for him to follow her; she would come back, for there, as she had left it, lay the Ayôdhya pot. Yes, she must come back. He could scarcely think of her without it clasped in her thin hands as she sat so silent; yet all the time she must have been thinking. He gave a little laugh, tender, half regretful. Dear little Azîzan! What a brute, what a fool he had been, to bring that look to her face! His brain was in a whirl, he could think of nothing save her shy, confident eyes. When all was said and done, did that world beyond the desert hold anything better, for all its parlance and pretension? Did it not come back in the end to the old ways, to those first principles? More than once he laughed recklessly at his own thought as, scarcely seeing the ground beneath his feet, he made his way homeward to the branded red-brick bungalow.

The factotum was standing in the veranda.

"The *mem sahib* is waiting for the *huzoor*," he said, calmly.

"The *mem!* what *mem?*"

"This slave knows not. She came half an hour gone, and said she would await the *huzoor's* return."

"Wait! where?"

The man pointed to the sitting-room. "In there, *huzoor*. She has since fallen asleep in the *sahib's* arm-chair."

George stared helplessly at the *chick* which, hanging before the open door, prevented him from seeing inside. Who could it be? Rose Tweedie? The mere thought sent the first blush of the morning to his cheek, by bringing him back with a round turn to civilization.

"Here, take these things!" he said, hastily, thrusting the picture and the pot into the servant's hand, "and see! wipe my boots—they aren't fit to be seen."

And as the factotum carefully brushed the dust of Hodinuggar from George's feet, the latter had forgotten everything in wonder as to who the "*mem*" could possibly be.

CHAPTER V

A LADY whom he had never seen before fast asleep in his arm-chair; the arm-chair of bachelors' quarters, which, having served as a deck-lounge on the way out, brings a solitary luxury afterwards to the bare sitting-room.

The present occupant appeared to find it comfortable, for she did not stir. It must be confessed, however, that there was not much to disturb even a light sleeper, for George's entrance was shy, and his surprise sufficient to petrify him for a time. She was dressed in a riding-habit, and a pair of neatly-booted feet rested on the only other chair in the room. Evidently she had made herself quite at home, for a helmet and veil lay with her gloves familiarly beside the cup and saucer set out on the table for the young man's breakfast. Altogether there was an air of proprietorship about the figure which rested in the chair, with throat and cheek sharply outlined against the turkey-red cushions; one hand was tucked behind the fair rumpled hair, the other rested slackly on the knee. This nameless peace increased George Keene's shyness, making him feel an intruder even in his own room, so that he turned instinctively without a word to leave it; as he did so, a glitter on the floor at his feet made him stoop to find a diamond pin. He stepped aside to lay it out of harm's way on the mantelpiece, and in so doing caught a closer view of the half-averted face.

When he had stepped out again on to the veranda he stood with his hands in his pockets and whistled softly, a habit of his when taken aback. A most surprising adventure indeed! An Englishwoman—a perfectly beautiful one into the bargain—at Hodinuggar alone! How on earth had she come there? From Rajpore, seventy odd miles of sheer desert to the north? or from the south? The chief's camp had certainly arranged to cross the sandy strip in that direction, perhaps on its return to look in on Hodinuggar; but that did not account for her being alone.

The factotum having departed to the cook-room, George, in order to avoid calling, strolled thither, intent on further information. In so doing he became aware of his groom at work on a strange horse. The *huzoor* was right, said the man with a grin; it was the *mem's*, and was it to have three, or four *seers* of grain? George, noticing the little Arab's hanging head, suggested a bran mash, and went on feeling as if he had tumbled into another person's dream. Yet no more was to be discovered even from the factotum. The *mem* had come, sent her horse round, and gone to sleep in the *sahib's* arm-chair. Furthermore, what did the *huzoor* mean to do about his breakfast? George, who was, to tell the truth, beginning to feel the pangs of hunger, hesitated between awaking his guest or taking his bath first. He chose the latter, moved thereto by the remembrance that he would be none the worse for a clean collar and all that sort of thing. But half an hour afterwards, when he returned to the veranda with the refreshingly clean look of a newly-tubbed young Englishman, the situation had not improved; it had become worse, for while the lady still slept, George had become ravenous; nor could he turn to his pipe as a palliative, from fear of her waking suddenly to find him reeking of tobacco; for he had always been a bit of a dandy, and fastidious over such things. This did not prevent him, however, from feeling injured, and telling himself that no woman, be she ever so beautiful, had a right to take possession of a fellow's breakfast as she had done. And yet it was not so much her fault as the detestable Indian lack of pantries and larders, which led to every plate and knife, every eatable—save the desert fowl in the cook-room—being, at it were, under the immediate guardianship of the Sleeping Beauty. Even if the store closet had been in the bedroom he might have "vittled free" cff sardines and captains' biscuit; but it, too, was in the sitting-room. And still she slept. At last, in sheer desperation, he determined to wake her, and, raising the *chick*, was beginning a preparatory cough when the sight of the breakfast-table suggested the possibility of a raid. The next instant his shoes were off, and the boyhood in him forgetful of the manhood as he stole in, with his eyes on the sleeper. She had a good conscience and no mistake, he thought, as he annexed the loaf and a tin of sardines. One of the seven sleepers, surely! This reflection came as he passed more leisurely to a pat of butter and a knife and fork, which he piled on the loaf with a spoonful or two of marmalade. Apparently she had no intention of waking for days! This thought led to a cup and some tea from the canister, and finally to a milk-jug, the latter proving fatal, for in returning backward with his *loot* through the *chick* its contents dribbled on to his best suit, and the effort to prevent this overbalanced the marmalade-spoon, which fell with a clatter.

Some people wake to the full enjoyment of their faculties, and with the first glance of those gray-blue eyes George saw that concealment—with half the breakfast-table clasped to his bosom—was impossible. He blushed furiously, and began to apologize, which was foolish, since excuses, if due at all, were clearly owed by the sleeper. She did not, however, make any.

"How kind of you not to disturb me before, Mr. Keene," she interrupted, in a charming voice. "Have you been in long?"

Her coolness increased his apologies. On the contrary, he said he had but just returned; only being in rather a hurry for his breakfast—

"Apparently," she interrupted again. "Dear me, what a very miscellaneous meal it would have been! But as I am awake, hadn't you better put it all down before the marmalade runs into the sardines? Then, as I am quite as hungry as you can possibly be, you might tell the man to bring breakfast."

George, if a trifle taken aback by her nonchalance, felt grateful for the opportunity given with such easy grace of getting at his shoes again before beginning explanations. On his return he noticed that she also had made use of the time to tidy her hair and restore a general daintiness of appearance. As he entered she was stooping to look under the table.

"It is a little diamond pin," she said; "I left it here with my gloves."

"No," he answered quickly, off his guard. "It was on the floor—I mean, it is on the mantelpiece."

"Thanks so much." She took it, gravely, ere going back to the arm-chair; then she looked at him archly.

"Was I snoring dreadfully when you came in the first time, Mr. Keene?"

For the third time since he had become aware of her presence he blushed. "Snoring! oh, dear, no," he began, angrily.

"That is a relief. I was afraid I must have been, to make you perjure yourself so; as if any sane woman could believe that you went about Hodinuggar in that costume! I believe you have been in for hours and hours. I'm so sorry, Mr. Keene, but you will forgive me when you hear my tale of woe."

George, with an odd little rapture at the thought, told himself he could forgive her anything because she was so beautiful.

"I'm Mrs. Boynton," she went on. "You will have heard of me, I expect, from Rose."

He told her he had heard of her from most people at Rajpore, which was the truth; but he did not say, which was also the truth, that their praises of her looks seemed to him miserably inadequate. No doubt, however, she saw this in his eyes, though she had too large an acquaintance with the expression to take any interest in it. Nice boys always admired her immensely, and this one looked very nice, with the beauty of cleanliness on him from head to foot. She detailed her adventures with that confidence in sympathy and help which is such a charm to very young men. To say sooth George deserved it, for he was one of those who are born to stand between their women-folk and that necessity for taking the initiative which —*pace* the strong-minded sisters—most women cordially detest, and which is the cause of half the nervous exhaustion of the present day. So, after a very short time, he took possession of her future even more decidedly than she had taken possession of his bungalow. Briefly, the case lay thus: Colonel Tweedie's camp, owing to the increasing heat, had changed its route slightly, and was due, as the incoming post would doubtless let George know, at Hodinuggar next morning. To do this it had doubled up two marches across the desert into one, so as to include some inspection work before turning at right angles along the canal. Owing to this, and some good sport on the way, every one had started by daybreak through the Bâr; that is to say, a hard waste-land dotted with tufts of gray caper bushes and stunted trees just high enough and thick enough to prevent one seeing more than twenty or thirty yards in any direction; beyond that the clumps became a continuous hedge shutting out the world. Colonel Tweedie and his immediate staff having ridden on in haste, the shooting-party, beguiled by the prospect of *obarra* (big bustard), had spread themselves through the jungle on one side of the track, followed by their horses and grooms. Mrs. Boynton, however, preferring such road as there was, was walking her horse along it in expectation of being rejoined, when the sudden firing of an unseen gun made her Arab bolt—first along the track; then, missing it at a bend, the beast had swerved into some bushes, where a thorny branch had caught in his long tail, making him perfectly unmanageable. After running about a mile he apparently broke into the track again and sobered down to a walk once more, much to her delight. Then a solitary traveller had passed, and assured her, as she imagined, that she was on the right road for the *sahib logues'* camp. So she had trotted on, until fearing there must be some mistake, as the others never turned up, she had been foolish enough to walk her horse back on its tracks, thus completely losing all her bearings, finally, at a fork in the almost invisible path, being forced to confess that she had not the least idea in which direction her destination lay—north, south, east, or west. The sun, therefore, was of little use to her as a guide. (Here her pretty smile grew a trifle tremulous, making George profusely indignant with the desertion.) Then apparently regaining her head, she remembered to have heard Mr. Fitzgerald—who, as Mr. Keene would know, had of course joined the camp on its entrance into his division—say that the more open country lay eastward, and so she had ridden as straight as she could into the shadows, that being her best chance of steering aright. (Here George grew clamorous over her courage.) Nevertheless, it had almost failed, she said, when on a sudden the great silver streak of the canal had appeared from among the bushes, and she had ridden along its banks till she came to a treeless waste with a big mound looming in the far distance.

"I knew it must be Hodinuggar," she finished, with a sort of caress to her own comfort among the pillows, "by Mr. Fitzgerald's description, and I knew you from Rose Tweedie's, so I felt it was all right. And now, Mr. Keene, don't you wonder I didn't snore, considering I had been in the saddle for eight hours!"

George protested it was virtue itself for her to wake at all; but that she would have the whole day to rest, as it was manifestly impossible for her to return to the camp—absurd, also, since it was to come on to Hodinuggar next day. He would send to the dewan and borrow a camel *sowar*, who would ride over with a note to the Tweedies', telling of her safety in the bungalow, and asking for anything she might require. For the rest, all he had was at her service.

"But I shall be turning you out of house and home, sha'n't I?" she asked, kindly.

The young fellow's eyes softened. "I don't think I ever thought of it as a home before," he said, with an embarrassed laugh at his own words. "But won't you come to breakfast? It's awfully nasty, I'm afraid—"

"Then we can fall back on the sardines and the marmalade," she interrupted, gravely. This gravity was with her a perfect art, and gave a great charm to her gentle raillery. Perhaps the food was nasty; if so, George, for one, did not mind, except for her sake. He thought of nothing save her comfort—of how he could welcome her to take possession of everything, himself included. Was she not the most beautiful, the most fascinating, the most perfect woman he had ever seen? Did she not deserve the best he could give her? So while she was writing a note for the camel *sowar*, George slipped away to give instructions to the factotum. The bedroom must be swept and garnished, the things pitched away anywhere. The drawers must be repapered, a towel put on the dressing-table, and—oh! what a beastly hole it was, he thought, as he left the man to his own devices, ruefully. But half an hour later his face cleared, for the factotum, having been in good services, had risen to the occasion. Not only was there a towel on the dressing-table, but two empty beer-bottles had been modestly draped, with the gilt ends of the *puggree* he had received from the dewan, into candlesticks, while the remainder of the muslin was festooned about the looking-glass. Azîzan's portrait stood on the mantel-shelf with the Ayôdhya pot in front, and a dinner-plate on either side; the arrangement being completed by two of his best ties knotted in bows about his hunting-crop and the kitchen fan. A tinsel veil, borrowed from the compounder of "eggsarse," did duty as a bed-spread, supported by his Cooper's Hill tennis-muffler as an anti-macassar. In the middle of the room the factotum still lingered, benign and superior, one hand holding a hammer and tacks, the other a pair of striped silks socks, with the decorative effect of which he was evidently enamoured. In addition, a figure swathed in white sat modestly behind the dressing-room door.

"It is my house," said the man, with a large smile. "Since it is not to be tolerated that the Abode of Princes should lack a female slave, the woman at my command takes the place of *ayah*. The *huzoor* may rest satisfied. Azîzan's (that is my house *huzoor*) knowledge of the *mems* equals this slave's of the *sahibs*."

Azîzan! The smile left George's lips, and before leaving the room he thrust the portrait into a cupboard, replacing it by an illuminated text which was lying neglected under a pile of velocity formulæ.

"The *huzoor* is right," declared the factotum, cheerfully. "The *mems* have them ever in their rooms. Lo! nothing is amiss."

George, as he turned for a last look, felt that the advice "Forsake not the assembling of yourselves together," emblazoned in Gothic characters, adorned holly and mistletoe, which a maiden aunt had sent him as a Christmas present, did indeed put a finishing touch to the solitude of the wilderness.

"But where are you going?" asked Gwen.

"I? Oh, they'll give me quarters at the palace, I expect. Perhaps I had better go over and see about it. Then I've inspection work, and—and a heap of other things. So perhaps I'd better say good-bye. I've told the servants about lunch, and all that sort of thing, and your traps will be here before dark."

A very nice boy, indeed, thought Mrs. Boynton, and showed her thought. So George went over to the palace feeling quite intoxicated because he had been instructed without fail to dine in his own house; and after he had settled about his quarters with Dalel, and had ridden off on his fictitious tour of inspection, he dug spurs into his pony out of sheer lightness of heart, and went sailing away over the desert, careless even of the direction in which he went.

Dalel meanwhile had repaired to the shadowy arches in a state of boastful superiority. His friend Keene was coming over to stop in the palace. They would play cards, and be jolly, and drink. And the lad always carried the key of the sluice-gate on his watch-chain.

"It is a chance, indeed," said Chândni, with a queer look. Then, after a time, broke in on Dalel's vaporings by snatching the banjo from the wall, and breaking into a respectable and plaintive love-song.

"Lo! thou hast thy way, and I have mine," she laughed, recklessly. "Let us see who succeeds best." So, slipping on the decent white domino, she set off for the palace, and turned down the dark passage leading to the women's apartments, since, without doubt, it was a chance which must not be neglected.

Between his desire not to disturb Mrs. Boynton too early, despite her kindness, and dislike to become a prey to Dalel at the palace, George, in the end, had to gallop his pony the last four miles, and then found himself with but ten minutes in which to dress; but he dashed up the narrow stairs leading to the odd little arcaded room placed at his disposal by the dewan, feeling confident in the factotum's forethought; and, sure enough, on the silk coverlet of the high, lacquered bed, lay his dress-clothes and white tie complete; nothing else, except his sleeping-suit. So, choice being denied him, he flung himself into ceremonious black, discovering, as he did so, that two or three jasmine blossoms and a sprig of maidenhair fern had been pinned into the button-hole of his coat. The factotum was evidently determined he should play the right game. He ran down the stairs again laughing, and wondering whence the man could possibly have procured the fern; then remembering to have seen a few fronds clinging far down in the creviced masonry of his well, into which the canal-water filtered. So the seed of this hill-born plant must have come with the water somehow, just as these strange items of knowledge regarding the shibboleth of dress-clothes and button-holes filtered mysteriously into the brains of these odd people. Life was really very amusing, and full of delightful surprises. Yesterday, waiting, without a collar, for a barmecidal feast; to-day, in swallow-tail and button-hole bouquet, going to dine with the most beautiful woman in the world! It was a fairy tale, indeed, with the branded bungalow illuminated out of all recognition, and, inside, more wonders still: a table set out with flowers, and Mrs. Boynton coming forward to greet him with a bouquet of jasmine and maidenhair amid the soft ruffles of her white dress. Then, if humiliating, it was still amusing to be obliged to confess that the attention came, not from his courtesy, but from the factotum's sense of duty. Then the very sight of the man himself, in spotless raiment, lording it over Mrs. Boynton's *kitmutgâr* was pure comedy. In fact when, dinner being over, George was left face to face with three napkin-swathed black bottles hung with foolscap tickets, "Port," "Sherry," "Claret," engrossed in the village school-master's best hand, he gave one look at Mrs. Boynton before exploding into laughter, in which she joined heartily. She would keep the menu, she declared, to her dying day, if only to show the folly of allowing fact to interfere with fancy.

Then by-and-by, when coffee came in, with the factotum diffident over the breakfast-cups, but triumphant over the under footman, with hot milk and sugar on the dinner-plate, they laughed again. Yet the laughter brought a moisture to George Keene's merry gray eyes. In a vague way the boy knew what had happened: knew that the most beautiful woman in the world had not only taken possession of house and home, but of body and soul. And he was glad of it, despite the moisture in his eyes; glad to the heart's core, as he chattered away confidentially while she listened graciously, thinking what a charming boy he was, and what an excellent husband he would make by-and-by for any girl. What an admirable son-in-law, for instance, he would have made had she had a daughter, and had he had money; for women of her sort view mankind chiefly from the matrimonial point of view, to which they give variety by importing into it all their female friends as possible brides.

"That reminds me," she said, as she listened to the hope that she was fairly comfortable, which George tacked on to his good-night. "You have the most fascinating blue pot on your mantelpiece. Where did you get it?"

"Do you really like it?" he asked, eagerly; "if so, you can have it."

"My dear boy," she laughed, "I don't mean to appropriate everything you possess."

He looked at her with shining, happy eyes. "But it isn't mine as yet; it belongs to some one, though, who wants to sell it; and if you would give it to me now I'd finish the bargain to-morrow morning, and you shall have it back by breakfast-time if it is to be had for love or money." The old formula came carelessly to his lips: love or money!

And about the same time, Azîzan, crouching behind one of the palace arcades, wondering when she would hear his footstep on the stair, was echoing the thought in another language. She was trembling all over from excitement and fear and hope —of what she scarcely knew—she did not understand. They had dressed her in her best, beneath the flimsy white veil, pretending to conceal the finery whose effect it really enhanced; so, surely, if he had thought her pretty before in that dreadful old shroud, he would be still kinder now. They had bidden her ask for the Ayôdhya pot, and take him to settle the price with her mother. But of this she was not sure; she was sure of nothing save that she must see him again—must see him to make certain he was not vexed; and then she would tell him that traps were being laid for him; at least, she might tell him. But, come what might, she must see him; aye! and he must see her as she ought to be seen!

Not a very safe thing for George to have found waiting for him in the moonlit shadows of the arcades, had he been in the same mood, even though all the plotting and scheming would have seemed incredibly absurd to him at any time, in any mood. It would have been so even in the dim light of the cook-room, where the factotum was putting away a copy of the menu among his certificates, as proof positive of his acquaintance with the appetites of the ruling race. Even there Chândni's snare would have met with the derision it deserved. But in the dark intricacies of palace politics it seemed simple enough, especially to one of her vile experiences.

But, as it so happened, George never went near the palace. He sat on the canal bridge till dawn, smoking one pipe after another, and looking aimlessly, dreamily, at the dark windows of the red-brick bungalow. No one could have foreseen this—not even the lad himself. He had no intention of outwatching the stars when the balmy air and a feeling of measureless content first tempted him to pause and set aside the forgetfulness of sleep for a time—if, indeed, it could be sleep, yonder, when she was in the desert, with God knows what ruffians. A rage grew up in him at the thought of Dalel and his kind, until the palace itself became distasteful. So, almost before he realized that he was on the watch, the gurglings of many camels, and the thuds of a mallet telling him that the advance guard of the camp had arrived, sent him across to the camping-ground in order to warn the tent-pitchers to be as quiet as possible.

"May the angels of the Lord pitch their tents around us

this night," used to be the favorite bidding prayer of a certain Scotch divine, when he ministered to a volunteer congregation, until one day a veteran happening to be there, said, audibly: "Then I'm hopin' they'll no mak' muckle noise wi' the tent pegs." A tale which shows the danger of imperfect local coloring; a fact which was to be brought home that night both to Dalel and Chândni. Since even then, George did not return to the champagne and the snarer; that incomprehensible love of the picturesque on which the latter had counted keeping him engrossed by the novel sight of a canvas city rising like magic from the bare sand. A novel sight, indeed! First, an autocrat with a measuring tape and pegs mapping the ground into squares; then, one by one in its appointed place, a great ghost of a thing, flapping white wings against a purple sky, to rise stiff and square above a fringe of even, silvery ropes.

It was not till a saffron-colored glint in the east startled him into the thought that he was a confounded ass, that George, out of sheer light-heartedness, ran all the way back and threw himself into the high lacquered bed to fall asleep before the saffron had faded into daylight. Perhaps it was as well, since even the Hodinuggar sun, which had been at work since the beginning of all things, might have stared to see a masher in dress clothes knocking into a Mogul palace with the milk. It stared instead at a more familiar sight: a girl, face down, on a bare string bed in the women's quarter, sobbing as if her heart would break.

CHAPTER VI

Naturally enough, George overslept himself. Naturally, also, he woke to feel himself hustled and bustled, for he was due to meet the incoming camp at the borders of his district at a certain hour—a feeling he proceeded to vent on the factotum for being late with the tea, which that worthy had carried over from the bungalow—an odd little procession, tailing off to the large-eyed village lads and lasses, learning, betimes, the customs of their rulers.

Then, George had promised an answer about the Ayôdhya pot, and now, even by hurrying, which he loathed, he could scarcely find time to seek Azîzan in the old place. Still, he did hurry; and leaving the camel which he was to ride gurgling in the court-yard, wasted five minutes in tramping up and down the flags in front of the mosque; finally, in vexation, returning by the short cut through the bazaar. In these early hours it had a deserted, yet still dissipated air, the few loungers to be seen looking as if they had been up all night. Only the quails challenged cheerfully from their shrouded cages. In the arched causeway, however, he came on Dalel Beg, almost offensively European in costume and manner, for he, too, was bound on reception duty.

"Aha! Keene, old chappie," he began, with a leer, "you sleep well after *burra khana* (big dinner—a feast) with the *mem!* By Jove! you keep it up late."

George could scarcely refrain from kicking him then and there. But the thought that these people had possibly put their own construction on his absence made him feel hot and cold with rage and regret. To avoid the subject—the only course open to him—he hastily held out the Ayôdhya pot which he was carrying, and asked the mirza if he had any idea to whom it belonged.

Now, the mirza's oblique eyes had been on it from the first, but at the question they narrowed to mere slits of compressed cunning.

"Ah! so! very good, I know. Yes! yes! It belongs to you, Keene, of course. Bah! it is worth nothing. I hate old trumpery matters. You are very welcome."

"You mistake, *sahib*," retorted George, haughtily. "This does not, did not, belong to your grandfather. It belongs to an old woman who lives near the palace. She promised to sell it to me, and now I am rather in a hurry to complete the bargain. *Mem* Boynton *sahib* wants it, and they leave to-morrow or next day."

Dalel Beg, who had been turning the pot over and over in his hand, laughed.

"So you say it is other—"

"Certainly, it is another," interrupted George, annoyed beyond measure by his manner. "It belongs, as I said, to an old woman. She has a daughter called Azîzan"—he paused, doubtful of putting Dalel on any woman's track.

"Azîzan!"—the mirza signed his attendants to fall back with unwonted decision before he went on—"Azîzan! Tell me, Keene; a young girl?—with eyes of light, like potters'?"

Evidently he knew something of, and was interested in, the girl, and George, now that it was too late, regretted having mentioned her name.

"Can't wait any longer now, I'm afraid," he replied, glad of the excuse. "Just send one of your fellows up to my quarters with the pot, will you? Thanks. I've no time to lose."

Left thus cavalierly, Dalel Beg scowled after the young Englishman; then, with a compendious oath, turned back to the side door whence he had emerged, and, stumbling in his anger up the dark stairs, appeared again in Chândni's presence. He almost flung the pot beside her as she lay curled up on her bed, and then, driven to words by her arrogant silence, began a volley of furious questions. What mischief had the women been up to? How came it that the English cub had seen Azîzan?—Azîzan who, after all, was his half-sister, one of the race, though they did keep her out of his sight. And that oaf, that infidel! His wrath was real; for, beneath the veneer of modern thought, the fierce jealousy of the Mogul lay as strong as ever.

Chândni gave a jeering laugh. "Thou art too handsome for the maidens, O Dalel! too wicked, also, even for the race. Thou needest one like me to keep thee straight. Lo! there is nothing to know, nothing to tell. Hadst thou asked last night, the answer might have been other. I set a snare and it failed; for thou wert right—the boy is no boy, but a milksop. May Fate send him death, and us a black man in his place! Else I stop not here."

Her jingling feet struck the ground with a clash, and she yawned again. In truth, she was tired of Hodinuggar, and longed for the Chowk at Delhi. Dalel, with a sneer adulterating his frown, looked at her vengefully. "*Wâh!* Thou art a poor creature—putting the blame on others, after woman's way. Thy wiles useless, forsooth, because the boy is a milksop. Then a strange *mem* comes, and he sits drinking wine — my wine, look you, for his servant required it of me — until the dawn; then comes home tipsy, after losing himself among the tent pegs." This was Dalel's version of the incident. It interested his hearer into provoking details by denial.

"It is a lie," she said, calmly.

"Daughter of the bazaars, 'tis true! Did I not wait till nigh three with champagne and devil-bone, yet he came not? Did not his servant tell me but now I had stinted them in wine? Did not the tent pitchers say he wandered like a madman among the pegs? Was he not at me, even now, to get this pot for the *mem*, this woman?" So far his anger had swept him past its first cause, now he remembered and harked back to it. "How came he by the pot, I say? How hath he seen a woman of our race?"

"Ask the dewan," she replied, coolly. "For me that measure is over. I will dance to another tune." And as she spoke, though her feet scarcely shifted, a new rhythm came to these jingling bells. "'Tis odd," she murmured, in a singing tone, as she lifted the pot and held it out at arm's-length, "we come back to this old thing at every turn, and now his *mem* wants it. Leave it with me a space, O Mirza Dalel Beg! I will set it yonder in the niche when I take the seed of dreams; it may bring wisdom to them." Dalel gave a contemptuous grunt.

"Thou art no better than an old spey-wife with thy dreams and omens and fine talk. Sure, the Hindoo pig from whom I took thee hath infected thee with his idolatrous notions."

"See I go not back to them, and him," she interrupted, quickly. "Leave it, I say, if thou art wise. If the *sahib* seek it of thee, say one of thy women knows the owner and makes arrangement. 'Tis true; and thou lovest the truth, O Dalel."

As usual, her recklessness cowed him, and when he had gone and she sat rolling the opium pellets in her palms, the Ayôdhya pot stood in the niche. Something had declared in its favor, and wisdom lay in humoring the mysterious will which, nine times out of ten, insists on playing the game of life in its own fashion. So she lounged back, half asleep and half awake, her hands clasped behind her smooth head, her eyes fixed on the shifting pattern beneath the glaze. The sun climbing up sent a bar of shine through a chink in the balcony roof. It slanted into the recesses, undulated over her curved body, and reaching the niche, made the Ayôdhya pot glow like a sapphire. But by this time Chândni was dreaming, so she did not hear the merry laughter of the cavalcade passing through the Mori gate on its way to the canvas city on the camping-ground; Rose Tweedie on a camel, the English side-saddle perched on the top of a native pad giving her such height that she was forced to stoop.

"Another inch, Miss Tweedie," cried George, gayly, "and you would have had to dismount. You will have to cultivate humility before trying Paradise?"

"Sure, Miss Rose is an angel already," put in Dan Fitzgerald.

But Lewis Gordon rode gloomily behind; partly because he himself was in a shockingly bad temper, partly because the camel he rode was a misanthropist. And these two causes arose the one from the other, since it was not his usual mount. That, when Rose Tweedie had taken advantage of Mrs. Boynton's absence to desert the *dhoolies*, which were the only other alternative conveyance across this peculiarly sandy march, had been impounded for the young lady on account of its easy paces. He remembered those paces ruefully as, with a low-pitched indignation, he wondered why she could not have stuck to the more ladylike *dhoolie.* Yet she looked well on the beast, and rode it better than most men would have done on a first trial—than he would, at any rate. But these were aggravations, not palliations. Still, when on dismounting she came straight up to him, her natty top-boots in full evidence—the huge mushroom-like *sola* hat borrowed from her father making her slim upright figure show straighter and slenderer than ever—he was forced to confess that if she did do these horrible things, she did them with infinite *verve* and good taste.

"I'm so sorry, Mr. Gordon," she exclaimed, eagerly. "Indeed I didn't know of the exchange father made till we had started, or I'd have stuck to the *dhoolie*—indeed I would. What an awful brute it was! I saw it giving you a dreadful time. Do let me send you over some elliman."

"I'm not such a duffer as all that, Miss Tweedie," he began.

"I didn't mean that; you know I didn't. But if you won't have elliman, take a hot bath. It's the next best thing I know for stiffness. You can tell your bearer to take the water from our bath fire. And thanks so much. I enjoyed the ride immensely. Mr. Fitzgerald raced me at the finish, and I beat by a good head."

"A particularly good head, I should say," he replied, out of sheer love of teasing, for he knew how intensely she disliked his artificial manner with women. The fact annoyed him in his turn. It was another of her unwarrantable assumptions of superiority. Nevertheless, he followed her advice about the bath.

Indeed, Hodinuggar for the rest of the day claimed suppleness of joint—in the mind at least. We all know the modern mansion, where, entering a Pompeian hall, you pass up a Jacobin staircase, along Early English corridors and Japanese landings to Queen Anne drawing-rooms; mansions of culture where present common-sense is relegated to the servants' attics. Hodinuggar was as disturbing to a thoughtful person unused to gymnastics; the more so because a certain glibness of tongue in slurring over chasms and ignoring abysses became necessary when, as fell to Lewis Gordon's lot, most of the day passed in interviews: solemn interviews of state, then personal interviews with an ulterior object, finally, begging interviews *pur et simple.* The other members of the camp, however, had an easy time of it, their attendance not being required; Dan Fitzgerald passing most of his day in vain hope of a tête-à-tête with Mrs. Boynton. He was on tenter-hooks to explain the feeling with which, on returning late to camp, he had found it in commotion over her loss; but Gwen, who always dreaded Dan when he had reasonable cause for emotion, avoided him dexterously; chiefly by encouraging George, who was nothing loath to spend his day in camp. At first the lad felt no little vexation at finding himself shy and constrained among so large a party; but it quickly wore off, and when he came ready dressed for tennis into the drawing-tent at tea-time, it seemed quite natural to be once more amid easy-chairs and knick-knacks, to see the pianette at which Rose sang her Scotch songs with such spirit littered with music, and to find her busy at a table set with all manner of delightful things to eat. He was boy enough to try so many of them that Dan had to apologize for his subordinate's greed before they trooped out, laughing, to the very different world which lay beyond the treble plies of the tent—that mysterious veil of white and blue and red which, during the camping months, hangs between India and its rulers.

No doubt the latter have their faults; but the bad name given by superficial observers to Anglo-Indian society is the result of that curious light-heartedness which springs from the necessity for relaxation, consequent on the gloveless hold India exacts on the realities and responsibilities of life. "Let us eat and drink and be merry, for to-morrow we die." This saying is hurled unfairly at pleasure-seekers all the world over, simply because the merriment has become associated with a low type of amusement. Change the verbs, and the blame vanishes; since to live happily is the end and aim of all morality. Then in India the pursuit of pleasure must needs be personal. There are no licensed purveyors of amusement; you cannot go to a box-office, buy tickets, spend the day seriously, dine at a restaurant, and take a hansom to the play; as a rule, you have to begin by building the theatre. So it is in all things; and surely, after a hard day's work in bringing sweetness and light (and law) within reach of the heathen, even a judge with a bald head may unbend to youthful pastimes without breaking the Ten Commandments!

But Colonel Tweedie was not bald, and he played tennis vigorously, in what Rose called the duffers' game, with Mrs. Boynton, the under-secretary, and Lewis Gordon, who pleaded short-sightedness as an excuse for not joining the Seniors against Juniors, where Rose and George challenged all-comers. Yet he owned it was pretty enough to see the former sending back Dan's vicious cuts with a setting of her teeth, ending in a smile either at success or failure; pleasant to see their alertness, confidence, confidentialness; to hear his quick "Look out!" evoke the breathless "I've-got-it," as the ball whizzed to some unguarded spot. It was a fierce struggle indeed, and the wide-eyed villagers who had trooped out to see the strange doings on their ancestral threshing-floor gathered instinctively round the harder game.

"*Ari*, sister!" murmured a deep-bosomed mother of many to her gossip, as they squatted on one of the heaps of chaff which had been swept aside from the hard, beaten floor. "That one in the short skirt is a *bûdmarsh*;* her man will need his hands." Yet an unrestrained chuckle ran round the female portion of the audience as Dan, overrunning himself in a hopeless attempt after the impossible, scattered a group of

* Literally, evil walker.

turbaned pantaloons, who, retreating with shaking heads to re-form farther off, muttered in wondering rebuke, "*Hai! Hai!* does not shame come to her?" But a third section ranged in rows gave an exotic "Hooray!" A ridiculous, feeble little cheer, started by a young man in a black alpaca coat, was accompanied by still feebler clappings; this was the village school with its master, claiming its right to be a judge of "crickets."

"You have the better-half of creation on your side, Miss Tweedie," remarked Lewis, when the games were over, and the men were resuming their coats. "What is more, the rising generation of the worser-half also. The boys were unanimous for the 'Miss,' we miserable men being left to the support of past ages. India is doomed! Another decade will see woman's rights rampant."

She turned on him readily, as she always did. "The boys applauded because the rising generation, thank Heaven, is being taught to love fair-play—even towards women."

"At it again!" interrupted Mrs. Boynton, plaintively. "Really I must get you two bound over to keep the peace."

"Then I shall have to hire another camel for my luggage," said Lewis, gravely, "for Miss Tweedie knocks me and my arguments to bits."

Gwen turned aside impatiently, saying in a lower voice, "How foolish you are, Lewis! One would have thought you would have tired of it by this time."

"On the contrary," he replied, in his ordinary tone. "The bloom is perennial. I wither beneath the ice of Miss Tweedie's snubs, and revive beneath the sun of her smiles like—like a bachelor's button."

And Rose did smile. Her contempt always seemed to pass by the man himself, and rest on his opinions. Even there, much as she loathed them, she was forced to confess that they did not seem to affect his actions; that it was impossible to conceive of his behaving to any woman save as a gentleman should behave. Yet this thought aggravated the offence of his manner by enhancing its malice aforethought, and made her frown again.

"Come, there is light enough for a single yet, Mr. Keene," she said, imperiously, and George, with one regretful glance at Mrs. Boynton, obeyed. Lewis Gordon looked after them, shrugged his shoulders, and strolled off to the mess-room tent.

"It really is shameful of Lewis to tease Miss Tweedie as he does," began Gwen, who, finding herself unavoidably paired with Dan, instantly started what she thought a safe topic of conversation. He looked at her with absent eyes.

"A shame, is it? But when a man likes a girl he is very apt—"

She broke in, with a petulant laugh, "Are you asleep, Dan? What could induce you to think that?"

"What? Why, love, of course! Set a thief to catch a thief. A man can't be in love himself without—"

He certainly was not asleep! But she managed to double back to safer ground. Yet his words recurred to her that evening during the half-hour's tête-à-tête which she accorded with the utmost regularity to Colonel Tweedie in his capacity of host; Rose meanwhile singing songs to the young men who gathered round the piano, leaving those two decorously to the sofa.

"There's a little song I want Mrs. Boynton to hear," called the colonel during the pause. "I forget its name; you haven't sung it for a long time, and I used to be so fond of it. A little Jacobite song—really a charming air, Mrs. Boynton."

Rose flushed visibly—at least, to the feminine eyes in the party—and shook her head.

"But you must remember it, my dear," persisted her father; "do try."

"Oh yes; please do try! I should so like to hear it," echoed Gwen, curiously, her eyes full on the blush. Rose, conscious of it, felt herself a fool, and looked still more uncomfortable.

"Talking of Jacobite songs," remarked an indifferent voice beside her, "I wonder, Miss Tweedie, if you know a great favorite of mine, called 'Lewie Gordon?'—don't laugh, you boys; it's rude. If so, please sing it. I haven't heard it for years; people are always afraid of making me vain."

She gave him a quick, grateful look, as, with a nod, she broke into the song:

"Oh, send Lewie Gordon hame,
And the lad I durna name,
Tho' his back be to the wa',
Here's to him that's far awa'."

She sang with greater spirit than before, a sort of glad recognition of his kindly tact leading up to the decision of the climax—

"Yon's the lad that I'll gang wi'."

And after all, amid the chorus of thanks, she heard him say, in his worst manner, "The lad I durna name! How like a woman!" And he added to the offence; for when the little under-secretary remarked, diffidently, that he had always understood that the song referred to Charles Edward, though whether to the old or the young Pretender he could not say, Lewis murmured, as he dawdled away to his nightly task of breaking up the tête-à-tête, that at any rate it referred to a pretence of some sort. But Rose had caught Gwen's appealing look from the sofa also, and, rising, closed the piano with a bang, and suggested a round game. If her intention was to punish the offender, who hated that form of amusement, she failed ignominiously; for he sat on the stool of repentance with perfect nonchalance, and when it came to her turn paid her such double-edged, charmingly caustic little compliments that she had to join in the laugh they raised. It was, in fact, past midnight ere the colonel, with many allusions to the delight of such company, said they must really go to bed, and they trooped in a body out of the big tent to seek their several quarters.

"I'm glad not to make a casual of you to-night," said Mrs. Boynton, softly, to George.

"I almost wish you were," he replied, giving a rueful look towards the red-brick prison on the farther side of the canal. "This is my home; that is exile."

Dan nodded his head sympathetically: "I know that feeling. It comes from jungle stations. And the bungalow does look cheerless in comparison. Odd; for one naturally associates a camp with wars and tumults, battles, murders, and sudden death—all the evils of a transitory world, in fact. But you must have noticed, Mrs. Boynton, the extraordinary air of peace, security, almost of permanence, which tents have in the moonlight. Look! might they not be solid blocks of marble fastened by silver cords?"

"I noticed it last night, when I was watching them being put up," began George, unguardedly, and Mrs. Boynton looked up quickly. Rose, who was leaning against a rope by the door of her tent, which stood next the mess, glanced along the line of the camp.

"Silver cords and marble blocks!" she echoed. "Yes; but it sounds like the New Jerusalem."

"I always thought," remarked Lewis Gordon, argumentatively, "that it was the tents of Midian; I'm sure some one told me so when I learned hymns. Or was it hosts of Midian and tents of Ishmael? Anyhow, they had nothing to do with paradise, and I, for one, have been prowling round long enough. So good-night, Gwen; don't grow wings in the night, please; it would be so disconcerting. "Good-night, Miss Tweedie."

Being close beside her, he held out his hand.

"Good-night; I hope you are not very stiff."

"I almost wish I were, for then you would sympathize with misfortune like a woman," he replied in a low voice, and as he passed to his own tent next hers, she heard him quoting the lines:

"Tho' his back be to the wa',
Here's to him that's far awa'."

She looked after him, her face showing soft in the moonlight; then, with a good-night to the others, disappeared in her turn.

George lingered, giving still more rueful glances at the bungalow. "I suppose I must be off, too. Oh, by-the-way! it's all right about the Ayôdhya pot. Dalel Beg tells me his women know the owner, so you will have it to-morrow. Good-night, Fitzgerald."

Dan, thus left alone to walk two tent-lengths with Gwen, felt that Fate was on his side at last; more probably she was, since her fine tact told her it was never wise to ignore his passion entirely. Besides, something in her shrank from treating him always as a mere outsider.

"I've been longing for this chance all day," he began at once, in a tone that was in itself a caress.

"Do you think I am quite blind?" she interrupted, a trifle petulantly. "The only wonder is that every one in the camp didn't see it also. You are so reckless, Dan! Of course, you wanted to tell me how you felt when I was lost, and all that—as if I couldn't imagine it;" she gave in to a smile that was almost tender as she spoke. "Why, Dan, I can see you, with a face yards long, and the whole camp, chief and all, under orders in half a minute. Fire-escapes, life-preservers, first aid to the wounded, everything mortal man could desire to avert disaster, ready before the rest had time to think. Do you suppose I don't know what you are, Dan?" The odd composite ring in her voice sank as she added, in a lower tone, "Sometimes I almost wish I didn't."

They had reached the place where their ways separated—hers to the last tent forward, his to the second row—and she held out her hand, smiling, to say good-night. His heart was beating hard at her half-reluctant admission of praise; besides, Gwen Boynton was not the sort of woman who could smile thus, and yet expect to end the interview then and there. Perhaps, again, she did not wish it so to end; in her relations with this man she often found it difficult to know what she did or did not desire.

"Gwen," he said, eagerly, standing close, with his warm, nervous hands clasping hers, "did you think of me—then?—when you knew you were lost, I mean. Did you, Gwen? I don't often ask anything of you, my darling; you might tell me; it isn't much to ask—did you, Gwen?"

She gave something between a laugh and a sob. "Did I? Oh, Dan, you know I did! There, that is enough; you said that was all you wanted. Good-night, Dan."

He went over to his quarters, happy as a king. As for Gwen, the personal influence his immediate presence had over her passed away quickly, and that which his real absence from her life invariably produced did not come to soften the curious dread with which she recognized that, in her trouble of the day before, her first thought had, indeed, been for him. How foolish she had been in letting him re-enter her life at all; but he had come back in her first loneliness when the future had seemed very black. Now it was different; now it was once more that choice between poverty and comfort which she had made in her girlhood, with what pain none save Dan—who, alas! always understood—would believe. And if the choice was necessary then, what was it now with her acquired habits, her knowledge of the world? They would both be miserable if they married without money; and then the thought of the bills came, as it always did, to remind her of the tie they imposed. Even if Lewis, whom she liked and respected, were to make up his mind to marry, she could not accept him without dismissing Dan; yet how could she dismiss him, even for his good, until that money was repaid? Poor Dan! he loved her dearly, and in a way she cared for him as she had never cared for any of her other lovers; and yet the decision which had turned out so comfortably ten years before was still the right decision. Many of those lovers had been as devoted to her, yet they had recovered from their rejection, as he would, doubtless. Then, suddenly, the remembrance of George Keene's admission—that he had been outwatching the stars—made her smile; he was a nice boy, who already deemed her an angel. But Lewis objected to wings, and of the two that was the most convenient—for the woman.

While she was coming sleepily to this conclusion, George had been looking after her interests, for on his return to the bungalow he had been startled by the sudden uprisal of a veiled female from a shadowy corner of his veranda. "I am Azîzan's mother," said a muffled voice. "The mirza sent me; I have been waiting the *huzoor's* return. There is the pot, if the *huzoor* will give ten rupees for it. It is much, yet the pot brings luck."

"Ten!" echoed George in delight, taking it from her. "Yes, you shall have that; then I owe Azîzan something also. Shall I pay yöu for her?"

"My daughter is as myself," replied the voice. "It is five for the picture, and ten for the pot."

George fetched the money, and counted it carefully into the shrouded hand.

"That is all, I think?" he asked.

"*Huzoor*, that is all. May the blessing of the widow and the fatherless go with the merciful Protector of the Poor."

But while he was thinking, as he undressed, how pleased Mrs. Boynton would be, the veiled figure was pausing in the moonlight to speak to the factotum.

"You have seen nothing, you are to say nothing; and the dewan sends these to the servant-people." Then, carefully, came fifteen chinks, this time into a clutching hand; and Chândni, hurrying back to the city, laughed silently to herself. The idea of bribing the *chota sahib's* servants with his own rupees would please Dalel, and put him into a good temper again; so, if this plan matured, her future would ripen with it. As she passed the sleeping camp she paused, wondering in which tent lay the *mem* who had succeeded so easily where she had failed. The lights were out in all save two, and the double row of gleaming white roofs struck even her insensibility with a savage recognition of undeserved peace and security. They were no better than she; no better than those shadowy, crouching figures of the village bad characters, set out here and there to keep watch and ward, on the principle of setting a thief to catch a thief—a plan which at least secures a deserving criminal, should aught occur. For it must never be forgotten that the strange hybrid between altruism and egoism, which we call a scape-goat, first saw the light in the East.

CHAPTER VII

One of the lights Chândni saw came from Lewis Gordon's tent. He was hard at work, not altogether from sheer industry. Sleep with him — oddly enough, in one claiming such serenity of temperament—had to be approached discreetly, and for many days past a disturbing current of thought had required the dam of good solid official business before he could trust himself safely to the waters of Lethe. He had not been constantly in his cousin's company for six weeks without learning to appreciate her infinite charm. She was emphatically a woman to insure a husband's success as well as her own. A man would never have to consider enemies with her at his side, whereas with many others — Rose Tweedie, for instance — it might be necessary to fight your wife's battles as well as your own. This comparison of the two arose from no conceit on his part in imagining that any choice lay with him. Simply he could not avoid comparing the only two women in his daily surroundings. At the same time, he was fully aware that Gwen would marry him if he asked her; and the question which had first assailed him in the hall at Rajpore recurred again and again, disturbing him seriously by alternate attraction and repulsion. He had seen too much of fascinating wifehood to care for possessing a specimen himself; yet Gwen would marry him because she considered it would further their mutual interests, and that, surely, was a more reliable foundation for a permanent contract than a girlish affection. Quite as pleasant, too, as the hail-fellow-well-met liking which seemed to be Rose Tweedie's notion of love; George Keene and she were positively like a couple of boys together. The remembrance jarred, though he went on working with a smile as he thought of her eager readiness to take up the glove on all occasions.

Rose, meanwhile, lay awake next door frowning over the

same fact, and then frowning at her own frowns; since what was it to her if Lewis Gordon were nice or nasty? He himself did not care what she thought, and would end by marrying his cousin; though, in his heart of hearts . . .

Rose sat up in bed angrily. What did she know or care of Lewis Gordon's heart? *Dieu merci!* Gwen Boynton was welcome to it; but she should not drag George Keene captive, as she seemed inclined to; George was too good to hang round a pretty woman, like Lewis . . .

This was intolerable! To escape the tyranny of thought she rose, slipped on her white dressing-gown, lit the lamp she had extinguished, and sat down to read a stiff book till she felt sleepy. The process was not a long one, for she was really fatigued, and ten minutes saw her turning down the lamp once more.

What happened then she scarcely knew; only this: a glare of light — a feeble crash. Then fire in her eyes, her face, her hands; fire at her feet, licking along the carpet and soaking up the folds of her filmy dress. The bed lay close at hand; she was on it in a second, wrapping the blankets round her, and beating out the runnels of flame, with eyes, brain, and body absorbed in the immediate personal danger. When that was over and she looked up she sprang to her feet on the bed with a cry, for the fire was everywhere, creeping up the sides of the tent, filling it with suffocating smoke! She wound her trailing skirts round her and made a dive for the first outlet— for her only chance of escape! The thick wadded curtain, swinging aside, let in a wind, making the smouldering cotton flame; but in the next instant she was out in the open, constrained to pause, wondering if by chance it was nothing but a bad dream. For the camp lay serene and peaceful in the moonlight: not a sound, not a sigh, even from her own tent. She stood, positively irresolute, staring back at what she had left. Was it a dream? Then, suddenly, a faint drift of smoke rose through a crevice in the cloth . . .

"Mr. Gordon! Mr. Gordon!" She burst through the chick, guided by the light in his tent to the nearest help. "Your knife—quick—my tent is on fire! Quick—or the whole camp will catch!"

The blood was flowing from a cut over her forehead, one arm showed bare through the scorched muslin, the draperies caught were singed and blackened, the stamp and smell of fire was on her from head to foot. Lewis started to his feet and stared stupidly at her.

"Oh, quick! Please, quick! Your penknife—anything. Cut down the tents. Mr. Fitzgerald said it was the only plan —the only . . ."

He had grasped the position ere she could finish, snatched up a hunting-knife, and was out, she, with a penknife, close at his heels.

"Good God! how the wind has risen," he muttered, as they ran. "No! not mine. The mess-tent first—the wind is that way."

As they flew past her tent, the scene seemed peaceful as ever, but ere the guy-ropes of the next were reached, a swirl of smoke and flame, prisoned until then by the outer fly of canvas, swept straight up into the sky in the first force of its escape, then bent silently to the breeze. So silently! not a roar, not a crackle; just a pyramid of fire, splitting the tent canvas into long shreds, which the wind flung in pennants of flame on the mess-tent as those two hacked silently at the ropes. There was no time for words, no time for thought. There was a quiver in the solid-looking pile, a shimmer in the moonlight as one rope after another recoiled like a snake from its strain; then a sudden sway, a crash of glass and china from within. Down! but with a creeping trail of fire within its folds.

There was no lack of helpers now — knives, hatchets at work right and left upon the ropes, lest the message of fire should find the tents taut. Colonel Tweedie, shouting confused orders in front; Dan Fitzgerald, after a quick inquiry if all were safely out, shouting clear ones in the rear row, where the danger grew with delay. The din was deafening, yet the flames made no noise. It was dark humanity yelling as it capered over the big tent, treading out the curling snakes of fire. Seen against the glare of a burning pyramid behind, they were like the demons in a mediæval judgment beating the lost souls down to the worm which dieth not.

Rose, standing to rest, now that abler arms were at work, felt a hurried touch on her shoulder, and turned to see Lewis Gordon holding out an ulster which he had fetched from his tent.

"Put it on," he said, unceremoniously, "or you'll catch cold."

She flushed with surprise; then, as she complied, realizing for the first time the havoc fire had made in her dress, continued the blush with an odd feeling of resentment.

"Where is Mrs. Boynton?" she asked, quickly, to cover her confusion. "I suppose you—I mean she is safe, of course."

"Of course. I haven't seen her, though; but I heard your father calling to her. She must be with him. I'll see."

"Mrs. Boynton? God bless my soul, isn't she with Rose?" cried Colonel Tweedie, who was still shouting orders to a crowd of coolies. "She answered me, and her tent is down. She must be out."

"Mrs. Boynton! has any one seen Mrs. Boynton?" Gordon's cry ran down the line without response. "Gwen! Gwen! The fools must have cut the thing down on the top of her." He had dashed up to the mass of ropes and canvas lying without beginning or end in hopeless chaos. "Gwen! Gwen! are you there?"

A muffled cry was audible now in the hush of the workers.

"Not stunned; that's one thing," he muttered to himself before shouting encouragement. Rose was at his elbow and caught his whisper. "The sparks, for God's sake, Miss Tweedie! I trust you. If the tent smoulders she may suffocate before we get to her. Coming, Gwen! coming directly."

But no obstacle against eager help was ever more successful than that tortuous heap of heavy canvas full of blind folds and entangled ropes, stayed fore and aft, and still fastened beyond possibility of removal to the bamboo strengthened sides, and the yet uncut guys. The seekers dived into the folds again and again to find themselves meshed, while Rose, with a sickening fear at her heart lest she should miss one, watched the sparks and shreds drifting by in clouds to settle here, there, everywhere; and as she watched, her swift commands rang out to the little band of helpers.

"Quick! quick! yonder by the corner. Another there! stamp it out! Quick! well done! well done!"

"What is it? What is it?" A new voice, this, above the turmoil. It was Dan Fitzgerald, running from the rear, grasping the truth as he ran.

"No! no!" he panted. "No use, Gordon; too long. Get to the guys, for God's sake! the thickest ropes, and half a dozen men to each. Colonel, the right corner, please, sir. Gordon, the left. Smith, round to the back—they are not cut—and see the pegs hold—they must hold. Miss Tweedie, a man to each stay as the front rises. I want the doorway—the door must show. Brothers," he continued, in Hindostanee, to the men fast falling into place, "we have to raise the tent again. Remember, the tent rises at the word. Gordon, are you ready?—all ready?"

He paused, gave a rapid glance at the sparks, and lowered his voice. "It has to be done sharp, Colonel, or—" Again he hesitated, between fear of letting the prisoner know her imminent danger and fear of not enforcing the necessity for speed. Rose understood the difficulty, and, racked by anxiety as she was, felt a thrill of recognition for Dan's quick thought which, even in such a moment, enabled him to remember that as Mrs. Boynton knew but little of Hindostanee, he could continue in that language. "The tent is certain to catch fire," he went on, "but it may be smouldering now, so we must risk it. Remember that I must get in and out before the canvas yields, or— So be sharp. Gordon, you give the word."

There was an instant's silence, broken by a voice. Then a shout, a heave, and Rose, straining at a rope as she never strained before, felt rather than saw something rise, pause, sink, and rise again, fluttering, swaying.

"Higher! higher!" shouted Dan, standing close in, ready for a dive at the door. "All together, Gordon! *Shâh-bâsh*, brothers. My God! it's caught already!"

A blot of shadow near her showed the coming doorway, and, half-clear as it was, she saw Dan dash into it with the cry, which was echoed from outside as a little runnel of fire quivered up the half-stretched canvas.

"Stand fast! stand fast!" shouted Gordon at the guys. "Run in, half of you, to the bamboos; they may hold longer than the stays."

Rose was at one in a moment, and clung to it, seeing nothing, thinking of nothing but that irregular square of shadow. When would he come through it again? Oh, those tangles within! how would he thread them? For the pole, having slipped from its supporting pegs, had slid along the ground, and would not rise more than half-way. So the inner fly and sides must be hanging in a maze—a maze of smouldering canvas. Horrible! —a burning pall! Oh, would he never come?"

Suddenly, in the tension which seemed to bring a silence with it, there was another cry. A great sheet of fire ran up the right ridge, and the men at the middle guy fell backward under the slackened strain of the parting canvas. Still the corners held. But for how long? Oh, would he never come out?

"Mr. Fitzgerald! Mr. Fitzgerald! be quick; oh, please be quick!"

A foolish, aimless little cry, yet somehow it raised a new idea in her mind. What if he had lost his way in that hideous tangle? She was at the blot of shadow in an instant, calling again and again. Too late—surely too late! for the bamboo lintel to which she clung frantically swayed. Not down yet? Yes, down, and she with it, half-kneeling still. She heard a cry from Lewis, bidding the others run in on the fire and stamp it out, but as she staggered to her feet, still holding the lintel, something else staggered into the open.

"All right!" She heard it plainly, before the great shout of relief rose up, drowning Dan's voice. When it had passed, and they crowded round him, he had set Gwen's feet on the ground and drawn the folds of blanket from her face, though his arm was still round her as she clung to him, scarcely believing in her own safety.

"Only frightened—half suffocated," he went on, struggling to get back his breath. "Couldn't some one bring her a glass of water—don't move yet—they will bring it to you here. It is all over—except the shouting."

Rose, standing aside, giddy with sudden relief, could hardly believe it could be over. Yet the coolies were rubbing themselves and laughing over their sprawl in the dust when the tent collapsed, and the tent itself was blazing away unheeded on the ground. Yes, it was over; and so quickly that George Keene, roused by the crash of the mess-room tent, came too late for anything save sympathy. He gave that to the full; not unnecessarily, for, in truth, the condition of the camp was pitiable. Lewis Gordon's tent, being the only one to windward of the original outbreak, was left standing, but the rest were either smouldering to ashes or severely damaged beyond the possibility of repitching without repair. The extent of other injuries must remain unknown until dawn brought light, and time allowed the fires to die out undisturbed; for any letting in of air while the wind remained so high might bring a fresh blaze.

Colonel Tweedie, looking a perfect wreck in his striped flannel suit, fussed about uncertain and querulous; while George and Dalel Beg, who had arrived from the palace, competed for the honor of putting up the ladies during the remainder of the night; Dalel, minus the least vestige of European attire, being re-enforced after a time by Khushâl Beg, breathless but dignified, bearing the dewan's urgent prayers to be allowed the honor of helping a beneficent government in its hour of need.

Dan, with an impatient frown on his face, waited for decision till his patience failed. Then he button-holed Lewis, who, amid all the wild costumes, looked almost ridiculously prim in his dress-suit, and expounded his views vehemently; the result being that the chief concluded in favor of the palace. If, as was possible, they might be forced into halting for several days, the old pile would hold them all, and a regiment besides. So, after a time, odd little square *dhoolies*, smelling strongly of *attar*, came for the two ladies; and in them, duly veiled from public gaze, they were hurried along, much to their amusement; the gentlemen, after a raid on Lewis Gordon's wardrobe, following suit, all except the under-secretary, who, coming last, found nothing available save a white waistcoat and a pair of jack-boots, in which additions to a pajama sleeping-suit he looked so absurd that the others sat and roared at him (as men will do at trifles when still under the influence of relief and excitement), until George carried him off to his bungalow, promising to return him next morning, clothed and in his right mind. Thus the night ended in comedy for all save Mrs. Boynton. To her, clothes were anything but a triviality, and as she lay among silk quilts and hard, roly-poly bolsters in the little strip of a room to which she and Rose were taken pending the preparation of a state suite up-stairs, she mourned sincerely over the probable fate of her wardrobe. Had it remained in the leather trunks, escape might have been possible; but, knowing they were to halt for a day at least, she had made the *ayah* hang up all the dresses round the tent. Poor Gwen seemed to see them, like Bluebeard's wives, in a row getting rid of their creases, and the thought of the under-garments which might be uninjured in the trunks gave her no consolation.

Rose was more calm, remembering that her riding-habit had, as usual, been removed in order to be brushed, and would most likely be produced next morning. Besides, she was worn out by the excitement, and forgot even the smart of a large scorch on her arm, in the memory of that five minutes during which she had watched for Dan to come out of the fiery maze. Despite her boasted nerves, the stress and strain of it all came back again and again, making her set her teeth and clench her hands. Yet Gwen, who had so narrowly escaped a dreadful death, was grumbling over the loss of her dresses. Rose, lying in the dark listening to the plaintive regrets, felt scornfully superior, not knowing that her companion was deliberately trying to forget, to ignore a like memory—the memory of her own feelings when Dan fought his way to her at last. If that sort of thing went on he would end by marrying her in spite of her wiser self, and then they would both be miserable. She was not a romantic fool, and yet a very real resentment rose up against him as she remembered her own confidence, her own content. She felt vaguely as if he had taken advantage of her fear, and that something must be done to prevent a recurrence of this weakness on her part.

If she could only pay back the money he had paid for her, matters would be easier to manage. As it was, even Lewis, with his easy-going estimate of women, would not stand the knowledge of her indebtedness to another man. Something must be done—something must be changed. That was the underlying grievance which found expression in petulant assertions that Fate was undoubtedly hard in making her fair. Had she been dark, like Rose, the part of Eastern Princess she would have to play until another consignment of civilized dresses arrived from Rajpore would have been fun. As it was, she would look a perfect fright.

She did not, however. Had she not been aware of this fact ere she made her appearance next morning in the long, flowing robes and veil of a Delhi lady, she must have gathered it from the looks of her companions. But she had appraised herself in one of the big mirrors in the suite of state apartments half-way up the stairs, and decided that she would wear a similar costume at the very next fancy ball.

This was in itself sufficient to clear all save immediate care from a mind like hers. In addition, even a stronger character would have found it difficult to avoid falling in with the reckless merriment which had seized on all the other actors in the past night's incident. Partly from relief at its comic ending, partly because of the charm of absolute novelty, the zest of the unexpected enhanced the pleasure of extremely comfortable quarters; for Lewis, in his capacity of personal aide, had decided against the dark state suite of apartments on the second story in favor of the roof above, with its slender balconies, long arcades, and cool central summer-house open on all sides to the air. Here, high above the sand-swirls, safe from the sun, they were far better off than in tents during the growing heat of the day. Gwen, leaning against a clustered marble pillar, looking down on the red-brown slant of windowless wall spreading like a fort to the paved court-yard below, said it was like living on a slice of wedding-cake—a solid chunk below, above, a sugar filigree—whereat George, delighted, assured her that the whole palace itself, viewed from afar, had always reminded him of the same thing. Filigree or no filigree, it was charming, and the central hall of the twelve-doored summer-house a marvel of decoration. Fast falling to decay, no doubt, yet losing no beauty in the process; since the floriated white tracery overlying the background of splintered looking-glass was so intricate that the eye could scarcely follow the pattern sufficiently to appreciate a flaw. Seated there in coolest shadow, you could see through the inner arches to the long slips of arched rooms on all four sides, and through them again to the sky, set in its rim of level plane; save to the north, where the view was blocked by the dewan's tower, rising a dozen feet or more from the terraced roof, with which it was connected by a flight of steps barred by a locked iron grille. Thus the roof lay secure from all intrusion except from the court-yard, whence an outside stair, clinging to the bare walls, gave access to the state-rooms below; and thence, still slanting upward, to the lowest terrace of roof. Rose, leaning over a balcony looking sheer down to where the servants, like ants, were running to and fro over the preparations for breakfast, declared that she would use one of the four little corner rooms of the summer-house as her bedroom. All it needed was a curtain at the inner arch, when it would be infinitely preferable to those dreadful rooms down-stairs, all hung with glass chandeliers, and with mirrored walls, which made her feel inclined to hang herself in sympathy.

"In the hope, rather," suggested Lewis, "of improving the style of the decoration," a remark which brought the usual frown to the girl's face. In truth, Rose Tweedie, in her trim riding-habit, did not suit her surroundings half so well as Gwen Boynton in her trailing, tinsel-decked robe. On the other hand, Colonel Tweedie would have done better in not yielding to the temptation of playing Sultan to Mrs. Boynton's Light of the Harem; for native costume does not suit an elderly Englishman. But the opportunity had been too strong for him.

"My dear father," said Rose, helplessly, when she first caught sight of her parent in a cloth-of-gold coat and baggy trousers. She might have said more had not Mrs. Boynton's grave compliment on his appearance sent the girl away impatiently to lean over the balcony once more, and wonder if they were ever going to bring breakfast.

To her, when he appeared, went Dan Fitzgerald, without even a look at the others.

"Thanks, Miss Tweedie," he said in a low tone. "I hadn't time to say it last night. I *had* lost myself, and your voice gave me the clew. However, it can only be '*thank you*,' and you have that."

Rose, with a smile, let his hand linger in hers for a second as their eyes met. Honest, friendly eyes. And George Keene also passed straight to her.

"Better? That is all right. By Jove, you were bad when I found you outside the fuss when the fire was over; you would have fainted if it hadn't been for the whiskey and water—which, by-the-way, I stole from Gordon's flask—"

"You didn't tell him?" interrupted Rose, quickly.

"Not I. I knew you wanted it kept dark about the scorch. It's better, I hope? Why! you have curled your hair over the cut on your forehead. What a dodge!"

His young face was overflowing with a sort of pride in her pluck when Mrs. Boynton came up. She was in the mood which craves attention, and some of her slaves had passed her by to give Rose the first word.

"What are you two discussing so eagerly?" she began. "Good-morning, Mr. Keene. How delightfully commonplace you look in exactly the proper breakfast costume for a young Englishman."

George blushed. He would have given worlds to say that she looked anything but commonplace, but was too young to venture on it; but he looked the sentiment, and Gwen smiled bewilderingly back at him; she was made that way, and could not help it.

"Isn't it quaint up here?" she went on, leaning over the balustrade and looking, as Rose had been doing, at the servants filing up the steps with silver dishes of sausages and bacon and all the accessaries of an orthodox English breakfast, regardless of the feelings of their pig-loathing hosts. "I declare, I have fallen in love with everything."

"Yourself included, I hope," added Lewis, joining the group. "Or, to put it politely, you have fallen in love with everything, and everything has fallen in love with you. And no wonder. The fact is, Gwen, that you do suit your present environment to perfection. I should not have believed the thing possible—but so it is." As he sat on the coping with his back to the landscape he bent forward, looking at her critically. "No," he went on, "I should not have thought it possible, but you look the part."

"It must be an awful thing to be a native," remarked George, fervently. His eyes were on Colonel Tweedie as he spoke. That conspicuous failure was, however, only partly responsible for his opinion. In a more or less crude form, the childish hymn of gratitude for having been born in order to go to a public school survives wholesomely among young Englishmen.

"I don't know," dissented Gordon, languidly, "a civilized conscience is a frightful interference with the liberty of the subject. Personally, I object to the native view of comfort, pleasure, and all that; but I can imagine some very good fellows preferring them. They are not nearly such a strain on the nervous system. For instance, Gwen, were you really the *shâh-zâdi* you look, there would have been no necessity for sending back those brocades over which I found you weeping half an hour ago. You would have appropriated them without demur; wouldn't she, sir?"

The colonel gave his little preparatory cough, and looked grave.

"It wasn't a brocade, Colonel Tweedie," protested Gwen; "it was simply the most lovely piece of old-gold satin in the world. It stood up by itself, and yet was absolutely invertebrate in its folds. Perfect! The same on both sides, too. I had half a mind to be double-faced myself, and take it when Mr. Gordon's back was turned."

"Why didn't you?" retorted the latter, cynically; you are the only one of us who would not be criminally responsible for the action. Isn't that so, sir?" He was mischievously amused by his chief's evident dislike to the subject.

"Should I be responsible?" asked Rose, surprised.

"Your father would be for your action; wouldn't you, sir?"

This was too much even for reticent dignity. "I—er—don't—I mean, doubtless; but—er—it is not—er—a subject which comes within the range of practical politics."

"I should think not," cried Rose. "My dear dad, fancy your being responsible for my actions! It isn't fair!" Her face of aggrieved decision made the others laugh.

"Perhaps it isn't, Miss Tweedie," remarked Lewis, gravely; "but I can assure you that we officials are all responsible for our female relations in the first degree. A merciful government has, however, drawn the line at cousins; so Mrs. Boynton could only lose her own pension if she was found out."

Gwen made a *moue* of derision.

"That is not much to risk. I wish I had known this before, Lewis! Do you think you could prevail on them to give me another chance with the satin?"

"What on earth is delaying breakfast?" fussed Colonel Tweedie, moving off. He hated persiflage, especially between his guest and his secretary.

"Coming, sir, coming," said George, leaning over to look;

"there is a perfect procession of silver dishes filing up Jacob's ladder."

"Oh, dem silver dishes!" hummed Rose, gayly, leaning over to look too. "How funny it is, isn't it?"

"Funny!" echoed Dan; it is simply appalling."

Perhaps the sudden sense of the utter incongruousness of it all accounted for the silence which followed, as they stood on the balcony which clung like a swallow's nest to the bare wall. Below them, beyond the court-yard, rose the shadowy arcades of the bazaar and the great pile of the Mori gate. Beyond that again the bricks and sand-heaps of Hodinuggar, with the village creeping up to be crowned by the grass palisade where the potter sat at work.

"Talking of bribes," said Dan, absently, after the pause, "I've often wondered how a fellow feels when he has been informed that her gracious majesty has no further need of his services. They seldom go beyond that, nowadays, but it must be bad enough."

"Very much so if the bribe has been insufficient," assented Lewis.

"Mr. Gordon, how can you?" began Rose, pausing, however, at the sight of his satisfied smile.

"You should adopt the sun, with the motto "Emergo," as your crest, Miss Tweedie; it would suit both your thoughts and deeds," he replied, teasingly.

"Don't mind him," put in Dan, "he always was weak in his grammar, and doesn't know that 'rise' must be the correct present tense of Rose."

"But really," persisted Lewis, when the laugh ended, "if a man had taken a bribe, the first thought to one of his *genre* would naturally be if the game was worth the candle. If he *hadn't*—why, dismissal from the public service is not always misfortune. There is the disgrace, of course, but personally I have never been able to understand the sentiment of the thing; it appears to me strained. Half your world, as a rule, dislikes you; it believes you capable of murdering your grandmother at any moment. Yet the fact doesn't distress you. It is inevitable that some people should think ill of you; so why should you care when they invent a definite crime for you to commit? It doesn't affect your friends."

"Well, I don't know," said George Keene, sturdily; "that's all very philosophical, but I believe I should shoot myself."

"No, you wouldn't, old chap, unless you wished people to consider you guilty."

"This conversation is becoming grewsome," put in Mrs. Boynton; "let us change it; though Lewis is right in one thing: government service seems to me a doubtful blessing—"

"But an assured income," interrupted Dan, with a laugh.

Lewis Gordon turned on him quite hotly. "I like your saying that, Fitzgerald—you, of all people in the world. Why, man alive, if I had your power I would chuck to-morrow, and die contractor, engineer, K.C.I.E., and the richest man in India!"

Gwen Boynton looked up in quick interest. "Really! do you mean that—*really*, Lewis?"

"I won't swear to the K.C.I.E. or the superlative, but Fitzgerald knows perfectly that I always say he has mistaken his line of life. We want hacks—people to obey orders, not to give them." As he spoke he glanced meaningly at Colonel Tweedie walking about fussily, and then at his friend's face.

Dan swung himself from the balustrade, where he had been perched. "Some one must give orders, and I mean to stick on for my promotion; it must come next year. So that is settled. Are you not coming to breakfast, Mrs. Boynton?" She met his smile without response as she turned away.

"Dear me! the others have gone in already, and I was so hungry. But one doesn't often get the chance, Mr. Fitzgerald, of considering an old friend in a new character. It was quite absorbing—for the time."

The balcony was left to the sunlight, and some one who had been watching it from an archway in the bazaar withdrew to the shadow, where she rolled the little pellets of opium in her soft palms, and prepared for her mid-day sleep. The burning of the tents was a real piece of luck. The *mem*—that was she, no doubt, in her native dress—would be in the palace for two or three days, and women were women, whether fair or dark. This one, too, looked of the right sort. Chândni's dreams that day were of a time when she would have the upper hand in Hodinuggar and become virtuous; it paid to be virtuous under the present government. Dalel should start a woman's hospital; then the *sirkar* would give him the water every year, and the necessity for scheming would disappear. In the meantime they must not be niggardly; that did not pay with women, since if they were of the sort to take bribes, they were of the sort not easily satisfied.

CHAPTER VIII

"Come and see our mad potter before you go home, Miss Tweedie," pleaded George Keene; "he really is one of the shows—isn't he, Fitzgerald?"

They had been doing the sights of Hodinuggar as an afternoon's amusement, tennis in a riding-habit having no attractions for Rose. Mrs. Boynton, however, on the plea of being *zenana* lady, had elected to remain on the roof, Colonel Tweedie keeping her company until the time came for his visit of state to the dewan on his tower. Lewis might have made the same choice had he been given it, but he was not. So he preferred loafing round the ruins to toiling after problematical black buck with the sporting party. He was a pleasant companion enough, as even Rose admitted, and was ready with information on most points, while between the references he would talk affably with Dan regarding the respective merits of Schultze *versus* brown powder, or some other equally absorbing topic, thus leaving the younger couple to themselves. So his change of manner stood out with unusual distinctness as Rose turned to him for consent to George Keene's invitation.

"As you please, Miss Tweedie; we are your slaves. A mad potter sounds cheerful. He is the man, I suppose, who made that jolly little pot Keene sacrificed to my cousin's greed this morning. When you are as old as I am, my dear fellow, you will keep the really pretty things out of the sight of ladies. I always do, nowadays. There was a little woman at Peshawer, I remember—she had blue eyes—who wheedled—"

"Mrs. Boynton was most welcome to the Ayôdhya pot," blundered out George, hastily.

"*Cela va sans le dire!* It is just because we love to give the pretty things to the pretty creatures that it becomes unwise to let the pretty creatures see the pretty things."

"Then it is your fault, to begin with," interrupted Rose, hotly.

"Exactly so. I'm sure, Miss Tweedie, you've heard me say a dozen times that we are to blame for all the weaknesses of women. They are simply the outcome of our likes and dislikes, and they will remain so until there is a perpetual leap-year."

"For Heaven's sake, Keene," said Dan, laughing, "lead the way to the potter's, or there will be murder done on the king's highway! Don't mind him, Miss Rose; he only says it to annoy, because he knows it teases. He doesn't really believe anything of the kind."

Lewis, his eye-glass more aggressive than ever, murmured something under his breath about the inevitable courses of nature, as Rose, with her head held very high, followed George Keene into the potter's yard.

It was a scene strangely at variance with the party entering it. Indeed, old Fuzl Elâhi, who had never before set eyes on an Englishwoman, would have started from his work had not George detained him with reassuring words.

"He tells his yarns best when he is at the wheel," he explained, as he dragged forward a low string-stool for Rose; "and I want you to hear an awfully queer one called 'The Wrestlers.' You know enough of the language to understand him, at any rate."

"Miss Tweedie is a better scholar than most of us," remarked Lewis Gordon, curtly, from the seat he had found beside Dan on a great log of wood—one of those logs so often to be seen in such court-yards; relics, perhaps, of some intention of repair long since forgotten. This one might, to all appearance, have fallen where it lay in those bygone days of which the potter told tales, when the now treeless desert had been a swampy jungle on the borders of an inland sea.

The afternoon sun, slanting over the grass palisades, played havoc with the humanity it found gathered round the wheel by sending their shadows, distorted to long length, across the yard, tilting them at odd angles against the irregular wall of the mud-hut beyond, and jumbling them all together into a conglomerate pyramid of shadow, with the potter's high turban dominating all as he sat silent, spinning his wheel. And as the clay curved and hollowed beneath his moulding hand a puzzled look came to the light eyes usually so shifty, now fixed on the riding-habit.

"It is not there," he muttered, uneasily. "I cannot find a clew."

George gave Rose the triumphant glance of a child displaying a mechanical toy when it behaves as it ought to behave. The potter was evidently in a mad mood, and might be trusted for a good performance. "Now, Fuzl Elâhi, we want 'The Wrestlers,' please. The Miss *sahib* has never heard it."

"How could she?" broke in the old man, sharply. "She does not belong to that old time; she is new. I cannot even tell the old tale if she sits there in the listener's place. I shall forget; the old will be lost in the new, as it is ever."

"Change places with me, Miss Tweedie," put in Lewis, with a bored look. "I am not regenerate out of the old Adam, am I, potter-*ji*?"

But as he rose, the pliant hand went out in a gesture of denial. "There is room on the log for both, and crows roost with crows, pigeons with pigeons. The big *huzoor* can sit on the stool if he likes; I know him; I have seen him many and many a time."

"Only once, potter-*ji*," protested Dan, as he and Rose changed places, and the wheel began to turn.

"The post is going from Logborough junction to St. Pottersburgh," murmured Lewis, discontentedly. "If we are going to play round games, I shall go home."

"Do be quiet, Gordon," put in George, eagerly; "he is just beginning, and it is really worth hearing."

But Lewis was incorrigible. "*Proxime accessit*," he went on to Rose. "What crime in your past *avâtara* is responsible for your being bracketed with me in this?"

"Oh, do listen!" protested George again.

"Listen! Who could help listening to that infernal noise? I beg your pardon, Miss Tweedie, but it is infernal."

Startling, certainly. A shrill moan coming from the racing, rocking, galloping wheel, as the worker's body swayed to and fro like a pendulum. It seemed to raise a vague sense of unrest in the hearers, a dim discomfort, like the remembrance of past pain. Then, suddenly, the story began in a high-pitched, persistent voice, round which that racing, galloping rush of the wheel seemed to circle; hurrying it, pushing at it, every now and then sweeping it along recklessly:

"It was a woman seeking something;
Over hill and dale, through night and day, she sought for something.
The wrestlers who own the world wrestled for her;
On the palm of her right hand wrestling for her.
'She is mine!' 'She is mine!' said one and the other,
While over hill and dale, through night and day, she sought for something.

"'Oh, flies! you tickle the palm of my hand;
Be off and wrestle down in your world.'
So they brought flowers and grass as a carpet,
Wrestling on as she sought for something,
Over hill and dale, through night and day, seeking for something.

"'Your carpet is hot, be off, you flies!'
So they brought her trees and water for cooling;
Wrestling on as she sought for something,
Over hill and dale, through night and day, seeking for something.

"'The grass grows long with the water,' said she.
'Be off, oh flies! and tickle your world.'
So they brought her flocks to devour the grass,
Wrestling on as she sought for something,
Over hill and dale, through night and day, seeking for something.

"'They have trodden my hand as hard as a cake.'
So they caught up a plough and ploughed her hand,
Wrestling on while she sought for something,
Over hill and dale, through day and night, seeking for something.

"'You have furrowed my palm, it tickles and smarts.'
So they brought a weaver and wove her lint,
Wrestling on while she sought for something,
Over hill and dale, through night and day, seeking for something.

"'Foul play! Foul play! Look down and decide.'
'Not I, poor flies, I must search for something.'
So they caught up a town to watch the game.
'He is right!' 'He is wrong!' cried old and young;
'He is wrong!' 'He is right!' And so war began.
While they wrestled away and she sought for something,
Over hill and dale, through night and day, seeking for something.

"'What a noise you make; I am tired of flies.'
So she swept them into a melon rind.
'Be quiet, flies! Lie still in the dark.'
She clapped her hand to the hole in the rind.
'I am tired of it all; I will go to sleep.
When morning comes I will seek for something,'
Over hill and dale, through night and day, I must seek for something.

"She rested her head on her palm and slept,
Down in the valley close to the river;
Slept to the tune of the buzzing flies
Wrestling and fighting about fair play.
And while she slept the big flood came,
And the melon pillow floated away,
Till a sand-bank caught it and held it fast;
And all within swarmed out to the sun—
Grass and herds and ploughs and looms;
People fighting for none knew what.
'I have made a new world,' she said, with a laugh—
'A brand-new world; and the flies have gone;
But the palm of my right hand tickles still;
Maybe it will cool when I find what I seek.'
So she left her new world down by the river—
Left it alone and sought for something;
Over hill and dale, through night and day, seeking for something."

The galloping wheel, which had responded always to the mad hurry of the recurring refrain, slackened slowly. Rose gave a sigh of relief and glanced at Lewis Gordon to see if he, too, had been oppressed by that shrinking recognition of a stress, a strain, a desire, such as she had never felt before; but he was leaning forward, his chin on his curved hands, intent on listening, so she could not see his face.

"By the powers!" came Dan Fitzgerald's voice above the

softening hum, "the old chap has made an Ayôdhya pot—the same shape, I mean."

"He always does when he tells this story," broke in George, quite pleased with the success of his entertainment. "I don't think he quite knows why he does it, however. Sometimes he says the woman was looking for one; sometimes that she always carries one in her left hand to balance the world in her right. But he invariably takes the unbaked pot to the ruins, and buries it with two of those odd little ninepins he calls men and women inside it. He is as mad as a hatter, you know."

"Several hatters," assented Gordon, fervently; but it is an interesting theory of creation."

"Now don't!" protested Dan, sitting with his long legs crunched up on the low stool close to the potter; "it is too human for dissection by the Folklore Society. But I'm impressed at one thing: the wrestlers; they are persistent figures in Indian tales, Miss Tweedie—are generally represented as giants; they are pygmies here."

"The *huzoor* is right and wrong," replied the potter, in answer to an inquiry of Dan's; "the *pailwans* were neither pygmies nor giants. They were as the *huzoor* is, two and a half *hâthu* round the chest; neither more nor less."

"That's a good shot," remarked Dan, in English; "forty-five inches, according to my tailor. You have an accurate eye, potter-*ji*, he added, in Hindostanee; "only half an inch out."

"Not a hair's-breadth, *huzoor*," replied the old man, mildly. "The measure of the *pailwans* is the measure of the *huzoor*. I have it here; my fathers used it, and I use it."

He sought a moment in the little niche hollowed, close to his right hand, out of the hard soil forming the side of his sunken seat, and drew from it a fine silken cord of brown, red, and cream-colored wool. It was divided into measures by small shells strung on the twist and knotted in their places.

"Hullo!" cried Gordon, eagerly; "that must be hundreds of years old. Those are sea-shells, and very rare. Simpson, at the museum, showed me one in fossil the other day; I wonder how the dickens the old man got hold of them?"

"Two and a half *hâthu*," repeated Fuzl Elâhi, absently; "the potter's full measure for a man in the beginning and the end." He leaned forward rapidly as he spoke, passed the cord round Dan Fitzgerald's chest, and drew the ends together. The curled spirals of the two shells lay half an inch apart. "So much for the garments," he muttered. "Yea, I knew it. The measure of a true *pailwan* to a hair's-breadth."

"And what am I potter-*ji*?" asked George, laughing.

The puzzled look came over the old man's face. "The *huzoor* may be a *pailwan* too. Times have changed."

"Rough on a fellow, rather!" exclaimed the boy, still laughing. "Here, Fitz! chuck me over the thing. Is that fair, Miss Tweedie?"

She laughed back into his bright face as he pulled his hardest to make the two second shells meet, then shook her head.

"Not on yourself, Mr. Keene. You are more of a hero than that, I should say."

The potter's eyes were on her, then back on George. "Everything is changed," he muttered again; "even the measure of the pots."

"Then you measure them, do you?" asked Gordon, to whom George had handed the cord, and who was now examining it minutely.

"Surely, *huzoor*, the first one of each batch; then the hand learns the make."

"Try what you are, Gordon?" suggested Dan.

"Not I. Here, potter-*ji*, catch! Miss Tweedie and I are, according to the best authority, abnormal; we are not ordinary pots; so I, for one, decline to be measured by their standard. And now, if some of us are to be in time for such trivialities as dinner, we ought to be going."

The potter rose also and stepped out of his hole. Seen so he was insignificant, his hairy, bandy legs almost beastlike, and contrasting strangely with the mild, high-featured face full of an expression of puzzled anxiety as he laid a deprecating hand on George Keene's sleeve.

"Wants *bucksheesh,* I suppose," murmured Lewis. "I have some rupees somewhere if you need them, Keene."

But it was not money; it was leave to speak to the *Mâdr mihrbân,* said the old man, humbly.

"*Mâdr mihrbân!* that's a nice name for you, Miss Rose," echoed Dan, softly. "'Mother of mercy'! a name to be glad of." She blushed as she went forward a step to ask, gently, "What is it? What can I do for you?"

He stooped to touch her feet with his supple hands ere replying. "*Huzoor,* it is a little thing. Fuzl Elâhi, potter of Hodinuggar, has a daughter somewhere. Perhaps she has gone to the *huzoor's* world; it is new; I do not know it. If the *Mâdr mihrbân* were to see her she might tell her to come back —just once—only once. I would not keep her. But now I have no answer when my fathers say, 'Where is thy little Azîzan?'"

"Azîzan!" echoed George, quickly. But the old man seemed to have forgotten his own request; he stood looking past the strangers, past the village, past even the ruins, into the sunset sky.

"I will send her—if I see her," said Rose, gently, with tears in her eyes; for George had told her the story of the lost daughter, and the sudden diffident appeal touched her. Yet the vast gulf between her and the old man, preventing even a clasp of the hand, touched and oppressed her still more as she left him standing beside his wheel.

"Well," said Lewis Gordon, when in silence they had reached the road once more, "you may call that amusement, Keene, if you like; I don't. When I get home I shall have a sherry-and-bitters."

"He *is* rather a grewsome old chap," admitted George, cheerfully. "I felt a bit creepy myself the first time I heard that song. By-the-way, Miss Tweedie, talking of creepiness, did I tell you about the Potter's Thumb? I didn't? Oh, that is a grand tale."

He told it, happily, as an excellent sequel to the show; while Dan, in one of his best moods, piled on the imaginative agony about Hodinuggar generally, until Lewis announced his intention of returning to the palace by a longer way. He would be late, of course, but that was preferable to having no appetite for dinner.

"By Jove! seven o'clock!" cried Dan, looking at his watch. "You and I, George, have to get over to the bungalow. We must run for it."

Rose watched them racing down the path, laughing and talking as they ran, with a troubled look.

"Fine specimens, Miss Tweedie," remarked Lewis, after a pause. "I don't think you need fear their cracking in the fire."

"I—I— " faltered Rose, taken aback by his comprehension.

"Am Scotch! That's sufficient excuse. I notice we seldom get rid of our native superstition. Besides, it was uncanny—the yard-measure, and the potter's thumb, and that horse-leech of a woman who was never satisfied. I felt it myself."

She knew he was speaking down to her as to a nervous woman, yet she did not resent it, because it was a distinct relief not to be taken seriously.

"I wish they had not measured, for all that," she persisted. "You will own it was odd, won't you?"

"Not so odd as Dan himself; he has been cracked ever since I knew him, and Keene is one of the sterling sort, certain of success; besides, he measured himself. Now, before you go up-stairs to dress, if your Scotch blood is still curdling, as mine is, have half a sherry-and-bitters with me. Crows roost with crows, you remember."

His friendliness beguiled her into playfulness.

"Crows, indeed! then I've a better opinion of you than you have of me. I thought we were meant for the pigeons."

"To bill and coo?"

If she could have boxed his ears it would have relieved her feelings. As it was she raced up-stairs in a fury without vouchsafing one word of resentment, and paced up and down her tiny room with flaming cheeks. Could a girl be expected forever and aye to be on the outlook for such openings? Of course Gwen Boynton would have laughed easily—would not have minded, perhaps; but then Gwen was charming; everything apparently that a woman ought to be.

Rose looked at herself and her dusty habit, in which she would have to go down to dinner and challenge comparison with Gwen in her silks and tinsel. Why should she? No one would care, no one would have a right to care, if she did stay in her room with a headache. The next instant she was ashamed of the impulse. What did it matter—they were welcome to their opinion. As for her, she would adopt no feminine excuse; she would leave those little devices to men's women. So she brushed her habit, and went out to join the others with a heightened color.

CHAPTER IX

Rose Tweedie's sneer against men's women lacked point, since it so happened that Mrs. Boynton, in the opposite corner room of the pavilion, was at the very moment setting aside the temptation of pleading a headache as an excuse for not appearing at dinner. And she had more reason to seek quiet than the girl, though a new dress lay ready on the bed; for Gwen loved to dazzle her world, and had spent some of her leisure in instructing a native tailor how to run up a length of coarse native muslin bought in the bazaar into a very decent semblance of a fashionable garment. But the pleasure of the trick had gone out of it; something had happened; something incredible, yet, given the surroundings, natural enough; something about which she must make up her mind. It seemed scarcely a minute ago since she had passed swiftly into the solitude of her own room in order to think. She, Gwen Boynton, in native dress, with a white, scared face, and something in her hand. Now she had to pass out of that room again as an Englishwoman, and the transition left her oddly undecided. Indeed, as she paused for a moment ere taking the plunge, with one hand on the embroidered draperies doing duty for a door, it seemed almost as if she were awaiting a command—some voice which should relieve her of responsibility. Then she smiled, and passed on to meet the surprised admiration of her little world; for she had never looked better, and she knew it. The creamy muslin suited her in its careless folds, her excitement showed itself becomingly in flushed cheeks and bright eyes, and the chorus of wonder at her cleverness made her gracious beyond compare as she deprecated their praise by saying they had been away so long that she had had to amuse herself somehow, and asking if there were not miles of muslin to be bought in every bazaar, and many men to put stitches in it; so any one could have done it. Rose, listening with a certain contempt in her look, told herself that Gwen said truth; any one could have done it who thought it worth while to take so much trouble for the sake of personal effect; yet a regret rankled somewhere mingled with a resentment which came as Gwen called attention, somewhat garishly, to more of her good works, by asking if they did not admire the room also. When Colonel Tweedie had gone off to the dewan's, she had consoled herself by pulling about the furniture; and did not the Ayôdhya pot look sweet on the corner stand she had improvised out of three bamboos, a brass plate, and a yellow silk scarf?

"You should have packed it away in your box at once," remarked Lewis, sarcastically. "Keene may repent his good-nature, or some of us might steal it. The color is certainly admirable." As he spoke he walked over to the stand as if for further examination.

"Don't touch it, please," cried Mrs. Boynton, hastily, "you—you will spoil my draperies."

"A thousand pities, when they are so artistic," put in Colonel Tweedie, glad of the opportunity. "That is dinner, Mrs. Boynton. "I've had it laid in the small pavilion so as to keep this as your drawing-room."

"Thanks! but everything is delightful—simply fascinating. In spite of what Mr. Keene said this morning, I begin to wish I were a native."

"For the sake of the satin?" asked Lewis, who was following close behind with Rose.

Gwen flashed a brilliant look at him. "No, not the satin. That game would not be worth the candle!"

Apart from the question of satin, however, Mrs. Boynton had excuse for admiring the *mise en scène*, and wishing to remain in it. The violet sky spangled with stars seemed made apparently but for one end—to hap and hold that terraced roof which was clearly outlined against it by the light streaming from the pavilions on to the fretted white balustrades. At the corners were shadowy cupolas, and there in the arched summer-house at the farther end, close upon the velvet darkness, showed a table set with silver and glass, fruits and flowers. At one end of it, so as to divide the ladies equally, sat Rose in her habit, doing the duty of hostess with a little air of gravity and preoccupation; at the other, Gwen, in her soft clouds of muslin, keeping the men in a state of admiring gratification through their eyes and their ears. They gathered round her, too, when, dinner being over, they adjourned to the balcony for coffee and cigars. It was deliciously cool; a faint breeze stirred Rose's hair as she sat a little apart from the others watching the twinkling lights go up and down the stair, which formed the only tie between that world on the roof and that in the court-yard below.

"We ought to go to bed early," said Lewis, coming to stand before her. "You are half asleep—no wonder after last night—and Gwen is what superstitious Scotch folk call 'fey.' Then, if we have to join that detestable hawking-party to-morrow morning, we shall have to get up at five."

"You needn't go unless you like," she replied, curtly. "Mrs. Boynton has begged off."

"I am not Mrs. Boynton's personal attendant, Miss Tweedie; I happen to be your father's—so duty calls." As he spoke he seated himself on the balustrade and leaned forward, his elbows on his knees, to watch the group on the other side of the arcade.

"If I didn't know that Gwen despises that sort of thing," he went on, in dissatisfied tones, "I should say that she had rouged this evening. Her way of showing fatigue, I suppose; though, of course, neither of you would have the common-sense to confess you were tired. Women are all ascetics at heart; at least, they believe in the virtue of martyrdom. They have different ways of showing it, that's all. Gwen spends her fatigue in dress-making and conversation—in other words, in trying to go beyond comfort into pleasure, and you, I'll go bail, haven't even a proper bandage on that scorched arm—"

"Mr. Gordon!"

"Yes. I saw you imagined I was blind; supposing we say

liked to imagine it; but I really had my eye-glass, Miss Tweedie. Besides, it doesn't require microscopic sight to see some things."

"What a profound remark," interrupted Rose, to hide her pleased surprise at his unusual consideration; at the same moment, Gwen's gay laugh rang out soft and clear. Either the sound or the speech annoyed the hearer on the balustrade, for he frowned as he slipped his dangling feet on to the floor. "As profound as I can make it this evening, for I am not ashamed to confess myself dog-tired. Couldn't tell a crow from a pigeon; so I shall be off. Good-night, Miss Tweedie, I wish you would persuade Gwen to go to bed. It is easier to give good advice than to take it."

Rose remained looking at the twinkling lights, and wondering if Lewis were really jealous of his cousin, till, seeing the others go back to the central summer-house, she followed suit.

"Tired!" echoed Gwen, sharply, in reply to her information that Lewis Gordon had stolen away. "Are we not all tired? I feel as if I had been up since the beginning of time, seeking for something I could not find; my bed, perhaps. Good-night, Rose."

They were an odd couple as they bent to kiss each other in that mirrored room, where the oddness was reflected again and again in the myriad scraps of looking-glass on the walls, each curved fragment giving and taking an eternity of Gwens and Roses bending to kiss each other.

"*I am tired of it all, I will go to sleep;*"
When morning comes I will seek for something.
Over hill and dale, through night and day, I will seek for something."

The remembrance evoked by Gwen's chance words sent a little shiver through the girl; and with it came a sudden pulse of sympathy for the woman who, now that she saw her close, did indeed look haggard and worn. "No wonder you are tired," she said, gently. "Even I feel as if I could sleep for days."

"But you are coming to hawk, surely?" broke in George, quickly. "Do please! It won't be any fun without you."

"Not a bit," assented Dan. "Gordon ordered your horse, I know, and told them to take you your tea at five punctually."

"You must go Rose," put in Gwen, with a shrug of her white shoulders. "Diana *Chasseresse* mustn't disappoint her votaries. I'm glad my habit was burned." She did not look it, and Rose, as she went off to her corner room, wondered if Gwen were jealous of her. The idea was absurd, but pleasing because of its novelty, and she fell asleep placidly over variations of the possibility.

But just over the way, with that dark, mirrored room between them, Gwen lay awake with one hand thrust under her pillow where she could feel a tiny paper parcel—lay awake asking herself questions. Should she keep it, or should she not? Should she say anything of the scene burned in on her memory, or should she not? She seemed to see it as a spectator, not as the only actor. A woman, in native dress, in that room set round with eyes; the Ayôdhya pot in her hand, and in her tinsel-edged veil the jewels which had fallen from its false bottom: jewels which, if sold, would buy her freedom; perhaps save her, and Dan, too, from a great mistake. It was a chance; a chance most likely known to nobody in the wide world save to herself; for who would knowingly have sold a pot containing three huge pearls and an emerald for ten rupees? Nor was she bound to give more to the seller for the discovery. Did not every one know that if land was bought, and coal, or tin, or anything was found in it afterwards, that was the buyer's good-luck? Facts like these, accepted apparently by the honest and honorable, go far to give such people as Gwen immoral support. Besides, no one could possibly know; she herself would not have known save for that chance slip, and the eyes made keen and eager through fear of some slight injury to the treasure. Then it was a means of escape from the danger which had come home to her so sharply in the past twenty-four hours—the danger of yielding to her own weakness about Dan; the new danger, suggested by his words, of her losing her hold on Lewis. Could he really be attracted by Rose? The events of the evening certainly gave color to the possibility. If so, there was no time to be lost; she must be free; free to do as she chose. No one could know; nobody would dream of bribing one so powerless as she; and even if the pearls had been put there knowingly, it was only her risk. No one else was responsible; Lewis had said so only that morning. Even that was a curious coincidence, pointing somehow to her acceptance of the luck.

So she argued, coming round always to the same thought, till the first glint of dawn brought sleep, as it so often does to weary eyes. Perhaps in the thought that the sun will rise, the world goes on, no matter what we do, or think, or say.

She slept so soundly that all the bustle of the hawking-party failed to disturb her; and when that was over, the long stretch of terraced roof lay empty of all sound or sign of life, save for the green parrots swooping and shrieking about the carven work. A pair of them had built in a loop-hole, where the young ones kept up a simmering, bubbling noise like a boiling teakettle; a comfortable, homely sound, strangely out of keeping with the foreign beauty of stone and sunlight and hard blue sky.

Down in the court-yard below two badge-wearers in scarlet and gold lounged on the stairs, barring the roof from intrusion, chatting to the passers-by, and discussing the news which had just been brought in by the camel which was crouching beside a pile of fodder in the centre of the yard, while its owner stretched his legs, cramped with riding all night across the desert, in front of the cook-room. Half-way up the stairs, on the landing leading to the state-rooms, Mrs. Boynton's *ayah* squatted, combining business with pleasure by being within reach of a call and her forbidden *hookah* at one and the same time. A bundle of letters lay beside her, intended as a peace-offering against the possible smell of smoke which might linger in her clothes. The sun climbed up silently, shifting the shadows on the silent roof. That was the only movement, till suddenly a figure in a white domino peered through the grille which barred the flight of steps leading to the dewan's tower.

Then, with the grate of a rusty key in a lock, the figure flitted silently as the shadows to the summer-house, and passed into the mirror-room. Perhaps the transformation which Western taste and Mrs. Boynton's clever fingers had wrought in its adornment was pleasing; perhaps it was the reverse. The *burka*, however, is of all disguises the most complete, since it blots out form, color, expression; even movement. The figure showed, indeed, like a white extinguisher in the middle of the room, until, with a swaying of ample folds, it glided over to the corner stand where the Ayôdhya pot stood out from Gwen's artistic drapery. Then something slid out from the extinguisher, still shrouded in white folds, raised the vase, shook it slightly, replaced it, and slid back again. A horrible, invertebrate, protoplasmic sort of action, calculated to send a shiver through the spectator. But there was none. The thing had the whole roof to itself save for that fair-haired sleeper in the corner-room, who lay with one hand clasping a little packet hidden under her pillow. Her dreaming face was turned to the doorway, in full view of those latticed eyeholes belonging to the *burka*, which, after a time, came to look upon her from the half-raised curtain and let in, with a shaft of sunshine, a vista of blue sky and marble balustrades, with two red-and-green parrots pecking at each other. It may have been the light, more probably it was the disturbing effect which the dim consciousness of other eyes fixed on their own has upon most people, which roused Gwen Boynton; anyhow, she opened her eyes suddenly and started up in bed, her heart throbbing violently, though the curtain had fallen, and not a sound was to be heard.

"Comin', *mem sahib*, comin'," came in immediate answer to her imperative call as the *ayah*, thrusting her *hookah* aside, snatched at the letters, and shook what smoke she could from her voluminous garments. A trifling delay, but enough to allow the thing up-stairs to flit round the summer house again—even to pause a second at the grille. "It makes too much noise; I will leave it open," it muttered, as it disappeared up the steps with the rusty key held in its formless clasp.

"Where were you?" asked Gwen, her heart still throbbing, "and who was that who looked in on me from the door? There was some one; I'm sure there was some one."

"Me, *mem sahib*," grinned the woman, readily "; me, *ayah*. Look in several times; *mem*, always *nindi per*. *Sota! Sota!* Sleep like *baba*. *Ayah* waiting close by to bring *dâk*. Many letters for *mem sahib*."

Mrs. Boynton looked at her doubtfully. It was not the *ayah* whom she had seen; of that she was certain. On the other hand, if the woman really had been sitting outside, it was more than probable the whole thing was a dream. No harm had come of it anyhow; so five minutes after she was dividing her attention between early tea and a long epistle from an absent admirer, for Gwen's victims were always excellent correspondents, perhaps because of that gracious indifference in which lay her great charm. A letter, therefore, had quite as good a chance as a man had of whiling away her kindly, sympathetic leisure. But when the *ayah* was brushing away at the pretty hair, her mind reverted to the question which had kept her awake. As so often happens—the learned say by unconscious cerebration—it appeared to have settled itself. Independently of Dan, or any secondary matter of that sort, money would be useful; most useful, seeing she had just lost the best part of her wardrobe, and had a season in Simla in immediate prospect. Now she came to think of it, Hodinuggar owed her some reparation for the loss it had inflicted upon her. Besides, it would be wiser to wait and see if the presence of jewels in the pot were suspected by any one or not. If the latter, it would be clearly flying in the face of a good Providence to mention her discovery. So, by the time she was ready to face her world, that world seemed quite simple and easy to face.

Chândni thought the same thing as she sat at the dewan's feet in the big balconied room of the tower overlooking the canal, telling him in whispers of the success of her plan so far. The jewels were no longer in the pot. The *mem* must have them, for, as she had found out through a *khitmutgar*, the *mem* had been alone during many hours, and had been making a mess in the room with trumpery pots and platters.

"She may send it back yet," said the dewan, cautiously. "Lo! I am old, and this I have learned through long years: Trust not a woman not to change her mind till she is dead."

The courtesan laughed. "'Tis as well for some men that she is born so, father. But a night's thought is as death to a woman. Life is too short to give more to such things, and that night is over without a sign. Give her yet one more, an' thou wilt; after that say that Chândni hath dug the channel. 'Twill be *thy* task to turn the water into it."

CHAPTER X

Among those things which come by nature, and are not to be taught, may be reckoned a pretty seat on horseback. One may be a good rider without it, a poor one with it; but when grace and skill are combined, a man certainly shows at his best on horseback. It was so with Lewis Gordon. He sat his lean little country-bred as if it belonged to him; not, as the usual phrase runs, as if he were part of his horse, for that is a description which ignores the essence of the thing to be described; that being, surely, the mastery a man has over something which is *not* himself. Part of his horse! The very words conjure up a man paralyzed to the waist and jelly above, agonizing over a cavalry seat!

If Lewis Gordon was grateful to Providence for one thing, it was for making and keeping him a light-weight, and thus independent on Australian and Arab mounts. The fourteen-hand-pony which he had picked up—a mere bag of bones—at a native fair, had to be hard held when trotting alongside of Colonel Tweedie's big waler, yet she had only cost him a tenth of the price. As she forged along, quivering with impatience, Bronzewing was a pretty sight, the sunlight shining red through her wide nostrils, and shifting in golden curves over the bronze muscles which were almost black in shadow. Rose Tweedie always admired it immensely, and, illogically enough, felt inclined to be more lenient to the rider. She told herself it was because he wore spectacles on horseback, and they were less offensive than the eye-glass which permitted so many variations of method in his outlook. She did not even fall foul of his indifference as he dawdled about at the hawking-party, a picture of aimless dejection; on the contrary, she had a sneaking sympathy with his feelings. It *was* dreary work watching unfortunate gray partridge beaten up from one bush by the coolies only to be pounced on by a hawk ere it could reach the shelter of the next cover. She also shared his disgust at Dalel Beg, who, in top-boots, red coat, and doeskins, took a keen interest in the gorging of the young hawks on the entrails of the still struggling victims, and gave shrill "yoicks" and "gone-aways" at each fresh flutter. Khushâl Beg, watching the sport from a bullock-wagon on which he reclined among cushions, was purely comical; his son purely offensive.

"I think," remarked Lewis, slowly, "he is the worst specimen of civilization I ever met; and I think this is the deadliest entertainment I ever was at; and both those facts mean something."

Rose laughed, and suggested that it would have been better if they had come across *obarra.* They, she had heard, were worth hawking. Her companion shook his head. "I've seen it on the frontier at its best. You lose the essence of sport. That, I take it, lies in pitting your strength, or skill, or endurance, against the quarry. In hawking you ride behind the skill, and, as the country is easy, the whole thing resolves itself into the pace of your horse: in other words, what you paid for the beast."

"Not always! I'd back Bronzewing against the field any day," cried Rose, impulsively.

He looked up with quite a flush of pleasure. "Well, she should do her best to win the gloves for you, Miss Tweedie." The reply came as naturally as the remark which had provoked it; but it made the girl feel suddenly shy and say, hastily,

"She looks as if she wanted to be off now; how that partridge startled her!"

"Not a bit of it. She is only longing, as I am, for a hunt."

"A hunt?"

"Yes; a partridge hunt. Have you never seen one?"—he gave a rapid glance round. "There are too many bushes here, but Keene may know of some fairly open country, with perhaps a thorn hedge or two for you to jump—that is to say, if you have had enough of this festive scene."

Five minutes after George Keene, Dan Fitzgerald, Lewis Gordon, and she were sweeping along in line across low sand-hills in order to dip down into a harder plain; a wide sweep of level, dotted sparsely with low caper-bushes, with here and there a patch of cultivation showing vividly green against its whity-brown frame of desert, and here and there a bit of plough ready for the summer crop. There is nothing more invigorating in the world than riding in line at a hand gallop across such country in the freshness of early morning; especially when the party has gay hearts and light heads. Rose felt it was worth all her purely feminine amusements put together, and, with a flush of enjoyment on her face, besieged Lewis Gordon with high-pitched questions as to what they were going to do; he calling back his answers, so that their voices rose above the rhythmical beating of the horses' hoofs.

"We are going without dog, coolie, gun, or any lethal weapon whatever, as the code says, to ride down and capture the gray partridge, or *Ammoperdix bonhami!* Have you seen it done, Fitzgerald?"

"Heard of it only. The pace must be good."

"Racing speed; no less. Therein lies the fun. He gave a quick glance at Rose's tackle, and frowned. "You should have a stronger bit," he began, when she interrupted him sharply.

"It is the same as yours."

"Perhaps; but a lady can't ride like a man, especially in this sort of work. If I had noticed it before I—"

"Nonsense! I always ride with a snaffle, and Shahzâd is as steady as a house."

"That is no argument. In my opinion a lady should—" The rest of the wrangle was spared to the company, for at that moment a partridge buzzed out of a bush at their feet. Bronzewing's equanimity gave way instantly, and with a snort of eagerness she burst after it, Shahzâd following suit, both beasts heading straight as a die after the quarry, heedless of their riders or their discussions.

"Give him his head, Miss Tweedie!" shouted Lewis, as he

shot past. "He has done it before, and knows the game! Off we are!" Off, indeed, helter-skelter, behind the gray-brown buzz of wings showing against a blue sky.

"Ride it! Ride it! Keep an eye on it! I'll do back!" came Lewis Gordon's voice, boyishly exultant, as with hands down he veered the mare a point or two by main force, until, as she caught sight of a heavier clump of bushes, comprehension came to the game little beast, and she headed straight for it.

"Where? Oh, where?" cried Rose, distractedly, to Dan Fitzgerald, who was now racing beside her.

"Right ahead—there—don't you see?"

Just a brown speck against the blue sky still, but skimming faster and faster to meet the brown horizon. Yes; there still—no—yes—*gone!*

Rose gave a cry, which was echoed by an exclamation from Dan, as instinctively they reined up, feeling the chase was over. George, hurrying up from behind, where his pony had been playing the fool, found them staring disconsolately at the bushes.

"Lost it, I suppose," said Lewis, as he joined them. "It is always difficult to keep it in sight on the horizon. However, you have had a good burst, Miss Tweedie. See! we started there—a good mile back. Have you any idea how you got here?"

"None! I suppose I rode, but I saw nothing save a sort of big bumblebee buzzing in front of me. Shahzâd did the rest."

"As I said, not for the first time, which confirms me in saying that he is only a Gulf Arab, for partridge hunting is a Persian sport. Only don't tell your father, please; he would never forgive me." As he turned in his saddle, resting one hand on the mare's quarters in order to speak to Rose, voice and face full of almost boyish enjoyment, the girl felt that it was a new development of his character, and that she liked it better than the old ones.

"Now, as we go along, I'll explain. That bird took us by

surprise," he went on, eagerly. "Four is an ideal number, though I've had rare fun riding partridge single-handed. Number one ought to make the pace, keeping eyes on the bird; number two keeps his on the going, so as to save number one from coming to grief over rough country; number three rides cautious, landmarks the flight, and is ready to turn if the bird breaks back—you can't when you're going full speed, unless the bird towers. Number four rides cunning, cuts off curves, and heads for likely covers—the whole aim being to press the partridge so hard that it has no time to settle in shelter, but, after skimming down to a bush, runs through and takes to wing again on the other side."

"And gets away, I suppose," muttered George Keene, still out of temper. "Don't see the fun of it."

"Wait a bit!" retorted Lewis, gayly. "Now you must remember that the rôle you have to play depends on how the bird breaks. There is no time to settle. The nearest in must ride it, the rest choose their parts as best—steady mare, steady!"

It was only a faint "te-titar, te-titar," in the far distance, but Bronzewing started, and even George's pony cocked its ears. Humanity went on breathlessly in line, the horses' feet at a walk giving out a hollow sound on the hard soil, on which the yellow sunshine cast hard shadows.

"Look out!" cautioned Lewis, in a whisper. "There's a partridge running on ahead; by you, I think, Fitzgerald."

"Don't see it!"

"Farther to the left; the mare sees it—we must trot a bit, or it won't rise fair—steady, lass, steady."

"I see it!" came in excited tones from George. "By the big bush, Miss Tweedie."

"That's another," cautioned Lewis again. "Take care and don't—"

Whir, buzz! whir, buzz!

"Ride it! ride it!" The cry came from two quarters; but Shahzâd was already extended, and Rose forgetful of everything save those brown wings low down against the horizon.

She was closer on them this time, for she could see their skimming swoop as they neared a heavy clump of cover; yet she felt she must lose them, as she had done before, when, to her relief, she saw Lewis shoot ahead, cutting across a curve.

"All right!" he shouted; "I'm on. Look out for yourself." There was a cut of his thong against thorns as he rose Bronzewing to a hedge Rose had not seen. But she had scarcely steadied herself in the saddle from the half-considered leap in his wake before the partridge was down and up again at right angles to its first flight; Lewis meanwhile bringing the mare round all he knew, and shouting, "Ride it, Miss Tweedie! ride it!"

Shahzâd, still steadied by the jump, was in hand and on the track in a second, snorting in mad hurry and excitement. The bird was not quite so fast this time, or Rose was riding straighter, for she saw the last skim of the wings change to running feet as it touched the gray-brown earth, which tinted so perfectly with its gray-brown plumage.

"Not there! not there!" came that warning voice from behind. "It's run on; the next bush—put Shahzâd over it."

A leap, a scurry, a flutter, and the quarry was up again, heading in its hurry for an impossible open, backed by bare plough. Bronzewing being now alongside, Rose found leisure to glance round for the others.

"Gone after the second partridge; I was afraid of it," called Lewis. "There's a hedge twenty yards ahead, Miss Tweedie; I'll mark meanwhile." She was over it, almost in her horse's stride; but the bird below the horizon was now a mere speck of darker brown against the plough.

"I've lost it! I've lost it again!" The despairing cry came from Rose's very heart as she tugged vainly at Shahzâd. When she succeeded in bringing him up, she saw that Lewis was slipping from the mare.

"All right!" he cried, cheerfully, dropping his white handkerchief on the ground. "That's the place I marked; it is somewhere about! Now for sharp eyes." Up and down the bare furrows he searched, followed by Bronzewing, her reins hanging loose upon her neck. Up and down, with such patience that Rose, gaining confidence, began to search also; only, however, to lose hope, as minute after minute brought no result.

"I don't believe it's here," she remarked, at last; and with the words saw Lewis Gordon stoop to pick up something she had passed by, thinking it was a clod of earth.

"Your first partridge," he said, with a kindly laugh, as he placed the bird upon her lap. There it lay unhurt, wide-eyed and motionless, as it had lain among the furrows.

"Why doesn't it fly away?" asked Rose, with a little catch in her breath, as she gently stroked the mottled back.

"It will soon; at present it's winded. Give it five minutes and we could ride it again. But we won't. It flew game, and I needn't ask if you enjoyed it." No need, certainly. The very horses panting, nose down, in each other's faces, seemed discussing past pleasure.

"It is safe from kites now," said Lewis. "Throw it up, Miss Tweedie."

The next instant a skimming flight had ended in a covert of thorns, and Lewis was on his mare ready to start. "It wouldn't head for the open again if we were to ride it, I bet," he said; "they get as cute as an old fox after a time. To your left, please; that rise yonder is Hodinuggar."

"But we might ride again, surely? It would give the others time to come up," began Rose, fiercely bitten with the game.

"Best not. The ground here is bad going—all littered with bricks, and you could barely hold Shahzâd that last time; a snaffle is hard work—for a lady." Rose refrained from open retort. Lewis had given her a morning's amusement, and she owed him something; for all that, she made a mental determination to ride partridge as often as she chose, with a snaffle or without it. His objection was only part of that wholesale depreciation of women which—here a partridge buzzed out of a bush, and partly from impulse and partly from sheer opposition, she gave Shahzâd the rein—a bit of bravado in which she reckoned without the excited horse—but ere she had gone fifty yards, she realized that it had the bit between its teeth. What was worse, she saw that Lewis realized it also.

"Look out for bricks!" he called, spurring Bronzewing alongside for a moment, "and don't try to follow when the bird breaks back, as it is sure to do, for cover." The words were still on his lips when the partridge towered and turned. Shahzâd, no novice at such tricks, pulled up short, nearly throwing Rose over his ears. Then with a bound he dashed off sideways, catching Bronzewing on the flank as she swerved, and throwing her rider's foot from the stirrup. The mare staggered, pulled herself together smartly, set her hoof on a loose brick, and came down heavily, while Rose, tugging vainly at her beast, went sailing away to the horizon, with the memory of that crashing fall seeming to paralyze her strength. When she did manage to turn, Bronzewing was on her feet; but her rider lay where he had fallen. The girl's heart stood still an instant in that utmost fear which will come first always — was he dead? Yet, as she galloped back, she told herself fiercely that it was impossible; people fell so often, and did not hurt themselves—but not, surely, to lie as he lay, with eyes wide open and one arm under him, as if he had pitched head-foremost. Rose had never seen an accident before, and at first all her helpfulness seemed lost in a senseless desire to gather him up in her arms and hold him safe. Then the thought of her own foolishness came to her aid. He had been right; women were no good; a man would have known what to do; and as she thought these things she searched, comically enough, in his pockets for a flask, as if unconsciously reverting to the man's first resource; but she could find none, and there was no water. What was to be done, save to chafe his hands and call to him vainly? while a perfect agony of negation clamored against her growing fear. He could not be dead; he was such a good rider; he must have fallen before, and yet he had not been killed—why, then, should he be killed this time? He could not be killed on such a bright, sunny morning, when they had been so happy—when he had been so kind; ridiculous, trivial, helpless little thoughts, such as make up the sum of such scenes.

Finally she rose, resolved by the depth of her very despair. Water and help she must have; if no nearer than the palace, then to the palace she must go. Shahzâd had taken advantage of liberty to seek a wheat field; but loyal little Bronzewing would carry her nicely with the stirrup over the saddle. The mare, however, distrusted strangers, and sidled off, still circling faithfully round her master. Then the girl's hopes and fears centred themselves on the immediate necessity for success, as she coaxed, wheedled, cajoled, forgetful of all else, till, of a sudden, Bronzewing paused to whinny, and Rose, looking round, instinctively recognized the magnitude of her past despair in the light of her great relief as she saw Lewis Gordon, raised on one elbow, looking at her in a dazed sort of way. She was on her knees beside him in a minute, confessing the past fear she had so strenuously denied while it existed. "I thought you were dead! I thought you were dead!" She was trembling and shaking all over, quite visibly, and he gave an unsteady laugh.

"Thumped the back of my head; that's all. No!"—a spasm of pain passed over his face as he sat up. "My collar bone's gone. Well, it might have been worse. The ground is uncommonly hard." Worse, indeed! Rose could not speak for a lump in her throat, but the loquacity of escape was on him. "Must have pitched on my shoulder, luckily. I don't in the least remember how it happened. We were partridging, I suppose, but my mind is an absolute blank, and no wonder; my head is just splitting, but I can walk home all right." And when she proposed riding Bronzewing for help, he negatived it firmly, on the ground that the mare wasn't broken in for a lady—a man never having such a strong hold on his individual quips and cranks as when he realizes that he has been within an ace of losing them altogether; whence the proverbial captiousness of convalescents. So she had to be content with giving him a hand up and walking beside him, feeling a sad trembling in the knees, joined to a general sensation of having gone to pieces; he, on the contrary, talking and laughing in magnificent, manly fashion.

"You had better tell me how it happened," he said, as they neared the palace. "People make such a fuss that it is as well to be prepared. Did you see me come to grief?"

Rose hesitated for a moment to own up; then she did it wholesale. "You told me not to ride because of the snaffle, but I did. I lost control of Shahzâd, and he charged Bronzewing. She put her foot on a loose brick, and—I'm very sorry."

"Stupid little beast!" he said, looking round at the mare, who was following them like a dog. "I suspect she wants re-shoeing." The evasion was kindly meant, but Rose regretted it; it seemed somehow to set her aside. But this was to be her portion in all things; for with Lewis in his room, scientifically bandaged by Dan and nursed by his cousin, Rose's part resolved itself into doing audience for her father's fussing. He had a capacity for it at all times, but Fate had provided him with special reasons for it now. Another delay, when it was absolutely necessary that he should hold a canal committee at Delhi early in the week. And how was he to manage without his personal assistant? Then there were private reasons for annoyance which he did not confide to Rose, but which that clear-sighted young lady fully understood. If Lewis had to remain a few days longer at Hodinuggar, his cousin would remain also; in which case Dan Fitzgerald would stay to look after them. Now Dan, ever since the fire, had been in the colonel's black-books. He had, as it were, thrust himself forward, and made himself conspicuous; besides, it was to be expected that any woman must feel a certain gratitude to a man who had saved her life. It was all of a piece—all the result of disobedience to his superior wisdom. Why had Rose set fire to the camp? Had he not warned her a hundred times against sitting up to read? Why had she charged Lewis? Had he not begged her fifty times to ride in a more reserved and ladylike fashion?

Rose could only fall back on George for comfort, and he, for reasons of his own, was utterly unsympathetic, declaring that a broken collar-bone was nothing, except an awful nuisance to every one else. To tell the truth, the only person in that up-stairs world who was satisfied at the new turn was Gwen Boynton, who felt that it suited her admirably in more ways than one. So she sat after lunch and talked with Colonel Tweedie in the balcony, until his ill-humor vanished in a bland flood of conviction that this eminently charming woman really was full of sympathy for his difficulties and thoroughly impressed with his responsible position. In fact, when she had apologized for returning to duty and her patient, he came and let loose his satisfaction upon his daughter. "Nothing," he said, "was more useful to a man having authority than the companionship of a really sensible woman of the world. It enabled you to do justice to yourself; to adopt the course you considered best without undue hesitation. Therefore, he would start for Raj-pore, as he had always intended to do, on the following day, taking Mr. Fitzgerald with him to supply Gordon's place. He knew something of the current work, and it would be a kindness, serving to show—er—that—er—there was really nothing against him at headquarters."

"That was very considerate of Mrs. Boynton," interrupted Rose, quickly. She saw the meaning of this manœuvre so far that it roused her resentment; yet, after all, it would be better for Dan than dangling about with a sore heart while Gwen nursed the sick man. Better for George, also, since the *partie carrée* could not consist of three and a dummy; George should talk to her, and be kept from dangling also.

So Dan himself was the only one to look blank at the proposal, and even he admitted its reasonableness when Mrs. Boynton pointed out the many advantages it would have. This was during the tête-à-tête which she allowed him in a bell-shaped cupola over their tea. To tell the truth, Gwen always behaved with the strictest and most impartial justice to all who had claims upon her, and she would have felt herself unkind had she allowed poor, dear Dan to go away feeling aggrieved. She was very sorry he had to go; or, rather, to be strictly accurate, she was very sorry that common-sense dictated that he should go. Had all things been consenting, there was no one in the wide world she would so gladly have had for her husband. Now when a woman of Mrs. Boynton's type, who is at all times kindly disposed to lovers, has an idea of this sort firmly fixed in her mind, she can be very kind, indeed, even in her dismissals. So Dan was perfectly happy after he had sat beside her, and given her a second cup of tea, and handed her the bread and butter; though he made wry faces over her lecture on the necessity for subordinating his opinion to Colonel Tweedie's.

"And Dan," she said, when the tête-à-tête had lasted long enough, "as you are going to Delhi, you might take a parcel for me to Manohar Lal, the jeweller's. It is quite small, but you might just send it around—the shop is in the Chowk—by the bearer. I wouldn't trouble you, but it is a chance, as you are going that way. It won't bother you, will it?"

"Bother!" echoed Dan, in the tones which men in his condition use on such occasions.

"Then I'll give it you now. I was going to send it by post, so it is addressed, and all the instructions are inside; but it would be safer if you took it, as you happen to be going."

She repeated the phrase as if to convince herself of its truth. Yet when, on returning with her commission, Dan seized the opportunity of taking the parcel to kiss the fingers which held it, she felt something of a traitor; even though, in sending the jewels she had found to be appraised, she told herself she had no other intention beyond, if possible, getting enough money to repay the loan she had so unwisely taken. That was all; and this chance of sending them to Delhi by a safe hand had decided her so far—no more.

"Good-bye, dear Dan," she said, "I always miss you so much when you go away."

That night Chândni reported progress to the dewan. The *mem's ayah* had let out that the big *Huzoor* Fitzgerald *sahib* was the greatest friend the *mem* had. She must be a regular bad one, if all tales be true. And the big *sahib* was going to Delhi, the most likely place in which jewels would be sold. She would write to her craft, who were good clients of the goldsmiths, and bid them keep a sharp lookout. It would, at least, do no harm.

"Thy father must have been the devil," said Zubr-ul-zamân, admiringly. "Yet will I reward thee, as thou hast asked, if all goes well."

"Does not all go well?" laughed the woman. "The fire and the fall?"

"And the girl?"

"Oh! nought of the girl! The lance-player hits not the peg the first time. That is done, for good or evil. The bridegroom, they say, comes next week. 'Tis well. We want no evil-eye to change the luck."

CHAPTER XI

THE *dîners à la Russe* on the roof had not passed unnoticed by the world below. How could they? Over such strange doings curious tongues must need wag, setting curious eyes to peep and peer, especially in the women's apartments, where life was so empty of novelty, and where a crowded, squabbling glimpse from some lattice of arrival or departure was all the inmates could hope for, beyond, of course, the ceremonious visit which the English ladies paid to a circle of selected wives. But there, in company-dresses and company-manners, the chief women of three generations had found it impossible to ask enough questions to throw light on the one absorbing phenomenon of utter shamelessness in their visitors. Indeed, after Colonel Tweedie's departure, disputes began to run high in that rabbit-warren of dark rooms and darker passages centred round the bit of roof, walled into the semblance of a tank, which lay to the right of dewan's tower. The elder women, led by the old man's last remaining wife, a still personable woman of forty, upheld the theory which has had so much to do with British supremacy in the past—namely, that the *sahib logue*, being barely human, must not be judged by ordinary human standards; as likely as not their women were not women at all. The younger party, however, consisting largely of Dalel Beg's many matrimonial ventures in the forlorn hope of a son, declared that the true explanation lay the other way—namely, in the excess of frail humanity; both positions being argued with that absolute want of reserve which is the natural result of herding women together, away from the necessity for that modest reticence which the presence of even their stranger sisters brings with it: that lack of reserve in the mind by which Nature compensates herself for the seclusion of the body, and which makes those who have real experience of the working of the *zenâna* system put their finger on it as the plague-spot of India—a plague-spot which all the women doctors sent to bolster up the system by exotic and mistaken benevolence will never cure.

To this war of words Azîzan listened listlessly as she crouched for hours beside that slit in the prison wall whence, on tiptoe, she could see the flag-stone before the mosque on which she had sat when he was painting her picture. She had ceased to cry, ceased to do anything save mope about in the dark, with dull, resentful eyes taking in the emptiness and hopelessness of all things, even her desires going no further than a vague wish that she could have seen the flag-stone where the *sahib* had sat, instead of that dull, uninteresting, unconsecrated one. In that house of languid, listless, useless women her dejection might have passed unnoticed, save for the fact that old Zainub, the duenna, began to be troubled with an old enemy—the rheumatism.

Up-stairs on the roof, the connection between Azîzan's tears and Zainub's sciatica would have seemed far-fetched, obscure; down-stairs, however, it was self-evident, clear as daylight. Briefly, Azîz had the 'evil-eye,' like her grandfather the potter, and she was using it as her mother had used it. Sixteen years ago, after nursing that mother in the damp dungeon where useless cries could be deadened, Zainub had nearly died of rheumatic fever. Not from the damp, of course; simply from the evil-eye; nothing, in fact, had saved her life then, save a promise to protect the baby. And now for the sake of money she had brought grief on the child, and unless that grief could be assuaged, the result was certain: she would die. The pains were already upon her, and a dozen times a day she cursed her own folly in helping Chândni—Chândni who, when the ruse failed, had thrown her over with a paltry fee. Yet old Zainub, even while she blamed herself, confessed that no duenna could have foreseen such a coil about nothing. But then the world was full of strange new wickedness; in the old time no girl in her senses would have met the suggestion of carrying on the intrigue on her own account, as Azîzan had done, with vehement denial, and glowering, unhappy eyes; the thought of them sent additional twinges through poor old Zainub's bones. George Keene, who had taken up his quarters in the state rooms of the palace, so as to be near Lewis Gordon at night, never dreamed how narrowly he escaped the invasion of an old beldame, beseeching him to remove a curse from her. He had for the time almost forgotten the Azîzan episode; even the surprise which the potter's mention of his daughter's name had aroused he set aside for the present. There would be time enough for inquiry when he was alone once more—when the absorbing interest of the present had gone out of his life.

So the tragedy down-stairs was completely hidden from those up-stairs; it is so often in India. Occasionally we gain a glimpse behind the veil; for instance, when the periodical scare as to the number of human brains required to keep up British prestige seizes on some cantonment—a scare which, it may interest the 'Peace with Dishonor' party to know, is apt to follow on any lowering of the lion's tail. Then there are two simple syllables, known doubtless to many readers of this veracious story, as they were to the writer of it, which if uttered casually—say in dinner-table conversation—will of a certainty lead to your servants leaving your service without delay. These things sound unreal—farcical, no doubt; so would George, as he handed their bread and butter to the ladies up-stairs, have deemed the fear which prompted old Zainub's wheedling words as she crouched by Azîzan's bed, plying her with greasy sweetmeats:

"Eat some my pigeon—a morsel, beloved! Why wilt not be comforted, child? Say what is in thy heart, and if Zainub's old hands can compass it, 'tis thine."

"I want nothing. Let me be," muttered Azîzan. Zainub rocked herself to and fro—partly in despair, partly to allay a sharper twinge of the enemy—and looked round dismally, as if for some inspiration of comfort. Not much to suggest it in those bare walls, inexpressibly squalid, and dirty beyond belief, save in the cemented floor, which underwent a daily sprinkling from a skin water-bag, and a daily lashing with a reed broom. There was a mark of the passage of that skin bag up the narrow stairs in a cleaner streak along the grimy walls, and a mark of that reed broom in the spatter-work dado of slush round the room. The smoke of rushlights blackened the arched niches, their oily dribblings seamed the once white-washed walls below, and centuries of cobwebs hung on the rough rafters. No furniture of any sort or kind, excepting the low stool on which Zainub crouched and the string cot whereon the girl had flung herself recklessly — not even resting fairly, but half on, half off, each listless curve showing her indifferent despair, her flimsy veil crushed into a pillow, her unkempt yet braided hair showing she had not thought of it for days; no uncommon sight in the *zenâna*, when so-and-so's "constitution is disturbed," as the phrase runs.

"Would it soothe thee to talk of it?" whined the old lady.

"No, no!" Azîzan sat up in sudden anger. "I hate him! I hate everybody!" Then, her own confused emotion being strange and new to her, she sought refuge, with a whimper, in her old sullenness.

"*Ari!* pretty one," replied Zainub, relieved at something tangible. "Thou art right to hate him. Yet grieve not, since he hath gained naught of thee. Thou hast passed him by scornfully."

On the face turned to the dirty wall something like a smile quivered. "He hath the pot—the Ayôdhya pot," murmured Azîzan, half to herself. "He kept that—he liked that." The duenna beat her shrivelled hands together and laughed shrilly.

"*Whâ illâh!* he hath kept it, sure enough, but he will rue it. Look you! I know not the ins and outs, yet will the pot bring evil. Yea, even though he hath given it to the *mem* up-stairs."

Azîzan was on her feet ere the words were finished, her eyes aflame, her whole figure trembling with excitement.

"He hath given it away! Mai Zainub, is it truth? He hath given it to the *mem!* Oh, how I hate them! It is mine! I will have it back—I will! I will!"

She flung herself once more on the bed, almost choking with her passionate cries, wild in her uncontrolled jealousy, while Zainub, mystified and half impatient, deprecated the foolish, impossible desire. Did she not want revenge? Well, the pot was to bring it about. It would bring money to the Treasury also; and before that consideration, what mere personal whim could stand? Finally, it was not hers, but the dewan's, who had a right to let the pot go as he chose. Azîzan's ultimatum came swiftly, with a savage gleam in her light eyes: "Then I will die, and others shall die too."

The girl was no fool; she could see through the secret of Zainub's docility by the light of many a covert allusion of her companions to those strange eyes. Well, if the power was hers, she would use it. Give her back the Ayôdhya pot or take the chance. Zainub crept away disconsolate; even with her life-long experience of the vagaries in which hysterical girls indulged, she demanded shrilly of High Heaven if there had ever been contrariety equal to Azîzan's! To set aside the possibility of revenge! Still, she must do her best, and if the *mem* had the Ayôdhya pot in the palace there was always a chance of being able to steal it. As a beginning, she spent some of Chândni's rupees on sweetmeats, and, hiding the tray under her domino, set off to pay her respects to Mrs. Boynton's *ayah.*

"The *burka* is certainly a most mysterious garment," remarked Gwen, as she leaned over the balcony just as Zainub shuffled through the court-yard on her errand. "Did I ever mention the fright I had one morning here? I awoke thinking that a pair of those latticed goggles were glaring at me; but it was only Fuzli looking in to see if I were awake. Still, it alarmed me."

"Women have a hard time of it," said Lewis, languidly, from the arm-chair at her side, where he was playing the part of interesting invalid, after four days of unwelcome fever. "How I should hate to have nerves."

"We are not a whole army of martyrs, however," objected Rose, swiftly; "I, for one, decline to be credited with them."

As she sat pouring out the tea with George Keene's help

her face rather belied her words. She looked fine-drawn and eager, her eyes bright yet tired. Gwen smiled confidentially at her companion.

"People in 'good times' never have nerves, so you and Mr. Keene have no excuse for them at present. By-the-way, you must have been successful with the partridges to-day, for I assure you, Lewis, they were not in to breakfast till past twelve." Not much in the words, much in the manner. It made Rose bring her cup of tea to the balcony, and stand looking with a satirical smile at the pair seated there before she turned to George.

"We think Mr. Gordon is in a 'good time' also, don't we, Mr. Keene? You should break something too; Mrs. Boynton would be quite equal to another patient." The crudeness, not to say rudeness, of her own words startled her into adding, hastily, "For she is a good nurse, isn't she, Mr. Gordon?"

"First-class for one," he replied, coolly; "but I doubt her managing three. Therefore, if Keene is going to break something, as you suggest, it would be as well if, for a change, you took some care of yourself. At present you look miserably ill."

Rose flushed into health at once. "I! Rubbish! If you have quite finished tea, Mr. Keene, let us go on with that match at tennis."

"There they go, supremely happy," commented Gwen, from her post of vantage, after a pause. "I'm a shockingly bad chaperone; but that is your fault, Lewis, for getting fever. Do you think *monsieur le père* will be *very* angry?"

He shifted irritably. "My dear Gwen, don't overdo it, for goodness' sake! I'm grateful; you know that quite well. But if you want me to believe that Keene is in love with Miss Tweedie I must decline to agree. The lad is palpably in love with you—like the rest of us. As for Miss Tweedie, I decline to have any opinion at all. Girls of her type are beyond me. She looks ill, of course; but no woman can stand half a dozen hours in the saddle before breakfast, and half a dozen singles before dinner, with, I suppose, half a dozen problems before lunch, and half a dozen books before bed. The thing's absurd;

and as you don't seem able to stop it, it is as well we are leaving Hodinuggar so soon."

His distinct loss of temper made Gwen change the subject outwardly, but retain it inwardly, as a justification of her tactics. They had been very simple. A word to George of gratitude for his care of Rose, and a playful remark about the latter's anxiety for the patient's comfort, had left the elder woman mistress of the situation. She was in no hurry, however, to bring it to a crisis. Time enough for that when they should have returned to civilization, and she had had that letter from the jeweller's, which might even now be waiting for a Mrs. Arbuthnot at the post-office at Rajpore. Perhaps she might not have found Rose so ready to acquiesce in her plans, through which the young girl saw perfectly, if they had not fallen in with the latter's convenience. It was easier that Lewis Gordon should believe her occupied with George, and better for the boy than dangling after Gwen all day; *he* was too good for that sort of thing. She told herself this, savagely, many times a day; even when, with a worldly wisdom beyond her years, she was playing the part of elder sister and confidante to the lad's ardent admiration. As for him, he was supremely happy between the occupations of worshipping the most perfect woman in the world and being companion to the jolliest girl he had ever known.

The day had been hot and sultry, unusually so for the time of year, and as the four stood saying good-night to each other for the last time on the roof, the sheet-lightning was shimmering in a faint haze low down on the eastern horizon.

"Rain," said Lewis Gordon, in an undertone, to Rose. "Lucky for that dusty *dhooli* journey to-morrow evening. In the meantime, I hope it may cure your headache."

"I have no headache," she replied, coldly.

"I'm glad you did not say no head; that perjury could have been proved. Good-night." He turned to his cousin, and let his hand linger in hers affectionately.

"Don't be alarmed if the storm is a bad one," he said, gently, with a smile.

"Of course I shall be alarmed," she answered, gayly; "then you and Mr. Keene will have no peace, for you don't suppose I intend to stay on the roof in order to be struck by lightning. I shall turn you out down-stairs at a moment's notice."

George, with adoring eyes on his divinity, suggested eagerly that if he returned to the bungalow the ladies could move down at once. Gordon no longer required any one at night, and it would be more comfortable.

"Nonsense," cried Rose, impatiently, "I don't believe it will rain. Anyhow, I shall stay where I am, storm or no storm."

"Nerves or no nerves," parodied Lewis, "Keene shall come into my room, Gwen, and I will order his to be got ready for emergencies. Then, if nature does convulse, you can seek shelter without disturbing us. Even Miss Tweedie will allow the wisdom of that arrangement from a masculine, and therefore selfish, point of view."

She did allow it inwardly. The worst of Lewis Gordon was his knack of being right in a way which forced her into disagreement. This consciousness accentuated her obstinacy, and even when Mrs. Boynton, pathetic and plaintive in a trailing white dressing-gown, sat on the edge of the girl's bed, beseeching her to let discretion be the better part of valor, she would not yield. She was not going to give color to Mr. Gordon's caricature of womanhood. Besides, it was close down-stairs; she had a headache and liked the air. Finally, she was not afraid of being left alone; Gwen could go down if she wished. As she watched the little procession bearing pillows and blankets file down the stairs, with the *ayah* in the rear, protesting that "big storm come kill *missy baba* for laugh old Fuzli," she felt glad to be left alone. Her head did ache; what is more, her pulses were bounding with a touch of sun-fever. It would be gone by morning, yet perhaps Lewis had been right also in saying that she had been exposing herself too much. The inclination to lean her hot head on the cool marble balustrade, and sit there under the restful sky, was strong; but with an instinct of fight she set it aside almost fiercely, and, after looping back the curtains of the corner-room so as to let in what air there was, lay down decorously; but not to sleep. A dreary, disturbing round of thought kept her awake, sending her back and back again to the same point: the assertion that she had certainly been overdoing it. That was the cause of her depression—until suddenly, causelessly, her native truth rebelled against the self-deception, and she sat up in the dark, pressing the palms of her hot hands together. What was the use of lying to herself? Was it not better to confess frankly that, with all his faults, Lewis Gordon interested her more than any one else in the world? Perhaps it was love; yes, she cared for him as she cared for no one else in the world; and was it not detestable to blush and deny the fact instead of being straightforward? At any time this indictment of her honesty would have been intolerable; now, with fever running riot in her veins, it forced her to exaggerated action. She had been behaving like a romantic school-girl in a novel. Well, in the future there should be no possibility of her denying the fact that she had wilfully, and without due cause, fallen in love with a man who did not love her. Yes, fallen in love! Her cheeks were flushed, her eyes shining, when the light of the candle she lit fell on them. As she passed quickly into the mirror-room the thousand facets gave back her eagerness, her determination, as she deliberately chose out Lewis Gordon's photograph from a folding-frame standing below the Ayôdhya pot. She stood for a moment looking at it, struggling with her pride; then she passed back into her room again and thrust it under her pillow. That was an end of all lies, at any rate! After that she would never be able to deny it—never be able to deny that she was a romantic idiot! She gave an odd, almost happy, little laugh as she crept into her bed again, where, after a time, she fell asleep, with one hand guarding something under her pillow—just as Gwen had guarded something in her corner-room a few nights before. No doubt it was the growing coolness of the night which soothed the girl; on the other hand, it may have been the testimony of a good conscience not ashamed to confess the truth.

The lightning shimmered over her sleeping face, and, as it

shimmered, showed a black arch of cloud looming from the east. By-and-by the wind rose, bringing with it the fresh, earthy smell of distant rain. It was now between second and third jackal cry; that is to say, the deadest hour in the Indian night, when even nature and dogs sleep. Yet there were two figures stealing round the base of the dewan's tower to the piled ruins of the odd wall, which had fallen on the potter's house long years before; fallen suddenly in the night, after just such a storm as that now sweeping up with the wind.

"*Ari!* heart's core!" pleaded a cracked voice. "Sure the rain begins even now, and God knows what the old stairs be like. 'Tis sixteen year gone since they were used. Holy Fâtima, what a flash! 'Tis no night for women-folk to be out; be wise and leave it. To-morrow, perchance, when they pack the things, I may lay hands on it."

"Be still, *mai!* What good to talk when 'tis settled! What didst say? Straight up to the hole in the wall, three steps down to the ledge, along that to the window-slit in the dewan's stair, so by them to the gate; thou hast the key. No! 'tis open, thou sayest! Is not that right? Lo! *mai*, 'tis easy."

"In the old days; but the lattice parapet is gone, they say, and a false step—oh, Azîzan, be wise! Would God I had not told thee of it!"

A faint laugh echoed into the pitchy darkness. "Thy aches and pains would never have reached the pot otherwise, O mother!"

The hint was not lost on old Zainub. She stumbled on hastily until a shimmer of lightning showed an opening half hidden by débris in the base of the tower, into which she crept. "See, here are the matches," she whimpered, "and witness, O Azîzan! I have done all, even to letting thee wear the old dress, since it pleaseth thee; though wherefore, God knows."

"'Tis light and strong," interrupted the girl, hastily. "Stay you here, mother; I will be back erelong."

A box of Swedish *tändstickors*, made for the British market, with a portrait of Mr. Pickwick on the cover, was an incongruous item in the scene, yet one of them looked tragic enough, as it sent a glow through Azîzan's brown fingers and showed a broken flight of steps.

"I will be back erelong," she repeated, at the first turn. Then the light went with her into the very heart of the wall.

Zainub sat crouching in the dark, shivering and groaning. "*Ai*, my sins!" she muttered, hiding her face from a sudden flash of lightning; "the pains of Jehannum are on me already. I perish of fear; the breath leaves my body." She rocked herself backward and forward ceaselessly, moaning and muttering, a weird figure guarding the stair, up which Azîzan was toiling by the light of other *tändstickors.* Beyond the possibility of a half-torpid snake, or a shower of loosened bricks from above, there was, as yet, no danger, even to one so unused to effort as this *zenâna*-bred girl. Thus she had time to think of what she was to do when she reached the roof. For one thing, she had to steal the Ayôdhya pot; for the rest she was not sure; but something ready for impulse lay tucked away in the waist folds of the old woollen dress. A glimmering slit, showing its arched top against a lighter darkness of sky, brought her back to the present. This must be the hole in the wall; and beyond it lay a chasm of night. She lit another match, and held it over the gulf. The flame burned steadily, for the stair, in winding through the wall of the tower, had brought her to leeward of the storm. Nothing was to be seen save the blackness of clouds above, the blackness of—God knows what—below! Then as she stood peering out into the darkness, a shiver of silent lightning revealed a silver plain far down beneath her feet, and above, to the right, silver balconies and cupolas. That must be the roof whither she was bound. The expenditure of more matches disclosed the three steps downward, and at right angles a ledge along the wall, ending in a buttress some thirty feet off. That must be the support of the dewan's stair. Both steps and ledge had once been protected by a latticed parapet; now they were edged by the blackness of the gulf. But the ledge seemed perfect as ever, and the rest was, after all, mere fancy; especially at night, when you could not see. Should she risk it? The match she held left indecision on her face as it flickered out. The storm, close at hand, took breath, as it were, for the onslaught in a long pause of intense silent darkness.

Then a sudden shimmer shot over the old tower, spreading a silver mantle upon the slender figure of a girl clinging to the wall.

Darkness again, and then once more the same sight — a girl with her face against the wall, moving step by step, slowly, deliberately nearer and nearer each time to the buttress. Then a little cry of fear or joy, too inarticulate for comprehension, rose on the still air, and when the next shaft of light came it found nothing but the bare wall. The figure was gone.

So much might have been seen by any watcher on the roof. But there was none; it lay still and deserted. The very wind, stirring the folds of the curtain Rose had looped aside, made no noise, and the light and the dark played their game of hide-and-seek in silence—an odd game in the mirror-room, and the arches on arches of shadow leading to it. Each separate scrap of looking-glass would blaze out like a star, sending a beam on the blue bowl of the Ayôdhya pot; then dive into the dark, again carrying a reflection of the scene with it in triumph: miles of shadowy arches, millions of blue bowls, glowing amid countless stars; thousands of looped curtains, showing a girl asleep on a white bed. But after a while the stars carried a new sight: a girl in a strange dress crouching by the bed. The lightning shimmered keenly over the group several times, bringing into glittering relief something held by the crouching figure, and something held close to a flushed cheek by the sleeping girl. The one was a knife, the other a photograph of a young man in an immaculate coat and irreproachable tie. Different things, indeed; yet the girls who held them differed little. They were both in dreamland; for Azîzan, as she crouched beside Rose, felt that she was in a new world. The whiteness, the stillness, the solitude, guarding the pure sleep of girlhood — the refinement, the peace—made her think involuntarily of the dead laid out for their last rest. She gave a quick little sigh; her hand relaxed its grasp; then tightened again, as a flash showed the photograph clearly. It was a picture of some one. If it was his picture, why, then— She struck a match softly and peered closer. No! She paused, taking advantage of the light to look at the sleeper. Rose stirred.

"Who is it?" she murmured, in the low, quick tones of those who talk in their sleep. The watcher's hand closed silently round the match, extinguishing it.

"I am Azîzan, *huzoor*."

The immediate answer had its effect. Rose nestled her head to the pillow once more, and from the ensuing darkness her breathing came soft and regular. Suddenly, with a crack, the thunder rolled right overhead, the wind hushed, the heavy drops of rain fell, each in a distinct plash for a second, then merged into a hissing downpour on the hard roof. Rose started up in bed, just as the quivering shaft of lightning blazed through the mirror-room upon a girl in an odd dress, holding the Ayôdhya pot close to her breast — a girl with odd light eyes. "I am Azîzan, *huzoor*." These words seemed still in her ears, recalling a confused memory of the potter and her own promise.

"Your father wants you, Azîzan," she said, half in a dream, and the sound of her own voice woke her thoroughly to darkness. Had she been dreaming? The wind, rising now the storm had broken, swept rain-laden through the open door, extinguishing the matches she struck hastily, so that the first glimmer of her own candle was echoed by the *ayah's* lantern, as the latter came paddling over the streaming roof with petticoats held high over her trousered knees, and shrill denunciations of the *missy baba's* obstinacy high above the storm. Rose Tweedie's thought flew to Lewis Gordon's warning, and his wisdom reminded her of her own foolishness. That was not a dream; she blushed violently over it as she thrust the photograph out of sight before her attendant rolled the bedding into a bundle and staggered with it down-stairs. As the girl followed ignominiously in the mackintosh and umbrella supplied by that injured official, she told herself she must indeed have had fever to commit such a ridiculous folly. Her ears tingled over the very recollection of what had perhaps saved her life.

Meanwhile, the girl with the Ayôdhya pot, whom Rose, in her absorbing shame, had decided must have been a dream, was stumbling down the broken stairs once more, her courage gone, her chaos of emotion reduced to one heartwhole desire to reach Zainub in safety. How she had crossed the ledge again she scarcely knew; but in the effort she had dropped the *tändstickors*, and as she felt her way step by step in the dark she was sobbing like a frightened child. Half-way down a displaced brick on the outside masonry allowed the lightning to glimmer over a sort of landing, where she paused for breath. "God and His Prophet! What was that huddled up on the next step?" She had to await another flash ere she could decide, and in the interval her heart beat with sickening, fearful curiosity.

"*Mai* Zainub! *Mai* Zainub!" Her cry of relief and content came swift as the flash. There was no answer save renewed darkness bringing downright terror. Still that was a human form she had seen! "*Mai* Zainub! *Mai* Zainub!" she called again. There was no flutter beneath the hand seeking the heart. Could she be dead! Then came a blaze of light, showing her the familiar face all unfamiliar; the fixed eyes wide open, the jaw fallen. The next instant she was dashing down the stairs recklessly; down and down, out into the open over the débris, anywhere so as to leave the horror behind. The wind caught her, the rain blinded her, the thunder cracked overhead as she ran on blindly, till with a cry she slipped on a loose brick and fell stunned against a mass of broken masonry. So she lay, looking almost as dead as the poor old duenna, huddled up on that landing in the secret stair where, with one final twinge at her heart, the rheumatism had left her forever.

An hour after, when the storm had passed and a faint grayness told that the dawn was at hand, a feeble light began to flicker about the ruins; up and down, up and down, as if it sought for something. It was Fuzl Elâhi, the potter of Hodinuggar, looking for his dead daughter. He had looked for her thus after every storm for sixteen years; and this time, with the Miss *sahib's* promise to send her back lingering in his memory, he sought in hope.

When the sun rose three things were missing from the palace at Hodinuggar — the Ayôdhya pot, Azîzan, and the old duenna.

Up-stairs, while George and Gwen and Rose, all for private reasons of their own, acquiesced, Lewis Gordon declared that some servant must have broken it in dusting the room, and, as usual, made away with the pieces. Down-stairs the same unanimity prevailed. Azîzan and Zainub had their reasons for running away; they would be found erelong, since no one near at hand dare shelter them, and the old woman could not go far. If the folk up-stairs had known of the disappearance downstairs, they might have connected the two losses; but they did not. So none of these three things were traced, and no one cared very much, especially Gwen Boynton. The pot might have reminded her of Hodinuggar, and now that she was leaving it, there were some things she intended to forget; besides, no one, now, could ever say she had taken the jewels.

CHAPTER XII

"I NEVER was so tired of any place in my life," remarked Mrs. Boynton. "It was not so bad at first; but nothing would ever induce me to attempt the wilderness again."

She was back in the big hall at Rajpore again, the centre of a circle assembled to bid her welcome; for Gwen was not the sort of person to come or go unnoticed. She looked charming in a new dress which she had ordered on the morning after the fire to be ready against her return. The band was playing, the dim lights were twinkling above the polished floor; people were coming and going through the swing doors, and Dan, devoted as ever, was waiting for his promised first waltz. A sheer bit of vanity, this promise on Gwen's part; she liked to re-enter her familiar world looking her best, and Dan was the best dancer in the room. Yet she lingered with her hand on his arm to glance at Lewis Gordon, who, still wearing a sling, stood on the outside of the circle trying not to look bored.

"And I don't think civilized people ought to go to those wild places and live in uncivilized ways," she continued, clinching the argument against Hodinuggar. "It is demoralizing, living on the roof without doors and windows. Look at my cousin; I don't believe he will ever settle down to work again."

"No locks had they, eh?" quoted Lewis. "I shouldn't have thought you were likely to approve of Arcadia anyhow, or Hodinuggar either. But I assure you, Graham, Mrs. Boynton played the Light of the Harem to perfection." She met the general chorus of belief with a little shudder, not all put on.

"I hope not! If I had thought that, I would have elected to stay in my room till I could appear like a Christian. But it only bears out my contention—civilized people should eschew barbarian environments; they are not safe."

"A bad lookout for me," laughed George, who had been given three days' leave in order to escort the party to head-quarters. Gwen turned to him in kindly familiarity.

"You! Oh, I'll except you as beyond temptation if you like. Shall you be here on my return? the next is ours, remember."

She knew quite well that the boy had remembered little else since she had given the promise half an hour before; but she knew also how sweet the reminder would be with all those older aspirants standing by. And she was always anxious to please when she could. Lewis Gordon, however, lifted his eyebrows and walked over rather aggressively to Rose Tweedie. "Why aren't you dancing?" he asked. "I am, unfortunately, a cripple; but Keene, I am sure, would be horrified if he saw you sitting down. May I tell him?"

"No, thanks. I don't feel up to dancing to-night. I fancy I have been overdoing myself a little over tennis and riding at Hodinuggar."

There was no challenge in her manner, but Lewis chose to suppose one.

"Your wisdom, Miss Tweedie, is of that truly feminine type which begins when the cake is finished. But it is refreshing to find you have these womanly weaknesses; without them you would be unassailable."

"If the carriage is here," remarked Rose, quietly, "I think I shall go home. If you see my father, Mr. Gordon, tell him I have done so."

His manner changed in an instant. "I will tell him now, and join you if I may, for a lift back to the club. I am out of it also; my brute of a bearer has bandaged me all wrong, and I must get it altered."

Rose, possessed of an ambulance certificate, would have liked to offer help, but had to be silent. Even on such a charitable errand, Mrs. Grundy would have been horrified at a visit to a bachelor's quarters. And while she acknowledged the limitation, Rose felt irritated by it as she stood waiting at the door for Lewis Gordon's return, and watching Mrs. Boynton skim by like a swallow under Dan's guidance. Why should the married women have all the chances?

"She waltzes beautifully, doesn't she?" asked Lewis, finding her so engaged.

"She does everything beautifully," replied Rose, coldly.

Not a good beginning for their drive together; but it was always so. As she watched the carriage taking her companion on to his quarters after it had set her down, she told herself, disconsolately, that they seemed to have a bad effect on each other, and to show to the very worst advantage in each other's company. She, at any rate, was never so painfully uncompromising in her condemnation of other people's foibles; perhaps because she did not care whether they existed or not. But she did care, dreadfully, when Lewis was in question; that was the worst of it.

Mrs. Boynton was not long, either, in leaving the hall; in fact, George Keene's promised waltz was but half through when she exclaimed at the lateness of the hour, and after salving over his disappointment with an invitation to tea on the morrow, bade her coachman drive home—an order, however, which she changed at the gates of the garden, so that the carriage instead of turning westward towards the civil station, chose the eastward road towards the native town; towards the post-office, also, which lay close to the Dekhani gate of the city. For a letter addressed to a certain Mrs. Arbuthnot should be waiting "to be called for," and at that hour, a few minutes before closing time, all but subordinates would have left the office; so a veiled lady asking for a letter would run no risk of being recognized. Yet, as Gwen Boynton drove home again along the dark mall with the expected letter still unread in her pocket, she told herself there was really no need for such precautions; only it was as well to prevent those gossiping native jewellers from advertising the fact that *Mem* Boynton *sahib* was so hard put to it that she had to sell her trinkets. That was all; yet each passing carriage as it flashed its lamp-rays on her face, seemed desirous of proclaiming the fact that she had been citywards to the eyes of its unseen occupants.

She felt a feverish desire to know who those occupants might be, and a distinct dislike to and distrust of the whole business rose up in her, making her glad to find time had run so short that she must dress at once for the dinner-party given to welcome her back to Rajpore. With a feeling of relief from immediate certainty she threw the letter still unopened on the sitting-room table as she passed it. But half an hour after when she returned, in her trailing white garments, the sight of it changed her mood. Better to know. After all, the things might be paste, and worth nothing; that would perhaps be the best ending to the incident.

She sat down by the table, and turned the envelope over in her delicate hands. It might mean so much; it might mean so little. And what, in either case, did she mean to do? She had literally no idea as with reluctant fingers she tore slowly at the envelope.

It seemed to her as if ages had passed before she realized that she was staring down at those few words telling her, briefly, that the jewels sent were worth six thousand rupees, and would she have the money in notes, or by bill of exchange?

How simple it was! No question of taking or leaving. Only whether it should be in notes, or by bill of exchange! And six thousand would not only pay Dan — if, indeed, she decided on that — it would also leave something over for the coming season at Simla. A welcome something, indeed, when all one's wardrobe had been burned; and people were so particular how one was dressed. Then if one came to think of it, did she not deserve some compensation for that loss of her dresses? Trivial thought going further towards decision than any of the others. So in the midst of her meditations a white-robed servant appeared at the door, saying, indifferently, "*Gordon sahib salaam deta.*"

Another triviality; yet she rose quickly, thrusting the letter into her pocket. So he had come already! She had known well enough that he would miss her; that he would come to seek her, but this was soon, indeed. "*Salaam belo.*" She gave the permission to show him in calmly, and yet the woman's triumph at her own power came uppermost, as awaiting his entry she turned to finish the fastening of a bunch of white gardenias. Her back was towards him, but he could see her, and she knew that he could see her, framed by the long mirror like a picture, her hair a golden setting to the diamond stars, her white arms whiter than her white dress — whiter than the furred cloak hanging loosely from her white shoulders, or the huge ostrich-feather fan dangling from her slender waist. Lewis thought instantly of Fedora in the ballroom scene; and then that, on the stage or off it, he had never seen a more utterly desirable woman to present as his wife for the world's approval. That is a feeling which decides many marriages.

"It seems a shame to trouble you," he began, "but the bearer *is* such a fool. The sling is always too high or too low, and I want to go to the club. I thought you wouldn't mind settling it, and I saw by the light in this room that you were still here."

Every word of this speech, though the speaker was unconscious of it, showed Gwen that her cousin had been thinking the very thoughts she wished him to think. Translated by her feminine *finesse* it stood thus: "You are too lovely to be bothered, but then you do everything so well. It is too deadly dull without you; so, knowing I could rely on your sympathy, I kept a lookout for some sign of your presence." Now, when a woman hears everything she desires in the words of a man, her reply is generally a return in kind. In this case words were of less importance than those pretty, soft, white hands so solicitous over his comfort.

"Is that better?" she asked. Her concern was absolutely honest, for she was a woman every inch of her; loving to cosset and care for her men-folk. Those hands were so close to his cheek that their softness seemed to thrill through him. After all, was it not a wife's part to flatter and cajole?—to make life soft and sweet? Who could do that better than she?

"Dear little hands," he said, laying his suddenly on one and pressing it tight to his breast. Then a quick passion blazed in his eyes. "Gwen," he cried, "ah, Gwen, how sweet you are!" The ring in his voice satisfied him. Yes, this was happiness! and the certainty made him stoop to kiss the face so close to his own. And then? She was beautiful as ever; he was cool as ever. The glamour had gone, the world was as it had been before his fate was settled; for he had settled it definitely, though he scarcely knew if he were glad or sorry for the fact.

"Am I to beg your pardon, dear?" he said, gently, looking into her gracious eyes; "or will you believe that you have spoiled me so that I cannot get on without the spoiler? Will you forgive me, and try and put up with me, Gwen?"

"Of course I will forgive you, Lewis," she began, plaintively; and then the lack of emotion in her own voice, her own heart, struck her disagreeably. Yet what else could she expect, when her first thought had been one of gratitude for that offer of six thousand rupees in her pocket? For all that she felt aggrieved, thinking, illogically, how different it was with Dan. Unwonted tears rose to her eyes, and made her face tender as she went on: "And why should I not spoil you, Lewis? You know I am always glad to help—anybody; and after all we are cousins—after all, there is always *that* between us." She did not know why she offered him this excuse, this loop-hole of escape. Not from calculation or *finesse*, certainly; yet it touched him as nothing else would have done; for he, too, had felt the flatness of it all—he, too, had thought vaguely that the sacrifice of his freedom deserved more solid satisfaction in return.

"Yes, dear," he replied, half playfully, "there is that; but there is something more, is there not, Gwen? At least I hope so, for you have spoiled me—I cannot do without you." It was her hand, however, that he kissed this time, and then the carriage being announced, he escorted her to it most decorously, taking care that her dress should not suffer from the wheel with all the attentive calm of a husband. The fact struck him ruefully as he went off to the club, feeling that his fate was definitely settled; though, of course, the matter need not be made public at once; Gwen would be sure to prefer that her season at Simla should be untrammelled by an open engagement, and he was in no hurry. Leave was inconvenient till the cold weather; so, during the rains, when people wanted amusement, they could afford them the excitement of the news.

Gwen's feelings as she drove to her dinner-party were of the same nature. It was settled, definitely settled, of course; but no one need know of it; no one must guess at it until she had given Dan his *congé*. It was the first time she had ever really put that thought into words, and the very suggestion made her heart sink. There would be no lack of emotion about that interview at any rate. Even the preliminary of paying back the debt seemed beset with difficulties. He was so quick to understand, so hard to turn aside once he had the least clew to her feelings. Finally, after much cogitation, she decided on waiting until she had actually received the money from Delhi. It would be more difficult for him to refuse the notes down on the table; besides, George Keene's leave would be over, he would have returned to Hodinuggar, and the possibility of confidences given under the influence of strong excitement would be over; for Gwen had not failed to notice the friendship growing between the two; indeed, in a way, she was vexed at what seemed to her a childish, almost absurd deference, on Dan's part, to the lad's opinion—Dan, who was his superior in every possible way; that is to say, if he chose to be reasonable. Last of all, the delay meant a closer proximity to that annual flight to the Hills, which would provide her with a safe retreat. So she set the idea aside for a time, and became cheerful over the respite.

George, having tea with her next day, thought her, if possible, gayer, brighter, more charming than ever; especially when his talk turned on his hero, Dan Fitzgerald. Now, no one had ever heard Mrs. Boynton say an unkind word of her neighbors; indeed, the peculiar *cachet* this gave to her personality made her remembered in after-years by all admirers, not so much as a beautiful, but as a perfectly gracious woman. To George, accustomed chiefly to the high-spirited freedom of sisters, this virtue seemed divine, the more so because the world generally disapproved of Dan—of his recklessness and want of reverence. Gwen Boynton, on the contrary, found nothing to regret, save that Mr. Fitzgerald was not the finest man *out* of the service, instead of *in* it; since, as Mr. Gordon said, he was too good to slave among men years his junior. Whereupon George, his young face full of importance, informed her, as a dead secret, that the reason Dan stuck to his colors was that a girl had promised to marry him whenever he got his promotion; that would be in the next spring at the latest, since as he, George Keene, was in charge of the sluice, no prejudicial contretemps could possibly occur. And Gwen, with an actual smile at the mystification, which so many women dearly love, reminded him that even when folk did their best, slips came between cups and lips. The lad laughed joyously.

"Oh, I don't venture to stand sponsor for the young woman, of course! I only meant that Dan would get his promotion if it depends on that gate being kept shut; I carry the key about with me, as Hare did in the 'Pair of Spectacles.' It's peculiarly inconvenient, of course, but as they say on the Surrey side, 'the villain who would reach it must pass over my dead body.'" Gwen, who had a fine taste, admired the determination underlying the jest. Mr. Fitzgerald, she said, was lucky in such a friend. Nevertheless, it might be a doubtful kindness, since the loss of promotion might induce him to seek fairer fortune elsewhere.

She insisted on this argument, even with herself, yet her heart beat uncomfortably fast when, delay having been extended to the limit of possibility, she sat awaiting Dan's arrival in the pretty room which was so like herself in its softness and its solid attention to comfort, beneath all the delicate tasteful ornamentations. The three thousand rupees in notes were ready for use in her pocket, and a long letter from Hodinuggar in George's bold handwriting lay on the writing-table beside the bouquet of flowers which Lewis had sent her from his garden that morning. From the next room came the sound of the *ayah* dusting out boxes against the immediate packing up. All Gwen's excuses for delay had vanished; yet she found it as hard as ever to face one man's confidence—the confidence which showed in his glad greeting. It forced her into beginning remotely, half affectionately, by regrets over his want of tact at the Delhi conference. It had not been an unqualified success so far as Dan's departmental popularity went. How could it be one when he had deliberately but savagely attacked the wisdom of his elders? True, the under-secretary had snickered in describing the scene, and even Mr. Gordon had laughed amid his vexation, saying that none knew better than he what a confounded ass Colonel Tweedie could be when confronted in public with new ideas. At the same time it had been needless, almost brutal, on Fitzgerald's part, seeing he had right on his side; that alone should have made him temperate. Of course, once his method had been suggested, no other was open to any one out of a lunatic asylum; all the more reason for mercy in bringing the fact home. So Gwen in her soft voice tried to convey her blame to the sinner, who, with his hands in his coat-pockets, stood before her trying to look penitent, and only succeeding in looking provokingly debonnair.

"But sure, it's the blatant stupidity of the world that is its greatest crime," he protested. "Don't I remember my mother saying to us, 'Ah, children, I don't mind your being naughty, I can whack you for that, but I will not have you stupid.'"

Gwen laughed. Who could help it over that picture of home training so utterly unfit for one recipient at least. Indeed, she was conscious of a wish that her companion were more dull; less full of eager vitality. It made that inevitable task so hard.

"Dan," she began desperately, in sudden resolve, "I want to talk about business. The fact is I've had a windfall of money lately, and so I—I intend to pay you back that loan of yours. It isn't fair—"

He was on his knees beside her to get a closer look at her face ere she had finished.

"What is it, Gwen?" he asked, rapidly, "you owe me nothing. What do you mean? There is no question of money between us," he went on, in answer to her silence, "there never was, but once; there never shall be again. Is it anything else, Gwen? Anything in which I can help? or are you only feeling afraid of the future? Tell me outright, dear."

Where was the good, she thought, petulantly, of delays and preparations, when he met her first hint in this direct fashion; yet against the grain, for she hated scenes, she took her courage in her hand and spoke up:

"Yes, I am afraid—afraid of the future for you as well as for myself. Oh, Dan! I really wish you would sit down like a Christian, and listen properly. Kissing my hand is no answer, and I am serious. This idle, foolish promise of thinking about it all seriously next year when you get your promotion is not fair to you. Don't laugh, Dan—it isn't. It ties you down, and prevents your doing yourself justice. And then it isn't fair on me."

He interrupted her quickly. "How is it not fair on you, Gwen? I don't see it. You do not like any one else as much as you like me; you know you don't. And if this half-promise to me holds you back from marrying some one you do not like as you like me, why then—" His voice lowered to tender gravity, "I thank God for it as I should thank Him for any good He sent into your life."

"You do not understand," she retorted, querulously. "Surely I am the best judge of myself, and there is no reason why I should want to marry some one else because I don't think it would be right to marry you. I should make a bad wife, Dan, to any poor man; and I should not be happy. Surely, surely, I ought to know best! It isn't as if I were the inexperienced girl I was before; I have been married for years, and I think—yes, I am sure—that I am happier as I am." Her last words degenerated into something between a laugh and a sob. It really was too ridiculous, too grievous that she, Gwen Boynton, with all her knowledge of the world, should not be considered fit to judge for herself.

"Married?" he echoed, thoughtfully, and something in his voice arrested her. "No, Gwen, my dear, you have never been married. You don't even understand what it means to be married; for your knowledge of it is all evil. That's the worst of it. Don't be angry, dear, I'm not going to lecture, like Mrs. Grundy, on the sin of a loveless marriage, or the degradation of one, like the sentimentalists. Surely, surely, a man or a woman may marry from pity, from honor, from self-devotion, and yet touch the perfection of the tie. But you—" he paused awhile—"you did not only lose the love of it, Gwen; the thing itself was never yours. The facing of life, hand in hand; two of you where there was but one before. See! There is my hand, Gwen, and there is yours. A difference, isn't there? But how close they fit, each to each! How close and warm"— he paused again to smile at her. "What is it the song says, Gwen, about giving your hand where your heart can never be? Fudge! It should be, 'How can I give my heart where my hand can never be.' Yes! there they are close. I am there too, my darling. Ready, always ready! Never again, Gwen, without the touch of a hand like 'children frightened in the night; like children crying for the light.' Never again, Gwen—never again!"

They were sitting together side by side on the sofa, her hand held in his so lightly that she could have withdrawn it without any effort. But it lay there in his clasp, as she sat listening to the soft voice. Listening on, even when it ceased, as if its spell lingered. They were not even looking at each other. Beyond the silent room, through the open door, the sunshine showed Gwen's bearer cleaning the lamps with a dirty duster. Not a romantic sight; but it is to be doubted if either saw it; for their eyes were blinded by the great darkness in which they found themselves, trustfully, hand in hand. At last, with a little shiver, she tried to move, but his fingers closed on hers more firmly.

"Too late, Gwen! Too late! You should have taken it away when you had the chance," he said, joyously. O Gwen, my darling, if we were married you would forget to be afraid, as you did just now; didn't you, Gwen?"

"I believe you mesmerize me," she replied, trying to jest;

"and forgetting bills doesn't help to pay them, does it, Dan?"

"So you are back at the money again. Well, I don't care. Money or no money; promotion or no promotion."

"No, no!" she interrupted, yielding as she always did to his decision; "that really is not fair—the bargain was promotion—it was indeed."

"Promotion be it," he assented, with a contented laugh; "though I can't for the life of me see what it has got to do with the matter."

"You would at least have more pay," she put in, wondering faintly the while how it came about that they should be discussing such questions when she had meant to be so firm. "I could not marry a pauper, could I?"

"Indeed, and indeed, it might be the best thing for you; then nobody would give you credit, dear, but me. And I—O Gwen, my dear, my dear—you might be bereft of everything—of all, save your own self, and sure I would give you credit for the *all* still. Credit!" he echoed to his own words, "isn't it absurd to be talking of it, as if either of us could be debtor or creditor to the other."

That was all she gained from the interview; that, and the unwelcome remembrance of full five minutes when the touch of her lover's hand and the sound of his voice had made her forget the world, the flesh, and the devil. But not for long. As she sat after Dan had gone, trying to comfort herself by the fact that one never knew what might happen, that they might all be dead and buried before the necessity of a choice arose, which, by-the-way, was her favorite consolation, she looked up to see the servant standing at the door, doubtfully expectant.

"What is it?" she asked, languidly.

"The *vakeel* of the Dewans of Hodinuggar, *huzoor*. He hath brought an offering, and desires an audience."

"The Dewans of Hodinuggar!" repeated Gwen, startled.

"The agent, *huzoor*. Shall I tell him the *mem sahib* is going to eat the air in her carriage? It is but to say something about a pot, he bade me mention. A pot that the *huzoor* fancied."

Gwen stood up, holding on to the table. "Now!" she said, after a pause, "show him in now."

Mrs. Boynton's neat victoria waited for its mistress long after the smiling, obsequious visitor had given his shoe-money to the servant and departed. Waited patiently till, as it grew dark, the *ayah* came out and removed the cushions and parasol. *Mem sahib* was not well, and would not go to the gardens; she would not go out to dinner either, so the horses could be put up. Then, the bearer coming into the veranda with the lighted lamps, a shrill altercation began over the shoe-money; the *ayah* asserting that when the visit was to a lady, her female attendant had a right to half, and even the grooms putting in a claim on the ground that they had been present. Their mistress, lying on the sofa where but a short time before she had sat hand in hand with Dan Fitzgerald, heard the dispute, and had not the courage to rebuke their greed. And yet the *vakeel* of the dewans had simply brought a message that, if the *mem sahib* would like another Ayôdhya pot similar in all respects to the last, one could doubtless be found and forwarded without delay. She had refused the offer promptly, decisively; but the fact of its having been made filled her with regrets and alarms. If—oh! how lonely she felt, without a soul to stand between her and trouble! Then Dan's words recurred to her, "bankrupt of everything, yet credited with all!" They brought no comfort, however—only a vague irritation against the speaker. But for him she would not have been tempted; but for him she would never have kept the discovery of the pearls secret—if, indeed, it was a discovery. Could it be a bribe? For what? Had they found out her entanglement with Dan Fitzgerald? Her vexation blazed up at the bare suspicion, and though every fresh proof of the attraction he had for her unstable nature invariably resulted in a recoil of the pendulum, she was conscious this time that it had never before swung back so far. He was to blame; yes, he was undoubtedly to blame for the whole miserable business! She knew herself to be too upset for Lewis Gordon's sharp eyes to be a safe ordeal; so, as he was to be one of the dinner-party, she sent an excuse, and spent the long evening in nursing her wrath; a very necessary process if Gwen Boynton was to bear malice, since her temper was of the sweetest. Even with this encouragement, the next morning found her ready with excuses for everybody, herself included. After all, matters were not so serious. Three days would see her safe in Simla, where six thousand rupees would be better than three, infinitely better than none; and it would be quite easy to keep her understanding with Lewis dark for some time to come. Then what proof could any one have that she had sold or even found the jewels? Who was to say that the pot had not been stolen, jewels and all? As for the jewellers who had bought them, they neither knew her name nor address. The only possible danger lay in weakly yielding to conscience in the way of attempted restitution. Besides, if the pearls were really meant as a bribe, surely those who offered it deserved to lose them and gain nothing; for, of course, the idea of gaining anything from her was preposterous.

She went to the hall that evening cheerful as ever, and exclaimed airily at the changes one short twenty-four hours had wrought in the shifting society of mid-April. The Grahams had left, the Taylors were to start that evening if there was room in the train laden with women and babies flying before the punkahs. Laden, too, with melancholy husbands conveying their families to the foot of the Hills, whence they would return to stew in solitude. Lewis Gordon divided these unfortunates, cynically, into two classes—those who would be sent home in charge of the *khansawah* with a menu of the first month's dinners, and an almost tearful injunction not to let the master, when he went out to dine, eat things which were likely to disagree with him; and those given over to the "bottle-washer" who "can cook a little, you know." And there was truth in his cynicism. Mankind is not like an amœba, all stomach, yet nothing can be closer to tears than two sights often to be seen during Indian hot weather: the one, a meal sent away untouched in favor of a clean whiskey-and-soda; the other, an elderly Mahomedan at a bag dinner-party waving the lobster-salad away behind his master's back, and presenting him with cheese and biscuits instead. There is full-blown tragedy in both. Tragedy also in Lewis Gordon's cheerful remark to his companion: "And, by-the-bye, Robinson has been ordered home by the next mail. They are afraid of abscess. So that jolly little house at Simla is going a-begging. He asked me if I knew of a tenant, but it is rather late in the day, I fear, even though he only asks half-rent."

"I'll take it," said Gwen, calmly. "Don't stare so. The fact is, I have had a little windfall of money lately, and I hate hotels. This will be almost as cheap, and much more comfortable."

"Infinitely so," assented Lewis. The house was fully a mile nearer his quarters at Colonel Tweedie's, and that was a great convenience, especially during the rains.

CHAPTER XIII

"SEND it back! It is hers! It is not mine! He gave it her! I stole it! Don't tell! Oh, send it back! send it back!"

Over and over again through the long hot days and nights, the murmur, in its monotonous hurry, blending with the hum of the potter's wheel. The old man had removed it to the farther court-yard, where he sat working feverishly, yet without avail, so far as the village people could see through the door, beyond which they were forbidden to go. The simple folk were agog at the potter's strange looks and strange ways. He never seemed to cease working; for even when the familiar sound of the wheel was hushed, an echo rose from within. Those were the times when he stood wistfully in the dark, airless hut, beside a restless head turning itself from side to side on the hard pillow, and keeping time to the monotonous rhythm of the murmurs, "Send it back—send it back!"

"Yes, dear heart, I will send it." Then there would be silence for a while; but only for a while, since the fever strengthened day by day. Small wonder, when all nature seemed in the grip of heat. The thermometer, we are told, is accurately divided into degrees; if so, the fallacy of such classification is self-evident, since every one with experience knows that the difference between eighty-four degrees and eighty-six degrees of Fahrenheit's instrument embraces the difference between comfort and discomfort. Between these two points that engine of torture, the punka, trembles ere it begins the steady swing which is only one degree less awful than the unsteady swing necessitating the occultation of boots and other light articles of furniture with a human head. Doubtless to the uninitiated it seems a trivial affair to loop a parti-colored rag through hooks in the rafters, and to attach to it a whitewashed board with a newly-starched frill tacked to its lowest edge, thereafter making mysterious dispositions of a leathern thong, the neck of an old whiskey-bottle thrust through the mud wall, and a circumambient flask of smelling-oil. But those who know what it is, on returning from a morning ride, to find the punka in possession of your home, feel a chill at the very thought such as the thing itself will never produce by legitimate means. The hot weather is upon one, and God only knows if fever, cholera, home-sickness, or sheer deadly ennui will allow you to pass through it unscathed as an honest gentleman.

George Keene, however, over in the branded bungalow, knew nothing of the horrors of hot weather in the jungles, and while poor little Azîzan lay moaning out her impotent repentance, was actually superintending the swinging of his punkas, which is equivalent to a man personally conducting his own hanging. He even, after the manner of engineers, took pride in a device which was to secure a perfect silence in the infernal machine, all unwitting of a time when, in the scorched darkness, it might be preferable to curse a monotonous scoop giving tangible excuse for wakefulness than to lie visualizing the unseen swoop, as of some vampire eager to suck your heart's blood. Those two degrees of heat bring a thousand other changes. Even at Hodinuggar, arid as it always was, they intensified the drought till a drop of water seemed as visionary a consolation to the parched horizon as it must have been to poor Dives in the fires of hell. The very canal denied its nature as it slipped past, yellow and thick with silt from the clayey defiles of the lower hills, each little swirl and eddy looking as if streaked and pitted in mud. Yet the chill of its snowy birth came with the flood, so that in the red-hot evening George's factotum used to call through the yellow dust-haze to the groom, who sat on the edge of the canal, apparently moored to his place by a soda-water bottle tied to a string. Then Ganesha, the groom, would haul in the strange buoy, and scramble up the bank with it rapidly, so as to give the master's dinner-drink a chance of being cool.

All this amused George Keene hugely—at first. He drew

caricatures of it for the rectory, and sent a very impressionist sketch of his world to Mrs. Boynton. It consisted of a dust-storm, a caper brush, and a rat-hole. She put it on the mantel-piece of the pretty drawing-room in the little house, among scented pine woods, where she was just beginning to appreciate the soothing effect of having a decent balance at her banker's. Her lady visitors laughed and said it was very clever, but some of the men looked queer and muttered "poor devil" under their breath. Not that George looked on himself in that light; on the contrary, Hodinuggar amused him. Its dreary antiquity was all new to him, and as he went through the cool, dark passages of the old palace on his way to play chess with the dewan, he learned to admire some things about it—notably the thickness of its walls, through which the sun never filtered, though it soaked pitilessly into his red-brick bungalow. Upon the roof Zubr-ul-zamân shrivelled under the heat almost as much as a certain figure, which still lay huddled up on the landing of the secret stair, in the thickness of the tower beneath him as he sat at chess. Below that again Khushâl Beg lay stark naked, like a huge baby, in a swinging cradle, which was pulled to and fro by a drowsy coolie, while a *bheestie* supplied the fat carcass alternately outside and inside with tepid water from his skin-bag; and as the *mushk* shrank Khushâl swelled visibly, horribly.

Yet farther, in the bazaar by the Mori gate, Dalel Beg, abandoning European fashions under the stress of climate, slept all day and waked all night—doing both more viciously than before, like a snake rendered lively and dangerous by the heat; but Chândni, from her cool arches, smiled calmly, even when "Ta-ra-ra, boom-de-ay" rose from the opposite balcony, which was now occupied by some one who could dance as well as sing. To tell the truth, she was glad to be quit of Dalel's amusement for a time. Such deviations from her control never lasted long, and this time she knew that the dewan himself was on her side. So she lounged about in the shadows, watching the pigeons in the niches, and rubbing her soft palms together. Sometimes a pellet of opium lay between them;

sometimes nothing at all, for it was a trick of hers; sometimes, on the other hand, it was a great deal—neither more nor less than one of the Hodinuggar pearls, which were as well known to all the jewellers of that part of the country as the "Koh-i-noor" diamond is to the keeper of the regalia. That was why Chândni, on her return from Delhi, whither she had gone ostensibly to learn new music-hall songs for Dalel's benefit, had laughed so triumphantly at her own cleverness as she sat at the dewan's feet, telling him what she had done.

"It was easy, with my cousin a jeweller; and we of the bazaar know a trick or two with goldsmiths. Manohar Lal hath the pearls, sure enough. All thou hast to do is to offer him a rupee more than he gave the *mem* (which will not be half their value). The Hindoo pig will take it, seeing it is better than having the yellow-trousered ones set on him as a receiver of stolen goods."

Zubr-ul-zamân looked at her approvingly from under his bushy eyebrows. She was a clever woman, but he would improve on her plan. He would put the screw tighter on the Hindoo pig, and get the pearls back in exchange for a promise to pay. So far, however, Chândni's plot had been unexpectedly successful. Both George Keene, by giving the Ayôdhya pot to the *mem*, and Dan Fitzgerald, by taking the jewels to Monohar Lal (as Chândni's spies said he had done), were mixed up in the affair. There was sufficient foundation for an *esclandre*, of course. But how would that help them? They did not merely want revenge, as is so often the case; they wanted the key of the sluice-gate. The courtesan, standing with wide-spread arms to fold her veil around her decently ere she left the dewan's presence, laughed shrilly at his difficulties.

"How? sayest thou. Who can tell? Save this: the *mem* will send for more if she gets the chance. That is our way. One rupee claims another. Bid the *vakeel* at Rajpore go to her and suggest a marrow to the pot. All things go in pairs, and we could send it through Keene *sahib*. For the rest we must wait. There is time yet, and if we are to work by fear of exposure, that comes ever at the last moment. I play for a high stake, as I have told thee, O my father! And I mean to win."

Then it was that the old man, with regretful thoughts of his past youth, had promised her one of the pearls in pledge for a future, when, if she succeeded, she would wear the whole necklace as Dalel's wife. That was how she came to be rolling the pearl against her palm lazily one moonlit night when George, who began to find the long, empty evenings, coming at the end of long, empty days, rather wearisome, strolled over, for the first time since his return from Rajpore, to see the potter, and while away half an hour in hearing some of his tales. Rather to his surprise, since he knew nothing of the novel freak for solitude, he found the outer palisade barred by thorn bushes, and going a little farther along to where it joined the mud wall, vaulted over the latter lightly into the inner court-yard. It was empty, and the door of the hovel closed. Supposing the old man to be absent, he was turning to go, when a low cough from within made him pause and knock. The next instant the potter burst out on him with eyes ablaze. "Devils! wilt not leave me in peace?" he began, before recognizing his visitor. Then his manner changed; he drew the door to behind him, saying hurriedly, "This slave mistook; the children tease. But if the *huzoor* wants songs he must come to the outer court. The wheel is there now. Will not the *huzoor* come?" He moved away like a plover luring an intruder from its nest; but George paused again to listen to a repetition of the quick, low cough.

"Who is that ill?" he asked, unwarily. The potter echoed the sound instantly.

"It is I who cough, *huzoor*," he went on, still moving away. "Pity of God, how I cough! And I have fever, too, mercy of the Most High! Fever always, with mutterings hard to understand. But 'tis no matter. We potters of Hodinuggar do not die; we go and come, we come and go."

He had reached the wheel and set it a-spinning. But it seemed pivoted askew in its new place, and whirled in fitful ovals. Then he looked up with a foolish laugh. "My thumb will slip often now, *huzoor*. Maybe 'twere better Fuzl turned no more pots."

The thought made him slacken the wheel to silence. He sat staring at it vacantly, while George looked at him, wondering at the change in the old man. His face had the weary, overstrained expression of those who have wilfully forsaken sleep—the look which comes to those who are on the rack day and night, beside a sick-bed. And George, remembering the cough, jumped to the conclusion that the potter had an invalid in the hut—most likely some female relation; whence his desire for secrecy. To be sure, the old man had often said he lived alone; but in India one never could be sure how far modesty interfered with the truth. So, being accustomed to such vicarious prescribings, the young man suggested he should send some medicine for the cough. His companion brightened up immediately. "It is not all a cough, *huzoor*," he replied, hurriedly; "it is fever. God! what fever! It is only a little cough, with a rattle, as of dead wheat straw, under my bosom as I draw breath; quick, quick, with curving nostrils, like a horse galloping fast."

The vivid accuracy of the word-picture made George realize an idea which had of late haunted his fancy: the idea of a hand-to-hand fight with death, alone, unaided, as the beasts of the field meet the destroyer. Here was some one doing it; dying, perhaps, of pneumonia, when others were being nursed through a finger-ache. The pity, the injustice of it struck him fairly. Then the potter's voice, going on softly, gave inconsequent answer to the vague doubt surging against the boy's youthful content.

"Not that it matters, as I tell myself in the night-season when I am worse. We of Hodinuggar do not die; we go and come, we come again and go." Something in his words, perhaps, seemed to arrest the old man's attention, and he paused.

"*Huzoor*," he said, suddenly, "I have something which belongs to the *Mâdr Mihrbân*. If the *huzoor* would write an address."

"Belonging to Miss Tweedie?" echoed George, in surprise.

"Do not thanks belong to those who earn them?" replied the potter, evasively. "If the *huzoor* could write. I have pen and ink. Lo! it is nought but a potter's work; and the miss was kind."

He fumbled in the niche beside his seat, and drew out a parcel done up in wax-cloth. Evidently a pot of some sort, thought George, beginning to print boldly, as one of his profession should, with the slant-cut native pen. The moonlight shone full on the potter seated at his wheel, and on the young Englishman stencilling Rose Tweedie's name. What was that rising on the stillness of the night? A murmur from the hut? George could not say for certain, as the old man set his wheel a-humming instantly; but once more the feeling of injustice, the flash of pity, came to disturb his self-complacency. The feeling lasted longer this time, and as he walked home his thoughts were full of that uncertainty which is so hateful to the young. The Mori gate showed black and white in the moonshine. A clash of silver bells rose from the shadows as he passed, and a pomegranate blossom fell at his feet. He took a step aside to crush it fiercely, passionately. It lay between that and picking it up; he felt uneasy. Life was so simple here, so confusing in its simplicity. To live and to die. Was that all? He spent the remainder of the evening writing to Mrs. Boynton, putting his heart into reserved, half-jesting hints at his own puzzles. And as he wrote, the potter, standing at the door of his hut, was listening to a murmur coming from the darkness within.

"It is sent, dear heart. She has it. No one shall know," he answered, softly. Then there was silence for a while, but only for a while. The murmur came again and again through the hot night, to be stilled by the same reply.

The post in due time brought Mrs. Boynton her letter. She read it with great interest, then promptly put it into the fire; her favorite maxim being that the keeping of letters was, at any rate, one reason for the slow progress of humanity, since improvement was dangerous when you were tied down in black and white to past opinions.

And the postman, after leaving the snug little house in the pine woods, came to Colonel Tweedie's with a packet for Rose. Half an hour afterwards the girl was sitting with the contents of the parcel on the table in front of her, puzzling her brains why any one should have sent her back the Ayôdhya pot, or one exactly like it. There could be no doubt about it, however. She took up the wrapper more than once; but the clear print, if unmistakable, was also unrecognizable. She felt carefully inside, hoping for a scrap of paper, a hint of any kind; but there was nothing save a few bits of crumbling clay, leaving a rough rim near the bottom of the pot. And all the time her first impression remained unaltered. There was a mistake; it had been meant for Mrs. Boynton. Undoubtedly it was meant for her. Under ordinary circumstances, Rose would most likely have taken the Ayôdhya pot over to the little house without more ado; but though she did not acknowledge it herself, she could not treat its occupant in an ordinary way. Besides, there was an element of mystery in the whole affair, and Rose hated mystery. The memory of her dream on the night of the storm at Hodinuggar annoyed her. She had slurred it over at the time, merely mentioning it as part of a feverish attack, but now she wondered if the dewan, or some one else, could really have arranged a theft. And gradually there grew up in her one distinct dislike to the whole business. She would have nothing to do with it. She would say nothing, but simply send the thing back whence it came. She would not even suppose that George had sent it; she would return it straight. After all, it might be another pot, and if she made a mistake in thinking this, they would know the truth at Hodinuggar.

A knock at the door roused her, and she slipped the vase behind another on the mantel-piece ere she said, "Come in."

"Only to say, Miss Tweedie," came in Lewis Gordon's voice from the threshold, "that I shall not be in to lunch. Your father has given me a half-holiday, and, like a good little boy, I am going to spend it with my relations. You will be at the Grahams' tennis, I suppose? We shall,"

"No. I shall utilize my half-holiday with my relations also," she replied. "Father and I will go for a ride. I don't often get him to myself."

"Then *au revoir* till dinner. How comfortable your little snuggery is. It and Gwen's drawing-room are the prettiest rooms in Simla."

Three days after this Chândni sat at the dewan's feet, once more holding the Ayôdhya pot in her hands.

"So I am right, O father!" she cried, with that shrill laugh of hers, "the *mem* hath sent for more. Lo! I shall wear the pearls erelong."

"If they are sent again, thou mayest lose them this time," retorted the old man; but there was no warmth in his warning; he had begun to believe in her luck. So the two sat in the purgatorial heat on the roof, imagining evil as unconcernedly as if the universe could hold no fiercer fire for the wicked. The pearls must be sent again, of course, and the parcel given to be addressed by Keene *sahib.* So much was clear; and Manohar Lâl might be told to offer a less sum this time.

"Thy father was the devil," remarked Zubr-ul-zamân again, this time more suavely, "and, pearls or no pearls, thou shalt have Dalel. For, look you, Khushâl is a water-butt, a grease jar, and Dalel has forgotten how to deal fair, even by himself; but thou hast brains. So bring thine ear within reach of a whisper. There is much to tell of Hodinuggar ways ere I forget with age."

She bent her head back till it almost rested on the old man's breast, and brought her flower-decked ear close to his mouth. One elbow touched his knee, the hand giving light support to her chin — the attitude of one all ears to hear; the dewan, still as a statue, nothing but a voice: a queer couple up there on the roof overlooking the red-hot red-brick house where George Keene was being introduced to what is familiarly called a "go" of fever.

Even that was, to begin with, somewhat of an amusement. A certain feeling of self-complacency comes with the first intermission. After the tortures and fires of the damned for some hours, the sudden and complete escape from them seems to redound to the credit of your constitution. You are confirmed in the impression that you are a fine fellow. But it is not long before the fever fiend can knock that sort of conceit out of a man, if it chooses. In George's case it did choose, and, having got him well in its grip refused, after a day or two, to let him go again. The factotum lingered round with something he called beef-tea, and another thing he called barley-water. Which was which, the patient, with his mouth full of Dead Sea apples and quinine, could not say; nor after a time did he very much care. He cared for nothing; unless, indeed, it was to get rid of that vision of the school-room in the rectory—a school-room with a cherry-cheeked boy roasting blackbirds at the fire. If you didn't twist the bit of brown worsted stolen from your sister's work-basket, then the birds slackened — slackened like the potter's wheel. Oh, it was a lifetime of twisting, or there you were plumb, burning with a horrid smell. When the factotum sat in the room the blackbirds didn't come; but then he breathed. Wasn't it rough that a man could not stop breathing for half an hour just to oblige a friend? Yet if the breathing beast sat outside, a "whittering" beast came in its place—"whitter! whitter!" under the bed, behind the boxes. That was the worst of a musk-rat: no one could possibly tell where it would "whitter" next. It wasn't its fault, of course; it meant no harm. Poor little beggar! what a rummy sight it must be, if the yarn was true, taking its kids out for a walk, tail by tail, in a string! And then, to his own infinite surprise and discomfiture, George's feeble laugh ended in a flood of tears—tears like a woman's, drenching the dry, hot pillow; that was one comfort; as good as a water-cart. So they came again between the laughs. For George, seventy miles away from a white face, was down with the worst type of jungle fever. Sometimes, when he felt a little better, the factotum brought out the medicine-chest, and between them they made wonderful compounds, which the latter administered when the master had gone back to the blackbirds.

It is a common enough experience, and George, not being a whit behind many another young Englishman, fought his way through it pluckily, while Ganesha, the groom, fished for soda-water bottles all day long, and the water-carrier circled round the house, cooling the dust with sprinklings, and keeping an eye on the punka-coolie during the factotum's absence over barley-water or beef-tea. Scorching nights, blistering days, devils in sparrow shape; the fringe of the towel pinned to the punka flickering your nose, yet sparing the mosquito fattening on your cheek. All this George knew till discomfort itself grew dim, and he ceased to care for anything in this world or the next.

Then, after a time, there was something dead cold trickling down his nose, and that surely was Dan's face. At any rate, it was Dan's voice.

"It's all right, dear boy. Sure, the doctor's ridden out too, and you'll be round in a jiffy."

It is an Eastern record of life which tells us of a love passing the love of woman, and even in these latter days one sees it more often East than West; perhaps, paradoxically, because men have so often to play a woman's part towards each other in India. Dan Fitzgerald in particular was as gentle as any Sister of Mercy, and stronger than most. To be sure, he sat on the bed smoking, and after a day or two his language over the barley-water was simply disgraceful. But by this time George had come back from "No Man's Land," and could remember a little booklet called *Home Comforts Abroad*, which had been given him by his grandmother. So Dan ferreted it out from the bottom of a box full of wire cartridges, and ordered the charcoal-brazier into the veranda. Then he stirred diligently, while George, propped up by pillows, read out the directions weakly, the result being that the factotum bore away a deadly mixture in triumph because, even with this surpassing love in his heart for the compounder, the boy could not swallow it. Nevertheless, wearied out by feeble laughter, he slept the first real sleep of recovery, and woke to extol the factotum's beef-tea. That functionary being thus appeased, the little red-brick furnace out in the wilderness became a home indeed; that is to say, an abode of love and peace and great contentment.

It was on the very day of promotion to an arm-chair and a cigarette that George received a letter from Colonel Tweedie enclosed in one from Rose. His eyes grew moist as he read it; he had to pause ere he could turn to where his companion sat busy over his share of the post, and even then his voice faltered.

"You—you *beast*, Dan!" The words were uncomplimentary; the tone was a caress. His hearer did not affect to misunderstand.

"Well, it will be jolly for you at Simla. The gayest fortnight of all just before the rains, and there's nothing like a whiff of hill air for killing the microbes. Besides, the Tweedie's house is awfully jolly to stay in."

"But you? You will be here," said George, remorsefully, despite the eager pleasure in his eyes.

Dan laughed. "It isn't the first time I've been in a jungle station. Are you thinking of the whiskey bottle again? Sure, I'll take a temperance ticket for the fortnight if it would make my keeper easier."

"Don't be a fool, Dan." He came round to lean over the back of George's arm-chair.

"Is that the thanks I get for warming a viper in my bosom? But I must get back to the office for a day or two first, then I'll start you off with my blessing and all the boiled shirts you have in the world; and more, by token—that picture of the girl with the Ayôdhya pot that's lying underneath them. Why didn't you show it me before? It's the best thing you ever did, and must go to the Exhibition. Always put your best foot foremost up at Simla among the big wigs. That is my advice."

"Which you don't follow yourself."

"But I do. Only my foot's a beetle-crusher, and the worms don't like it. So that is settled, and we will tell the washerman about the white ties. And look here, George, I'll bring the duplicate of that key back with me; then you can take yours and I shall know—"

George's hand went up to the back of his chair as if to find another; then he changed the *venue* with an odd little laugh.

"Give me a light, old man. I—I can't keep this cigarette going, somehow."

As Dan stooped over him their eyes met. That was enough.

CHAPTER XIV

THE angel Azrael had turned aside from other doors in Hodinuggar besides that of the red-hot bungalow across the canal. Fuzl Elâhi, the potter, sat once more at his work with the old calm on his face. The wheel was back in the inner yard again, where the westering sun sent a creeping shadow of the high wall almost to the edge of the spinning circle. It spun so slowly that the eye could see the blue outline of a pot upon the moulding-pirn.

"*It was a woman seeking something.*
Over hill and dale, through night and day, she sought for something.
Foul play, foul play! look down and decide.
Not I—"

The chant stopped in a start. There was a grip on one shoulder, a thin, brown hand over the other pointing accusingly at the wheel.

"Why didst lie to me?" panted a breathless voice, low yet hard. "Why didst say thou hadst sent it to her. Why? Why?"

"I lied not, heart's delight—"

The slackening wheel, as his hands fell away from it, showed the Ayôdhya pot, as if in denial of his words; yet he repeated them gently, looking back the while at the girl who had crept from the open door of the hut behind him. "I sent it, but it hath come back, as all things do in Hodinuggar; as even thou didst, Azîzan. Be not angry with thy father. Lo! it is fate."

She set his deprecating hand aside roughly. "Let be, father—if father thou art. I tell thee 'tis the pot. Give it me here. Yea! 'tis so—and thou hast put a false bottom of new clay to it. Wherefore?"

The old man's forehead wrinkled in perplexity. "I do it always. Let me finish the task, Azîzan. Chândni the courtesan will give money for it, as always; then thou shalt have violet-sherbet to allay the cough. Pity of me, how thin thou art!"

In truth, the girl was emaciated to skin and bone, and her small face seemed all eyes; yet, although she swayed as she stood from sheer weakness, there was energy and to spare in her grip on the Ayôdhya pot. "Chândni!" she echoed; then suddenly the fire died down, the tension of her hold slackened. "Lo! wherefore should I care if it be lies or truth," she muttered to herself; "the old man is crazy, and 'tis the dewan's when all is said and done—not hers. Here, take it, poor soul. I care not now, so I be left in peace."

"Art not angry with thy father, Azîzan?" he asked, humbly; but there was no answer. He watched her languid retreat to the hut almost fearfully. "Lo! she forgets the things I have remembered, and I forget those she remembers," he murmured, before he broke once more into his chant with a quavering voice. This forgetfulness of the girl's, showing itself so often, was a perpetual wonder to the old man, who never for an instant doubted that she was his daughter returned to him. "Nay! but thou knowest, beloved!" he would remonstrate against her ignorance. "Hast not played in the Mori gate, and bought sweetmeats of old Bishin, perched on my shoulder like any tame squirrel?"

"Mayhap, mayhap!" she would answer, impatiently; "I care not. There was a Hindoo girl, I remember, who did not weep as the others used to do. Life was a dream, she said. She would forget it soon in another. Mayhap 'tis true, and I have forgotten."

It suited her to deceive the old man. When she had first realized the position, she had been too weak to do more than wonder at it. Then, by degrees, while she still lay helpless, the potter's talk, her own recollections of old Zainub's hints, joined to the extraordinary similarity in those extraordinary eyes, had given her a shrewd guess at the truth; and with it came a fierce, savage delight in her inheritance of witchcraft. It meant revenge: revenge and safety. The potter deemed her a ghost from another world, and the village-folk should think the same. So she hid herself away in the dark hovel, spending the long hot days in dreaming of a time when she could creep out on some moonlit night and frighten the wits out of the world which had wronged her. For her whole nature was jangled and out of tune, and she hated everything and everybody, herself included. Nor was her little world unwilling to be frightened. Gossip of the strange doings at the potter's house already began to pass from mouth to mouth—voices had been heard, sights seen; finally, *Mai* Jerun's longed-for son had been born with a distinct thumb mark, and had died. The only person, in fact, who could have allayed these fears lay shrivelling into a mummy with the heat on the old secret stairs; so that Azîzan might have wandered through the village had she chosen, without fear of anything save sending the women into hysterics, and making the men give themselves up as doomed to die. She did not care to wander, however; she cared for nothing save to sit crouched up at the lintel of the hovel-door, and stare into vacancy until the dawn sent her back to the darkness within. The potter found her so when he returned from taking the pot back to the Mori gate late in the evening. The fading daylight struggled still with the rising moon, making confused havoc among the shadows, and giving an odd iridescence to the dust-laden air. From without came a barking of dogs, an occasional cry; every now and again a group of bleatings from the goat-pens—all the every-day commonplace sounds of village life; and in the court-yard the same lack of outward novelty. Only an old man with his *puggree* off, eating his supper of *bâjra* cakes and water beside a sick girl.

"*Ari*, beloved! cough not so," came his tender voice. "Lo! I will go for the sherbet. Dittu was away when I passed his shop but now. And see! I will seek out the *sahib* ere he leaves to-morrow, and ask for more medicine. It did thee good." The girl's breath came faster.

"Leaves? Wherefore?"

"He hath been ill, dear heart; so Chândni says. He goes to the *mem sahib* in the hills."

Azîzan's hand clutched the old man's arm. "And the pot! What of the pot?"

He shook his head. "Maybe it was for her; I know not. Cough not so, beloved. See, I will fetch the sherbet." He bent over her as he rose in gentle pleading. "Go not from me while I am away, Azîzan! Lo! I will be back erelong." She gave a short laugh and sank back, still breathless from her fit of coughing.

"Go! whither should I go? God knows!"

The old man sighed, and as he turned away he looked back more than once at the listless, dejected figure. So it remained for an instant after his had disappeared through the outer yard, then, as if galvanized, it rose suddenly, and the thin arms were flung out passionately.

"She shall not have it! Chândni shall not give it to her! She shall not! She shall not!"

Five minutes after, trembling half from weakness, half from sheer hurry, Azîzan was on her way through the village wrapped in a white sheet which she had snatched from the hut. What she was going to do she scarcely knew, just as she scarcely knew whither she was going. Though within a stone's-throw of her birthplace, the path down which she struggled was as unfamiliar to her feet as the tempest of emotion was to her mind. A fever of excitement, anger, mistrust of everything and everybody, surged through her veins. The road was silent, deserted; but even had it been thronged the girl would not have hesitated. Amid all the confusion one thing was certain: Chândni must tell the truth—she must be found and made to tell the truth. But where? Yonder was the Mori gate; she had seen that before through the lattice, and that at any rate would serve as a landmark. She would go there first and see.

As she came within earshot of the tunnelled causeway a woman's voice rang out in shrill laughter from the dark recesses to the right. Her first instinct was to pause; then second thought made her keep straight on her way as if to pass through, till at the farther end of the causeway she turned and sank down behind a plinth to the left. It was as if a shadow had disappeared. A minute to regain her breath, and then she crept farther into the darkness, where, unless some belated gossiper should choose that side of the arch, she was secure. From over the way came a clash of anklets, and a low, full voice, contrasting strangely with those high trills of laughter, assured her that she had come straight upon her quarry. The rest was patience, till sooner or later the woman would be left alone. Sooner or later the laugh must cease; sooner or later even wickedness must tire and turn to sleep. So the girl sat crouched into herself in the curiously impassive attitude of her race, her thin arms round her thin knees, whereon her small chin rested. Not a very startling sight outwardly, though to describe what lay within is wellnigh an impossible task with an audience of Western ears. For Azîzan's knowledge would be, to such ears, incompatible with her ignorance; her jealousy and passion, with her patience. Such an audience must remember an upbringing foreign to their experience, and imagine her still as a statue, though the blood raced like liquid fire through her limbs and throbbed like sledge-hammers on her temples.

The moon, sinking slowly, sent a slanting yellow light through the dust-haze visible beyond the arched causeway; the village dogs ceased one by one the nightly challenge to their fellows; but still the laugh went on. Would wickedness never tire? The wonder and her own heart-beats lulled the girl into a drowsier patience. She woke to silence, and, standing up, strained her eyes and ears into the shadows. Not a sound. She stole softly across the causeway, slipped into the recesses on the right, and listened again. A low breathing from one corner made her feel her way towards it, and her touch, light as the breeze, hovered over a figure on the ground wrapped from head to foot in a sheet like a corpse. A servant, doubtless; certainly not the woman she sought. She would not choose so airless a spot. But there must be rooms above, and a roof above that; it was worth a trial before going on towards the bazaar. Slowly, for she knew nothing of where she was, Azîzan groped her way to some winding stairs, thence to a suite of low chambers, empty of all save pigeons rustling and cooing at her step in the dark. Upward again till, at a turn, an archway gave on a terraced roof not six feet square; and there, lying on a string-cot which from its narrow resting-place seemed suspended in mid-air, she saw the soft curves of a woman's figure outlined against the moonlit dust-haze beyond. Not a place for a sleep-walker's slumbers, not even a place for a restless one; but Chândni slept the sleep of the unjust, which, nine times out of ten, is sounder than that of the just. Her conscience never troubled her; she belonged to a race apart from the customs and creeds of the people—a race born to the profession of panders and prostitutes, openly, shamelessly.

So, not being afraid like other women-folk of sleeping in the moonlight with her face uncovered, she lay carelessly as she had thrown herself down, her tinsel-set veil thrown aside by one arm thrust under her head, the other stretched almost straight into the gulf of dusty air glittering faintly like the ghost of a sunbeam. Beneath its filmy net-covering the bold sweep of her bosom rose and fell softly with its burden of the past day's faded jasmine chaplets. They gave out a last breath of perfume as Azîzan's thin brown fingers closed round the sleeper's throat.

"If you stir," said the girl to the startled eyes, as they opened, "I'll kill you! Feel!" Only a prick above the heart, but joined to that scorching, stifling grip it was sufficient to send the coming shriek back from Chândni's lips. She lay terror-stricken, staring at the wild light eyes which, catching the moon rays as they dipped to the horizon, seemed to glow with a pale fire. This was no ghost! it was something worse than that.

"Why didst send the Ayôdhya pot to her? Why? Give it me back!"

Chândni slackened all over in sudden relief; if she could

have laughed with that hand on her throat the shrill sound would have no doubt risen on the hot air. So that was all! Nothing but jealousy! Of all things in the world the easiest to rouse and to allay by lies; and she had plenty of these at her command. So many, that poor Azîzan, after a time, wondered sullenly how she came to be sitting amicably on the string-cot beside the woman she had meant to coerce.

"Poor little chicken!" said the courtesan, in contemptuous consolation. "So thou wouldst have killed me, thy best friend. One who seeks to destroy the *mem!* 'Twill be the ruin of her, look you, and then he will have none of her. That is their way. She will not get him; so pine no more, child. Lo! I will teach thee to have lovers and to spare."

"I want no lovers," muttered the girl, angrily. "If 'tis to harm her—and thou hast sworn to that—I care not; and thou hast sworn to let me be also. That is enough."

As she rose, folding her white veil around her, Chândni felt sorely tempted to give the little push which must have overset the weak balance and sent Azîzan to certain death below. But the thought that if looks told the truth Fate would do the work for her erelong and without scandal stayed her hand. Besides, the knowledge that the girl was alive and intent on revenge might be of use in dealing with the palace if they showed themselves traitorous to her claims. So when she had watched Azîzan go stumbling down the stairs, Chândni rolled over lazily to meet the midnight wind which was springing up, and shortly afterwards fell asleep like a child. She was in dreamless slumber long before Azîzan, who had sunk down on a step of the silent causeway, hoping to regain strength for the homeward journey, had felt equal to the task. A deadly despondency had replaced her excitement; yet beneath this again lay a dull resentment against Fate. If she had understood, if she had known—as Chândni seemed to know—the ways and thoughts of these white people, she might have done better. She had meant no harm—no harm in her world, at least—for she was not bad. He might, as Chândni said, turn away from the *mem* for being wicked, but he would never have had cause to turn away from her if she had only known. She never would have done anything to displease him—never have done, or said, or looked: the sting of painful memory drove her from her resting-place to stumble on recklessly in the direction of a twinkling light upon the mound. That must be the potter's house, he must be watching for her, and there she would at least find shelter. But it was not the house, it was the potter himself seeking for her among the ruins. His face, by the light of the cresset he carried, showed haggard, and its anxiety soothed her, even while it sent a new pain to her heart. He was unhappy at losing her; and—ah God!—how her own heart ached. Must it always be so when those you loved were lost? Then, would he feel so if he had to turn away from the *mem?*—would it send that pain into his heart?

The question was insistent, imperative, as, scarcely listening to the old man's deprecating delight, she followed him into the darkness of the hut. Even there it haunted her. Through the long night, through the long, hot day, as she lay huddled up out of sight, it came back again and again. Would he care? And if he did care, would she be glad or sorry for his pain?

The moon and the setting sun were disputing possession of the world again, and George lay on a lounge-chair in the veranda of the red-hot bungalow. The air was fresher, if not cooler there, and the factotum within was disturbing the foundation of the round world in attempting to pack his master's things; among these, Azîzan's picture, and a parcel which had been sent from the palace addressed to Mrs. Boynton. Something, it was said, she had asked the *vakeel* at Rajpore to get for her. The lad, though still weak, was joyous to the heart's-core in the knowledge that another hour would see him on his way to spend his holiday in the society of the most perfect woman he had ever seen. That was how he viewed the future—Gwen in full focus, the rest of the world out of it; even poor Dan, who was at that moment riding his hardest across the desert to take charge of the subdivision at its uttermost limit, and so give the boy every possible second of his leave. Not a very just estimate of relative values, but a very usual one when Narcissus is absorbed in the reflection of himself.

"*Salaam alaikoom*," came a breathless voice behind him. He turned to see Azîzan, who had sunk, as if exhausted, on the veranda steps. He stared at her, silent with surprise, in which a certain shamefaced annoyance was mingled. He had no desire to be reminded of her existence at present, and even if, as he had felt inclined to suspect, there was some mystery about her, he could do no good by inquiring now, on the very eve of his departure.

"I have come for the pot, *huzoor*," she began without preamble; "they took it from me. Lo! I was poor, and the poor have no voice. Justice, justice!"

"Took it from you?" echoed George, his annoyance increased at this plunge into the past. "Do you mean by force?" She nodded. "But," he went on, "you sold it. I gave the money to your mother when she came here—on the night the huts were burned."

"My mother died before that, *huzoor*. It was not my mother who came, but a bad one from the palace. It is true that I never sold it, never got the money. And now I want the pot back again. It brings luck. I will not sell it."

"But why didn't you come at once and tell me?" asked George, angrily; "then I might have done something; now—"

She interrupted him eagerly.

"Your slave has been ill, as the *huzoor* may perchance notice." Her wistful tone made George look at her more closely.

"Very ill, I should say," he assented, shortly. "You are not fit to come so far. Why did you? Why didn't you send some one else?"

"I thought the *huzoor* would not believe unless he saw me," she said, after a pause. "I heard the *huzoor* was going away to-day, and I wanted the pot. Surely he will give it back! The Protector of the Poor has so many things; his slave has but this one thing."

Her face was outlined against the white pillar beside which she sat, and, with all the languor of sickness on it, still showed strong in its entreaty. Something in it struck George with regret, even amid the pressing desire to kick somebody which her words had aroused in him. "Give it back," he echoed, savagely; "of course I would, if I could; but I can't; it was stolen—"

"It has been found again, *huzoor*."

"Perhaps; but I haven't found it. I'm very sorry, my good girl, but I haven't got it."

"The *huzoor* mistakes. He has it. It is in the parcel that came from the palace. They took it from me again to send it back to the *mem*."

George stared at her, unable to believe his ears. "Took it again—then you were the thief? Is that it?"

There was a slight pause ere she replied. "The *huzoor* always speaks the truth. I stole it—but it was mine."

George gave a low whistle; then a sudden grimness came to his face. "And you say it is in that parcel they sent addressed—by Jove if it is," he added in English, as he rose hastily. A minute after, when he returned from within, his face was still more grim. "Here, take it," he said, thrusting the blue curves of the Ayôdhya pot at her, as if in haste to be rid of it and her. "When I get back I'll inquire, and if what you say is true—" He paused, reduced in his anger to thinking incoherently of Dalel and horsewhips. How dare he send it *her*, mixing *her* up, as it were, in such a discreditable affair. "Well," he continued, looking impatiently at the girl; "that's all, I suppose. You don't want anything more, do you?"

The attitude in which she was sitting reminded him perforce of the sunshine glowing on the blue-tiled mosque and the sideling pigeons; of a past of which he did not care to be reminded, and a hardness crept over his face.

"That is all," she replied, rising to go. "But the *huzoor* should not be angry; the pot belonged to this slave."

"Angry," he echoed, with a sort of lofty consideration; "why should I be angry with you? Every one has a right to his own, surely. Now you have got it, go home and get stronger, my child. *Salaam*, Azîzan!"

"*Salaam, alaikoom, huzoor.*"

He took up his cigar again, relieved to find it alight, for he felt that he needed soothing. On his return, Dalel must be brought to book and smashed; meanwhile he was not sorry that the cursed pot had finally passed into the hands of its rightful owner, for it had a knack of appearing and disappearing in a way which annoyed his common-sense. Now he need never see it or its owner again. One palpable reason for the latter probability made him give a compassionate glance after the thin, small face, on which consumption had set its mark indubitably—the face which he had seen for the last time.

No, not the last! She, too, was pausing to look back from the gateless gateway, guiltless of a fence on either side, which served no purpose save arbitrarily, uselessly, to divide one portion of a dusty road from another. So he saw her outlined against the shadows which softened the havoc sickness had wrought in her young face. A graceful figure, seen, as he had painted it, against the purple mound of Hodinuggar, with the pot clasped to her breast. Yes, when Mrs. Boynton saw the picture she would be pleased; that is to say, if he showed it to her at all. Perhaps it would be better not to do so, since she must not be mixed up with anything discreditable.

The thought absorbed him, and when he looked up the shadows were empty.

CHAPTER XV

Ten days had passed since George, after many hours of deadly discomfort, found himself admitting that the world was not such an intolerable place, even in India; that, when all was said and done, there were some things in it worth looking at. Those who have experience of these convalescent journeyings will know at once that this must have been just about that turn of the upward-trending road where a bridge slants the *dhooli* across a dry torrent-bed, so that the traveller can see a stream of pink oleander blossoms filling the narrow ravine. The morning sunshine lies yellow on the red, parched hillocks, the red rocks crumble from thirst, but the heat-hidden water proclaims its presence beneath them by that glory of flowers; nothing else, far or near, suggesting moisture, save, perhaps, the candlestick euphorbea, reminding one vaguely of the Ark of the Covenant. Not a very welcome reminder, surely, in this land of drought, where even a deluge of rain would be a blessing. So, at least, thought George, all unwitting of the times, now close at hand, when a racing, roaring demon would fill that valley, and the oleander flowers would seem adrift, and the arch of the bridge echo to the metallic churnings of the boulders below; until, maybe, it would take a fancy to join them, and leave travellers staring at each other across an impassable torrent.

Another turn or two and the candlestick-bush is left behind. The red-flowered indigo hides the dry, red soil, and from it rise strange shrubs with spare foliage and abundant blossoms: yellows and whites and lilacs, with here and there a pomegranate, vivid green and crimson. A sweet scent fills the air from gray aromatic herbs, among which the wild bees keep up a perpetual hum. It is the land of honey and honey-bees—butterflies also; there goes a purple emperor, and, by Jove! yonder is one of those swallow-tailed whoppers you have seen somewhere in a glass-case. The head sinks back upon the pillow again, tired, content to watch the scarlet flash of a sun-bird. Was that a fern hidden in the crevice of the yellowing rocks? Yes; parched, dwarfed, but still a fern. So on and up until the coolies set the *dhooli* down on a bit of real green grass beside the tiny trickle of the stream where they slake their thirst, and some one from a shingled hut, hung with flowering, fruiting gourds, brings the *sahib* a red-brown earthen pot. A land of milk, this; somewhat smoky, no doubt, but still milk. Over the tops of the fragrant pine-trees something blue climbs up into the skies. Can it be a hill—the hills "*from whence cometh our help*"? The memory, perhaps, of some early morning service in the old little station church comes over you. The punkas swinging overhead, the deputy commissioner reading the Psalms, the involuntary stir northward of the small knot of worshippers as the words sank straight into their hearts, bringing thoughts of dear faces looking down on the heat-sodden plain. Yes, those are the hills; for as the coolies slither through the slippery pine-needles, the faint blue mist, blending into clouds, rises, and the headman, pausing, points to a cluster of white dots. Those are the *sahib logue's* houses. The path steepens; George pulls up the neglected shawl as shelter from the growing cool, and, as he is hurried along the curving road to find old familiar friends in every flower and leaf, his renewed vitality expresses itself, oddly enough, in the inward conviction that here at last is a place in which one could die comfortably. Not that George, or any other convalescent in his position, contemplates the possibility of death. Why should one, when life has suddenly become attractive; when one can breathe instead of merely drawing breath; above all, when it is safe to go out into the garden without a hat, and pick a carnation for your button-hole before strolling over to have tea with the best woman in the world?

Those ten days, therefore, passed like wildfire. George knew no more how he had spent them than how he had spent all his money—chiefly, it may be said, on sweets at Peliti's, kid gloves, and new ties. It was the first time the young fellow had ever been let loose on equal terms with the very best of society—a society, moreover, bent on amusing itself. That he should follow its example was a foregone conclusion; and it must be owned he certainly got his money's worth in solid enjoyment. There is always one particular period in the life of every man and woman when the sun seems to stand still in the heavens on purpose to make pleasure perpetual. This had set in for George, and it had its usual effect in giving a fine-drawn, eager expression to his face. Small wonder, perhaps, seeing that, as a rule, he never went to bed till three in the morning, and that the days passed in one ceaseless round of amusement. It seemed incredible even to himself that not a fortnight past he had been agonizing at Hodinuggar on beef-tea and barley-water. But then Hodinuggar itself was incredible; almost as much so as the fact that he had proposed to wear his old white shirts, washed by a desert washerman, at Simla! They were thrust aside in a bottom drawer now, and their place filled by brand-new ones from a European shop; for how could one dance with the most perfect woman in the world in a shirt that had no deportment? How, in fact, could you do anything without reference to the certainty that your unworthy self would form a part of perfection's environment? That is what it comes to when a steady, honest young fellow like George falls down on his knees to worship a pretty face and a gracious smile. No doubt it was not a very admirable occupation; but it seemed so to him, as it seems to that majority of mankind which does not ask itself questions; and this simply because he had been taught, as we have all been taught, to look on sentimental love between the sexes as something almost divine. Thus, the real issues being hopelessly confused, this new feeling of passionate worship had all the effect of a religion upon him, and other things besides old shirts were thrust out of sight, among them Azîzan's picture. The idol should not see it till the depths of deceit regarding the Ayôdhya pot had been fathomed, lest in any way perfection's ears should be sullied by a queer story. By-and-by, when, on returning to Hodinuggar, he had time to unravel the mystery, he might send the portrait to her as the best piece of work he had ever turned out; but now? Why now, as usual, it was time to ride over on the hired pony—of whose mane and tail you were inwardly ashamed—to the pretty little house among the pine woods, and there, in Paradise, try to forget that but three days more leave lay between you and Purgatory. Certainly not an admirable occupation; but the novelty, the excitement, the supreme pleasure had gone like wine to the boy's head, producing that exalted condition of mind and body which has been described as leaving one in doubt whether to have another whiskey-and-water or to say one's prayers and go to bed.

Lewis Gordon, standing in the back veranda, watched the young fellow ride off with a frown. "It's too bad of Gwen," he murmured to himself, as he went back to finish dressing. "I can't think what the fun can be. But the boy's having a good time; that's one thing. And I suppose we all have to go through it some time or other."

When he had done putting himself into an extremely dandified racing kit, he passed through into the office again and began work steadily on some files. He was not on leave, and if he had to ride a steeple-chase at half-past four, that was no reason why he should waste an hour in dawdling down to Annandale beside Gwen's *dandy*. There was no reason, either, for his doing duty with Colonel Tweedie and his daughter, who had ordered their horses at three. Time enough if he galloped down at four, when the road would be pretty clear, instead of being clogged up by a perfect procession of women and coolies masquerading in ridiculous costumes. Whence it may be inferred that Lewis Gordon was in a bad temper. As a matter of fact, he had been so ever since he arrived at Simla, despite the welcome he received from Gwen's constant smiles, exquisite dresses, and admirable lunches. Perhaps he was conscious that some one would have to pay for all these amenities, and the prospect of responsibility in the future weighed on him; not in a pecuniary point of view, but in reference to the fact that the debtor would be his wife; for, like most men of his *genre*, he was fastidious over the duties of women in any way connected with him. Anyhow, he was distinctively dissatisfied with his world as he sat, buried shortsightedly up to his nose in piles of paper, his racing colors, white with a crimson hoop, looking ridiculously out of keeping with his occupation. A clatter of hoofs told him that the colonel and Rose were off. He could see them from his window passing a turn of the road below his house, their figures outlined for the moment against the dim blue of the valley. She sat straight, certainly, and as he watched her a smile came to his face as he remembered the partridge hunt, to be replaced immediately by a frown. For the memory of Hodinuggar conjured up that of Dalel Beg, who had come up to Simla for these races, and had, in Lewis's opinion, been making himself most objectionable. There was no reason on earth, of course, why Dalel should not come; no reason on earth why the governor-general should not shake hands with him, or any one else—that was part of the duty for which governors-general were paid; but that Gwen Boynton should shake hands with him and allow him to speak to her familiarly was different. That was a matter of feeling, not a matter of reason. Apart from the question of color, Dalel was an objectionable brute; could scarcely be otherwise, considering his upbringing. That much of this was sheer insular prejudice on Lewis Gordon's part may be true. If put to it, he would have frankly confessed to many another objectionable brute with a white face; but that the dark skin should enter into the question is at present inevitable in India, because it is typical of a variety of theories and practices which make real social intercourse between the upper classes of the two races an impossibility—*at present.*

And, to say sooth, Dalel was not nice outwardly or inwardly. Even the best tailors in Simla could not make him look aught but intolerable in his elaborate riding-gear, as he paused on his way to the race-courses before a small shop in the bazaar — a dark hole of a place, squalidly bare of all save a sign where, in crooked lettering, it was announced that "*Munohrlall of Delhi Jewler gold works*" was ready "*tobyandsell.*"

"No news of the pearls yet?" asked Dalel, in an undertone,

of the man in dirty white *dhoti* and low turban, who came out hastily to cringe at his stirrup.

"*Huzoor*, no; the *ayah* saith they have not come. Perhaps the *chota sahib*—"

A measured shuffle of footsteps and a gay laugh arrested the deprecating voice. It was Mrs. Boynton, carried by four men arrayed in white; she herself a vision of angelic spotlessness. Beside her, his hand on the shaft of her *dandy*, his young face intent on hers, came George Keene. It needs great ignorance, or great experience, to walk in this fashion without appearing either ridiculous or unseemly. George looked neither —only extremely happy.

"Who was that?" he asked, as his companion bowed.

Her little gloved hand, resting so close to his, tightened nervously. "Dalel Beg. He bowed to me."

George gave a quick glance backward. "By Jove! so it is. What cheek!" He thought so honestly as they passed on between the irregular rows of shingled huts, leaving the group before the jeweller's shop looking after them curiously. Past the bazaar, down many a turn, till a bare zigzag showed on the hill-side beneath them; below that, again, a green oval of valley set in trees. The eye following each angle of descent could see, as it were in terraces, an almost continuous stream of *dandies*, *rickshaws*, and ponies, all bent towards that grassy oasis where a tent or two gleamed white, and a crowd of humanity already swarmed like bees.

No gayer crowd in the universe than this; though, even as it passed downward, a man with a sober face and a telegram in his pocket passed upward on a sorry errand. But ten minutes before, that telegram, handed in to the club tent, had hushed the laughter into silence for a while. "Cholera, of course," said some one, after a pause. "I heard yesterday from Galbraith; it was getting rather stiffish in those parts. Poor old Jackson! After all these years, too." And then the recipient had ridden off in hot haste, because the widow of his best friend was coming down at four o'clock, with his wife, to see the steeple-chase, and it would be best to prevent *that*, if possible. A sorry errand, indeed; past those holiday-makers, to whom he had to give back greeting, irrespective of that death-message in his pocket. Even to the pallid, pretty-faced wife, raising herself eagerly from her pillows, to ask if Mrs. Jackson had heard from *her* husband that morning. She had had no letter; but, of course, Mr. Jackson would have mentioned it if there had been anything wrong with Charlie. Doubtless, Mr. Jackson would have written, came in answer to the wistful eyes, ere the messenger rode on, full of that wrathful, surprised grief which such scenes bring to the average Englishman. And it must not be forgotten that it is in such scenes as these that the foundation of all that is best in our Indian Empire is laid. Going to the Hills! Whose fault is it that the phrase conjures up to the English ear a vision of grass-widows, flirtations, scandals, frivolities? Surely it is the fault of those who, telling the tale of a hill-station, leave out the tragedy of separation, which makes British rule in India such a marvel of self-sacrifice, both to the woman and to the man. Yet below, in the club tent and round the shady ring, the laughter went on after its brief check; Mrs. O'Dowb, whose husband had held Hill appointments ever since he had married a big-wig's daughter, improving the occasion against her bitterest foe, Mrs. Larkins, by declaring that some women had no sense of duty, and seemed to forget that they had sworn at the altar to cherish their husbands. To which her little enemy, using the sharp tongue which captivated mankind generally, assented smilingly; she herself knew women who could not be brought to understand that their absence must be a far greater comfort than their presence. Whereat there was war.

A gay crowd indeed, with here and there a surge, accompanied by murmurs of "Your Excellency," and a steady circle round some recognized leader holding her court. Not much interest, on the whole, save in a knot of men near the betting-tent, where Dalel Beg, hand in glove with a shady lot of fellows from a newly-opened hotel, went swaggering about with his jockey's colors pinned to his coat.

"I'm not on duty to-day," replied a handsome man to Gwen

Boynton's inquiry, why he was not, as usual, in his tent. "A contingent of bad lots brought their ponies up and rushed the meeting. They do it sometimes, and then it isn't good enough for old stagers. All we stewards can do is to keep them as straight as we can, and that isn't easy. Weight for weight, inches for inches, Mrs. Boynton, I'll back an Indian *gymkhana*, where nobody has any money to pay—and all the subalterns think they know something about a horse, especially their own—to lick creation in sheer crookedness. And when the profession come down like a wolf on the fold, as they have done to-day, it is crookeder still. And all about a *pari mutuel*, for the most part." The look of disgust on the speaker's face was almost comical.

"Poor Major Davenant!" smiled Gwen, sympathetically. "But the chase will be good. Mr. Gordon is in it."

"I wish he weren't," said the major, briefly—a wish echoed by Rose Tweedie, who stood within earshot. For the last half-hour she had been trying to keep her eyes away from the zig-zag—now almost deserted—on the opposite hill-side. An ineffectual attempt—ineffectual as her wish; for there, coming down at a rattling pace, was an unmistakable figure. She clasped her hand tighter on her riding-whip, impatient at her own nervousness, and went on talking to George Keene.

"No; you aren't a creditable patient. You don't look a bit better than you did a week ago; I'm not sure you don't look worse. And you have only three more days; you should ask father for an extension."

Mrs. Boynton turned round quickly. "What a splendid idea! Do, Mr. Keene! Rose will back you up, and so will I. You mustn't go before the club ball."

The young fellow flushed, but shook his head, with a laugh. "And poor old Dan down in the wilderness! Not I. It is only excess of amusement, Miss Tweedie; I shall soon get over that at Hodinuggar." His face sobered at the very thought.

"Poor fellow!" murmured Gwen, in an undertone, and he brightened up again.

"How many gloves was it to be on Bronzewing, Miss Tweedie? You promised to back her against the field, if you remember," came a voice, making Rose start. How nice he looked, with his covert coat just showing the white and crimson! She hated herself for thinking such things, and yet she thought them all the same. It seemed to her, sometimes, as if she were always thinking of him; but she had given up hating herself for that. That had to be faced and kept secret, like this strange feeling of dread. She had seen dozens of men ride steeple-chases before without a flutter at her heart; but now—

"You bet? Then I lay you three to one against. You need not pay, lady-fashion," interrupted another voice ere she had time to reply. It was Dalel Beg, swaggering along, fresh from a vice-regal handshake, to assert his rights in society—notably with Mrs. Boynton, much to her tall companion's horror; for he had done his best on two occasions to get the offender kicked off a race-course. The mirza's flabby hand was now thrust out at Rose, but the riding-whip seemed a fixture in both of hers, as it would have been if the hand offered had been fair instead of dark; for there was a certain class of men with whom the girl never shook hands. Lewis Gordon, watching her with curious impatience, as he often did in society, had often been forced to confess that her instincts in this respect were generally right. This time her refusal gave him distinct pleasure.

"I don't bet lady-fashion," she replied, coolly; then, turning to Lewis, went on in the same tone: "I believe I did promise, Mr. Gordon; so perhaps Major Davenant wouldn't mind half a dozen pairs to one on the mare."

"Double the odds wrong way up," smiled the major, crossing over to her side; "you wouldn't make your fortune as a book-maker, I'm afraid. However, I'll take it, if you will let me hedge for you."

"You don't know Bronzewing; I do."

"You don't know the field; I do. In fact, Gordon, if I had had any idea we were to be inundated with down-country ruck I should have advised you to scratch. They don't want outsiders."

"They will have to thole them, as we say north of the Tweed," replied Lewis. As a rule, he was shy of admitting his Scotch birth, and the pronoun sounded sweet in Rose's ears.

"What an arrant pirate you are, Gwen," he said, in a low tone, as he took the place beside her *dandy* vacated by Dalel Beg, who had returned to her for consolation, after his rebuff from Rose. "You have been betting against me, haven't you, dear?"

"Against Bronzewing, you mean. What chance can she have against the Confederation's Arab? If you were riding *it*—and I am so badly off for gloves." She looked at her lavender-cased fingers plaintively—as pretty and well-dressed a picture of gracious womanhood as the imagination could paint. The fact was mollifying, and brought admiration to his eyes.

"Don't see it. Seems to me you are not wanting anything. What a jolly shawl that is—too good, surely, to be crumpled up that way." He was right; a white cashmere, with a broad bordering in faint grays and lavenders is hardly the thing for a dust-cloak. Perhaps she was aware of the fact; anyhow, she colored up.

"Not at all; I bought it for a mere song. Isn't it time you were weighing in, or something of that sort? They have been ringing a bell."

"Directly. You see, I'm dressed ready."

"Yes, I see; you look so nice."

Rose might have made the remark with far more fervor than Gwen could conjure into it, yet the latter scored the point. Lewis strolled off, feeling less dissatisfied with life than before. Men are trivial creatures when in the hands of that trivial creature—woman.

To a large proportion of men a horse-race is a most uninteresting affair; to the majority of women a mere accessary to a misused wedding-breakfast or a somewhat spoiled *fête champêtre*. This one was no exception to the rule, and the interest of the resident racers being reduced to a minimum, there was little excitement beyond the immediate circle of the tents.

"Game little beast, that of Gordon's," remarked Major Davenant, as Lewis cantered past; "pity he hasn't a chance, but I'm afraid she is out-classed. By George! they are off—no! that's a pity"—a short man standing close by laughed—"for Gordon. I know that beast—seen him down country; he is warranted to wear out the temper of any but his stable companions. Is Bronzewing keen, Miss Tweedie?"

"Very."

"I thought so; there! back again. Gordon looks pleased, doesn't he?" His face certainly showed vexation, his hand did not; and as he turned the mare to face the starter again, he leaned forward to pat the fine bronze neck. There was a greater interest this time as the pace slackened to a walk.

"Splendid line," commented the major; "now then. Oh, dash that mare! No! by Jove, that was well done!"

"For the dun!" echoed the short man. "Smart, very. Wonder how he managed it?" for, as the flag fell, Bronzewing had reared straight on end, only to shoot forward with a bound which more than compensated for the delay on which the others had counted.

"Didn't you hear?" cried Rose, clasping her hands tight. "It was the partridge's note did it. He—Mr. Gordon—gave it. You heard it, didn't you, Mr. Keene?"

"Yes; I heard." He was as excited as she was. "By Jove, what a sell for that dun brute! Look! there they are. He is in—right in to the posts; trust Gordon for that!"

Now to be in to the posts means something, when you have to go twice round a course which follows the narrow oval of a valley—except at the ends of the ellipse, when a less clever-footed beast than Bronzewing might find trouble in the sharp curve.

"Oh, how badly that man rides!" cried Rose. "He can't hold his horse—ah!" She felt a wild inclination to cover her eyes—to get away—not to see; for as the horses rose to a stone-wall, a sudden swerve of his left-hand neighbor carried Lewis Gordon's foot clear out of the stirrup.

"All right, Miss Tweedie; over, like a bird. But you are

right; Green rides—badly." And the short man looked at the major comprehensively. "Jimmy," called the latter, quickly, as the horses were seen again at the end curve, as they came round on the winning-post for the first time, Bronzewing fourth, and ousted from her inner place by Blue-and-White, who was making the pace over the straightest bit in the course, "get me all you can from them on the mare, in Simians—gold; I should like to let those fellows in."

"But she is behind—ever so far behind," interrupted Rose, divided between regret and relief that she would not have to watch a reckless tussle at the end, with its thousand possibilities of mishap.

"There isn't a beast near her at the jumps, and if Gordon—he's saving her now, Miss Tweedie—gets the inner lap again, top and bottom, it is as near a moral as racing ought to be. Lord! how she took that water! Well done, little 'un, well done!"

He was almost as excited as George, who was craning forward to catch a last glimpse of the trail of bright colors skimming round the farthest turn behind some trees.

"By Jove! he is in again; and how Green is riding him. Stick to it, man, stick to it! Game little lady! not an inch to spare, and over it, as if she had the floor to herself. They mean Blue-and-White to win, that's clear. Ah! now it's on the straight; now Green will shoot! Hum—not much to spare in that cross. Green's in—that's an end. Blue-and-White wins unless he makes a mistake." Major Davenant put down his field-glasses with a sigh. On they came, the red hoop and the green almost neck-and-neck close in to the posts; keeping pace half a length behind, in the clear, Blue-and-White, saving breath for his awkward beast at the last hedge; behind them a trail of colors, like a pennant streaming backward. Now they are at the sharpest corner, and a murmur rises as Bronzewing shoots ahead, making the Green give way.

"Hullo, what's that," cries the major—"a foul? Did anybody see it?"

No time for an answer as yet. Green, seeing his work over,

slacks his pace, and there is nothing but an easy hedge and a couple of hundred yards galloping between the crimson hoop, Blue-and-White, and the winning-post. Inch by inch Bronze-wing gives way before the swinging stride of the Arab, but she presses him hard—too hard for the last fence, easy as it is. They rise almost at the same second. It is the mare's last chance against those longer, clumsier legs, and she gains it. Blue-and-White sways in his saddle as his beast, touching the rail, staggers, jumps short, and rolls over easily. Green, half a length behind, is alongside in a second, but a second too late; for Lewis Gordon wins by that second, and no more.

Rose, who for the last minute has been completely blinded by the beating of her own heart, was left alone amid feminine congratulations, the men having gone to offer theirs in person to the winner.

"Oh, Jimmy, my boy, I wish I'd said thousands," mourned Major Davenant, as he passed his pal in the outer tent.

Jimmy whistled softly. "Just as well you didn't; they claim a foul for Green, and it looks bad. I wish you had been on. Williams and Grey are such duffers, and that Souter—" A shrug of the shoulders completed his meaning effectually.

"A foul!" echoed the major, sadly. "Well, I must own it seemed like one to me. What does Gordon say?"

"Looks black as thunder. Go inside and see; most of the field swear to it, but it isn't like Gordon."

There was not much judicial serenity about the inquiry which was being made, nor much of the circumstance of justice either: a bare tent, a cane-bottomed chair or two, the weighing-machine, where Lewis still sat listening to Dalel Beg, who was volunteering information. An Englishman in like position would have been told to hold his tongue, but what are vaguely termed political considerations affect the question in regard to the native nobility, especially at headquarters.

"I beg your pardon, I'm sure," interrupted one of the judges, diffidently; "but if you will allow me, since the claim is made, perhaps Mr. Crosbie — that is, I think, your name, sir — will kindly tell us what occurred." The man in green silk bowed

—a gentlemanly-looking man, with a suspicion of past military training in his carriage.

"I regret it exceedingly, and I am sure it was quite unintentional on Mr. Gordon's part; but there can be no question about the foul. As most of those present can bear me out in saying, I had taken and kept the inner place fairly. Mr. Gordon was riding for it also. At the corner-post his mount was too eager, and the foul occurred—so violently that, as you see, two buttons have been almost wrenched off my breeches. I quite admit that I recovered an outside place without delay, but I beg to remind the judges that the race was lost by a second."

"And I beg to remind the judges," added the Blue-and-White Jacket, "that I was on a level with Mr. Crosbie and Mr. Gordon, a little farther out, and saw the whole affair. It was not Mr. Gordon's fault, but the foul was indubitable."

"And what have you to say about it, Mr. Gordon?"

"I?" He rose, quietly, and went over to Green Jacket. "I should advise Mr. Crosbie to try benzine; it's the best thing I know for taking paint off breeches—doesn't stain in the least. By-the-way, Davenant, I've often told you that it is a most awkward post. It's just on the angle, and if you haven't perfect control over your beast, it is almost certain to go the wrong side, as Mr. Crosbie's did, and then if the thing is newly painted, you—you spoil your clothes." He turned on his heel as he drawled out the last words, and walked away.

"I utterly deny. I—I— It is impossible," stuttered Green and Blue together.

Lewis Gordon looked back from the door. "Exactly so; I leave you gentlemen to settle how Mr. Crosbie got that red paint on his left knee, when, according to you, he was hugging the post with his right. It is an interesting question, and I shall be glad to hear the judges' decision, when they have arrived at it." He was in a towering temper, despite his cool words, and Mrs. Boynton felt quite a pang of alarm, as he apologized, curtly, for not being able to wait for her, as he was in a hurry to get home to some important work. That, however, as she noticed, keenly, did not prevent him spending five minutes beside Rose Tweedie in eager conversation. Of course, Lewis Gordon was not such a fatuous idiot as to allow the mere gain or loss of half a dozen pairs of gloves to affect his arrangements for the future; but it certainly affected him in the present, and Gwen was quite aware of the fact. She felt glad that the proceedings of the *pari mutuel* were strictly confidential, and as she went home, listening gracefully to George Keene's adoring small talk, her mind was full of care. Now at these periods of life when the sun stands still in the heavens, and a man acquires the art of talking about the most trivial details in a tone which is a caress, he is apt to pall—unless the caress means as much to the woman. So Gwen sent George home from the turn up to her house, and went alone through the scented pine woods, where the long shadows lay across the path. Her face, now there was no need for a smile, looked haggard and anxious; utterly out of keeping with the luxury of her surroundings, and the comfort of the flower-decked veranda, where the *ayah* stood waiting for her mistress, and some one else, too, in highly-starched muslin, and a low-wound white *puggree*, showing a triangle of pale pink folds about the forehead. A smirk was on his face, a wooden pen-box under his arm, and an attendant was squatting beside some more boxes done up in a Manchester handkerchief.

"*Mem sahib* see my thing. Gold-work, Delhi work, Cashmere work—all work."

He thrust a card into her hand. "Manohar Lal, from Delhi."

She turned away quickly. "I don't want anything. *Ayah*, how often have I told you never to let these people come?"

"Manohar Lal say he know *mem sahib*," murmured the *ayah*, sulkily, moving off with the wraps.

"No need to buy, *huzoor*," said the crafty lips. "I have good things to look. Or I buy. Anything. Gold-work, silver-work, pearls. I buy three big pearls of lady in Rajpore last month. Shall I open boxes, *huzoor*?"

"Yes, you can open them," said Gwen, quickly.

CHAPTER XVI

DEODARS and soft green stretches of turf surrounded by a map of Asia in high relief. Silver streaks of rivers at the bottom of the map, snowy peaks and passes at the top of the map, just as if they were set there to show comparative lengths and heights. Such was the scene from the ridge chosen out for what is called a râjah's picnic. What râjah or mâharâjah, what nizâm or nawâb, matters not. Some one of the many feudatories who crowd to prefer their claims to something at Simla had asserted his dignity by giving a picnic to society; and society had consented to come and eat *pâté de foie gras* and drink champagne on a hill-side at the expense of a man to whom one or other of these two things was an abomination. That is the case in a nutshell; and so long as the *pâté* was not bought cheap from a box-*wallah*, and the champagne was drinkable, nobody cared whether the host was or was not performing the whole duty of a man in tempting his fellows to do those things which he himself considered worthy of purgatorial pains. But, then, to nine-tenths of the guests the host was a mere lay-figure, imported into society on certain occasions to give it local color by the display of gold tissue and diamonds.

Barring the shock it gives to first principles in some minds, a râjah's entertainment is generally pleasant enough; even more so when it takes the form of a picnic, which, by-the-way, the natives translate adroitly into *pâgul khâna* (fools' dinner). This one was no exception to the rule. Two huge, flat-roofed tents, open on all sides save for a deep flounce of gay appliqué work, and supported by flower-and-fern-wreathed poles, served as marquées, where a most elaborate lunch was laid out in a style worthy of the great Simla caterer. What the cost was to be per head to the unfortunate noble playing the part of host is a trivial detail.

So to him was the lunch itself, seeing that in this particular case the host was a Hindoo of the strictest caste—too pure, too proud even to sit down at a table spread with such abhorred viands. His part consisted, therefore, in receiving the company in a Cashmere shawl tent with silver poles, yawning between the handshakes, and thereafter, when the outcasts were safely started on the champagne and the *pâté*, jolting back joyfully in a *jhan-pan* to Simla in order to purify himself in unmentionable ways before starting his own dinner. The next day or the day after he would pay the bill, some official would be told off to congratulate him on the success of the entertainment; perhaps if he were a great swell to say that H—— E——y had enjoyed it immensely. And then the only thing remaining to be done would be to enter the cost in the state accounts, under what heading outsiders cannot presume to say; possibly civilization!

But none of the guests troubled themselves about these details. The sky was blue as blue could be, the gray bloom on the spreading deodar branches glinted white in the strong light, the shadows beneath them showed black. Across the valley, contours of terraced crops round a cluster of apricot-trees showed the village sites. Blue air between you and them, blue air between them and the snows, blue air giving a thousand iridescent tints to the plains which rolled up into the southern sky beyond the dotted range of Simla; and below you, drifting up the valley like grazing sheep, little fleecy mist clouds, inconsequent, hopelessly astray.

"Poor things, how lost they look," said Gwen, gayly pointing at them with her white-lace parasol."

"A fellow-feeling makes us wondrous kind," quoted one of her circle. "Mrs. Boynton knows what it is for a heavenly being to be condemned to earth."

"That sounds prettier than it is—an angel astray! Lewis, defend me from my friends!"

She turned to him with the prettiest air of appeal, the sweetest confidence in a regard which to the outside world was cousinly—to those two something more. Such a bait seldom fails to rouse a man's vanity, even if it leaves his heart untouched.

"My dear Gwen," he replied, readily, "there is no need for defence. The angel is not astray, since you are here with us and we are in paradise."

George Keene applauded with both hands as he sat at her feet looking out over the plains. Once more it seemed incredible that there should be such a place on God's earth as Hodinuggar.

"Well, some of us will be sitting at the gate thereof, disconsolate, ere long," remarked a man leaning against a rock with a cup of black coffee and a cigarette. "By-the-way, Keene, we might share a *tonga* the day after to-morrow."

"Mr. Keene is not going," interrupted Mrs. Boynton quickly. "No one wants him down there, and we need dancing men dreadfully. Miss Tweedie has spoken to her father about it."

"And you?"

The question, which came almost in a whisper, was answered by a smile only, but it brought a sort of mist to George Keene's young eyes as he looked out over the plains again. The spiritual exaltation of it all was almost too much at times for the hard-headed young fellow who had clothed his own honest uprightness with a woman's softness and sweetness in order to worship it. Now, as a matter of fact, Mrs. Boynton had said nothing to Colonel Tweedie about the lad's leave; still, as she fully intended doing so in the course of the afternoon, her smile was perhaps excusable. What is more, she kept to her intention. Half an hour afterwards any one rash enough to do so might have interrupted a tête-à-tête that she was conceding to the colonel in the shade of a large deodar-tree, to one side of a level stretch where two mud tennis-courts had been laid out. But no one did. A certain officialdom prevails in Simla society, and the heads of departments have recognized rights and privileges. The colonel, however, would scarcely have admitted that he owed his good-fortune to his seniority, for he felt juvenile in a new lounge-suit with very baggy trousers—quite the thing for lolling about in on the grass while a pretty woman leaned over the shafts of her *dandy* which she was using as a seat, and asked for your opinion on a number of trivial, personal questions. Yet Gwen Boynton was in earnest about it all, to judge from her eyes, as she let the conversation drift further afield.

"He is such a nice boy. One of those boys who make a woman think how delightful it would be to have a son in her old age. But he looks as if he would be the better for another week among the hills, and I suppose even *you* cannot manage that."

He smiled condescendingly. "The lieutenant-governor might object, of course."

"Then you can! O Colonel Tweedie, if you would! He really isn't fit to go down, and Mr. Fitzgerald, who is as strong as a horse, could easily stop at Hodinuggar. He wouldn't like it, of course, but it wouldn't hurt him. Only"— She paused, looked at her companion, and shook her head gravely.

"Only?" echoed her elderly admirer; the heart which had melted at her cavalier mention of Dan stiffened again at what might be consideration for that most ill-advised person.

"Only George won't consent to that, I'm afraid. He has such a ridiculous attachment to Mr. Fitzgerald. And I suppose it would be quite impossible to leave the place even for a few days without a really first-class man in charge. What a comfort it must be to you to have officers on whom you can rely, like Mr. Fitzgerald."

Colonel Tweedie gave his little preparatory cough. "No doubt; no doubt. At the same time, I'm not aware that Mr. Fitzgerald's presence er—is—is—er—indispensable. The fact is, my dear Mrs. Boynton, that owing—er—to previous occurrences, we were anxious to keep him out—er—of the responsibility as much as possible. In fact, but for his own request, I should not—er—have arranged for him to take Mr. Keene's work at all. To refuse, however, would have—er—given rise to—er—unfounded comment, and so—"

She interrupted his halting mixture of dignity and desire to be at once considerate and captious with a sigh.

"Poor Mr. Fitzgerald! He has been unlucky, and I suppose if anything were to go wrong when he was there you would have to take notice of it. How dreadful for him. Perhaps, after all, it would be better for George to go back. One would need to be omnipotent to carry out all one's kindly impulses, wouldn't one, Colonel Tweedie? And we women are so helpless."

He leaned forward and laid his hand close to hers, as it rested on the framework of the *dandy*. "Unless you have a stronger arm at your disposal, as you have now—my dear lady, if only for your kindness to my daughter—and, as you say, young Keene is not quite the thing. Besides, I—I mean you—I mean there are privileges which—"

What those privileges were remained unexplained, though Gwen, no doubt, had a shrewd guess at them, for just at that moment Dalel Beg, having no fear of departments before his eyes, came swaggering up in a bright-green velvet coat.

"Aha, you there! Hi! you *khitmutgar!* Bring me champagne cup. Jolly, Tweedie, ain't it?"

The colonel's face belied the epithet, but the new-comer was not one of those who look for support to their surroundings. He was a law unto himself only. "You see I wear swagger clothes like you, Mrs. Boynton, râjah *sahib* old-style man, so I come as native of India to please him. He is neighbor, Mrs. Boynton, by Hodinuggar down waste-water canal cut. You give him water, sir, he give you laces on laces!"

This time the colonel's expression was a study; but Gwen, despite her usually keen sense of the ludicrous, did not add a smile to the mirza *sahib's* crackling laugh.

"I regret"—began the head of the department, loftily, but Dalel's mind was full of one thing only, and that was himself; his immense superiority over the râjah *sahib;* his equality with the *sahib logues.*

"Hi, *khitmutgar! Ai! soor ki butcha! kyon nahin sunte ho?* (Oh, son of a pig! why don't you listen?) *Ek* glass curaçoa.

Cup what you call hog-wash—eh, Tweedie? Râjah, poor chap, know nothing about cup. *Khausamah* do him in the eye. Hee-hee. Poor old chappie. Gone home to do *poojah* and have baths. What rot."

"Will you take me to get a cup of coffee?" said Gwen, hastily, to Colonel Tweedie, "I won't trouble you to bring it here; it spills so in the saucer, and then it drops over one's best frock."

The courteous excuse for escape, which came naturally to Gwen's lips, pleased neither of her companions. The gracious instinct prompting it, which to Colonel Tweedie seemed quite uncalled for, was totally lost on the mirza. He scowled after her, muttering something as he tossed off the glass of curaçoa, and went off to bestow his favors elsewhere. A minute or two afterwards George Keene ran up to the empty *dandy* and pushed his watch and chain under the cushion. "She won't mind," he said, half aloud, "and it's safer there than in the tent. Wouldn't do to lose it here, of all places in the world. All right, Markham, I'm coming. Spin for court. Rough? Rough it is. If I'd only known they were going to put me up in the doubles I'd have come in flannels."

With coat and waistcoat off, however, his white shirt-sleeves rolled up, showing young, white, round arms, and his Cooper's Hill scarf doing duty for a belt, George looked workmanlike enough to play in the impromptu match of civil against military; and being of wholesome mind and person, straightway forgot the round world in the effort to keep one ball a-rolling. The sun hung in the west above a frilled edging of lilac-tinted hills, the snows began to glisten, the valleys on either side grew fathomless as the mist rose from the streams dashing through them. On the ridge itself the deodars sent long shadows eastward, though the yellow sunshine seemed to crisp the tufted parsley fern, among which civilization grouped itself in cliques and sets for afternoon tea, and in which the servants, decked in gorgeous liveries for the occasion, flitted about like gay butterflies. A great content was on all. Perhaps the memory of an excellent lunch lingered with the men, the gratifying consciousness of being well dressed with the women; but the most of them felt that it was good to be there, transfigured, as it were, on a hill-top, forgetful even of Simla, whose shingled roofs showed on a jagged outline to the south.

Yet Gwen Boynton, who, as a rule, would have shown her best in such a scene—a situation—a society, pleaded a headache as an excuse for getting away early; so that when George came back to where he expected to find the *dandy*, she was already on her way back to Simla.

"What is it, Mr. Keene?" asked Rose, who was mounting her pony close by.

"Oh, nothing, only I put my watch and keys under the cushion of Mrs. Boynton's *dandy*, and now she has gone off. If you should see her on the road, you might tell her. I have to play a return match—bad luck to it."

"You don't look very unhappy," laughed the girl, as he finished the task of putting her up by giving sundry professional little tugs at her habit to make it sit wrinkleless. "And oh, by-the-way, it's all right about your leave. Father has arranged it; he told me so just now."

"How good you are! If I could only leave my interests in your hands always, the future would have no terror for me, as they say in the melodrama. Good-bye, Miss Tweedie, till dinner-time; and you won't forget about the watch, will you? I don't want Mrs. Boynton—"

"I'll take care she doesn't make off with it," interrupted Rose, wilfully unsympathetic, as she moved away at a walk. A hundred yards or so along the broad ride which had been cut for the occasion in the hill-side from the high-road to the picnic-place, a zigzag bridle-path led down into the valley. Rose had never ridden that way, but she knew that once at the stream below, a recognized short cut would take her direct to her destination. At the worst she might have to dismount and lead her horse for a while, and there was something decidedly fascinating in a downward path at all times; more especially when every step showed something new stealing into vision out of a blue mist. In addition, she would avoid the rush of people, and of late Rose Tweedie had found a large portion of her fellow - creatures very tiresome; perhaps because humanity is only gifted with a certain capacity for liking, and she expended too much of hers on one person. The first mile or so fully justified her choice. The path, if steep, was safe; and after passing over a small bridge she was about to follow a track apparently leading down the right side of the ravine, when she heard a faint shout behind her to the left. With her experience of the Himalayas she stopped instantly, knowing she must be on the wrong path, and retraced her steps, expecting after a few turns to come on the shepherd or coolie, who, having seen her from above, had raised the warning cry. Instead of this she met Lewis Gordon, riding at what was really a break-neck pace for the style of path. He pulled up suddenly. "Miss Tweedie, you don't mean to say it was you I saw on the other bank? I had half a mind not to shout; for a man with a clever pony could do it easily. What a piece of luck for you I did."

She flushed up at once. "I'm afraid I don't see it in that light. I've no doubt I should have done it as easily as a man, and it is annoying to be brought back half a mile out of your road for nothing."

"Unless that road happens to be a mile longer, as it is in this case," replied Lewis, coolly; "but you really ought not to have tried the short cut alone. Your father, of course, had arranged to meet the lieutenant-governor, and Keene couldn't get away; but if you had asked me I should have been delighted to do my duty—I suppose you wouldn't let me say my pleasure; that is reserved for my juniors."

There was a certain snappishness in the conclusion of his speech which somehow appeased Rose's wrath. The futility of many proverbs has scarcely a better example than that which sets the orthodox number for a quarrel at two, when almost universally it is either one or three. For the spectacle of another man losing his temper is almost sure to soothe the first offender, unless dispassionate humanity appears in the form of a spectator. So Rose said sweetly that he was always very kind, and that she would certainly have asked him to accompany her if she had anticipated any difficulty, since no one could give a better lead-over than Bronzewing and her rider. And then, having reached the valley and a broader path, they dawdled along it at a walk, beside the very edge of a stream splashing and dashing over its pebbly bed, and curving round tiny meadows just large enough to serve as a stand for some huge walnut-tree. The soft mist they had seen from above, now they were in it, only intensified the blueness of the shadows or the gold of the sunlight following the contours of the hills. Down in the hollows the maidenhair fern grew like a fairy forest; out in the open great turk's-cap lilies rose higher than the blue-and-white columbines; and in every cranny the potentilla hung out its bunches of scarlet, tasteless, strawberry-like fruit.

Thus, side by side for a mile or more, they dawdled along a level grassy path, as if there were no such thing as effort in the world; as if civilization and comfort, dinner and bed, all the necessaries of life, in fact, did not lie two thousand feet or so above their heads.

"This way, I'm afraid," said Lewis at last, turning his pony into a road joining the path at right angles—an engineered road with drains and retaining walls; scientific, uninteresting, guiltless of ups and downs, facing the ascent evenly.

"Oh dear!" cried Rose, in tones of regret, and then they both laughed—laughed so gayly that the peace of the valley went with them, and the sound of their light chatter echoed up the zigzagging road to where glimpses of a *dandy* toiling on ahead showed through the trees. Its occupant, looking downward, could see them far below: the girl in front, the man behind; their voices becoming clearer and clearer until, just at the last turn where the zigzag merged into the high-road, each careless word was distinctly audible as they came scrambling up below the retaining wall, which at this point carried the branch to its junction with the main road. Gwen Boynton's hand closed tight on the shaft of her *dandy*, partly in sympathy with her thoughts, partly because the coolies swung round the last corner sharply. The wall, not two feet high at the turn, sloped rapidly up to some fifteen feet before ending in the one which supported the big road above. As is usually the case, it was built in steps or terraces, giving the required slant backward. Just as the *dandy* was at the turn, a horseman followed by two mounted orderlies came clattering along the road. Perhaps this frightened Rose's pony; perhaps the sudden swerve of the *dandy* to get out of the new-comer's way just as the girl was about to pass it actually forced her mount into shying and backing. Anyhow, it did. There was a struggle, a rattle of stones over the edge, a slip, then a jerk forward, as the beast found a momentary foothold for its hind-legs on the narrow step some two feet down.

A cry of dismay broke from the spectators, for, with the next movement, a fall backward seemed inevitable; but it ended in one of relief as Rose wheeled the pony clear round with swift decision, and, giving it a cut with her whip, leaped it into the road below.

A bold stroke for life instead of death; and even so, as the pony came on its knees with the shock, it seemed for an instant as if both it and its rider must go rolling over and over down the side of the hill. The next moment they had both struggled to their feet, and stood quivering all over; but safe and absolutely unhurt.

Lewis, who had pulled up at the corner, aghast with impotent horror, was beside her, almost incoherent in his relief and admiration.

"And—and—I only had a snaffle," said Rose, with a tremulous laugh not far removed from tears. She felt it imperative, if those were to be controlled, that they should descend to commonplace at once, and she was aided in this purpose by Dalel Beg, who, having reined in at the sight of a disaster for which he was partly responsible, was now standing by Gwen's *dandy* oblivious of apology.

"*Shâhbâsh!* Well done, indeed! Pretty! Pretty! You are rippin' rider, Miss Tweedie. If you ride race, you win like Gordon. Aha! Gordon. I congratulate you for lucky accident of paint. That Crosbie take me in, also. He swore it was foul, Mrs. Boynton, and I thought I saw foul—you believe that, eh, Gordon?"

Lewis—to whom the temporizing decision of the judges that, foul or no foul, Mr. Crosbie was out of the race by having been at the wrong side of some post at some part of the course had been irritating—scowled up at the group above.

"I am sure you saw foul," he replied. "Now, Miss Tweedie, if you please! The beast is all right, and the sooner you get home for a quiet rest the better."

He was so occupied with the shock to her that he scarcely seemed to realize that it must have been one to his cousin also; though Rose, as she passed the *dandy*, paused to say that she was absolutely unhurt, and that it was nobody's fault but her own for riding an unsteady pony in the hills. They had gone on nearly half a mile before she recollected George Keene's message.

"I don't see the necessity for going back at all," said Lewis, crossly, "but since you are so determined to obey orders I'll go. If you ride on at a reasonable pace I'll catch you up again in no time. What was it he left in her *dandy*?"

"His watch," called Rose after him. As he galloped back his temper was none of the best. He objected to a great many things: to George's familiarity with Gwen; to Rose's familiarity with George; and, as he came on the *dandy*, to Dalel Beg's familiarity with it, for the mirza had dismounted and was walking along with his hand on the shaft, just as if he were an Englishman. The sight and thought enlarged the focus of Lewis's displeasure, making it include Gwen.

"It was only a message from Keene," he said, curtly, in reply to her welcoming smile. "He asked Miss Tweedie to tell you, but she forgot; so I came back. He put his watch in your *dandy* to keep it safe."

"His watch!" echoed Gwen, feeling at the same time among the cushions. "Yes, here it is! Lewis, what am I to do with it? Won't you take it?" For without drawing rein he had turned his pony and was riding off. He looked back carelessly.

"Keep it, I suppose, till Keene comes to claim it; that won't be long."

As he rounded the next curve in the road, Mrs. Boynton and Dalel Beg were left face to face with George Keene's watch between them. It had a Chubbs key attached to the chain, and Dalel Beg's eyes, as he stood beside the *dandy*, clothed in a green velvet coat and European rowdyism, were attached to the key. Gwen's were on Lewis's retreating figure, and there was real jealousy and anger at her heart.

An hour and a half later, George, galloping the hired pony along the mall, after the manner of very young men on hired ponies, pulled up at the side of Mrs. Boynton's *dandy* in pleased surprise.

"I'm so glad!" she exclaimed, before he could say a word. "There is your watch." As she handed it over to him their eyes met, and his took an expression of concern.

"I'm afraid your headache is very bad; you should have been at home hours ago."

"On the contrary it is better," she replied, quickly. "I came by the low road and dawdled. Besides, I had to call at the dress-maker's, and she kept me waiting for ages. By-the-way, Colonel Tweedie says you are to have another week's leave."

"So his daughter told me. How good you both are to me; only Hodinuggar will be worse than ever—afterwards." He would have liked to say "after paradise," but he refrained. She gave a nervous little laugh.

"Don't think of it yet. I hate thinking. It does no good, for one never knows what mayn't happen. You are safe for a week anyhow."

As she lay awake that night in defiance of her own wisdom, thinking over the matter in all its bearings, she told herself that he was safe for more than a week. Everyone was safe. At the worst Dan might lose his promotion, but even that would be no unmixed evil if it forced him into independence. Indeed, if he knew of her worries, of the snare laid for her, of the covert hints about an *esclandre* involving both him and

George Keene which were wearing her to death, he would gladly sacrifice something for the sake of safety. If by any chance the sluice were to be opened during that week of absence, how it would simplify the whole business! And after all, what had she done? Nothing. Surely a woman might go and see her dress-maker sometimes and leave her *dandy* outside? Was it her fault if the dress-maker lived in a house close to the bazaar, in full view of Manohar Lal's shop? Was it her fault if the coolies slipped away to smoke their *hookahs?* Was it her fault that the key of the sluice was behind the cushions of the *dandy*, and that Dalel Beg knew it was there? What had she done? What had she said? Nothing. Had she not set aside the mirza's suggestion that she should look in on Manohar Lal's new jewellery on her way home by saying that she had no time—that she must go to the dress-maker? Had she not hitherto refused to listen to hints or threats? Had she not even defied Manohar Lal? And now would it really be her fault if any one had taken advantage of her absence?

Gwen turned her face into the pillow and moaned helplessly, telling herself that never was woman before so beset by misfortune. She had meant no harm, yet George had given her the pot, and Dan had taken the jewels to Manohar Lal's. There was no proof, of course, against her or any one else; but the *esclandre* would kill her. That must be averted at all costs.

CHAPTER XVII

Mrs. Boynton was physically incapable of being constant to anything disagreeable, even to her own thoughts. The love of ease which came uppermost in her made it impossible; so as she sat waiting for George Keene on the following evening she had forgotten the vague remorses and regrets which had assailed her the night before. All she chose to remember was that both George and Dan would be away from Hodinuggar *if anything happened.* What more could anybody ask from one in her position? She made a pretty picture in the pretty room. A wood fire blazed on the hearth, a scent of English flowers filled the air. Everything—from the books on the table to the graceful figure in white satin and pearls on the wicker-chair—told a tale of delicacy and refinement; of what it is the fashion nowadays to call culture. On the mantel-piece, among a Noah's Ark of china beasts, and supported by a placid brass Buddha, George Keene's sketch of the dust-storm, the *kikar*-tree, and the rat-hole struck a dissonant note in the general harmony; but Gwen's ears were too much attuned to content for her to notice it. Briefly, she was full of solid relief; not only because escape from a tight corner seemed assured, but that such relief had come in the nick of time; for Lewis Gordon had been over to tea, saying things which made it imperative that something definite should be settled about Dan's promotion and prospects. Saying, for instance, that he was sick of doing orderly duty at the Tweedie's house, and wanted one of his own; that she needed a firm hand to prevent her wasting her pension on *pari mutuels.*

Beneath these jesting complaints she had seen real discontent and a determination for a change in the future. And was he not right? Her whole mind gave its assent to his wisdom. What an unspeakable relief it would be to find herself back in a straight path; not only for her own sake, but also for the sake of others — of those two especially whom she had implicated all unwittingly. But for them she would have defied the plotters; but for them she would never have stopped to flatter Dalel Beg, and take shawls and ornaments at nominal prices from Manohar Lal; to do any of those things, in short, with which their covert hints had forced her to rivet the chain which bound her to deceit. At least, so she told herself; but then she was a proficient in the art of playing the thimble trick with her own mind, and as often as not was really incapable of saying where the motive-power of her actions lay. So, as she sat in the wicker-chair waiting for George Keene, she felt quite virtuous over the sacrifice of her honorable instincts on the shrine of friendship. Even *if anything did happen*, all real blame would lie with Colonel Tweedie for allowing both George and Dan to be absent; but what was blame to the head of a department? It slipped from him like water from a duck's back. And then in regard to the water itself? Even Lewis allowed that the poor people might just as well have it as not.

"Keene *sahib salaam deta*," said the servant, interrupting her soliloquy of smooth things. She rose, with outstretched hand and kindly smile.

"Punctual, as ever; we shall be in time for number two—" Then she paused abruptly, in careless surprise. George, who had been told off as escort during the three-mile *dandy*-ride to the town-hall, was still in his light morning-suit — smart enough in his new shirt and tie, and with a carnation in his button-hole, but still scarcely in the costume for a bachelors' ball. "What is the matter? Aren't you coming?" she asked, quickly, as he stood silent, yet disturbed—the sight of her having always the nature of an electric shock upon him.

"To see you so far, of course. To the ball? I'm afraid not. You see, I have to start to-night."

"Start? Where?"

"For Hodinuggar; where else?" He spoke lightly, but his face contradicted his tone. When is it a light matter to leave Paradise?

"Nonsense!" broke in Gwen, sharply, startled out of all sane negation. "You must not go."

"Must, I'm afraid," he echoed, and his voice was a trifle unsteady. "You see," he went on, more confidently, "I ought never to have taken that offer of extra leave. I knew it at the time, but I thought Dan would stop, and the temptation—however, I'm off now."

"Now?" she echoed, in her turn, still lost in her surprise.

"To-night, I mean. Of course I have no chance of a *tonga*, so I must go by *dhooli*. It's a bore, but it can't be helped."

This phrase seemed to bolster up his manliness, and he smiled at her. Such a pleasant-faced boy; so clean, so wholesome, so full of promise for the future. A pang shot through Gwen's heart, and roused quick opposition to unlucky chance.

"But why? It isn't as if you were keeping him—I mean Mr. Fitzgerald. We settled all that; he goes back to Rajpore, all the same."

"So Gordon told me this afternoon. That is why I must return; the place must not be left alone, of course." As he stood leaning against the mantel-piece his eye caught his own sketch, and he took it up mechanically. "To think I shall be back in that hole the day after to-morrow," he said, with a short laugh. He felt very sore, yet determined to face his pain in dignified fashion. "Meanwhile," he added, "you must not be late. Is that your cloak?"

The futility of being tactful, even for your most familiar friends, was being born in upon Gwen Boynton with the remembrance of her own certainty that Dan Fitzgerald's return to Rajpore must be necessary to the lad's acceptance of the leave. And here he was declaring it to be the stumbling-block! The thought sapped the very foundation of her general security, and made the results, which this change in his plans might produce in hers, strike her confusedly. She set aside the wrap he held out to her with quite a nervous hand.

"You are very foolish. Nobody wants you to go. Even Dan—"

"Perhaps," he interrupted, feeling quite set-up by her evident regret; "but if anything were to go wrong, you know, I should never forgive myself."

The words were, to a certain extent, quite meaningless to him; he did not even seriously contemplate the possibility of what he suggested, yet they roused her fears, her regrets.

"But if anything were to go wrong," she answered, forgetting caution in her eagerness, "it would be better you should be away. Surely you must see that it would be better for you both to be away—if—if *anything should happen.*"

He smiled indulgently. "But nothing would happen while I am there. And it means such a lot to Dan. I think I told you he is engaged to a girl—"

"Yes, yes! I know—I know— But, as I said, if I were the girl—" She broke off hurriedly, then began again: "George, what has that to do with the question? Nothing will happen, of course, and then you will have lost your pleasure for nothing. Don't go! It is foolish. It is unkind—when we all want you to stay—when I want you—I do, indeed—you will stay, won't you, George? Just to please me!"

To do her justice, she seldom stooped to use her own personal charm, as she did then, wilfully; but the case was urgent—the boy must not go. George stared at her incredulously for a moment.

"Don't," he said, in a low voice, "please don't."

"But it is true, George," she went on, laying her hand on his arm. "I do want you to stay. I do, indeed."

His hand met hers suddenly, almost unconsciously, to fall away from it again with a gesture of quick renunciation.

"No, no!" he began, in the same low tone; "it isn't true; how can it be true?" Then his whole nature seemed to cast reserve aside, and his voice rose passionately. "Why should you care? I have never thought you could; never! I swear to you, never! How could I? Do you not see it is only what you are to me, not what I am to you. What does that matter? But for the other—for what you have been, and are, and will be all my life? Oh! that is different. Yet you know well enough—you must know—for I can't tell it, not even to you."

And there, English boy as he was, she saw him on his knee, stooping to kiss the hem of her garment. It was cut in the latest fashion, full round the edge and bordered by pearls of great size. They might have been of great price also—the Hodinuggar pearls, for instance—and George been none the wiser. He saw nothing but a blaze of light through the open gates of heaven, showing him a woman, transfigured, glorified. And she? There was nothing before her eyes but a boy at her feet—a very ordinary boy, whose every-day admiration she had accepted carelessly; yet it was she who, covering her face with her hands, shrank back, as if blinded. "Don't!" she cried, in sharp accents of pain. "You don't know— I—I don't like it."

He was on his feet again in an instant, blushing, confused. "I—I beg your pardon," he stammered; "I don't know what induced me to—to behave—like—like a fool."

In sober truth, he did not, being all unused to self-analysis, and far too young to understand his instinctive recoil from the cheap cajolery which had caused his outburst. But she was older; she understood. He would not let her stoop, and yet —ah, God! how low she had stooped already! So the emotion she had wantonly provoked in him caught her and swept her from her feet.

"Oh, George!" she cried, coming a step nearer, and thrusting her hands into his, as if to hold him fast and make him listen; "it was a mistake! I meant no harm—no harm to anybody—least of all to you."

"No harm!" he echoed, blankly. "What harm have you done?"

She looked at him, realizing her own imprudence; yet for all that not sufficiently mistress of herself for caution. A worse woman than she might have kept silence; but she could not. The shame, the dread of betraying the lad who trusted in her so fully forced her on.

"Don't ask, George!" she pleaded. "I can't tell you—indeed, there is nothing to tell. Only you must not go down to Hodinuggar now. Believe me, it is better you should not. I can give you no reason, but it is so. Don't go, George, for my sake."

"For your sake," he echoed, still more blankly. "Why—I don't understand—Mrs. Boynton, I—" He paused; his hand went up in a fierce gesture, and came down in still fiercer clasp on the mantel-piece. His eyes left her face, shifting their startled, incredulous gaze to his own grim jest, leaning against the brass Buddha. "Unless—"

There was a dead silence.

"If there is anything to tell," he said, at last, "tell it to me, for God's sake—it would be better—than this. Why am I to stay—for your sake?"

Tell! How could she tell the horrible truth? And yet if he knew all he might be able to help. Then the need for support, the craving for sympathy, which at all times make it hard for a woman in trouble to keep her own counsel, fought against the evasion suggested by caution.

"Oh, George, I meant no harm! I did not, indeed."

The weak appeal for mercy, which presages so many a miserable confession, struck cold to the lad's heart. He walked over to the table and flung himself into a chair, hiding his face in his clasped hands.

"You had better tell me everything," he said, in a muffled voice; "then I shall know what to do. Don't be afraid—it—it won't make any difference."

Once more his words aroused her self-scorn, and made her forget herself for a time. "But it must make a difference," she cried, hotly, crossing to the table in her turn, and seating herself opposite him. "Yes, I will tell you; it is the only thing to be done now."

She was never a woman given to sobs and tears, and even through the shame of it all there was a relief in telling the tale.

"Yes, yes!" he said once, interrupting that ever-recurring plea of her own innocence of evil intent, "of course you meant no harm. So you took the jewels and sold them to Manohar Lal for six thousand rupees." The fact recounted in his hard, hurt voice seemed to strike her in its true light for the first time, and she looked up wildly from the resting-place her head had found upon her bare, crossed arms.

"Did I?" she asked, pushing the curls from her forehead. "Yes, I suppose I did; it seems incredible now. Oh, George, what shall I do? what shall I do?" It did seem incredible; and yet his fears as to what she might yet have to tell him proved his credence of what he had already heard.

"You had better go on," he answered, dully; "I can't say what is to be done till I have heard all." The sound of his own voice shocked him. Was it possible that he was sitting calmly listening to such a story from her lips, and asking her to go on? The curse of the commonplace seemed to settle upon him, depriving him even of the right to passionate emotion.

"Is that all?" he asked, wearily, when she had told him of everything save of the empty *dandy* waiting outside the dress-maker's shop. That seemed beyond her powers. The question came more from the desire to help her along, should there be more to tell, than from curiosity or fear, since from the very beginning he had been vexedly conscious of his own relief in remembering that she had returned his watch and chain before she had even reached home. The query, however, suddenly roused in her a fierce resentment against her own humiliation. Every syllable of that story, now that it was told, seemed an outrage on that love of smooth things which were her chief characteristic, and a sort of vague wonder at her own confidence made her answer, swiftly: "That is all I know. Is it not enough?" In her anger she told herself that what she said was the bare truth. What was there more to tell save merest possibilities?

Her reply left George face to face with action, yet he sat on silent, unable even to speak. At last he rose, and, coming to where she leaned, face downward over the table, stood beside her with quivering lips. "I am sorry," he began; then stopped before the fatuity of his own words.

"Do you think I am not sorry, too?" she broke in, recklessly, raising herself to look him full in the face. "I wish I were dead, if that would help; but it won't. Something must be done, and done at once, George! Why should you go down? To stay is so simple, and it will hurt no one. Believe me, it is the best—best for us all." She was back to the position she had taken before her appeal to his passion had recoiled upon herself; but he could not follow her so far, and he gave a bitter laugh.

"For you and for me, no doubt! But for Dan? Remember what the possible loss of promotion means to him. Besides, I have promised. No! I must go down; that much is certain."

"And after?"

For the life of him he could not tell. He seemed incapable of thinking of any course of action save the palpably proper one of going straight to the chief and telling him of the plot laid against the sluice-gate, his instinct for this remaining clear and well-defined amid all the confusion. As he stood silent, almost sullen, she laid her hand quickly on his arm. "You will not be rash, George. For my sake, you will not."

"Whatever I do will be for your sake," he said, unsteadily.

"And you must not be angry with me. Indeed, indeed I meant no harm at first, and afterwards I was so frightened—so afraid of you all. Oh, don't be angry with me, George!"

He set her hand aside with a hopeless gesture, and turned away to hide the tears in his eyes. She did not understand, and a great dumbness was upon him. He could say nothing. After all, what was there to say? She had done this thing meaning no harm, and he must save her, and himself, and Dan from the consequences somehow. He took out his watch mechanically and looked at the time. Barely ten o'clock. So it was impossible to destroy heaven and earth in half an hour.

"It is time you were going," he said, in quite a commonplace tone. "You had better go. Gordon—and the others—might wonder."

It was the first time he had even hinted at the supposition that some definite tie existed between her and her cousin; this and his cynical acceptance of the fact that in the tragedy of life action must be swayed by the desire of the spectators as much as by the emotions of the actors themselves, brought home to Gwen her crime against the boy's youth. For the first time she broke into a sob.

"Oh, George, why did I do it? why did I do it?"

Why, indeed? A pitiable thing, surely, to stand silent without an answer. Pitiable also for the woman, forced by worldly considerations into self-control; into bathing her face and perhaps powdering it, certainly rearranging the pretty, artful curls, and so setting off through the dark to the town-hall, as if nothing had happened. For what loss of liberty is comparable to that entailed on the possessor of a fringe which will come out of curl, even with the damp of tears?

The first clouds of the coming monsoon were drawn over the heads of the hills like an executioner's cap, and George, riding the tired pony behind the *dandy*, felt as if he were following the funeral of a faith condemned to death. A dreary little possession this, despite its goal, as it wound its way through the dark chasm of the valleys on the one side, and the dark shadow of the hills on the other. And then, like some enchanted palace set between earth and sky, that pile upon the ridge sending long beams of light and fitful snatches of dance-music across the ravines. So familiar, yet so strange. Then, finally, the twinkling lamps, the crowd of *rickshaws* and *dandies* blocking up the angles and arches, the red carpet in the porch, the red streak of baize climbing up the white stairs. He kept that pearl-edged garment from the dust till she reached them.

"Have you settled on what you are going to do?" she asked, in a low voice, as he held out his hand to say good-bye.

He shook his head. "I'll settle it, somehow; you needn't be afraid."

"I am not afraid. But if the worst comes to the worst . . . I will not let others suffer for my fault. So be careful, for my sake."

"Whatever I do will be for your sake; you know that."

He stood watching her go up the stairs—up and up, until

the last trail of that hem disappeared amid the colored lamps and flowers. That was the end of it all—of all save Hodinuggar, and the desire to kill somebody. First of all, however, safety for her; and that might be secured by money. During that three miles' ride his thoughts had been busy over possibilities, and one of them made him turn the tired pony's nose towards Manohar Lal's shop instead of homeward. There was no power in India like the power of the rupee; and that, with the club still open and half a dozen young fellows, as reckless as yourself, ready to back the chance of your living to pay your debts, was not difficult to borrow for a month or two. Especially when there was something — not much, but a few hundred pounds or so—to come when the dear old governor—George choked down a sob in a curse at the tired pony for stumbling over the ill-paved alley.

The dawn had broken when the patient beast pulled up for the last time by the veranda of Colonel Tweedie's house. A drowsy servant dozed against the long coffin-like *dhooli*, the bearers crouched outside, nodding in a circle round a solitary *hookah*.

"The *huzoor*, having lost chance of the mail, may perhaps delay till eve," suggested the half-roused torch-bearer, mechanically corking up his useless bottle of oil, at the sight of the growing glow in the east. George, his face flushed, yet haggard, stood for an instant looking over the pine woods, where, had the light been stronger, he might have seen the angle of a little house among the trees. After all, why should he not stop now, if only to see her gratitude? Twelve hours' delay was not much, especially when she was safe. Why need that be the last sight of her?—going up the stairs with the pearls! . . . pearls.

An hour afterwards, when the sun tipped over the lower hills, to make the morning-glories, festooned from rock to rock, open their eyes, they opened them upon the coffin-like *dhooli* going rapidly downhill to the accompaniment of shuffles and grunts and recurring protestations that the *sahib* was "*do mun puccka.*" If the heaviness of heart could have been measured, George might have weighed a ton.

Even at the best of times the *descensus avernus* from the cool hills to the hot plains is never easy, and in this case Paradise lay behind, Purgatory in front.

"I am so sorry Mr. Keene has gone," said Rose Tweedie at breakfast. "I shall miss him dreadfully." Lewis Gordon's eyebrows went up superciliously.

"No doubt; but he was right to go, in more ways than one."

Colonel Tweedie, busy over a virtuous plate of porridge and milk, which, in some mysterious way, he regarded as a sign of youth, gave his preliminary cough.

"I scarcely agree with you, Gordon. In my opinion, there is—er—a savor—of—of—insubordination; or, not to speak so strongly, a want of respect in this sudden departure. Of course the zeal, and the—the desire to do his duty—are pleasing in so young a man. At the same time, a little more confidence in—er—the judgment of—"

"Mr. Gordon wasn't thinking of that, father," interrupted the girl, with her gray eyes showing some scorn for both her companions. "He meant to imply that George—Mr. Keene—was better away from Simla."

"Your perspicacity does you credit, Miss Tweedie. I did mean it. He has been going rather fast, and will be none the worse for saving up some more rupees at Hodinuggar."

"If he had the money to spend, I don't see why he shouldn't spend it in having a good time," retorted Rose, quickly. "He won't ask you to pay the bills, will he?"

"Hope not, I'm sure; but the bearer brought quite a little pile of them to me this morning, by mistake."

Rose bit her lip. "Perhaps you will be so kind as to tell your man to put them back in Mr. Keene's room. I'll forward them when I write. Are you coming with me to the Grahams' this afternoon, father?"

But Colonel Tweedie was not to be diverted from the head-of-the-department frown he had been preparing.

"I am sorry to hear it. To say the least, it is bad taste to —to—"

"Leave I O U's instead of P P C's," remarked Lewis, flippantly. "But really, sir, I don't see how he could help it, after all. He had to go in such a hurry."

"I deny the necessity," continued the colonel, pompously. "I fail to see any just cause for setting his opinion against that of—of his elders and superiors."

"Unless he had a private reason of his own," suggested his daughter.

"My dear Rose, a public servant can have no private reasons."

There was an epigrammatic flavor about this remark which, to the colonel's ears, completely covered its absolute want of sense. He felt vaguely that he had said something clever, and that it might be as well to let it close the subject, which he did by answering the previous question as to whether he would go to the Grahams'. Certainly, if it did not rain; but the barometer was falling fast, and a telegram had come to the office that morning to say the monsoon had broken with unusual violence at Abu. It might be expected north at any moment. On which the two fell to talking about dams and escapes, inundation, cuts, and such things, while Rose, indignant with Lewis, yet disturbed at the confirmation his hints gave to her own fears, sat thinking over what had been said. George had been reckless; there could be no doubt about that. Had not one of her particular partners last night told her that he had left George playing poker at the club but a half hour before? George, who had declared he had no time to put in an appearance at the ball?

When breakfast was over she went into the lad's empty room for the bills and took the opportunity of giving a housewifely glance round, to see that nothing had been left behind or taken away in the hurry. The former, certainly; for there was the bottom drawer quite full: old shirts and ties, a rather battered pot-hat, and, beneath the whole, a picture. She stood looking at it blankly. What a very odd coincidence! The girl of her dream! The girl with the quaint dress and the Ayôdhya pot clasped to her breast. Why had George brought it up to Simla and never shown it to any one? Why, when the pot was stolen, had he said nothing about the girl? Though, on the other hand, she had kept silence about her dream. She puzzled over it for some time; at last, finding certainty on only one point—namely, that for some reason or other George had wished to keep the picture secret—she took it away to her own room; for she was of those who regard the unspoken wish of a friend to be quite as binding as any they may express.

Just about the same time Gwen Boynton, still in her bed, was looking at something else George had left behind him, but this had only an envelope carefully addressed to her. It contained two pieces of paper signed by Manohar Lal: one a receipt for a diamond necklace on which the six thousand rupees had been lent; the other, a later date, giving a quittance in full for the same, plus interest.

How simple! Why had she never thought of such a plan before? But where could she have raised money enough to buy freedom? Besides— She buried her face in the pillow in a vain desire to shut out the conviction which rushed in on her, as she recognized that if the plotters had gained what they wanted from the empty *dandy* outside the dress-maker's shop, they would naturally be quite ready to deal with George and take money for a security they were already pledged to give; which, in fact, they would have given, since the canons regulating bribery in India are strict in regard to value returned for value received. Every penny, therefore, of the money George must have paid for these papers was so much clear, unexpected gain to Manohar Lal—*if the plotters had already attained their object.*

Still she was safe; and even if anything happened, nobody could blame George. Now she had had time to consider the whole bearings of the matter, she told herself such blame was impossible; while, as for Dan, if he would only leave government service and make money, she was read to marry him tomorrow! She had woven a conscience-proof garment for herself out of the old hair-splitting arguments long before

George's *dhooli* had reached the level plain. When it did, the clouds had banked themselves against the higher hills, shutting out the boy's farewell glance. As he climbed into the country gig, in which forty miles of dusty road had to be covered, the barometer was falling fast, and the driver remarked cheerfully that when the rain came the cholera would increase. It had been bad at the third stage that day, and one of the coolies belonging to the government bullock-train had died on the road, about five miles farther on. The *sahib* might, perhaps, still see the body lying there.

CHAPTER XVIII

The last twelve hours before the advancing rains break over your particular portion of the fiery furnace!—who can describe them? Who having once endured them can need description as an aid to memory? The whole world one incarnate expectation—blistering, parched, like the tongue of Dives: the heavenly drop of water for which you long squandered on the hot air, moist with a vanguard of vapor, so that the breath you draw is even as the breath you exhale—if, indeed, you breathe at all; if, indeed, by sensation or touch or temperature you can differentiate yourself from the sodden heat of all things, or get rid of the conviction that, like the devils in a still hotter place, you are an integral part of the business!

And Hodinuggar, on this sodden July day, had small hope of future improvement to lighten the burden of the present, for it stood on the edge of the rainless tract, in the debatable land of meteorological reporters. Not more than a shower or two from that southwesterly column of cloud was due to bring up its scanty average of rainfall, which came, for the most part, from electrical dust-storms, and suchlike turbulent, undisciplined outbreaks; so the heat lay over it hopelessly, and even the peasant, patiently awaiting the return of the smith who was to mend his ploughshare, did so more from habit than from any expectation of having use for the tool in any immediate future. After all, waiting was the chief occupation of his life: waiting for something to grow, or for something to be reaped; waiting for some one to be born, or for some one to die. So the smith being absent over some work at the palace, why should he not be waited for, even though the sun was setting red behind the heat-haze? For one thing, it would be cooler to tramp home with the ploughshare on your shoulder. A tall, grave, bearded man was the peasant, sitting with his back against the wall, his hands hanging listlessly between his knees. The painted girl in the balcony above looked down and told him the news, calling him father, respectfully. No question of her trade here, with this dweller in the fields; only a pious "God keep us all" ere she became voluble over Shumshere the zither-player's seizure by cholera that morning, as he lay fighting quails in the street. Doubtless he was dying, now the sun was setting; any moment the wail might arise from that seventh arch down the colonnade, where he lodged. Whereat the long beard below wagged slowly over the fact that the great sickness had visited the hamlet, also bidding a crony or two wait no longer for anything—not even for ploughshares or rain. And then, to solace themselves, both courtesan and peasant quenched their thirst on great chunks of watermelon bought for a cowry from a heap of green-and-red fruit which had just been shot off a donkey's back into the dust at one corner of the Mori gate, the donkey meantime browsing at the edge of the pile, unrebuked.

"*Ari*, father! There it is! Did I not say so?" remarked the painted one, as a low moan rising to a banshee shriek broke the sodden stillness of the air.

"*Rain! rain!*" ejaculated the peasant, piously. "It is a bad year for sure, rain or no rain."

So, having finished his watermelon, he broke a morsel of opium from a lump he carried in a fold of his turban, rolled it under his tongue, and dozed off, still propped up against the wall. And the sunset faded, leaving the world hotter than ever, though in the crypt beneath the staircase in the Mori gate the air was cooler than outside, despite the fire which flickered fitfully over the blackened arches. It flickered also on the silver bracelets circling Châandni's round brown arms as she lay curved across a string-bed, her jingling feet swaying softly in time with the tinsel fan she waved above the bold outlines of throat and bosom. And the fan in its turn kept time with the flicker of the fire and the wheezing breath of a smith's bellows rousing the charcoal embers into dancing flame, or letting them die down to a dull red glow.

"Thou art long, O *Lohar-ji*," she said, looking backward at the bare bronze figure crouching before a low anvil. "All these hours to make a key, when thou hast a mould before thine eyes too!"

"True, O mother; but the key is not as our fathers' keys, and the hand lacks cunning in new patterns. Lo! I had made one for the treasure-chest of kings in half the time. But there! 'tis done. See how it fits its bed—like the seed of a pomegranate to the shell. God send it may do its work fairly and well!"

"God send it may for thy sake, smith-*ji*," she replied, indifferently. "Here, take the rupees, and have a care no key is forged to unlock thy tongue regarding this matter. The dewan is old; but there are others behind him, and behind him again, and Chândni behind them all." The reckless triumph of her words rang through the low arches as she brought her feet to the ground with a clash.

Five minutes afterwards she was looking down on a slender key lying in Zubr-ul-zamân's nerveless hands.

"I have won the prize," she said; "the pearls are mine."

The hands quivered, and the keen old eyes seemed to seek her out from head to foot, revelling in her beauty and her boldness. Then the light died out of them, the head sank again. "The game is played," he muttered, "the game is played."

"Yea; it is played indeed." The woman's contemptuous laugh echoed out into the dark night, through which George Keene, on a hired camel, was making his way across the desert—not by the usual road, since that meant delay and Dan's questioning eyes at Rajpore; but by a side route, branching from the railway farther to the south. A hot night—an intolerable smell of camel—dust in the eyes and nose and mouth—dust and ashes in the heart; even the twinkling lights of the palace homelike and welcome in the endless darkness of all things. The consciousness of doing your duty soothes the mind, but is powerless before bodily discomfort; and George was wretchedly uncomfortable. To begin with, a high-paced camel driven at full speed is not an easy method of conveyance; nor does the necessity for having its unwashed attendant bumping in the after-saddle add to the charm, even though that saddle be to the leeward of you—for which Heaven be thanked! And then the lad had had nothing to eat since the hastily swallowed breakfast at a rest-house, save some smoked milk and tough dough-cake brought him at the village where he changed camels. So, as he bumped through the silent night on the bubbling, breathing, silent-footed beast, with that other breathing beast behind him, more than half George's slender hold on the joys of life lay in the prospect of supper, even though it must be one of the factotum's barmecidal feasts. Such things defy the mind, especially when that mind is lodged in a young and healthy body. Thus, while he could set his teeth over the remembrance of that half-hour during which his world came to pieces in his hand, he could not prevent himself coming to pieces on the camel. A dark night indeed—so dark that the red-brick bungalow showed only by the white arches of the veranda a ghostly colonnade rising out of the shadow. The servants' houses, too, dark as the night itself, and silent as the grave. George, stepping ankle-deep into yielding sand, called once, twice; then, giving in with irritation to his knowledge of native slumber, walked over in the direction of the cook-room—too sandy for snakes; besides, booted as he was, they would hardly reach him. Necessary thoughts, these, now that he was back in Purgatory, with death, for aught he knew, coiled in the path; they came back to him naturally, as part of the environment of life. Another call without the screen of tall grass, sacred to the modesty of the compounder of egg-*sarse;* then an impatient setting aside of the mat at the entry.

"They might as well be dead!" he muttered, angrily, going up to a string-bed set in the centre of the little yard, whereon he could just distinguish a figure long enough to be a man. "Get up, you lazy brute!" cried George, shaking it by the shoulder. No answer; and he drew back hastily, shouting for some one—any one.

A twinkling light from the stables; a drowsy exclamation

from behind the hut. So, out of the surrounding dark came timorous steps, a hand bearing a cresset, a doubtful face or two peering at the intruder, then yielding to surprised salaams; finally a sudden breaking into garrulous clamor: "*Ohi! Ohi!* 'Tis the *huzoor* returned! and the *huzoor's* faithful servant hath been summoned by the Lord. Lo! if the *huzoor* had but come three hours ago there would still have been a *khitmutgar* in his honor's house. But it was the great sickness, *huzoor*, which waits not; all day long ill in the *huzoor's* cook-room with great patience. *Ohi! Ohi!* the *sahib* must be hungry; and, lo! where is he who gave the *sahib* meat fit for his rank? O, my sister! O, bereaved one! O, widow! put thy grief from thee, and prepare food for thy master; in duty sorrow finds solace."

"Is—is he dead?" asked George, standing, dazed, looking incredulously at the sheeted figure dimly visible by the flickering rush-light. He had seen the man asleep thus dozens of times. At the question, another sheeted figure, which had crept from the hut into the circle of light, broke out into a gurgling cry: "*Ohi! meri admi murgya! meri dil murgya! murgya!*" (Ah! my husband is dead! my husband is dead!) And one or two later arrivals, in like disguise, crouched beside the voice, joining in the strange, low whimper of the conventional wail. George fell back a step or two, repelled to his heart's core, shocked out of speech.

"Weep not, O widow!" snivelled the water-carrier, who, being the only Mohammedan male present, felt impelled to the duty of consoler. "Didst not give him beef-tea? Aye! and barley-water likewise? even as to the *huzoor* when he was stricken, and did not the master arise to health thereby? Wherefore, is it not the will of God, plainly, that the man should find freedom? Therefore, place thy heart on comfort. He will be buried at sunrise, *huzoor*, so the *sahib* will have no more annoyance; and by the fortune of the Most High there is even now to be had without delay a servant who can cook—the one who is dead is as nothing to him—faithful to salt, having many certificates, mine own wife's cousin, a—"

George, who by this time was half-way back to the dark house, cursed him and his wife's relations utterly; then bade him bring a light somehow. Meanwhile, scarcely conscious of what he was doing, the lad had groped his way into the room where he had first seen *her*, and, stumbling against a chair, sat down mechanically, resting his head on the back over his crossed arms. Would the light never come? and when it came, what would it reveal? More dead men, waiting to be roused? Oh, horrible!—most horrible!—the remembrance of that— No! no! no! he would not think of it. He would think of that other face, asleep on the red cushions of the easy-chair; but that was dead, too. The face of a dead ideal! Ah! the light at last, thank God! and he could be sensible.

Whatever it showed George, he showed it a mask, terrible in its needless pain, ghastly in the hunted, shrinking look in the young eyes which used to be so bold. Even the water-carrier, dense as he was, saw it, and understood vaguely.

"This is bad word that the *huzoor* should return like this. It is not fitting his honor. If he had only waited till Fitzgerald *sahib* comes back—"

"Comes back!" echoed George, dully. "Why should he come back?" Yet he knew quite well in his own mind that Dan, too, had judged it wrong to leave the fort unguarded, as it were. His mind wandered to the love he bore this man, while the water-carrier went on volubly about the *sahib* having gone off in a hurry that morning, and being very angry about something he had lost; something that the *sahib's* base-born personal attendant had said must have been stolen; as if—

George, looking at all things with uncomprehending eyes, suddenly lost patience, cursed the speaker, quite quietly this time, and bade him go about his business.

"Your honor's *khitmutgar's* widow can cook food, if the *huzoor*—"

George did it a third time, solemnly. When he was left alone he glanced round quickly, as if uncertain of what the room might contain. The easy-chair, with its red cushions; a bare bed—brought in, doubtless, for the sake of the larger room and cooler air—a dirty table-cloth on the table, littered with the crumbs and plates of Dan's last meal, left, in slovenly native fashion, to await deferred cleansing. A half-empty whiskey-bottle and a water-*surahi;* that, at any rate, was something, and his hand went out to them instinctively. Even in his general confusion, however, the precepts of modern hygiene remaining clear, he deferred to drink till they brought him some tepid soda-water. Such precaution was necessary with cholera in the compound. Whatever else it may do, civilization certainly intensifies the dread of death. The peasant and the courtesan had munched melon in the very shadow, but George's cultured nerves had no such courage. He was no coward, but he had received a shock which was bound to make its mark on the highly sensitized mind and body; bound to weaken them for the time.

Ah! that was better. The room did not seem quite so dreary. Another soda? Yes, another soda. After that the outlook itself seemed less dreary. Dan had been right in saying that he, George, did not know the temptations of stimulants. Temptations? If they brought you up to your bearings with a round turn in this fashion—why, he felt twice the man he had been five minutes ago! Now he could think; now he could see clearly; now he could reason, and decide what ought to be done. To begin with, *she* was safe. Those papers, joined to little Azîzan's confession of having stolen the Ayôdhya pot, made it quite impossible to prove that she knew anything about the jewels. As for himself, that did not matter, though for a fact he was quite as safe as Dan. That is to say, the palace devils might raise a scandal, but the break-down of their case in regard to *her* would show it was all no more than revenge for their failure; for they would fail, of course. So far nothing had happened. There was no water in the overflow cut; he had made sure of that as he came along. And now that he was on the spot, he could do quite as much, off his own beat, to prevent treachery as any one—the colonel and all the department to boot—could have done, had he reported the whole affair. To-morrow the guard would be changed and doubled, to provide against any violent attempt; an unlikely event, however, as such an assault would take time, and he meant to pitch his tent down at the sluice, so as to be on the spot at night. During the day he could watch from the bungalow. Against other and more stealthy treachery he was also provided—absolutely; so absolutely that he gave a short laugh as he drew a couple of Chubbs' keys and a new lock from his wallet. But that, also, was for to-morrow; there remained to-night. No! not to-night, since already it was past one o'clock. What wonder that he was tired! did any one in the wide world know or care how tired? He stood up sharply, every vein tingling now; his whole mind aglow, despite his weariness. He must have something to eat first, of course; his very determination insisted upon that; but not from those plague-stricken purlieus out yonder—cautious civilization insisted upon that. Biscuits or something in the cupboard. As he crossed over to it, the memory of his raid while *she* slept among the red cushions returned to make him laugh again.

> "And when she got there,
> The cupboard was bare."

The childish doggerel fitted the occasion, and left him smiling at ship's biscuits—the last resource of hunger by sea or land—left at the bottom of a tin. Dan certainly *was* a bad housekeeper. The comedy of his disappointment struck him; the tragedy, needing the sequel to develop it, remained invisible, like a photograph in film-embryo. Dry work, ship's biscuits, in a fiery furnace, with a ten-pound thirst upon you and whiskey-and-soda within reach. When he stood up again the weariness seemed to have crept upward, leaving nothing alert save his brain. Had he ever been so tired in all his life? As tired as *she* must have been when she fell asleep in the chair he was just passing. His hand lingered on the back of it for an instant, almost caressingly.

By Jove, what a furnace outside! Lighter than it had been, however, because of the suggestion of a moon low down in the heat-haze. And there was the potter's lamp, twinkling like a star above the domed shadow of the Hodinuggar mound. Queer old chap—queer start the whole thing, if one came to think of it; a crazy, irresponsible creator, as Dan had called him. Why not he as well as another? Who knew? who cared?

He stood for a space, looking out with sensitive seeing eyes to the broad shadows, formless save for the pin-point flicker of the potter's light. Face to face at last, he and Hodinuggar; between them the sliding water, mother of all things.

"*Hath not the potter power over the clay?*" If that was all the light amid the shadows of life, better far were darkness! If that— He turned quickly, beset by uncontrolled, passionate contempt, uncontrolled passion for some action, and beneath his shaking hand the lamp on the table flared out smokily. A poor protest, yet the dark was better—darkness and rest, if rest could come to one so tired as he was, as it had come to *her*. Not that it mattered if he were tired or not.

Five minutes after, the twinkling light, could it have reached so far, would have found him fast asleep, peaceful as a child, among the red cushions where *she* had slept. But even Azîzan's eyes, keen set as they were by devotion, could not pierce the darkness. The cresset was in her hand as she stood looking out from the yard towards the other bank of the canal.

"It hath gone out again," she murmured; "a servant, likely, on no good errand; and the old man tells me the truth, I think. Another week ere he returns. I would it had been sooner, so that I might have warned him. But there! 'tis the same; the task is mine in the end."

As she crossed back to the hut she paused an instant to look, by the cresset light she shaded with her fingers, on the figure of old Fuzl Elâhi asleep, in the open, beside his wheel.

"Poor fool!" she said, softly, as if to the sleeper. And after that even the potter's light disappeared, leaving both sides of the sliding water to darkness.

The dawn came and went; the sun climbing up into the sky turned it into brass—a brazen dome, in which the sun itself seemed merged and lost. Yet still George slept on, undisturbed even by the water-carrier's cautious peepings through the chink.

"Lo! the *huzoor* is young, and he was broken into pieces by thy bad animal," he said to the camel-driver, who was impatiently awaiting payment. "Sleep is even as food and drink to him; and, besides, ere he wakes, my wife's cousin, whom I have sent for, will be present to cook my lord's breakfast. There is great virtue in being *majood* (*i. e.*, created on the spot), and the man who cooks one meal hath himself to blame if he cook not many. If thou art hurried, go. Who wants thee and thy evil-smelling brute?"

So George slept on; and when he woke at last, it was to the confused, unreasoning consciousness of those who have been drugged. He stared around him incredulously, until, out of the mist, as it were, the empty whiskey-bottle on the table grew clear, accusingly clear, and he sprang to his feet, becoming aware as he did so of a racking headache. Undoubtedly he had been drinking—not, perhaps, without cause, he added, as memory began to return. The next instant he was at the door. Yellow haze, yellow heat, and through it a silver streak steering to the south!

That was all he saw, but that little changed the whole world for him in the twinkling of an eye. The sluice-gate was open! The devils had won! they had won! they had won!"

What use is there in saying that he felt this, that he felt that? What use in pointing out whether anger or regret came uppermost in the conglomerate of passion? As a matter of fact, George felt nothing consciously; not even when, after an hour or more, he came back to his red-hot bungalow out of the red-hot air.

He sat down, then, at the table, now cleared of last night's crumbs, and re-laid by the wife's cousin with that superfluity of covers which marks new zeal in India, and tried to think of what he had thought, or said, or done since he first caught sight of that silver streak steering southward, where no streak should be. But after a time he found himself deeply interested in reconstructing the pyramid of five forks intertwined, with which the new hand had adorned the table. What a fool—what an arrant fool he was, to be sure! Even if there had been any one upon whom to use the revolver, he would most likely have lost his opportunity or missed the beggar; but there had been nobody, and he might as well have left it at home, lying on the table ready, as it was now. The sluice-gate had been opened, not ten minutes before he woke, by a key—a key which had broken in the lock, making it impossible to close it again till it had been repaired. Of course, there was the other key and the new lock; but what need was there to hurry now? No power on heaven or earth could hide the fact that the sluice-gate had been opened. For months to come miles on miles of crops, ripening to harvest, would proclaim the failure, the treachery! "As ye have sown so shall ye reap." Concealment was impossible—that much was certain; and the certainty brought with it an odd sort of content. Since it was all his fault from beginning to end, it was quite right that he should suffer. Yes! Opened quietly, while the guard was eating his dinner; opened quietly, while he, George, was asleep—why not say drunk at once? that was nearer the truth.

And the dewan! George's listless hands tightened as he thought of that brief interview with the old man on the roof, his own torrent of reckless abuse, the courteous regrets and replies ignoring his very accusations. But those palace devils could afford to eat abuse! Zubr-ul-zamân had played, and the game was won indeed. But how? Half mechanically George drew out the key attached to his watch-chain and looked at it, carelessly at first, and then carefully. And what he saw there, clinging to the inner surface of a ward, changed heaven for him in the twinkling of an eye, even as the silver streak of water had changed the world.

A very simple thing: only a piece of wax.

How long he sat there staring at it he did not realize. The yellow haze outside grew ruddier with the sinking of the sun; the water-carrier, shadowed by the white-robed aspirant to the dead factotum's duties, hovered about the veranda expectantly.

"What do you want, you fool?" bawled George, looking

up, surprised at his own anger, surprised that anything should touch him save the thought that *she* had known—must have known; that *she* had done it—must have done it.

The man edged in through the chink, signing to the white-robed one to follow his example.

"Only to bring the *huzoor* this," he began, noisily; "only to bring this proof of honesty to the feet of justice. Lo! it was found even now by this man, with a foresight and quickness to be commended, in the *sahib's* own room, *huzoor*, beneath the matting, thus causing the face of the big *sahib's* ill-begotten servant to be blackened by reason of his base insinuation of theft! Theft! How can there be theft in a house where the water-carrier is as I am, and the *khit* will be as this one—my own wife's brother, *huzoor*—"

George broke out suddenly into dull laughter. "Oh, go to blazes with your wife's brother; put the thing down there on the table, I tell you, and go. Go! Do you hear?"

Anger and something more than anger was back in his tone when he ended, and the water-carrier, knowing his master's voice, fled. The white-robed one, with the courage of ignorance, risked all by a salaam.

"At what hour will the *huzoor* please to dine?" The young man looked at him curiously, feeling that the world was past his comprehension.

"The usual time, I suppose."

As well this fool as another; as well to-morrow as to-day. Everything was trivial, commonplace. The interruption had somehow brought home the reality of what had happened to the lad, and his head sank on his crossed arms once more in utter dejection. *She* might have told him, warned him. Surely when he had promised *she* might have done so much for his sake, and Dan's—by the way, what was it that Dan had lost, and that chattering idiot had brought in with him? George's right hand trembled a little as he reached over the table to take a plain gold locket on a slender chain. It was familiar enough to him. Dan wore it night and day, and many a time had George chafed him about the young woman! No wonder the dear old man was vexed at the thought of losing it. Losing it or losing her? In the keen thrust of this thought the locket slipped through George's fingers, and, falling, opened. So it lay, face upward, while the boy sat staring out into the open, blindly intent on the remembrance that after all it was not a case of whether a man or a woman should suffer; it was one woman or *another*—the woman *he* loved, or the woman *Dan* loved. A hundred thoughts beset him, but, analyzed, they all resolved themselves to this: his love or Dan's. To save *her* from even a breath of scandal he was willing to bear the blame; but how could this be without imperilling Dan's future? No! if the worst came; if he could find no way—yet surely, surely, there must be some way, some simple way of taking all the responsibility on his own shoulders. If not, then *she* must be brave, she must tell the truth and save this woman whom Dan loved, whose face— He looked down at the locket.

"*Gwen!*"

The sound, barely a whisper, scarcely stirred the sodden air. After a while he pushed back the chair slowly, and crossed to stand once more looking out over Hodinuggar. It seemed to have a fascination for him; yet his mind held but one thought: to find some place where there were neither truth nor lies, where he need say nothing. That surely would settle it. "*No you wouldn't, old chap—not unless you wanted them to believe you guilty.*" Lewis Gordon's idle words, as they stood laughing and jesting on the balcony yonder, but a few months ago, came back to him—the only living memory in the chaos of his present pain. The scene reproduced itself before his haggard young eyes. Yes, that would settle it; and, after all, he was guilty. Why had he not told the colonel? Why had he slept? Why—

The sound was louder now; yet not loud enough to disturb the servants, chattering across in the cook-room over the chances of perquisites under the new régime. Loud enough, for all that, to deafen the lad's ears forever to questionings of truth or untruth.

He lay on his back, face upward, and a faint stream of

blood oozing from the blue bruise just over his heart traced a fine girdle round his breast—perhaps to show that the potter's thumb had slipped, and the pot had cracked in the firing.

Maybe a fiery furnace and a red-hot bungalow are trying even to the best of clay when it is fresh from the moulder's hand; but that is neither here nor there. The fact remains that George had run away from truth and untruth, from himself and his fellow-men, but most of all from Hodinuggar and the crazy, irresponsible creator; yet could he have realized the fact, no one in the wide, wide world would have been more incredulous of his own action.

And as he lay dead, with a bullet through his heart, the barometer upon the mantel-piece was falling faster and faster, while Dan, with a telegram in his pocket, was riding all he knew across the desert to open the sluice-gate against the biggest flood within the memory of man—to open it so far and no farther, and to prevent any weakening of the channel for a while. Too late! For already the peasants were knee-deep in their own fields, breaking through every obstacle which might stem the rising water. And still the barometer fell faster and faster; but the only one who could have understood the silent warning had deserted his post.

CHAPTER XIX

She was waiting for darkness, like many another woman in India; waiting for the veil of night to destroy the veil of man's contriving. Not so much because she dreaded to show her face in the daylight, but because it suited her to keep up the mystery of her appearance. Waiting, however, for the last time; since, once her work of warning was done, there need be no more concealment, no more playing like a cat over a mouse with the palace-folk. Once that was done she would forget caution and kill some of them; for her own death was nigh, and revenge would sweeten the end of life. As she sat, her back against the wall, her knees drawn up to her chin, Azîzan had no very distinct plans for that revenge. First of all, the Ayôdhya pot must be taken from its hiding-place in the stair of the old tower. That, with its secret bribe of jewels, would prove to the *sahib* that there was truth in the tale she had gathered during her nightly wanderings as a ghost about Hodinuggar. When that was done, she would be free, in some of those nightly wanderings, to kill the dewan, or his son, the man who had killed her mother. Perhaps she might be able to kill both, and yet have some strength left for Chândni — Chândni, who had told her so many lies. For there was a fire now in Azîzan's light eyes which quite accounted for the consideration which the courtesan had shown the girl when, more than once, Chândni had wakened to find them looking at her. By-and-by, the latter had decided, a stop must be put to this masquerading through the village; at present it would be unsafe, when so much depended on good-luck; thus Azîzan had hitherto been unmolested. Indeed, Chândni herself had taken malicious pleasure in countenancing current tales of the return of the potter's dead daughter; and once when Khushâl Beg, during his son's absence, had deemed it well to single her out for favor, she had sent the hoary old sinner back to his swinging cradle like a quaking jelly, from abject fear of what he might meet on the way. It was only when she was on the roof with the old dewan that she ventured to speak in whispers of a time when this mad girl should be taught her own impotence for good or evil. But in the meantime this freedom from interruption, and the dread which the mere thought of her roused in the simple village-folk, all conspired to increase Azîzan's faith in her supernatural power. As she sat in the growing dusk, no doubt of her own success assailed her. The *chota sahib* had returned, so said the old man, who, with all his craziness, was to be trusted. Therefore, in less than an hour, he would know all, since the day was dying down quickly, smothered in a hot, hazelike smoke; not a shadow anywhere—just a dull darkness, growing momentarily, as the dull darkness had grown upon her mind day by day. For all that, she had the power. The potter might mould the clay, the palace-folk might plot and plan; but she, the woman with the evil-eye, was stronger than they.

"Azîzan! Oh, thou art there still. Heaven be praised!" The cry roused her from a sort of dream, to find the old man beside her, breathless as from running, his mild face, seen dimly in the darkness, full of piteous entreaty. "Go not from me this night, O heart's joy! Leave me not again in the storm!"

"The storm! What storm, poor fool?" she asked, indifferently.

He laid his trembling hand on her arm. "Listen! Thou canst hear the noise of many waters. They came before, so the fathers sang, and made a new world. Down yonder at the palace, where thou goest, 'twill run like the race of a river, and the stones of the old wall where thou liest will be crumbling into it. Go not there to-night, O light of mine eyes! It is safe here on the heights."

"There is no water," she answered, with a short laugh. "There will be none, save in the canal. The *sahib* will see to that, now he hath returned."

"How can he see, when he is dead—"

"Dead!" she echoed. "Bah! thou liest! He is not dead. There is no water, and there is no death—" She broke off suddenly, silenced by his look as he stood, with one hand raised, as if listening. In the breathless air a strange whispering reached her ear, and like an arrow from a bow she flew to the gap in the palisade, whence she could see the dip between the river and the canal-bank, and beyond that silver streak again to the bungalow dotted down upon the level plain.

"*Dohai! Dohai!*"

The Great Cry—the blind human cry of her race for justice—burst from her instinctively. The next moment found her bare-faced, in the open, on her way to prove if the old man spoke truth about death also.

"Azîzan, go not! Leave not the House of Safety! It is the Flood of the Most High! Go not! ah, go not!"

His unavailing plea came back to him unanswered from the night, which had fallen suddenly, as the dust from below sprang up electrically to meet the dust above, and hide everything from sight. But through the thick veil that rush of running water rose louder and louder as the girl sped on her way. That was true; so much of what the old man had said was true; she had seen it. There was a river by the old palace. Was the other thing true also? Was the *sahib* dead? Had they killed him? The darkness, as she ran over the bridge, lightened a little, so that she could see a great swirl of yellow water shooting past the piers not three inches below the keystone of the arch. Lower down it had found the sluice-gates open, hurled them from their foundations, and carried them with it as it burst through the embankment, weakened by the new-made cuttings of the villagers, and raced in a mad river, to fling itself against the mound of Hodinuggar, tearing down yard after yard of crumbling sand as it turned abruptly from the collision to try conclusions by a flank movement. Azîzan saw none of this—nothing but the dim white arches, where she had waited once before.

"*Sahib! Sahib!*"

No answer; and in her eagerness she crouched down at the closed door, tapping softly.

"*Sahib! Sahib!*"

Only a quarter-inch planking between them; that was all. For they had left him as he fell, till some other white face should come to accept the responsibility of interference. Yet it did the work as effectually as all the barriers of custom and culture which had divided them in life.

"*Sahib! Sahib!*"

Could it be true? It must be true that he was dead; otherwise he would surely hear her cry!

"*Sahib! Sahib!*"

As she crouched she might have put out her hand and taken his, but for that trivial quarter-inch of wood between them; but he did not hear. Because he was dead? Perhaps; yet even in life he had not heard—he had not known. The light in the potter's yard lit by her passionate love and care had only served to arouse his contempt—better darkness, he had thought, than such a light as that.

"*Sahib! Sahib!*"

At last she rose and stumbled across to the servants' quarters, seeking the certainty which she must gain, somehow. A light glimmered behind the grass palisades sacred to her namesake's modesty, and from within came the eager yet subdued tones of gossiping women. Azîzan crept close, and, crouching in on herself, held her breath to listen.

"Lo! I content myself with good-will towards all men," came the widow's voice, self-complacently. "Yet, O Motiya, wife of Gunga the syce, I make bold to aver that this is no more nor less than a judgment on—"

"What! Dost think it to be really the Flood of Destruction?" broke in Motiya, whimpering.

"*Ai, pârgul!*" (fool), who cares for the water? It flows south, not north; so we are safe. No! 'tis the *sahib's* death. Mayhap 'twill teach other folks' relations not to be in such a hurry to thrust themselves into other folks' service, against the custom—"

"But—"

"*Ai teri!* wouldst deny my right—the widow's right? *Ai meri admi!* thy *sahib* is dead, and there is none to see justice done and employ thy relations! *Ai! meri dil murgya! murgya!*" As the renewed sense of her wrongs rose in the familiar wail, the women from within joined in it dutifully. Without, the girl, with her hands clinched and her wild eyes straining into the shadows, seemed to be so caught and carried away by it also that her shrill voice echoed theirs instinctively.

"*Ai! meri sahib murgya! Ai! meri dil murgya! murgya!*"

The women, scared to death at the unexpected aid, stopped suddenly, and the young voice rose alone: "*Ai! meri dil murgya! murgya!*" The sound of her own wailing brought home to her the truth, rousing her passion, her grief, her anger, to madness; and in one swift desire for revenge she turned and ran.

"*Meri sahib murgya!*" The wail echoed over the wild swirl of the flood as she crossed the bridge once more. It was trembling now before its doom, as the water rose inch by inch. And could that be rain?—that large warm drop upon her hand, so large that it ran down between her fingers—another on her upturned face blinding her? If those were rain-drops, and many of them came, it might indeed be the Deluge of the Most High. And if it were? Had not the end of all things come to her already? Yet, as she ran, she looked curiously into the sky. Not a cloud visible; only an even haze of gray vapor, through which now and again a great drop splashed down upon her, warm and soft.

"*Ai! meri sahib! meri sahib!*" No more than a sob now; yet even that she hushed as the Mori gate showed black before her. Should it be Chândni? No, not yet. But for Dalel and the hopes of him, the woman would have cared nothing for water or no water. So she passed on through the causeway. One or two villagers, hurrying like her through the darkness, talking in scared whispers of the strange flood, fell back from her path, terrified. A knot of men in the bazaar huddled aside as she slipped by like a shadow; even in the court-yard of the palace the watchmen, gathered round one pipe for the comfort of companionship in such uncanny times, gave no more than an uneasy glance at the half-seen figure which they did not care to challenge.

Should it be Khushâl Beg in his swinging cradle? He had betrayed her mother, and the knife she carried was long enough to reach through the fat to his heart—long enough to do the mischief when held in reckless hands, even if aid came to the unwieldy body. No, it should not be Khushâl, either. Let him wait awhile, since he had done little to harm the *sahib*. The true quarry lay higher, in the old man up yonder in his nest, like a bird of prey, seeing all things with his keen old eyes, plotting and planning with his wise old brain. But for him the others had not been; but for him the *sahib* would have been alive, and now he was dead. Each step of the stairs as she labored up them seemed to need that cry of "dead! dead!" to help her on her way; and they left her breathless on the first platform of the roof, where those huge drops of rain were falling in audible thuds upon the hard plaster—faster and faster. This was not rain; something must have given way in the sky, and, as the old man had said, it was *Tofhân Elâhi*. So much the better for her purpose. In the arcades on either side faint figures, glimmering white in the shadows, showed where some of the servants were sheltering. So much the better, also, since she might find the old man alone; not that she cared for that, either, save in its greater assurance of success. He would not be in the pavilions at this time, but in the room to the north end of the tower, of which she had heard the woman speak; the room with the big jutting balcony whence you could see north, east, and west—everything except Hodinuggar itself.

By this time the rain-drops, falling faster and faster, had become a sheet of water, streaming straight down with such curious force that she staggered under it. A little sun-baked fireplace against which she stumbled dissolved to sheer mud ere she had recovered her balance, and a loosened brick in the last step upward rolled down, beaten from its place, ere her foot touched it. It was the *Tofhân Elâhi* indeed, though every moment the sky grew lighter, and she could now see her way clearly.

"*Meri sahib murgya! murgya!*" She kept the wildfire glowing in heart and eyes by the murmur, until, through an open door, she saw what she sought: an old man seated still as a statue at a chess-table. With a cry she darted forward, snatching at the knife in her girdle; then paused abruptly. Where was the hurry? he could not move. So, with a half-laugh of exultation, she turned back deliberately to bolt the door — a strong door, as befitted one living on the favorite sleeping-place of despotism. It would need time to force an entry—more time than she would need to do her work. Meanwhile she must look at this arbiter of her fate ever since she was born; this tyrant whom she had never seen. A wreck of a man, with his head on his breast! Was that all? But as she came nearer, the light, such as it was, from the wide-arched balcony, aided by a cresset smoking in a niche, showed her something of the youth in his eyes. Perhaps it showed him something of the age in hers, for the dewan paused with one query on his lips, then began again with another going closer to the root of the matter—as if in appreciation of the resolve on her face.

"Hast come to frighten me, as thou frightenest the villagers, O Azîzan, daughter of the potter's daughter?" he asked, coldly. He was defenceless, save for craft of the brain, and he knew it.

"Nay; I have come to kill thee, Zubr-ul-Zamân, Dewan of Hodinuggar," she replied—"to kill thee, as thou hast killed the *sahib.*" A sound which might have been a laugh reached her as she took a step nearer, brandishing the knife; perhaps it was that which made her pause again; laughter was hardly what she had expected.

"I did not kill the *sahib*, fool. He killed himself for love of the *mem sahib* — the fair *mem* who took the Ayôdhya pot."

The girl fell back the step she had taken, and the hand bearing the knife went up to her forehead in a gesture matching her sharp cry of pain. The truth struck home; yet she caught at denial desperately. "Thou liest! She did not take it. I took it, once, twice. I have the pearls—the Hodinuggar pearls. I—I—not she—"

One of those curious spasms of life came to the wreck of a man as it turned to look at the girl more closely. "So! Thou also hast brains. 'Tis the woman's *yog* nowadays. My son and my son's son have none. Thou shouldst have been my granddaughter, Azîzan, had I but known. Thou mayst be now."

His granddaughter! Of course. She had suspected so all her life, had known it to be so for months, yet she never realized the fact till now; and an odd, inexplicable sense of kindred rose up in her against her will.

"I shall kill thee, no matter who thou art!" she cried, quickly.

"Wherefore? What harm have I done to thee, Azîzan? 'Twould have suited me better had the *sahib* fancied thy face. Thou hadst thy chance."

Something in her shrank back abashed before the naked truth of the old man's words. She had her chance, according to her world, and she had failed. She had failed utterly; and yet something else in her—strange, incomprehensible—clamored against the verdict. The deadly weariness, the passionate apathy she had felt so often before came over her. The knife dropped to her side, and, half mechanically, she looked out through the arches of the balcony to where the red-brick bungalow should stand. Nothing but sheets of water streaming from above and from below—a rush, a roar. Suddenly, on the floor, *pit-pat, pat-pit,* in half a dozen places. The rain had conquered the thick domed roof.

"It is *Tofhân, Elâhi,*" she said; and even as she spoke a babel of voices rose at the closed door.

"Open, open! The river saps the foundations! *Ari, bhai!* Is he dead that he hath no fear? Beat it down! O dewan *sahib!* O servant, who hath closed the door, open! open!

Nay!—without a smith 'tis hopeless—and I tarry not—listen! —there goes more of the wall—open! fools—open!" . . .

Amid the roar and rush, the vain blows and shouting, the old man's eyes were on Azîzan's, not so much in appeal as in command. He could not move; his faded voice would never reach through the clamor; his only safety lay in her obedience. But she shook her head; then crouched down as if to wait till they should once more be alone—crouched in her favorite attitude, her back against the wall, her knees drawn up to her chin, the knife still clasped in her hand ready for use. A louder roar came from without, a rattle as of bricks mingled with cries of caution and alarm; then gradually the blows and voices dwindled away from the ceaseless clamor of the rain, and the intermittent rumblings of falling masonry, as the smallest crack widened beneath the pressure to a breach, and bit by bit the solid walls seemed to melt away.

"Why didst thou not open the door, Azîzan?" The words in the great silence were just audible to the girl.

"Because I did not choose." Again the odd sound like a laugh came from that bent figure.

"The woman's reason. Why didst thou not choose, Azîzan?" There was no anger, scarcely a trace of anxiety even, in his tone. He was no novice to the ways of women, and the girl's face told him that his chance of life was almost gone. What must be must, and death came to all—to the mad fool, in her turn. The sombre fire of her eyes met his sullenly; but she made no answer, save to lay the knife down quietly on the sill of the arch against which she leaned. The steel rang clear upon the hard red sandstone. The old dewan's wrinkled hand hovered for a moment over the pieces on the board, then fell back upon his knees. So they sat staring at each other silently, in the bow of the balcony. There was nothing more to be said. She had chosen; why, she knew not. And as the clamor of the rain and the rush of the river rose higher and higher, Zubr-ul-Zamân's head sank upon his breast with the old formula:

"*Rani ki mât; khel ho-chukha*" (Queen's mate; the game

is done). The woman's reason or unreason had conquered the strength of the world. But that was no new thing to the old dewan's wisdom.

But to the people outside in the open, huddling together under the pitiless downpour for safety's sake, it was more or less of an amusement to wonder how long the old tower would hold out against the mad stream sapping at its foundations. Not long; for already the ruined wall had gone, disclosing a portion of the secret stair where Zainub, the old duenna, lay, parched up almost to a mummy—a hideous sight, no doubt, had there been light enough to see it; but there was not, and the refugees upon the higher ground could discern nothing but the block of the old tower and the swirling water below. A faint light came from the balcony of the room, where the dewan was known to be; and as they watched it, people speculated how the door came to be fastened. Perhaps it had swung to, perhaps— Well, he must be dead, or would soon be dead, since rescue was impossible. And, after all, he had lived his time; Khushâl had been saved from his swinging cradle, and then there was Dalel away up at Simla. Rulers enough for a poor country-side, if God spared it from the *Tofhân Elâhi;* and if not, why then the old man was at least better off than they, exposed as they were to the elements—far better; both he and the outcasts in their straw-huts, which would hurt no one even if they fell. So the first in the land was as the last, and the last first. *Sohhan Ullah!*

As the rain slackened the night grew darker, until even the block of the tower ceased to show against the sky, and the little company of watchers could only hear the thunder of its fall.

"God rest him!" muttered a peasant, muffled into a formless bundle in his blanket. "He was a hard master, and the new one may be harder still. There will be a good crop, anyway."

And down on the very edge of the boiling stream, when the rain ceased, a light went twinkling up and down. It was the potter looking for his dead daughter, as the débris of the old wall, beneath which she had been buried sixteen years before, crumbled away, bit by bit before the furious stream.

CHAPTER XX

The dawn broke upon a new world as far as Hodinuggar was concerned. Where the desert had stretched, thirsty and dry, lay a shoreless sea. Where the streak of silver had split the round horizon in halves, the double line of the canal-banks looked like twin paths leading to some world beyond the waste of waters. They steered straight out of sight on either side, almost unbroken save for the great gap where the sluice-gate had stood. There the stream still swept sideways, to circle round the island of Hodinuggar, bearing, like an ark, its company of refugees from the surrounding plains—a little company, which straightway, taking advantage of the coming sun, began to wring out its wet garments and spread them out to dry, until the general air of washing-day reduced the tragedy of the past night to the commonplace. And, after all, what had happened? An old woman or two had been drowned, the dewan and his tower swept away. But the world held too many old women and more than enough of nobles. For the rest, it had not been the flood of the Most High; and though death came to all in the end and the loneliness of it must be dreary, still it was somehow more terrifying to die in batches, wholesale.

So, clothed in their white, new-washed robes like the elect, they went down after a time in companies, to see the extent of damage done to their belongings, and test how far it was possible to wade through the water towards the village homestead or two which rose above the flood. Canalwards, of course, passage was barred—would be barred for days, until the stream ceased flowing or a boat was brought. So the horseman, picking his way flounderingly along the northern bank, might be the only survivor of the big world beyond, and they be none the wiser—for the time. It was Dan Fitzgerald, who, after an enforced shelter at the half-way village, was wondering who could have taken the responsibility of anticipating the telegram he carried in his pocket by opening the sluice-gates, and so, in all probability, saving the big Sunowlie embankment farther down. For it had been opened; that was evident to his experience at once. Without the lead of current to cut, the flood would have swept on to do its worst elsewhere. Well, whoever had done it, be he watchman or dewan, he would deserve something at the hands of the department, and be the past record a bad one, this should have its reward—its just reward—if he could compass it.

Ten minutes after he had driven the chattering servant from the room, and grief-stricken, yet convinced into a sort of calm acceptance of the inevitable, had lifted the poor lad's body tenderly to the bed. He scarcely even thought of a reason; perhaps there was none. Dan, in his rough-and-ready life, had seen such a thing before; had known the useless search for some adequate cause. And was there not cause enough for a sudden loss of balance? The race down from Paradise to Purgatory? The intolerable journey, the horrible home-coming; and then the cursed bottle he had left! The remembrance sent his whole mind into useless regrets. If he had only ridden faster, if somehow he could have been there in time to prevent the loneliness, the awful desolation of it all. He had been through it himself; he knew what it had been to him. Perhaps, taking his own excitability as a standard, he over-estimated the effect on George's nature. At any rate, as he stooped mechanically to pick up the revolver round which the dead boy's hand had still been closed, he felt that given the necessity for sudden return the rest might be inferred. And then beside the revolver he saw the open locket, with Gwen's smiling face still staring up at him. *Gwen!* Great God! what did it mean? His own locket, of course, and yet— He sat down at the table, white as death, looking first at the pretty face, then at the still figure on the bed, now decently shrouded from the glaring light of day. And by degrees the color returned to his cheeks. No! it could not be so. She was not cruel, only careless; and ah!

what a grief this would be to her! Besides, George was not the one to put life-long regret into a friend's life. So among other incidents of the terrible home-coming had been that of learning who Dan's sweetheart was; that had not happened at Simla; that could not have been the cause of the lad's sudden return. It was a relief. But why had he come? The new lock and keys lying on the table gave him a clew, and his quick wits suggested danger to the gates. Then the thought struck him suddenly, in a flash, confusedly, almost irrationally, that it had been done for his sake and hers. He was on his knees by the bed in a minute. "O George, George! why did you do it?" And in the answering silence came a decision, impulsive, yet unmistakable. Such blame as could be taken, he would take. No one should know or dream of failure. No one should ever say, "Ah, poor fellow, he shot himself; must have been something wrong, you know." Rapidly he counted the cost, the possibility of concealment. Hodinuggar, separated from him by an unpassable stream, could not be taken into account, and he must accept the risk there; it would be not much if the servants' tale was true, if they had only discovered their master's death when the storm began, and had done no more than send word to the palace. If so, no one had seen the body save those four or five servants who loved their master and worshipped rupees; and beyond even rupees, peace and quiet, instead of the dangerous rakings up of the past, following always on the advent of the police. Then for the department itself. Whether George had opened the sluice when, as the servants said, he went out in the middle of the day, or whether the palace-folk had done it, the department, in either case, owed the opener a debt of gratitude. If the latter, the Moguls would be glad to keep silence; if the former, even if they set up a claim for compensation to the ruined tower, they would have been due so much had he, Dan, arrived in time to carry out his orders. So half an hour afterwards one of the servants started along the path to the outer world with a telegram to headquarters, and that evening, when the flood subsided a little, Dan chose out the driest spot he could find in the sandy compound, and read the Church service over his friend's body. No one should know—except some day, perhaps, Gwen, when she came there as his wife. Then he would tell her the pity, the needlessness of it all; yet the needlessness had this virtue in it: that concealment was possible. The flood had swept away the error, if error there had been.

The telegram reached Colonel Tweedie next morning, among many more, telling of disaster and death along the line of the great canal. Yet none was more pitiful than this:

"*Opening of the sluice-gate, as ordered, saved Sunowlie embankment, but palace injured. George Keene died yesterday of cholera. Very prevalent here. Details by post.*"

"Dear, dear," fussed the colonel, "how very sad! What a blow to poor Mrs. Boynton! She is so tender-hearted, and really she was almost unnecessarily interested in that boy." They all thought of her; even Lewis Gordon, as, yielding to that odd desire to see for one's self, which besets us all when bad news comes by telegram, he sat looking at the flimsy message of evil. Yet his first words were of Rose.

"Your daughter will feel it also, sir—feel it very much, I'm afraid." Then he paused, to resume in more ordinary tones: "I had, I think, better start at once, sir. I can report all along the line, and wire if your presence seems necessary. I hardly think so, and it is useless inconveniencing yourself for nothing."

Colonel Tweedie bridled. "I am not accustomed to consider my own convenience as against public service," he was beginning, pompously, when Lewis cut him short.

"I'm afraid I wasn't thinking so much of you, sir, as of Miss Tweedie. This will be a great blow to her." He thought so honestly, and as he jolted down the hill in a *tonga* half an hour afterwards he told himself he was glad to escape from the necessity of seeing her grief, even while he was conscious of a certain curiosity to know how she would take the news. There was no such difficulty in imagining Gwen's behavior. He could almost see the pretty, pathetic face keeping back its tears, and hear the soft voice saying with a little thrill in it that George was the nicest, dearest boy she had ever met, and that she would never forget his kindness—never—never! As he thought of this his expression was not pleasant; for Gwen had, in his opinion, done her level best to turn the lad's head. In saying that sort of thing she must surely know she was talking bunkum; a man, at any rate, would call it so, though perhaps it was not fair to judge a woman's by a man's standard of truth. Gwen, doubtless, was as genuine as she knew how to be—as genuine, anyhow, as Rose Tweedie, with her pretensions of utter indifference to all sentiment. Well, poor girl, she was face to face with realities now; for she had certainly cared a good deal for George—even to the extent of keeping him from Gwen's wiles. Poor George! a fine young fellow who, for one thing, had been saved a bad heartache. Lewis Gordon had intended passing on as quickly as possible to Hodinuggar, but, being delayed by settling endless requisitions for repairs, had barely reached Rajpore ere Dan Fitzgerald returned, reporting that there was no reason for him to go out. Permanent repair was impossible till the rains should be over, as every lesser flood must run down the channel cut out for it by the deluge, and everything to assure the future safety of the palace had been done. Barring the dewan's tower, not much damage had, after all, been done, as the jewels and treasure in the vaults below had been saved; besides, the bumper crops which would follow on the inundation would more than compensate for any loss. There was a certain anxiety in Dan's face as he said this.

"Well, even if they were to claim," replied Lewis, complacently, "the saving of the Sunowlie bank would be dirt-cheap at a few thousands. It cost us over two lacs, and I was in an awful funk about it, thinking we must be too late. I tried to intercept poor George with a wire, knowing he would take the order quicker, as he was already on the way."

Dan's whole soul leaped towards the possibility. "Then he got it, after all! I was wondering—" He paused, angry at his own imprudence.

"Wondering what?" asked Lewis, impatiently. "I was going to say I missed him, and then I didn't see how you could possibly get there in time. By-the-way, when did you get my wire?"

"About an hour after you sent it off," said Dan, uneasily. He did not care for Lewis Gordon's sharp, practical eyes on these details.

"That is to say, ten o'clock on the morning of the 6th, I suppose. Good riding, indeed! And that reminds me. The report from the râjah's people which came through your office says that the water first ran through the cut about middle-day on the 6th. Manifestly impossible. You had hardly left for Hodinuggar. 'Tis a trifle, of course, but you had better stamp on the inaccuracy, and show you are on the watch, or they will go on to cooking generally."

"Yes," replied Dan, slowly. This simple difficulty in concealing the discrepancy in the time had escaped him before, but he was fully alive to it now. Most men in his place would have set the question aside at all costs for further consideration, and risked the possible consequences of the evasion. But Dan's mind was of a finer temper; he could trust it to thrust home at any moment. This is the true test of power, and it is only the second thoughts of the commonplace which are better than their first; so he took the occasion calmly, knowing his man.

"But they are right—I did not open the gates. I believe George did, but even of that I am not sure. However, you shall judge for yourself. I don't ask for confidence, of course; I haven't the right; but I expect you will give it all the same."

Then boldly, plainly, yet with one reservation, he told the tale of what he knew and what he surmised. George had shot himself—of that there was no doubt. The sluice had been opened in his, Dan's, opinion, by treachery, of which George at Simla had received some hint, and he had arrived too late to prevent; though this also was mysterious, since the gates had not been opened till long after George's arrival. The guard at the sluice had been drowned or had disappeared. The new dewan, Khushâl, professed pious ignorance. Only this much was certain—the Sunowlie embankment had been saved; George had taken the responsibility on himself, even to the death, and the flood had made it possible to keep his memory from stain. For the sake of his friends, was not this desirable? This hint, no more, he gave of the inner tragedy connected with the locket. Yet as those two men sat looking at each other across the littered office-table, their thoughts, all unknown to each other, flew to the one woman. But the memory brought tears to Dan's dark eyes, and left Lewis hard as the nether mill-stone in the conviction that Gwen was at least morally responsible for George Keene's death. It came to him as a certainty, yet a contemptuous tolerance came with it. She had not meant, of course—women never did—to play fast and loose with the boy's heart; yet she had done so. He had spent too much money, he had been careless; honest, perhaps, though even that might not be so. No one could tell; why should they tell now, when it was all irrevocable, when no harm could come out of it save to the poor boy himself? A good sort he had been—too good for such an end. And then, even for Gwen's sake? He felt very bitter against her, very sore; yet such things must not be said about his future wife as might be said if the truth were really known. "I suppose it had better remain as it is," he said at last, moodily. "Cholera has served its turn in such a case before—one of the advantages of living in a land of sudden death. Poor George! I dare say there was treachery."

Dan, shading his eyes with his clasped hands, was silent for a minute. "If there was, he had no part in it. I wonder if you remember a conversation on the balcony at Hodinuggar about what a man would do in such a case. 'No, you wouldn't, not unless you wanted to be thought guilty.' Do you remember saying that, Gordon?" Lewis nodded; it was not a pleasant memory. "I can't tell you the whole; but I am convinced that George shot himself to save me. He knew—what perhaps you don't—that I was engaged to a woman—"

Gordon pulled some papers towards him impatiently, and took up a pen as if to end the subject. "I suppose it is always '*cherchez la femme*'; yet it does not seem to me an agreeable factor in existence."

"*Cherchez la femme*," echoed Dan. "Why not? They are our mothers and sisters, our sweethearts and wives, after all. And have you ever thought, Gordon, what it must be to look back over a lifetime, and see next to nothing that you would rather have left undone? Or, if you are pious, to take a sort of pride in pillorying yourself for a cross word as a taradiddle? There isn't a man in a million with that record; half the women one meets—aye, half the women one *patronizes*—have it. Perhaps it's small blame to anything but fate; yet still they have it."

"Or think they have, which has the same effect. You remind me of a countryman of yours, a doctor I knew once. 'The sex,' he said, 'can't do wrong, and when it does it's hysteria.' However, let us leave that poor lad to rest in peace; in a way, that is more worth looking to than the happiness of any woman who has ever been born. And look here; make the tale of reports complete and send them to me, and I'll consign them, dates and all, to oblivion. That is the beauty of official mistakes; you can pigeon-hole them and no one is the wiser, unless, indeed, some personal motive crops up; but that is not likely. So far as I can see, it is to no one's interest to make a row—not even if there is a woman at the bottom of it all."

There was a concentrated bitterness in his tone due to no cynicism—rather to an intensity of pain. For if Rose Tweedie belonged by birth to that strange latter-day development which unconsciously sets passion aside both from mind and emotion, and will none of it spiritually or physically, Lewis belonged to that still larger class of men who have driven it from the mind; who say openly that it is despicable, but that the world cannot get on without it; who insist, in a breath, in its unworthiness and its necessity. Gwen, he said to himself, after Dan had gone, was very womanly, and capable of ruining any man in a week if she chose, and then being sorrowfully surprised at the result. Still, it would be unkind to wound her unnecessarily by telling her that result, the more so because she would certainly tell other people, and Rose Tweedie might break her heart over it. Even if the pigeon-holed mistake were found out, they might get up a fiction about the telegram having reached George, after all. The compensation might have to be given; but even in that case he could see no reason for raking up the mud. Nevertheless, a week after, when he and Dan were again seated opposite each other at the office-table, he felt vaguely uncomfortable; for the schedule of the dead lad's debts, which lay between them ready for the administrator-general, showed an item of six thousand rupees, borrowed on his note of hand, backed by some youngsters, on the very day he left Simla.

"It was a first holiday, you know," said Dan, regretfully; "and Hodinuggar is such a hole! There were the races, you know—and—"

"*Cherchez la femme!*" quoted Lewis. "I don't blame him; not a bit. I spent more than that, I remember; but if there had been an inquiry, Fitzgerald?"

Dan shook his head, and sighed fiercely. "Yes, I know. For all that, he was straight—straight as a die! My only regret in keeping the thing dark is that some one has got to go scot free.

CHAPTER XXI

A SHIVERING woman in one pannier; in the other, such things as a breathless fugitive can gather together in one half-hour. Between them the hump of a camel—a camel which every instant seems as though it must split into halves as its long splay legs slither and slide in the mud covering all things. Such was the method of Chândni's flight from Hodinuggar. Not comfortable, but, under the circumstances, necessary; nor was she altogether unprepared for that necessity. People of her trade know what to expect when they are attached to petty intriguing courts, where one ruler's meat is invariably the next ruler's poison. Besides, in this case she had to reckon on Khushâl Beg's anger at the repulse she had given him on more than one occasion—given him, of course, with a view to future possibilities with his son Dalel; but that rather increased than diminished the offence. And now her patron, old Zubr-ul-zamân, was dead, Khushâl had supreme power, and, what is more, three pearls were missing from the Hodinuggar necklace; three pearls which could be easily traced home to her safe-keeping, *and no further*, if need be. So, at the first hint of inquiry, Chândni had deemed it wiser to seek the protection of the only man who knew something, if not all, about the intrigue which had ended so strangely in a providence setting aside the necessity for any intrigue at all. Dalel chose to remain at Simla, where, no doubt, he was amusing himself hugely.

Well, she would not interfere with his amusements. That had never been her plan. She would only resume her empire over his weak, worn-out wickedness. And yet the flight entailed horrible discomfort. The splaying camel was to her what a bad passage across the Channel is to a fashionable lady. As she clutched wildly at the sides of the panniers, she decided that life was not long enough for a repetition of such experience. If she returned to Hodinuggar at all, it must be in a position which would insure a different style of locomotion. Even the night journey by rail, cooped up behind iron bars in the wild-beast-cage-like compartment, labelled in three languages for "modest women," was in comparison comfort itself. Huddled up decently into a shapeless bundle, she could at least think over the odd turn affairs had taken, and make up her mind what had best be done. The first thing, of course, was to bring Dalel to her heel. That ought not to be difficult, for though, the water having been procured, he might, like his father, find it convenient to underrate her services in the matter, she had one or two good cards to play in her adversary's strong suits which might with care save the trick; at any rate, they ought to prevent any reckless disregard of her claims.

First, they wanted the pearls; and now that the dewan was dead, she was the only person who could tell them the ins and outs of that transaction. Next, they wanted payment of the heavy *douceur* promised to them by the râjah for good offices in making it possible for the water to irrigate that basin of alluvial soil to the south. But now the dewan was dead, they would find difficulty in proving that anything had been done; that the flood was not responsible for all, unless she chose to help them with her evidence. For the rest, give her Dalel and a bottle of champagne to herself for one hour. If in that space he did not come back, as he had done a dozen times before, to her empire of evil, she would have none of him. He would be dead to all she had to offer in the fullest perfection; he would be beyond her influence, as it were, and so useless for her purpose. She was not going to marry a fool in order to wear a veil and live with a lot of women.

By this time two coolies were carrying her up the hill from Solon in a thing like a bird-cage slung on poles, so small, so square, that she had to sit crossed-legged and bolt-upright. But though she could not sleep, even with the aid of opium, and though the hill-sides after the first rush of rain were clothed with tinted blossoms, and the winding valleys were green as emeralds with the young rice, Chândni never parted the thick patchwork curtains which shrouded her from the public gaze until the setting down of the *dhooli* warned her of an opportunity for a gossip and a pipe. Then her feet came over the sides with a challenging clash of silver bells and a quick stir round the sleepy, sun-sodden stage, where travellers and coolies and sweetmeat-sellers lay huddled together in the shade. Even the cowboy, driving his cattle from the bales of fodder on their way up for *sahib logue's* ponies, paused to look at her with a grin, while his beasts ate on. The bees were flitting from flower to flower, a golden oriole flashed through the green transparency of the walnut-trees. Below the branches the great emerald hearts of the yam leaves outlined themselves against the sapphire distance of the valley, which was divided from the sapphire distance of the sky by the glittering diamond spikelets of the snowy range. And this in turn was echoed and re-echoed in every receding distance by the pearly clouds dividing one sea of ether from another. In all this world nothing worth a look, apparently, save Chândni, the courtesan, swinging her silver anklets over the edge of the *dhooli*—to judge, at any rate, by those human eyes.

She did not go straight to her destination, but paused at a house in the bazaar, where such as she were all too welcome. There was never any mincing of words or thoughts with Chândni. To one end she had been born a Kunjeri, and to this end she lived to the best of her ability. So she paused to clothe herself in clean, clear muslins, and hang great garlands of tuberose and jasmine about the column of her massive throat, to redden her lips, and give a deeper shadow to her eyes; looking at herself the while in the thumb-mirror, worn on her left hand; no more, no less intent on appearing at her best than many a person who has not been born to that end—many a decent, respectable person, with powder-puff and curling-tongs, who would be dreadfully shocked at having her innocent half-hour before the cheval-glass likened to Chândni's most reprehensible occupation. Perhaps the difference lies in the size of the mirrors; at any rate, it is not probably apparent elsewhere.

Mirza Dalel Beg was living, she knew, as the upper-ten of the natives love to do, in a European house; why, is, in five cases out of six, a mystery. The sixth, no doubt, has acquired exotic tastes; the remaining five, no doubt, consider it good style to pretend them, and so, after paying roundly for the privilege of toilet-sets and dinner-services, prefer the *bheesti* with his *mussuck* to a lavatory, and a big platter on the floor to all the neatly laid dining-tables in creation. A curious example of the fascination which useless comforts have for some people came to light during one of the many embassies from Cabul which British diplomacy, or the want of it, has inveigled into India. During its stay there, district officers were instructed to provide the whole horde of barbarians with houseroom in European fashion, to avoid invidious distinctions. So, as a rule, the local Parsee was invited to furnish a requisite number of empty houses with the necessary rep curtains, French clocks, Britannia metal teapots, and German prints needed for the night's hospitality. Next day, so runs the tale, there never was a soup-plate to be found. Occasionally the guests packed up a French clock; once, it is affirmed, a sponge-bath went a-missing; but unless they ate them, that embassy must have gone back to Cabul with some hundreds of dozens of soup-plates stowed away among the official presents of watches that won't go and guns that won't fire. And soup is not a national dish in Afghanistan.

So Dalel Beg had rented a house, which he got cheap, because three of its tenants had died of typhoid-fever—a pretty place enough, shut in somewhat by the ravines which furrow the lower part of the ridge, but with an outlook beautiful beyond belief over the plains. The single dahlias, refuse run wild from many a garden above, found foothold in every cranny of the rocks, and the morning-glories climbed over the broken palings fencing the narrow path from the steep *khud*, which seemed to leap at one bound to the pale blue of the valley below. Chândni, on her way to seek Dalel, looked out at it distastefully, reached forth a strong ring-bedecked hand, appropriated a yellow dahlia which she stuck behind her ear, and called; then the bells clashed again as she walked with a free step over to the veranda of the house, raised the *chick* and looked in, while the *dhooli*-bearers squatted down beside the railings, and, apparently, resumed a conversation begun in the bazaar. For the rest, sunshine and silence.

Chândni, dazzled by the glare outside, could see nothing clearly. The room seemed to her unaccustomed eyes crammed full of useless things. Then suddenly there came a shrill, unformed voice.

"Go away! we don't want you. Mamma, send her away. Go, I tell you! The mirza is married now. I am his wife."

Not more than fifteen by the look of her, with a frizz of hot-pressed light hair over her forehead, and a skin which gave one the impression of being bleached, perhaps, because of the coal-black eyes set in the narrow, sharp face; yet with a certain attractiveness about the figure, dressed as it was in the height of fashion, with sleeves to the ears, and a waist requiring the surgical bandage of folded silk to prevent it breaking in two. His wife! Chândni looked from her full height and magnificent development at her as distastefully as she had looked at the view from the terrace. Neither was to her liking; they appealed too much to the imagination. This one was better, though past her prime and pulpy; drowsy, too, from the snooze she had been enjoying on the sofa—still with a torrent of capable, tell-tale abuse for the intruder.

"*Ari*," laughed Chândni, contemptuously, when the fat lady paused for breath, "so thou too hast been of the bazaar. But I want not thee, or the half-fledged thing who calls herself a wife; I want Dalel. Where is he?"

"Mamma," cried the unformed voice, in English, breaking down over its own feeble passion, "send her away, I tell you! The mirza will be back soon, and she must not be here. Don't fool with words. Call the servants. *Ai, budzart!* (base born); I will throw thee down the *khud!*"

Chândni laughed again—laughed louder—as in response to the girl's cry a face showed itself behind her.

"Salaam, O *bhai!*" (brother), she said, nodding her head at the new-comer. "Ah, 'tis thou, Mohammed; look you, this image saith she will fling me down the *khud*. If it came to force, my pigeon, I know which would have the mirza. But I will not fight for him thus; he is not worth it. So he fancies thee! God help him! Sure, thy mother is the better woman."

"Come, come, Mother Chândni," urged the servant, in answer to shrill commands. "This is no place for thee now. These are *mems*. And he hath married her," he went on, fast and low. "Yea, 'tis true; the *nikkah* hath been read, so abuse is vain. Come, thou canst see him elsewhere."

"Nay; I will see him here — here with his *mem*," retorted Chândni, airily. Then she turned swiftly on the elder woman, who, going to the door, was about to call for further assistance. "What harm shall I do thee, fool, who art as I am with a piebald skin, or as this one, who would be as I am had God made her a woman. Lo! ask thy servants who Chândni the courtesan is, and what she has been—aye, and will be, if she chooses!"

It was an odd scene: the room, decorated into bastard civilization; the girl, depending on a lack of pigment in her skin for all her claims to *memship*, that being the only trace of her unknown European father; her mother, without even this distinction, yet clinging to her taint of Western blood as to a patent of nobility — clinging to it desperately, in fringe and furbelow — in fashion generally; before them, against them, Chândni, in her trailing white Delhi draperies and massive garlands, a figure which might have stood for some of those strange solemn-eyed statues, half Greek, half Indian, which are found buried in the sand-hills of the frontier. There was a little crowd now of dark, expectant faces at the door, towards which she nodded familiarly.

"Go back, O brothers! I do no harm. 'Tis not my way with women-folk. I wait the mirza's return. Then, if I am not wanted, I will go. Lo! Chândni the courtesan hath no need to keep a man in a leash; she hath no need to have the *nikkah* read, my little pigeon, as thou hast. *Ari!* so the pictures in the papers Dalel used to bring me are true, and 'tis a beauty to have no body and a big head."

Beatrice Norma Elfrida D'Eremao, presently Her Highness Mrs. Dalel Beg, gave a little scream of rage, and stamped her tiny, high-heeled shoes on the floor. Mrs. Lily Violet D'Eremao, her mother, known in her time by many a different sobriquet until she settled down to sobriety and the education of a fair daughter, screamed too, in voluble abuse; but they were both quite helpless before the white-robed figure standing between them and the sunlight, with a laugh on her red lips.

It did not leave them when into the midst of the scene came Dalel Beg, got up in his dandy riding-gear, only the folded *puggree* remaining to tell the tale of his birth, perhaps because the ideas within the head it covered needed some such excuse for their existence. His face was hideous in its sheer malice; livid, not with passion or fear, but from that hatred of opposition which belongs to his race. And Chândni, recognizing this, swept him a low salaam, graceful to the uttermost curve in each finger—a salaam which would have made Turveydrop die of envy, a salaam such as one sees once or twice in a lifetime. A minute before she might have given it in derision; now she yielded it to the lingering majesty in this pitiful representative of a long line of tyrants.

"Long life attend my lord," she said, in those liquid tones of set ceremony which her class pride themselves in acquiring—and even among them Chândni had a silver tongue; none near her, so the report ran. Dalel Beg's eyes saw, his ears heard; they would not refuse their wonted office. And yet as he took a step nearer he raised the hunting-crop he held.

"Go!" he cried, "go! Mohammed! Fujju! turn this scum of the bazaars from the door!"

"Which scum of the bazaars?" she asked, coolly. "This—or that?"

It was not scorn exactly; it was an indifferent contempt, which seemed to leave no denial possible, and which held action arrested.

"Which is it to be, mirza *sahib?*" she asked again, crossing swiftly to where the girl stood, as if to measure her height against that small, insignificant figure. "There is not much to choose between us except in the outside—and thou hast eyes!"

"Fujju! Mohammed! Ditta! Scoundrels! turn her out! call the Kotwal! Turn her out, I say!" shrieked the mirza, fast losing all dignity in a sort of animal admiration for this woman who, he knew, would come back to him at a word—a word he dare not give; which, as yet, he did not wish to give.

"Softly! softly! O my brothers," came that soft, liquid voice. "There is no need to touch Chândni the courtesan. The master hath his right, and I will go. I only ask a word, and sure my words are better for the ears than hers."

Incontestably true, for mother and daughter were now at the highest pitch of the Eurasian accent, aggravated by hysterics. The men stood uncertain, siding, every one of them, with that which was familiar.

"The word is this," she went on, boldly: "I have done my part. Is there to be payment?"

Dalel's face lost its last trace of dignity, and settled down into mere spite. "So! it is payment. Lo! mother-in-law, hold thy peace! 'Tis nothing but a bad debt—a debt without a bond! Payment! Go, fool, and ask it of the old man—the old devil who was drowned. Ask not here; here we need all the money we can get!"

Then, in his delight and content in this opportunity of malice, he forgot a suspicion of fear which had been with him hitherto, and turned to the girl with a leer and a laugh. "Aha! we want the oof ourselves, don't we, Tricks. Lo! I give you gold watch and chain to-day. I give you gold bangle to-morrow, if you good girl. But that one—nothing—nothing." He echoed the last words jeeringly in Hindostanee, cutting with his whip towards Chândni as one cuts at a dog to frighten it from the room. Perhaps he was nearer than he thought for; anyhow, the uttermost end of the lash touching the silver bells on her ankle, set them jingling—a slight thing to make two women cease their cries and half a dozen men or more hold their breath involuntarily; yet it did.

"Lo! thou hast given me something, O Mirza Dalel Beg,

which no man hath given before to Chândni the courtesan. It is enough. I go." So far dignity went with her. But at the door she turned to give the women back in their kind, and with interest, the abuse they had given to her. Even with a despicable cheat like the mirza there was a reputation to keep up; he was at least the descendant of worthy men who had done their best for such as she; but with those two — women even as herself, without her claims?

Yet ere she was half-way back to the bazaar she had forgotten them and their abuse; forgotten everything save that clash of the silver bells. That was an end, an end forever, to Dalel. In a way she was glad; for he was unendurable when sober, not much better when drunk. Now nothing remained save the necessity for compensation and revenge. If the Moguls would not pay, there were others who would. The *mem*, for instance, who had taken the pearls. And those who had spread it abroad that the *chota sahib* had died in his bed, they would not care to have their truth impugned. They had bribed the servants, no doubt, the dewan was dead, and they had held the water sufficient inducement for silence in the others. But she? She had had nothing, and she meant to have something. And then when she had got her money's-worth for silence, she would go and sell that silence to the râjah; unless, indeed, by that time the Moguls had bidden higher for her speech. Without her, the question as to whether the bribes were honestly for favors done could not be settled. She would begin with the *mem;* not by demanding money, but the pearls; since, most likely, they had been disposed of, and the difficulty of getting hold of them again would, as it were, increase her power of screw. If at the end of a month the *sahib logues* defied her, she would offer her silence or speech to the highest bidder and give her evidence for either. After that a merry life, even if it had to be a short one. Even the mere taste of comparative freedom she had had that morning in the wooden house in the Simla bazaar had aroused the old reckless instincts; and before the evening was over the news that Chândni, singer and dancer from Delhi, had come to the place was on the tip of every native's tongue.

CHAPTER XXII

Mrs. Boynton had behaved very much as Lewis Gordon had anticipated on hearing of George Keene's sudden death from cholera. She had wept honest tears over the dear lad, even while she could not help feeling happier than she had done for months, because of the flood which had come and gone, sweeping away with it all her difficulties, all her troubles. Yet it brought her one unavailing regret: that she should so unnecessarily have put the bitter pain of hearing her confession into those last days; that he should have gone down to his death, not thinking unkindly of her—the dear lad would never have done that—but hurt, disappointed, unhappy. She would have liked him to see a certain letter which lay in the drawer of her writing-table—a letter addressed, sealed, stamped, ready for sending, which she had only kept back one day. Only one; yet, but for that lucky chance, it might have fallen into Dan's hands while George was ill, and brought needless pain into another kind heart; for there was, thank Heaven, no more need for humiliation and confession and promises of restitution. She had torn open the letter in order to read it again, and had been quite satisfied with its straightforward avowal of responsibility and firm intention, should difficulties arise, of taking the whole blame upon herself. Then she had put it away again as a perpetual witness to her repentance and amendment. And surely these virtues had a right to forgiveness!

One person, she knew, would do more than forgive if he knew all, and this knowledge, joined to the sense of loss which his prolonged absence from her environment always produced in Gwen Boynton, made her think very tenderly of Dan, who wrote her such kind, sympathetic letters from Hodinuggar about the dear lad. *He* was not jealous and full of evil imaginings like Lewis, whose temper had certainly not been improved by his visit to the plains. Though she did not consciously feel the need of something stronger than the cousinly affection she had for the latter, there is no doubt that the shock of her own lapses from strict honesty, joined to that of George Keene's sudden death, had made her disinclined for final decision; so the fact that Dan would, from pressure of work, be unable to get leave that year, and Lewis, from the same cause, was not likely to be urgent in love-making, suited her capitally. She would have time to recover her tone. To this end she proceeded, with a curious strength of purpose, to dismiss the nightmare of the past from her mind. It was over. What had been, had been. She would reach out to the things which were before— No, not reach out—she would not again be premature; she would let fate and luck have their say to the full.

One small fact showed the state of her mind exactly. She dismissed her *ayah*, giving her as a parting present most of the articles which Manohar Lal had forced her into buying from him. The woman sulked, yet held her tongue, no doubt knowing through her patron, the jeweller, that so far as he was concerned the *mem* was safe; besides, when all was said and done, the *bucksheesh* was sufficient, and under no circumstances could she have expected more. So, on the whole, life went pretty smoothly in the pretty little drawing-room where poor young George had sat with his head on the table, dazed and stunned by his bitter pain.

Over the way, however, in Colonel Tweedie's house, things were different. Lewis Gordon, up to the ears in endless calculations, yet had time to notice that grief suited Rose very ill. And grief, forsooth, for a boy who had not cared a pin for her, who had run into debt and gambled and lost his head completely over another woman; who, if the truth were known, had shot himself because—to take the most charitable view of the matter—he had not the pluck to bear disappointment. Naturally, a young fellow felt being fooled—more or less—by a woman, because certain instincts were the strongest man had—as a man. But one expected something more, or less, in a gentleman. And there was Miss Tweedie, who depended for attractiveness on the *beauté du diable*, looking pale and worn over a mere sentimentalism; since she herself would be the first to deny that she had been what he, Lewis, would call "in love" with George. Finally, although he, knowing to the full Gwen's responsibility of the boy's suicide, had every right, if he chose, to be hard on his cousin, why should this girl, who knew nothing, stand aloof and show her disapproval so plainly?

"You don't understand girls," said Gwen, easily, in reply to some hints of his in this respect; "dear Rose can't help huffing me at present. I should feel the same towards any one who had to my mind stood between me and my dear dead."

Lewis shifted irritably in his chair and wished to goodness she would talk sense.

"Sense! Why you yourself are always blaming me in your heart because that poor boy thought me the most perfect woman in creation. You know you are! As if it were my fault. As if I ever encouraged such an idea in any one, or set up for being perfection."

It was true enough. She never posed as anything but a woman *pur et simple.* That was one of her charms in his eyes, and the injustice of cavil at what he really liked made him say more gently, "I don't suppose you could help it, dear; and perhaps Miss Tweedie can't, either. I don't pretend to understand women — have enough to do to understand the atrocious English men put in their reports. But I wish you would come over sometimes as you used to do; the girl oughtn't to be allowed to eat nothing and grow so disagreeably thin."

Gwen gave an odd laugh. "Well, I'll invite myself to luncheon to-morrow. It is bad for the girl, and so useless into the bargain."

The common-sense of the last remark lingered in Lewis Gordon's mind comfortably as he went home. In more ways than one it was quite useless to dwell on George Keene's unfortunate death. No doubt Rose, if she knew all, would judge Gwen very hardly — not only Gwen, but those who, knowing as they did, went on as if nothing had happened. But Rose Tweedie, the fates be praised, was not his judge. And yet when he passed the window of her room on his way to his own, she was, in sober truth, sitting in judgment on the figure she saw for a second between the draped curtains. He had been over as usual to Mrs. Boynton's; to the woman who had been the last to see George Keene, and yet would say so little about the interview; to the woman who was no doubt to blame if, as her father said, George had run into debt and gambled and lost his head. Lewis must know all this—perhaps more; yet he went on approvingly. By-and-by he would marry this woman, for they were engaged, of course, even now. Was not that enough to make any one who cared for him as she cared—Rose leaned forward over the book she was studying, and tried hard to bend her mind also to its consideration.

Despite these thoughts, she received Mrs. Boynton on the next day without a sign of disapproval; for Rose, like most unmarried girls at the head of a house, was intensely proud of her position. In society, if she did not care to speak to Gwen, she would not speak; if she did not care to have her in the house, she would not ask her; but if she came, as she did now, uninvited, she was nothing more nor less than a guest, to be treated as a guest should be treated. Perhaps Lewis Gordon had an inkling as to her graciousness, but Colonel Tweedie saw nothing but a renewal of those amenities, the loss of which he had so helplessly deplored during the past fortnight. It had put him out considerably, and left him completely puzzled as to its cause. Certainly not to any change in his mind, for it had broken in on a steadily growing conviction that he would not only like, but that he also ought to ask, Mrs. Boynton to marry him. Rose was too much alone; she brooded, as the former had kindly pointed out, over life, and fancied herself in love with subordinates. She was too sensible for that sort of thing to be real, but the constant companionship of a woman of the world was a necessity to a young girl. It is surprising how many second marriages are inspired by secondary considerations of convenience, and still more surprising why such considerations should then be thought virtuous, moral, blameless; yet be deemed *anathema maranatha* in first marriages. But there are some things which, as Dundreary pointed out, "no fellah can find out"; one being the curious ethical code which has quite obscured the real issues of marriage, and thus made it possible for quick-witted men and women to quarrel desperately with each other about their own feelings in regard to something else which is not marriage. Colonel Tweedie, however, treated his secondary reasons with the greatest respect, and beamed pompously round the luncheon-table as he announced his infinite regret that the duties of his responsible position made it necessary for him to leave such pleasant company sooner than he otherwise would have done. Mrs. Boynton, however, would readily understand that councils of state were paramount to the public servant. Whereupon Gwen, after her fashion, took the edge off his anguish by saying that she also had to be home early, seeing she had promised to interview some dreadful Madrassee creature who had been recommended to her as an *ayah*.

"Why did you send old Munia away?" asked Rose, suddenly. They had risen as they were speaking, and she had been standing by the window, listening, with a certain weariness in her face, to her father's ornate regrets.

"The old reason: '*I do not like thee, Dr. Fell,*'" laughed Gwen. "I suppose it is very illogical—therefore, as Lewis would say, very womanly; but I can't help disliking my world by instinct."

"That is monstrously unkind," broke in the colonel, eager as a boy over the opportunity, "when your world cannot help doing the reverse." There is something very satisfactory, apparently, in a compliment to the person who makes it, and the colonel felt and looked very lighthearted over his.

"When you have got rid of us all, Miss Tweedie," said Lewis Gordon, in a low tone which yet covered Gwen's little laugh, "you should go out and have a jolly ride. I'm not using Bronzewing: she frets at waiting, so she is at your disposal, if you care—" He paused in quick surprise.

Such a very little thing upsets a woman's balance at times, and Bronzewing had been the very subject over which they had quarrelled the day of his accident. It was very foolish, but the look on her face made him turn hastily from the window to his cousin, and catch at the first thing likely to give the girl a chance of recovering herself.

"I believe your *ayah* is coming here, Gwen; at least, I see one of those little covered *dhoolies* descending from your house; and if there are to be *purda nishin* women about, sir, it is time we were going."

"Don't be ridiculous, Lewis! It is somebody going to pay a visit to the *khansaman's* wife. The *ayah* wouldn't dare to come here; and if she did, I am not going to make a *zenâna* out of Colonel Tweedie's drawing-room."

"But you could go into Rose's sitting-room, of course," protested the colonel; "couldn't she, my dear?"

"But, indeed, good people," began Gwen, laughing, "it can't—" Just then a servant, entering stolidly, announced a woman waiting to see *mem* Boynton *sahib*.

"I told you so!" cried Lewis, joyfully; "and, as a matter of fact, we ought to be off, sir. It will take us a good twenty minutes to the Secretariat."

"Show the woman into the miss *sahib's* office," cried the colonel, fussily. "Rose, my dear—" But the girl had taken the opportunity of escaping through the open French window.

"Please don't mind," said Mrs. Boynton. "I know my way about this house; at any rate, I ought to, seeing how hospitable you have been always. Good-bye; I hope your interview will prove more pleasant than mine is likely to be." Their ponies were waiting, and she stayed to give them a parting nod as they rounded the last visible turn of the path leading to the Mall. Gwen always added these pleasant, friendly touches to the bareness and business of life; they came to her by instinct, and she herself felt cold and cheerless without them. Then, very well satisfied with herself, she crossed the long matted passage which ran from end to end of the house separating the portion Colonel Tweedie reserved for his own use from that occupied by the office. Here, beside her father's private room, was Rose's little study, and beyond that again Lewis Gordon's quarters, and the big glazed veranda where the clerks sat designing.

It was quite a tiny room, and it seemed to Mrs. Boynton as she entered it to be over-full of perfume; possibly from the vase full of wild turk's-cap lilies on the table. The window was shut, too, and Gwen, as she made her way to the most comfortable chair with scarcely a glance at the white-robed figure standing in the shadow of the curtains, gave a quick yet languid order to set the glazed doors wide open.

"They are best shut, if the *huzoor* does not mind. I have that to say which requires caution."

These round, suave tones, with almost the nightingale thrill in them, belonged to no *ayah*, surely! Gwen looked round hastily. No *ayah's* figure either—tall, supple, unabashed. Instinctively the Englishwoman stood up and confronted her visitor, more curious than alarmed. Even to that ignorance of native life which is so typical of the *mem sahib*—an ignorance not altogether to be deprecated—the woman's trade was unmistakable. That was writ large in the trimness and cleanliness, the spotless white, the chaplets of flowers, the scent of musk and ambergris filling the room. All the more reason for surprise at her presence there. Yet, even so, curiosity outweighs indignation and resentment in Gwen's cold questioning.

"Who are you? What do you want?"

The answer came quick: so quickly that it left the hearer with the breathless sense of pained relief that the worst is over which comes with the clean, sharp cut of the surgeon's knife.

"I am Chândni of Delhi. I want the Hodinuggar pearls which the *huzoor* took out of the Ayôdhya pot." No mincing of the matter here; none of that beating about the bush which, as a rule, Gwen loved. Yet the directness did not displease her; it seemed to rouse in her a novel combativeness, taking form in similar effrontery and cool assertion.

"I don't know what you are talking about," she said, indifferently, "and I don't want you. Go!"

Her Hindostanee, though limited, was naturally of that imperative order, and suited the occasion; yet it evoked one of Chândni's shrill, mocking laughs.

"The *mem sahib* forgets. She is not, as I am, a daughter of the bazaars, and if it comes to words, Chândni hath two to her one. So I come quietly to ask reasonably for my rights; not to dispute, after the manner of my kind. There is no need to tell the *mem sahib* the story. She remembers it perfectly. She knows it as well as I. But this she does not know: the pearls are mine, and I will have them back, or their price, in revenge!"

"I think you are mad!" cried Gwen, more hastily. "Go! Go, instantly, or I will call the servants."

"That were not wise! Lo! I know all about the papers of safety which Manohar Lal gave in exchange for the *chota sahib's* rupees. But the pearls went not once but—twice."

"Twice!" The involuntary echo had a surprise in it which angered the courtesan.

"Yes, twice! The *mem* knows that as well as I do. The Ayôdhya pot—"

"Was stolen from me in the palace," put in Gwen; "you stole it, I dare say."

Again Chândni laughed. "If I did, what then? The *mem* got it again, and sent it back through the post for more pearls. But we did not send it thus; we sent it by the *chota sahib*, who gave it to the *mem*, and she sent the key in return. The papers are about the first pearls. These are the second; and there are no safety papers about them."

"It is not true—it is a lie! He never took them—he never gave them to me!" cried Gwen, her courage, oddly enough, failing before what was to her an absolute, novel, and unfounded accusation. "I will not listen! Go! or I will call."

Chândni took a step nearer, lowering her voice. "What! wouldst let the truth be known, when thou canst conceal it —forever? Give me the pearls, and no one shall know—no one shall cast dirt on the *mem* and on the *chota sahib*—no one shall know how he took the bribes for you—no one shall know thou didst beguile him as men are beguiled—"

"I—I did not! It is a lie! I—" fáltered Gwen, falling back till Chândni's hand closed like a vice on her wrist.

"*Wah!* What use to deny it to me? Do I not know the trick? A word—a look; no more. What! do men send bullets through their hearts as Keene *sahib* did for no cause? *Ari*, sister! we know better."

The jeering comradeship was too much for caution, even though the story of poor George's death passed by as wanton lies. Gwen, struggling madly, gave one scream after another for help, and, breaking from her persecutor's hand, turned to fly. At the same moment Rose, who had been in her father's study for a book, burst through the door and stood bewildered at the scene.

"Send her away! She tells lies—lies about me and George—lies about everything. Oh! have her sent away, Rose. Please send her away." The girl, clasping the hands with which Gwen clung to her, turned on the intruder angrily, and an indescribable hardness and contempt came to her face as she took in the meaning of the figure and its dress.

"How dare you come here? Go this instant. Put on your veil, hide yourself, and go! Impertinent! Shameless!"

There was no answering laugh here. "The *huzoor* speaks truth," replied the courtesan, quietly. "I have no business here. I came but to see the *mem*, bethinking me she might listen better in the house of those who were friends to the *chota sahib*—" But Gwen's immediate terror had passed, leaving her face to face with future fears.

"Don't listen, Rose," she interrupted, in English; "you should never listen to what women of that sort say about any one. She frightened me at first with her lies, but the wisest plan is to send her away. I'll call a servant." Chândni, listening to the quick whisper, smiled.

"The *mem sahib* wants silence," she said, nodding her head, "but silence is ever unsafe unless tongues are tied. And mine will wag—if not here, then elsewhere—unless I get the Ayôdhya pot."

Rose gave a quick exclamation; but Gwen's hand was on her

arm, her voice full of passionate entreaty. "Don't, Rose! don't speak to her. I can tell you it is all lies: some rigmarole declaring that after the pot had been stolen from Hodinuggar it was sent back to me at Simla; that I returned it again. There isn't a word of truth in it. I never—"

But the girl set aside the detaining hand with an impatient gesture, and crossed to where Chândni stood watching them. "You have made a mistake," came the clear, unfaltering voice; "the Ayôdhya pot was not sent to the *mem sahib*. It was sent to me, and it was *I* who returned it. What then?"

The frank admission brought a curiously similar expression to those two listening faces; it seemed to leave both abashed, uncertain, so that Rose had to repeat her clear question before it gained reply.

"What then?" echoed the courtesan at last, somewhat sulkily. "How can I tell if this be so; and if it be so, how can I tell what must come? Only this I do know: the pot went to Keene *sahib* the day he left. He gave it to some one; let that some one answer. I care not who 'tis, so long as I have my pearls that were hidden in the pot."

"Pearls! There were no pearls in it when it came to me," cried Rose, quickly; then, remembering the jagged edge of clay she had noticed inside, she turned to Gwen. "Did you notice anything like a false bottom when you had it before?"

The face into which she looked paled. "You don't understand," cried Gwen, petulantly; "the woman says that the pearls were put there after it was stolen; so how could I notice anything when I tell you I never saw—never heard anything of it again? I told the woman so just now; I will tell her again before you. Then I must, I will, have her sent away; she has no business here."

But Chândni's recklessness had grown in the interval. "I care not who has them. See! there are three of us here in this room who have handled the pot; let her who hath it and its hoard speak truth, and save the *chota sahib*. For he had it sure enough; of that there is proof."

"Three of us!" repeated Rose, absently, as if struck by a

thought. Then, obeying a sudden impulse, she went over to a portfolio standing in one corner of the room. "You mistake," she continued, her eyes full on the courtesan, "there are not three but four of us. Look! Keene *sahib* painted that."

Chândni fell back, averting her face from the portrait of Azîzan which Rose placed against an easel on the table. "The evil-eye! the evil-eye! God save us from the witch!" she muttered, thrusting out her right hand in that two-fingered gesture which is used against a baleful glance in both East and West.

But Gwen, pressing closer, looked at the picture with a dawning light of comprehension on her face. "Did he paint that? How pretty it is! And it explains—it explains—a—a great deal. He gave her the pot, I suppose. Well, it is a pity, but one ought not to be—"

"Ought not to be what?" interrupted Rose, quickly, with a fine scorn in her face, scarcely less concealed than the contempt with which she turned to the other woman, as she went on: "You both seem to know more about this picture than I do," she said, superbly. "Perhaps you can tell me whom it represents?"

"My dear Rose," expostulated Gwen, aside, "don't, for pity's sake, ask that creature. What would your father say if he knew? You may mix yourself up—"

"Whose picture is it, I ask?" repeated Rose, unheeding. Then, in the silence of Chândni's smile and Gwen's frown, she turned passionately to the portrait itself. "Why don't you speak and shame them? You look as if you could tell the truth, and if he made you so it is true!" The very vehemence of her own fanciful appeal imposed on her as she stood as if waiting for a reply. It came with a laugh from Chândni. "She! She was another of the *chota sahib's* friends. The miss saith true; there are four of them here. Which will give back the pearls and save him?"

"Save him from what?" cried Rose, disregarding Gwen's appealing prayer for her to leave the mad woman to the servants. "What has Keene *sahib* done that you can dare to threaten?"

The girl's bitter contempt roused Chândni's innate savageness. After all, she was the mistress, and this girl, despite her courage, was in her power; what is more, she should learn it. "From what? From the shame which comes to the *sahib logues* when their pretence of honesty is found out—from the shame of having friends—the shame of taking jewels for those friends—the shame of being untrue to salt—ask the *mem* how it is done; she knows. The shame of sending the key of the sluice-gate so that the water—" Her voice had risen so far with each sentence; now it ended in a gasp and a gurgle.

"Open the door, please," said Rose to Mrs. Boynton, who gasped also in intense surprise of the girl's swift action. "Don't struggle, fool!" she went on, in the same hard tones, only the dead whiteness of her face and a catch as she drew breath telling of the wild passion surging in her veins. "I won't choke you if you hold your tongue." Once before Chândni had felt a girl's grip on her throat—a hot, straining grip. This was neither. It was the grip of a strong, healthy hand, made vigorous by constant use. Those fierce fights over bat and ball with the dead lad had had their share in the sheer muscle of her defence of him, before which Chândni's large softness gave way, leaving her not even a slandering tongue.

"Put the veil over her face, if you please! I won't even have it known who dared to come here!" continued the girl, forcing the woman backward step by step till they reached the door; then she pushed her from it magnificently. "Now go! and tell what lies you like elsewhere."

But her face changed as she turned, when the door was closed and bolted, to Gwen Boynton. "Is it true? For God's sake, tell me if there's a word of truth in it, and I will find the money."

Gwen dissolved into helpless tears—tears at once of vague remorse and a very real sense of injustice. "True! Oh, Rose, how can you ask? Of course it isn't true. I wouldn't have done it for the world. Indeed and indeed I never saw the Ayôdhya pot again, and I don't believe George did. He was the soul of honor, and so good—so good to me. It is all wicked, wicked lies; unless, indeed, that girl— But there, I dare say she was bad, like that horrid creature. Perhaps they stole the pot between them, and are now trying to blackmail us."

"Stole the pot!" repeated Rose, slowly, remembering for the first time her dream on the night of the storm at Hodinuggar. "Yes, that is possible; and yet"—she looked at Azîzan's picture, and then back at Gwen, who was dabbing her eyes with a soft pocket-handkerchief—"you are sure?" she began again.

"Of course, I am quite sure," retorted Gwen, whose remorse had vanished into anger at this impudent attempt to amend and enlarge the text of a past incident. "I never saw or heard of the pot again. I may be weak; I may have done things, for which I am sorry, in the past; but whatever you may think, my conscience is clear. And as for the sluice, Dan opened it by order. Besides, there was the flood. It is all an attempt to blackmail me, and I won't be blackmailed. I have done nothing they can take hold of—nothing, nothing."

Rose gave a sigh, almost of dissatisfaction. If it really was a case of blackmailing, payment would be but a temporary relief. Perhaps, as Gwen had suggested, the girl in the picture was in league with Chândni, and yet she did not look that sort. Nor did she look as if— Rose glanced from the pure oval of the cheek and the fine long curves of the mouth to Mrs. Boynton's tear-stained face, and frowned.

"Some one has the pearls," she said, "and George's memory must be saved—somehow."

CHAPTER XXIII

"Come in." The words were given in an impatient tone, for Lewis Gordon was busy, and he hated being disturbed—especially when, as now, he had taken his coat off, literally as well as figuratively, before a difficult file. The garment hung on the back of his chair, which, in obedience to a fad of his, was the only one in the office; a second one, he declared, being easily sent for if required, while its absence shortened many a trivial interruption. Otherwise a comfortable enough room, with a large French window set wide on a magnificent view of the serrated snows resting on the wall of blue distance, and framed by the curved tops of a forest of young deodars. The day was bright as a morning in the rainy season can be; bright by very contrast between the brilliant lights and shadows in earth and sky; bright as a rain-cloud itself when the sun shines on it. A fresh breeze came in with Rose Tweedie through the opening door, and blew some papers off the table.

"I beg your pardon," came in duet, as Lewis fumbled blindly for his coat, his eye-glass having deserted him in the surprise, after the manner of eye-glasses. As he did so he felt injured; not that he was such a crass idiot as to be outraged by a pair of shirt-sleeves in himself as in others. But he knew quite well that no man can look dignified when struggling even into a lounge-coat, and he liked to be dignified, especially with Rose Tweedie. His irritation, however, hid itself under a different cloak; that is to say, annoyance at a most unusual intrusion. Perhaps she read the expression of it in his face, for her first words were an excuse.

"I came here—to your office, I mean—because I want to ask you something, and I didn't want you to feel hampered—not as a friend, you know." Her eyes met his in confidence of being understood so far, at any rate, and he gave rather a stiff little bow.

"You are very welcome. Won't you take a chair—the chair, perhaps I ought to say? I've been sitting all the morning and shall be glad of a change, unless you require some time. If so, I will send—"

"No, thanks; I prefer standing also," she interrupted, with a quick flush. "I only wanted to ask you a question. It is about George Keene."

"Yes," he replied coldly, unsympathetically; and yet he was noting her anxious eyes and haggard face with a sort of angry wonder why she should make herself so unhappy. Rose's fingers held nervously to the edge of the table by which she stood.

"Have you any reason—I mean is there, officially, any reason—to suppose that the Hodinuggar sluice was opened before the flood came down, or before Mr. Fitzgerald—" She paused, with her eyes on Lewis's face. She had lain awake almost all the night thinking of Chândni's threats and hints, and with her clear sight had seen that their worth or unworth depended largely upon the official report of what had actually happened at Hodinuggar. To her father she could not go without danger from his want of judgment; there remained Lewis, who was always just, always to be trusted in such matters.

His heart gave quite a throb of dismayed surprise at her question, and forced him by contraries into still greater chillness of manner. "I'm afraid I can't quite see your right to ask me such a question as yet. Perhaps if you could give me a reason—"

"Oh, yes; I can give you a reason," she interrupted, with a ring of scorn in her voice, "though I think you might credit me with a good one where George is concerned, surely. Only, if I have to tell, you had better send for the chair. I thought perhaps you would understand—for once."

The bitterness of her tone did not escape him, and accentuated his annoyance. As he handed her the chair and leaned negligently against the table, his hands behind him, he told himself that he was in for a *mauvais quart d'heure* with the girl. Man-like, she would expect to know all; woman-like, she would expect sentiment to outweigh official integrity. These thoughts did not serve to soften his heart towards the dead lad even at the beginning, and as her story unfolded itself his face grew sterner and sterner. But hers lightened; it was an infinite relief to have his advice, his help, and she told him so frankly, even while she appealed for it.

"You needn't even answer my question, Mr. Gordon," she went on, earnestly. "You will know so much better than I do what had best be done. I thought of going to see the woman myself--"

"You didn't go, I hope," put in Lewis, hastily.

"No; I made up my mind to ask you first. You see, if there is no truth in all this—no truth whatever—"

"That is unlikely, I warn you," interrupted Lewis. "These women—really, Miss Tweedie, if you follow my advice, much as it may pain you at the time—you will leave this business alone, absolutely alone. It is not one with which — excuse me for even alluding to the fact—a girl such as you are should meddle. Unfortunately, we men have to face these things, and they are not pleasant—even for us."

"You speak as if you thought George was guilty," said Rose, hotly. "What right have you to do that?"

"I may have more right than you suspect. Believe me, Miss Tweedie, I am heartily sorry—especially for you—and, so far as is compatible with the facts, I will do my best to avoid official *esclandre* should this matter really crop up. In the meantime I am afraid I must decline to interfere in what Mrs. Boynton, you tell me, stigmatized as an impudent attempt at blackmailing. She has her faults, no doubt, like everybody else, but she has, excuse me for saying so, more knowledge of the world than you have. In fact, you could scarcely do better than take her advice on this point."

The girl, with a frown on her face, rose from her seat slowly. "Then you refuse to find out the truth. You are content to let this suspicion lie upon—upon me, and your cousin?"

Lewis smiled. "That is rather far-fetched, Miss Tweedie, surely. The idea of suspicion with you is simply absurd, and as for Gwen! Well, I know you are ready to admit she has her faults, but she has called this claim impudent blackmailing, and you must excuse me if I incline to believe her."

"And for George Keene? Do you suspect him? Are you going to allow his memory to be smirched?"

"I have told you I will do my best. For the rest, he must take the consequences of his own acts, I'm afraid. Indeed, I am sorry—very sorry," he added, hastily, impelled to it by the look on Rose Tweedie's face; it had grown ashy pale. Yet she stood steadily before him, her eyes on his unflinchingly.

"Then there is truth in it. You had better tell me. It would be kinder to tell me, if you can."

Perhaps, after all, it would. Perhaps if this scandal had to come to light, it would be better she should be prepared; and even if it did not, was it not wiser she should know the real truth about George Keene, and so be able to judge him fairly? Not a bad boy, of course; that talk of bribery was no doubt false, and he had done no more in other ways than hundreds of boys in a like position. Even at Simla he had only run wild a bit, and for that he was not the only one responsible. Still, when all was said and done, he had shot himself, and that alone made the task of whitewashing him an impossibility if these women chose revenge.

"Yes, there is some truth in it," he said, gravely. "If you will sit down again, I will tell you everything I know, and then you can judge for yourself. I should like you to understand, however, that, in spite of appearances, I don't believe George lent himself to anything more than—what you would—not you, perhaps—but most of us would expect in a young fellow of his age and his position. Life is—is rather intoxicating to—to some of us." So, leaning against the table, he told her the truth, trying to do his task calmly and kindly, yet beset by a certain impatience at the still figure seated in his office-chair, its elbows among his files, the coils of its beautiful hair showing beyond the hands in which the face was hidden.

What business had it there? What business had the thought of its pain to come so close to him—closer, even, than his own reason, his own sense of justice?

"And you have known that he shot himself from the beginning?" she asked, raising her head suddenly to look him full in the face. He assented, with a distinct self-complacency.

"Then what did you think made him do it? Then—before you knew anything about the debts—or the opening of the gates?"

The self-complacency vanished. "There are many reasons, or want of reasons, for that sort of thing, Miss Tweedie," he said, evasively. "I did not—I mean it was impossible to say absolutely, and that is why I acquiesced in Fitzgerald's plan. It was more convenient to every one concerned."

"Much more convenient," echoed Rose, sharply. "And you have known this all the time, and not—" She broke off, as if incredulous of her own half-uttered thought.

"Certainly I have known it, and we would have kept the secret, Fitzgerald and I, but for this unfortunate business," he retorted, and his tone was not pleasant.

"Ah, *he* is different—*he* did not know! *he* thought George had done it for his sake—to screen him! But you! What did you believe?" The girl's very voice was a challenge.

"I must say, Miss Tweedie, that I scarcely see how my belief affects the question, or, pardon me, what it matters to you," he replied, taking refuge once more in his indifference.

"Do you not? Then I do. Not that it matters now," she added, in sudden passion, "for I will have my way in the future. If you won't help me, I can't help that; but I will have the truth. I will go down to this woman in the bazaar and make her tell me. Whether her story is a lie or not, there shall be no more concealment. I will not have it."

"And George Keene's memory?" he suggested, angered almost beyond his self-control by her unmistakable defiance. "My advice is unwelcome, of course; but if you took it—and Mrs. Boynton's—only that is unwelcome, too—you might avoid all scandal. I cannot say for certain that it would, but as I have told you I would do my best—officially, even, I will do my best. That seems to be an offence also for some reason, but I would do it as much for the sake of the department as for the boy's. You, I know, think only of him—"

She turned upon him like lightning, carried out of herself by her scorn, her passion. "Of him! I was not thinking of him at all! I was thinking of you—of you only, as I always do. Why should you not know the truth? You will not care a pin whether I think of you or not. And I? I care for nothing—nothing so long as you do not blindfold yourself wilfully—so long as you are just and honest. Oh! you may think I am mad—perhaps, if what you believe about men and women is true, I am; but it means everything—everything in the world to me that you should be so—just and honest; because, what you are is more to me than all the world beside. That is the truth." The last words came slowly, as the fire of her passion died down; yet there was no uncertainty in them. "I suppose I oughtn't to have said this," she went on, turning from him to lean her elbows on the table and rest her head on her hands wearily. "But you won't mind, and I don't care. It can't hurt any man to know that he is loved—it can't."

Loved! The word sent a thrill through the man such as he had never felt before. Loved! Was that what she meant? The thought broke through even his armor of surprise. He stood for an instant, looking down at her; then turned slowly and walked to the window—to return, however, in a second, with quick, clear steps, breaking the silence of the room. "What do you mean? I can't believe it. What do you mean?" he asked, imperatively; but his impatience would not wait for a reply in words. Her face would give it truly; that he knew, and he stooped over her, taking her by the wrists in order to draw her hands apart. Then she turned to him, bravely enough.

"Rose!" It was almost a cry, as, stooping lower still, he knelt before her, his eyes on hers, incredulous, yet soft. Then, suddenly, still clasping her slender wrists, he buried his face upon them in her lap. "Oh, I am sorry—I am sorry!" Never since, as a child, he had said his prayers at his mother's knee, had Lewis Gordon so knelt to man or woman. And something of the child's unquestioning belief in an unselfish love came back to him, joined to a perfect passion of the man's clear-sighted remorse and regret.

"Don't," she said, gently bending over him. "Please don't. There is nothing for you to be sorry about; indeed, there isn't."

Nothing to be sorry about! Once more he echoed this girl's words to himself, with that strange thrill, as, recovering his self-command, he stood straight and stiff beside her, conscious only of one vehement desire to care for and to protect her. "What is it you want me to do?" he said at last, unsteadily. "Tell me, and I'll do it."

Then, woman-like, she began to cry; it is a way the good ones have when they succeed in imposing their own will on those they love. "I don't think I want you to do anything—particular," she answered, trying to conceal her tears. "I don't know; besides, I would much rather you did it your own way."

If the uttermost truth could be told about a man's emotion in such scenes, as it can be regarding a woman's, it would have to be confessed that Lewis Gordon came very near to crying, also, over this foolish, unconditional surrender on Rose Tweedie's part. For he understood the irresolution of a generous nature before its own success, and, what is more, the woman's desire to give the man she loves the glory of gratifying her belief in him. He felt quite a lump in his throat, and had to seek escape from the tenderness of one sex in the decision of the other. In nine cases out of ten these are but different methods of showing the same emotion.

"I will go down and see this woman to-day; and then—" He paused, not in order to think over his next move—that, undoubtedly, would be to see Gwen Boynton—but to overcome a dislike to mentioning her name, which suddenly assailed him. Why, he scarcely knew, save that it seemed mean, unmanly. Rose, however, saved him from the necessity by again repeating, this time almost abjectly, that she would rather not know

—that she would be quite content to leave the matter in his hands.

"Thank you," replied Lewis, in such a very low tone that it was almost a whisper. It did not lead, however, as might have been expected, to a silence, but to a louder, more aggressive gratitude. "I have to thank you—for many things. I won't affect to ignore or set aside what you did me the honor of telling me just now. That would be sheer impertinence on my—" Now, when he had got so far in a perfectly admirable sentiment calculated to soothe both her feelings and his own, why he should suddenly have found his hands in hers again, his heart full of an unpremeditated assertion that he was glad she loved him, cannot be explained logically; but so it was. Yet before the scared look in her eyes his own fell; he loosened his clasp, and the appeal died from his lips. There was no place for him, or his questionings, in her avowal; that hedged itself about from intrusion with a dignity he recognized. So what remained, save to pass on with as much dignity as *he* could compass to the work assigned to him? "I will come in and tell you what I have done this afternoon, about five o'clock," he said, quietly; "that is, if it is convenient."

"Quite, thank you." The baldest, most conventional of tones on both sides. The baldest, most conventional holding open of the door for her to pass out—to pass out from a scene that would linger in his memory—in nothing else. The descent to normal diapason comes sooner or later, no matter how highly strung the instruments may be to begin with—and the most melodramatic of incidents fades into padding. But in real life this return to the commonplace generally leaves some of the actors dissatisfied with the way the scene has been played. Lewis Gordon felt this distinctly when he was left looking at his own chair, as if he still saw a girl's figure seated there, her elbows resting on the litter of official papers, and the great coils of her burnished hair showing beyond the hands which hid her face.

"It can't hurt any man to know he is loved!" She had said so; but she was wrong. It did hurt confoundedly. So that was what she meant by love, was it? If any of the trivial interruptions which Lewis Gordon so much dreaded had come during the following five minutes they would have found the coveted chair vacant, though the owner's face was buried in his hands among the files and reports. Apparently he gained little consolation from them; for when he resumed work he looked about as upset and disordered as a tidy man can do when he is cool and properly clothed. Nor did they gain much from him during the next hour, which ticked away remorselessly from the chronometer by which Lewis loved to map out his day. He thrust them aside at last impatiently and ordered his pony, thinking that maybe when he had got through that visit to the bazaar he might feel less of a duffer and not quite so much knocked out of time. And yet she had said there was nothing to regret—that he would not care—that it would not matter to him if she thought of him or not!

It was a queer world! He set his teeth over it as he rode reluctantly between the shingled arcades of the big bazaar and then through a narrow paved alley, pitching, as it were, sheer down into the blue mists of the valley below. And so on to the balconied house where, from inquiries at the Kotwâli, he learned that Chândni was lodging. The task before him was a disagreeable one; yet he swore inwardly as he thought that, but for his abject capitulation, Rose would have attempted it herself. Rose! Yes, he began to understand that the feminine world could not be divided into two classes. There was a third composed of one specimen: Rose—and Rose only. And as he went on, the very cleanliness and order, contrasting so sharply with the dirt of surrounding respectability, struck him offensively on the girl's behalf, while the giggling in the lower story gave him a vicarious shock, and the obsequiousness of his introduction into the higher one where Chândni sat secluded actually made his cheek burn. "It can't hurt any man to know that he is loved!" He set aside the haunting words angrily, and began his task so soon as the patchwork drapery at the door fell behind him, leaving him face to face with white-robed, salaaming grace.

"See here, my sister! This is for the truth. 'Tis not often thy sort are asked for it; but I ask nothing else. I will take nothing else."

Checked thus in her languid welcome to the unknown guest, Chândni looked distastefully at the hundred-rupee note thrust into her hand, then at the giver; though both were to her liking. The latter she recognized instantly as having been among the party at Hodinuggar, and the recognition showed her that her seed of slander had taken root already. So far, good.

"My lord shall have that which he requires, surely. Wherefore else are there such as I?" she replied, and the cynical truth of her answer convinced him of her wit at once. He acknowledged it, frankly, when half an hour afterwards he felt himself baffled by the calm simplicity of her story. Most of it he had already heard, but the details proved more unpleasant than he had imagined possible. Azîzan, it appeared from Chândni's account, had been a palace lady, with whom George had had clandestine meetings, over which he had first become mixed up with the intrigues about the water. The key of the sluice had been sent from Simla, whether by the *mem* or the miss, or the *sahib* himself, she did not know—she could not say. Was she not telling *huzoor* the bare truth she knew to be true, and nothing else?

"And how much do you want to keep all this quiet?" he asked, calmly, when she had finished. It was as well to know her price, at any rate. For an instant the immediate temptation to take the bird in the hand made the courtesan hesitate. Then she struck boldly for higher game. "The pearls, *huzoor!* —the pearls or my revenge!" This man with the cool, refined face, and the contempt which made her involuntarily remember the *miss sahib's* also, affected indifference now, and would most likely offer her some paltry sum. But she could afford to wait for the change which was sure to come; for she was not in the least afraid of anything Lewis could do, and, without being absolutely insolent, took care to show him the fact as she lolled about at her ease chewing betel ostentatiously. She had nothing to gain here by affecting delicacy, so he might see her at her coarsest and worst; it contrasted better with his brains. The result being that Lewis Gordon came into Gwen Boynton's drawing-room for his next interview looking depressed: partly because he had been riding through a tepid shower-bath; for recurring rain had washed away the bright promises of the morning and was falling drearily over the rank, dank grasses, and beating down the fringes of delicate ferns growing upon the dripping branches of the oak-trees, until they lost shape and became nothing but a green outline against the gray mist. Within, however, by the light of a blazing pine-wood fire, Mrs. Boynton looked bright yet soft, like a pastel painting or a figure seen in a looking-glass; for she soon recovered from her emotions, and took pains to hide their effects even from herself. So the fact that she had lain awake half the night wondering if by chance Chândni's impudent lies had been prompted by any flaw in the chain-armor of security which George and the flood had forged for her, did not show on her face. For they were lies: even that tale of the dear lad's death, which had given her such a shock at the time, was nothing but the vile woman's wicked, cruel invention. Rose had evidently heard nothing and still knew nothing of it; besides, Dan did not know; and even if he had wished to keep the pain of such knowledge from her, Lewis, with his jealous blame, would have been sure to have used it to point a moral—a pointless moral, nevertheless, since George could have had no cause for despair. Had not the flood come to end even the anxiety? unless, indeed, there was any truth in the tale about the portrait. Yet why should truth be supposed in one incident, when causeless, wicked lying was evident in all the others? No; it was an impudent attempt at extortion, and must be met by denial. Therein lay safety both for her and for poor George Keene's memory; the conspirators would never face the evidence of those papers which they knew she held. So, as her cousin came in she greeted him with a smile, changing to sweet concern at his ill-looks.

"I have a headache," he replied, curtly. "No wonder; the smells and the general abominations of the bazaar are enough to kill one, and I had to go down there. Besides, I'm damp, and I've had no lunch. Isn't that a long-enough catalogue of ills? No, thanks—don't order anything for me. I'd rather have a cup of tea by-and-by." It was the worst thing for him, he knew that; nothing but a quiet cigar and a man's drink would have restored his balance. But he told himself, captiously, that he had been in a melodramatic atmosphere all the morning, and might as well go in for it to the bitter end. He felt demoralized, and so, almost out of contrariety, put himself at a further disadvantage by rushing at his fence.

"Gwen," he began, abruptly, "I've come to ask you for the truth." He did not hand her a bank-note, as he had done to the other woman; yet the thought crossed his mind bitterly that one of sufficient value might be useful; and though he set it aside, of course, as utterly unworthy, the knowledge that it had been there remained. In common justice he had no more right to prejudge Gwen's implication than he had to prejudge Rose Tweedie's. Of course, there was the fact of George Keene's suicide against the one, but that was no new thing. She had been judged on that count before, and he had decided to save her from the pain of knowing it. To that decision, also, he meant to keep if it were possible. Gwen's heart gave a great throb; she understood in an instant that the crisis had come sooner than she expected; yet she was prepared for it.

"I suppose Rose Tweedie—" she began, coldly.

"Yes; Rose Tweedie asked my advice, and I've been down to that woman in the bazaar. She sticks to her story; so now I have come to you—"

"If you had come to me first, Lewis," she interrupted, with a vibration of real anger in her voice, "I would have warned you not to waste your time in playing Don Quixote at Rose Tweedie's bidding. The woman is an impostor and should be treated as such. I would have sent the police after her yesterday, had I thought it wise to take even so much notice of her lies. And now you have been to see her! It is too foolish, too annoying! And all because Rose went crying to you, I suppose, about her lover. Her lover, indeed! You are very soft-hearted, Lewis! Perhaps some day your desire to console will lead you into taking his place."

He stared at her. That sort of thing was so unlike Gwen's usual sweetness. But his surprise did not equal his confusion, and his common-sense showed him her possible wisdom. "Miss Tweedie did not cry over her lover, I assure you," he began—feeling, in very truth, that the young lady in question had meted out more blame than sympathy—"and I did not choose to allow such tales of you to pass unnoticed."

"So you listened to them again!" retorted Gwen, in rising anger which she wilfully exaggerated—"listened to what a common woman in the bazaar had to say of me! Really! I am obliged to you, Lewis! And she, I suppose, told you that I had stolen the pearls and the pot, and then taken it and a fresh bribe from poor George? Well, now that you have come to me at last for the truth, I tell you, as I told Rose—who perhaps did not repeat it—that I have never seen the thing since the night of the storm at Hodinuggar. So I have less to do with it than she; since she confesses it was sent to her, and that she sent it back on the sly. Did she tell you that? And have you been asking her for the truth, also? or am I the only one who has to be questioned like that creature in the bazaar?" Gwen had never looked better than she did, with the unwonted fire of real indignation lighting up her face, and Lewis Gordon felt vexed that it awoke no thrill in him. Was he really allowing Rose Tweedie's open mistrust to bias him? The idea made him reply more gently than he might otherwise have done.

"Perhaps you are right to be angry with me," he said, quietly. "I beg your pardon if I have hurt you; but indeed it seemed best to me at the time. Perhaps, as you say, it would have been better to wait awhile until, for instance, I can consult with Fitzgerald. I wired him to-day to come up on three days' urgent private business. He knows a lot."

Gwen gave an odd sort of laugh, not unlike a sob, and her face softened. "I'm glad he is coming," she cried, passionately; "very glad. He always understands, and he knows." Yes, he understood and trusted her—would stand by her even if he knew of that one fatal mistake—whereas Lewis would treat her as a Magdalen! as if she, Gwen Boynton, were a fit subject for a penitentiary! "Yes," she repeated, slowly, "I am glad he is coming. You did the right thing there, Lewis, at any rate."

So with this small consolation he had to make his way back to give his report to the girl who had told him that she loved him. Another delicate task, and he felt himself detestably awkward over it; the more so because Rose herself met him as if nothing unusual had occurred.

"Well," she asked, eagerly, "what news?" He told her briefly that there was none. He had had three versions of truth—her own, Chândni's, and Mrs. Boynton's, and there seemed nothing to be done save wait for Dan's arrival. He might be able to throw some light on the subject; he was the only person, at any rate, who was likely to do so.

"You forget the girl—the girl of the portrait, I mean," suggested Rose, quickly. He frowned; there were some things which he did not intend to tell Rose, and the story about Azîzan was one of them.

"She disappeared, they say, just before we reached Hodinuggar. I should like, by the way, to see the picture, if you don't mind." He stood looking at it in silence for some time. "And that, you say, was the face in your dream?" he asked at last.

"The face, the dress, the pot clasped so to her breast. I seem to grow more sure of it every hour. And I am certain now that it was she who said 'I am Azîzan.'"

"That sort of certainty grows upon one unconsciously," he replied, after another pause. "I confess it is odd; but you can hardly believe it really was the potter's daughter. She has been dead these sixteen years. You think it was her ghost, perhaps; but did George paint the ghost?"

Rose stood silent, her hands clasped tightly. "Who knows?" she said, slowly. "One knows so little. When I think of it all—of that strange old man with his refrain, 'We come and go, we go and come'—I seem to feel that odd, uncanny sense of helplessness which one has during a storm at sea when you realize that the waves are not moving at all, but rise and fall, rise and fall forever in the same place. It is the ship which drifts within their power, giving them their wrecker's chance once more; and now you will say that I am superstitious, but I almost regret that you should bring Mr. Fitzgerald into this business at all. You remember the potter's measure? Think of it, and how poor George himself—" She paused, her eyes full of tears.

Lewis, watching her, told himself he would never understand women-folk. Here was a girl overflowing with fanciful sentiment in some ways, who yet, apparently, had none to spare for the one subject round which sentiment was supposed to cling—love and marriage. In addition, here were two women, both of whom he desired to help, and yet they were at daggers-drawing about the best method of giving that aid. If he pleased one, he displeased the other; and, anyhow, he got no comfort out of either.

CHAPTER XXIV

"NAY, thou hast given me enough, O mirza *sahib*—more than a free woman cares to have," said Chândni, with a shrug of her massive shoulders. "Thou hadst thy chance to pay me fair."

Dalel Beg, clad in his European clothes, and perched, in all the isolation of an esteemed visitor, in the cane-bottomed chair of state, felt he would like to be on a level with those jeering lips, as he used to be at Hodinuggar. Not for the sake of desire only, or for the sake of revenge, but for a mixture of both. As usual, the very audacity of her wickedness fascinated him; yet now that wickedness was directed against himself, he could have strangled her for it.

"Pay thee! how can I pay thee," he whispered, "when those low-caste white swindlers with whom I betted will not pay what I have won; when those white devils of women turn the place into a museum, until every Parsee in the bazaar threatens to summon me to court?"

It was not much more than a week since he had defied Chândni in the presence of the said white devils; but the interval had not been pleasant. Beatrice Norma Elfrida's mamma knew all about Chândni's long years of hold on the mirza *sahib*, and he was totally unaccustomed to the nagging of wifely jealousy. Besides, something had happened which had opened his eyes to the danger of allowing the courtesan to have a free hand. A proposal had been made to the Canal Department to allow water to run permanently along the sluice cut; the râjah who owned the land to the south having spent a whole season at Simla in order to work the oracle, and the flood having come opportunely as a warning to the experts that it might be wise to provide a more satisfactory outlet for the surplus water. Now in this case Hodinuggar, which would benefit but little by the plan, being for the most part barren desert, might, by judicious application of the screw, make the râjah pay for its consent, as a considerable portion of its best land would have to be taken up for various works. This sort of secret intrigue, these almost endless ramifications of rights and dues, underlie the simplest transactions in India, and are recognized by its people as an integral part of administration. Besides, Hodinuggar itself, in lieu of compensation for damage done—which, for various reasons, it had not yet claimed, one being a delay on the part of the râjah in paying the promised fee for the opening of the sluice—might manage by the same judicious diplomacy to secure some trifling hold on the water supply; something, in short, which might be used as a screw for the extortion of a perpetual, if small, revenue. But for all this, silence as to the past was necessary. This, to European ears, may seem almost too fine-drawn to be worth consideration. To Dalel Beg and Chândni it was quite the reverse; for he came from a long line of courtiers born and bred in such intrigues; men whose trades had passed with the corrupt courts of other days, while the memory of it survived in their title: Dewans of Hodinuggar; not Nawâbs or Nizâms, but Dewans; that is, in other words, Prime Minister. And she? Every atom of her blood came from the veins of those who for centuries had woven a still finer net of woman's wit around the intrigues of their protectors. It is this extraordinary strength of heredity towards virtue as well as towards vice which, in India, makes the cheap tinkering of Western folks, who are compounded of butchers, bakers, and candlestick-makers, so exasperating to those who have eyes to see. If English philanthropists would spend their motley benevolence on the poor, the diseased, the drunken of their own country, it would be better both for it and for India, where the death-rate is no higher, drunkenness is comparatively unknown, and poverty is neither unhappy nor discontented.

Thus, Chândni and Dalel were well matched, as she leaned back in her cushions with a laugh. "So she spends money! Lo! since thou hast married a *vilayeti* wife, thou canst advertise, as the *sahibs* do, in the papers, that thou art not responsible for her debts. There is no sense in stopping half-way, as thou hast done. Thou shouldst have gone to a *missen* and been baptized, instead of making that half-caste girl repeat the 'Kulma' on the promise that thou wilt not in future claim the right of the faithful to other women. Yea! yea! I know the trick."

"If I have," muttered Dalel, vexed, yet pleased, at her boldness, her shrewdness, "such promises are easily broken. Divorce is easy."

"If thou hast money to pay the dower to her people, not otherwise; so both ways thou art snared."

That, she told herself, was always the result of trying new ways of wickedness instead of keeping to the old ones. She did not, and, on the whole, felt contemptuous over her adversaries so far. The miss *sahib's* arms were strong, for sure, but the men were worth nothing; not even the long *sahib*, who had come blustering to her about the pearls.

Dan Fitzgerald, dangling his long legs disconsolately from Lewis Gordon's office-table, allowed as much himself.

"The fact is, I ought to have killed her," he said; "only I didn't feel up to it to-day, after my journey. Oh, you may smile, Gordon!" he went on, more eagerly, his face losing some of its dejection in his love of the extravagant, "but it is true. That sort of woman doesn't belong to our civilized age. We are absolutely at a disadvantage before her. There was I, strong as a horse—as the mad old potter said, with a hero's measure round the chest—driven to words and threats of a policeman. I couldn't, even at the time, but think of that old sinner Zubr-ul-zamân, and what her chance would have been with him. Just an order, a cry, and then silence. Sure one feels helpless at times, when one stands face to face with that old world. What's the use of strength—what's even the use of brains—nowadays, except to make money? There was I, with that woman, I give you my word, at the end of her tether; but it was the hangman's rope for me if I went a step closer; and so I didn't."

"If you didn't," remarked Lewis, grimly, "there isn't a civilized man who will. So we had better try something else. Still, unless that woman is silenced, we must face an inquiry, and then the facts of poor Keene's death must come out. By the way, Miss Tweedie knows them, but we have agreed to keep them, if possible, from my cousin. There is no use—"

"I'm glad of that," interrupted Dan, with a sudden quiver of his mouth. "I should be sorry to have that memory spoiled." He was pacing up and down the room now, his hands in his pockets, the brightness of his face absorbed, as it were, by a frown.

"Gordon!" he said, abruptly, "I'd give everything I possess if I could lay my hands on that cursed pot. Not that it would satisfy that horse-leech's daughter unless it contained the pearls —which isn't likely—for I believe the whole story is a myth. But the thought that it is somewhere visible, palpable to the meanest fool on God's earth, is maddening. Or if we could say to that she-devil, 'Do your worst!' Oh! why didn't you send that wire sooner, and save poor George from his needless death?"

"Why didn't you tell the truth about it at first? You might as well ask that. It would have been better, as it turns out, if you had; but who could tell? As it is, I'm quite ready, as I told you before, to burke everything I can, in conscience; but, as far as I can see, it will do no good. If that woman breaks silence, the main facts must come to light."

"I wish I had killed her," said Dan, regretfully.

"And I wish she were dead," replied Lewis, cynically; "that is the difference between us. You are active, I'm passive; but we don't either of us seem to be of much use."

That was the truth; and they had to confess as much to Gwen Boynton that afternoon. She looked a little haggard as she listened, though she protested bravely that, in her opinion, that vile creature would never dare to put her lies to the proof. But they were playing at cross-purposes: for she could not tell them of the papers she held in absolute disproof of the first accusation; and they wished, if possible, to save her from the knowledge of George Keene's suicide. Perhaps if they had set their own feelings aside and told her, she might even then have confessed her lion's share in the blame. But only perhaps; for she was a clever woman, capable of seeing that her confession would do no good, and that she had, as it were, lost her right to save poor George from suspicion. Besides, she had brought herself to believe in the duty of denial; for, like many another woman, she required a really virtuous motive before she could do a really wrong thing. In sober fact, even in her worst aberrations from the truth, never losing hold of a fixed desire to be amiable and estimable. To this self-deception, as was natural, Lewis Gordon's half-hearted belief was gall and wormwood; while Dan's wholesale confidence was balm indeed. She could not refrain from telling him so when the former, pleading stress of work, left the latter alone with her beside the cosey little tea-table glittering in the firelight.

"Now don't spoil it all, dear, by wanting me to marry you to-morrow," she added, half laughing, half crying, when his pleasure at her words showed itself. "We are all too busy for such talk, and too sad—at least, I am. He was so good to me—you don't know how good. I shall break my heart if this vile creature succeeds in sullying his memory."

"It will not be your fault, dear, if she does." A chance shot may hit the quarry truer than the best aim, and Gwen turned quickly towards him with a little cry.

"Dan, you will prevent it, won't you? You are so clever, and really it is for my sake as well. For my sake you will, won't you?"

"I do everything for your sake—you know that," he answered, simply. Gwen stared at him as if she had seen a ghost. Perhaps she did—the ghost of a dead boy, who had said those very words to her in that very room not a month ago.

"Gwen, what is it?" came Dan's voice sharply, anxiously. "What is the matter—tell me!"

Yes, the past was repeating itself. George had begged her to tell him also, in much the same words; and in her selfishness, her fear, she had yielded and put a needless pain into a life passing to its close. She would not yield again; in denial lay her duty.

"Nothing is the matter," she echoed, "save this: that you say we can do nothing. I do not believe it. God will never let these lies prevail; he will never let my poor lad's memory suffer—never, never!"

If her mind could have been taken to pieces and strictly analyzed as she gave utterance to this burst of real feeling, it would have afforded fruitful study to a whole college of psychologists. Yet the mental condition described as "sitting in a clothes-basket and lifting yourself up by the handles" is quite common to humanity of both sexes, though women are the greater adepts in the art. Mrs. Boynton was really a firm believer in a Providence which was bound by many promises to help the virtuous. George, therefore, had a claim to its assistance. The fact that Providence might possibly have appointed her as its instrument was a totally different affair. So good faith and good feeling made her voice thrill as she went on fervently answering Dan's doubtful yet admiring face. "Oh, you mayn't think so; you perhaps don't believe as I do, Dan, in a 'Providence which shapes our ends, rough hew them as we will'; you don't—"

"Don't I?" he asked, catching fire, as it were, more from his own thoughts than from her words. "Oh, Gwen, my dear! it's little you know of me, then, if you think that. Don't I see it—who but the blind do not—in everything? Isn't it that which makes me content to go on as I'm doing? Gwen! it's because I know that it is bound to come; that sooner or later you will take my hands in yours, as I take yours just now. Yes, Gwen, it's fate; but when will it be, my dear—when will it be?"

She was never proof against this mood in the man; this tone in his voice. "Oh, Dan!" she cried, with a petulance that was all feigned, "didn't I say you would be asking me to marry you to-morrow if I was so rash as to tell you that you were a comfort to me? As if that had anything to do with it."

"Sure, it has everything to do with it!" cried her lover,

fondly. The future, in truth, gave him few fears. It was the present, with the chance of annoyance, if that venomous woman remained unscathed in the bazaar, which caused him anxiety. On the other hand, it was the future over which Lewis Gordon frowned as he sat trying to make up his mind about his own feelings. The present was unpleasant, but it was palpably clear that they must face the possibility of scandal boldly, when in all probability Chândni's story would break down utterly as regarded everybody save George. He, poor lad, had brought this on himself. But when all this was over, he (Lewis) was going to marry Mrs. Boynton. No doubt about it, for it was too late to judge her for that other fault—far too late. He had condoned it with the full knowledge of what he was doing, and the fact that Rose Tweedie's subsequent scorn had awakened a tardy blame did not alter the past. At the same time, he had an insane desire that Rose Tweedie should be brought to see this as clearly as he saw it. In fact, the idea of talking over the matter with her, and perhaps taking her advice on it, had an attraction for him; and though he heaped contumely on himself for the mere thought, it lingered insistently. It was partly that which made him pause to knock at her sitting-room door on his way to the drawing-room before dinner. She would be glad to have the last news of the miserable affair, he told himself, but in his heart he knew that was not the real reason—that he himself scarcely knew what the reason was. Reason? There was none. Only a foolish curiosity to understand better what this icicle of a girl meant by love. It did not seem to hurt her, at any rate. But as he entered to see her sitting there by the fire, the reading-lamp on the table lighting up her dress but leaving her face in shadow, he seemed to forget all these thoughts in the friendly confidence of her greeting.

"I'm so glad you have come. I was wondering if you would. What news?"

He shook his head. "None. We have all had our chance and failed."

"Not all," she answered, quickly, pointing to Azîzan's portrait, which showed dimly above the mantel-piece, against which he leaned. "You forget the girl; she has not yet said her say."

The unreality, the strangeness of it all, struck him sharply, not for the first time, as he replied, after a pause:

"And never will; she is dead. Fitzgerald managed to get that out of the woman to-day. She must have been hidden away, as a punishment, most likely, in some dungeon of the tower, for her dead body was found among the ruins—by—by the old potter. Yes, I know what you are thinking of; but that is impossible. He was always searching about, you know, and so it was more likely he would find—something—than others. It is a coincidence, I admit, but the fact of the death seems undoubted. The woman let it out in her anger—Fitzgerald is not a nice cross-examiner, I expect—and tried to glaze it over afterwards. Perhaps it is as well; her story may be best unknown."

"I don't agree with you," said Rose, quickly. "I have been counting on her help, perhaps more than I realized, and now that her chance is gone—" The girl's eyes filled with tears, and her voice failed her for a moment. "It seems as if we could do nothing more to save him."

"I'm afraid not. You see, once we begin to question outsiders we show our hand. There is no alternative between the silence and defiance which Gwen advocates so strongly and a bold and open inquiry. In my opinion, it is time for the latter. You see my cousin is not quite a fair judge; she does not know that so far Fitzgerald and I have concealed George Keene's suicide, and that from purely personal motives we—or, at least, I—cannot have this scandal sprung on me by an outsider. He would take the risk, he says; but I, in my position, conceive that it is not my duty to do so. He, however, has suggested that we four shall meet and talk it over finally before I take any action, so I took the liberty of asking Gwen to come down to-morrow morning. It is Fitzgerald's last day, and something must be done before he goes down. I don't see the use of this meeting myself—we have all, as I said, had our chance; but it can do no harm, and it may satisfy Gwen—and you."

"I am satisfied already," she replied, gently. "You could have done no more than you have done. I see that now."

"I am glad," he began, and then stopped short, realizing that he was not glad of the evident finality in her meaning. Was she contented that things should end as they had begun? Had her passionate interest in him died down with his obedience to her orders? A sorry reward, surely! A most perplexing result.

"I shall be glad," he corrected himself, almost angrily, "when we have got out of this muddle. Of course, I have heard before of such intrigues. But I never came in personal contact with that sort of thing before. It is maddening. I scarcely seem to know whether we are in the nineteenth century or the ninth. Ever since we met at Hodinuggar we seem to have got mixed up with some antique dream; the whole thing is absurd—scarcely credible."

As he spoke the dinner-bell rang, and he held the door open for her to pass from the consideration of these things to the well-appointed table, worthy of a house in Belgravia, where the dark-skinned, white-robed servants handed sherry with the soup and vinegar with the salmon quite as naturally as Jeames or John in their plush liveries. But heredity was here also; Jeames's father may have been a day-laborer; but not one of these could not have answered, truthfully, "*Huzoor*, my father was servant to so and so, or so and so, in the Great Mutiny time, and his father served such and such a *sahib* in the Sutlej campaign, or in Cabul, or somewhere else"—faithfulness or unfaithfulness to salt being a different question; though that also might be one of heredity. Such thoughts strike one sometimes after years of complacent blindness, and on this evening they increased the sense of unreality which had already taken possession of Lewis Gordon. Nor did a remark of Colonel Tweedie's on his daughter's improved looks during the past few days amend matters. He felt that he might be living in that twenty-ninth century, when humanity may reasonably be supposed to have educated itself out of some frailties, as, in the necessary glance at the young lady's face required by decorous assent, he met a perfectly unconscious, happy smile; so full of friendly confidence that a positive gladness glowed at his heart that she should be content with him. Nevertheless, he made one more effort to get back finally to the every-day world by riding over to the club after dinner and listening to the gossip of the day. There was nothing wrong with the world. It was going on as usual. He played a game or two of pool, talked gravely with Major Davenant over some new rules intended to prevent such another *fiasco* as the last race-meeting, heard the latest official canards, and listened, more patiently than usual, to some boys who had to go down from leave next day, bemoaning the general beastliness of the country as a residence for an English gentleman. It was only, so the verdict ran, fit for niggers. Yet even this demonstration, that life in the main was commonplace as usual, did not restore Lewis Gordon's general indifference. And the knowledge that this was so made him more than ever determined to carry his point when, next morning, the four met in Rose Tweedie's room to settle the course of events.

The rain, after a downpour in the night, had ceased; or perhaps had become too light to make its way through the thick, white mist which had settled down like cotton-wool upon everything, blotting out the world. There was not a breath of air, not a sound, save occasionally a soft *pit, pat,* as the vapor, condensing on the roof, dropped into the hearts of the rain lilies which fringed the veranda with their upturned orange cups. Yet it was neither dark nor dull, as on a cloudy day. The whiteness of the mist was almost luminous, and through the wide-set windows sent a faint glow, like that from newly-fallen snow, on the faces of poor George Keene's friends, and showed still more clearly on the even surface of Azîzan's portrait, as it stood upon the mantel-shelf. Rose stood beside it, looking beyond everything in the room, beyond the row of orange lilies, into the cotton-wool mist which seemed bent on suffocating the house and its inhabitants. There was silence in the room; the silence which comes to a discussion when the last objection has palpably fallen through, and a conclusion, absolutely satisfactory to no one, seems inevitable. Gwen, a flush of excitement on her cheek, lay back among the cushions of her easy-chair nervously turning and twisting the rings upon her fingers. Dan Fitzgerald, who was seated close beside her, had evidently been the last to speak, and was now leaning towards her, his eyes fixed with kindly encouragement and sympathy on her face. Lewis Gordon, his elbows resting on the table, apart from the others, looked half-regretful, half-resentful; the look of a man who knows he must take the initiative in a singularly disagreeable duty.

At last, through the silence came Rose Tweedie's voice, reluctant, yet with a sort of challenge in it. "I suppose that is settled, and that we can none of us suggest any other reason why we should delay longer."

"I have told you before," broke in Mrs. Boynton, "that I have every reason to believe that no action will be taken by this woman; that she will never court inquiry."

"I did not mean that," replied Rose, still with the same note in her voice. "I meant that if none of us have any further knowledge beyond what we have already discussed, Mr. Gordon's plan for a private, yet open inquiry, with my father's knowledge, seems the best. I, for one, have none. I know nothing, absolutely nothing, in favor of delay. Nothing that would prevent the possible danger to George Keene's memory."

Lewis Gordon followed fast on her words in swift, vexed comprehension of her challenge. "I fancy we are all able to say the same, Miss Tweedie. If we agree, I may have to speak of something I should not otherwise mention, but it is no reason for delay. On the contrary, it is a reason why open inquiry will be the safest, even for George Keene's memory. I know nothing better. I wish I did."

"Nor I," said Dan Fitzgerald, then paused, and, rising from his chair, crossed to the open door, whence he looked out, as Rose had done, beyond the rain lilies to the mist. "I know better than any of you what George was, I know better than any of you what he did, and if this is settled I, too, will have to tell something to his credit—something that will make inquiry the better for him. Yet I'd give all I possess to save the necessity for it. But I'm lost"—he stretched his hands out impulsively into the mist—"lost as any one might be out yonder—lost, as the lad's own explanation is lost in the mystery of his death. It's hard to say so, George, but I can't help it."

He spoke as if to somebody out of sight, and Gwen Boynton sat up suddenly, nervously, with a scared look in her eyes.

"I think you are all wrong," she said, querulously. "The woman must know that proof is against her story; but you will not believe it, and so I cannot help it, I cannot, indeed." Her voice died away to a sort of sigh, and she sank back again clasping her hands tightly together. Rose let hers fall from its grip on the mantel-piece. Dan's tall figure leaned more loosely against the lintel, and Lewis Gordon mechanically turned the leaves of a book lying beside him on the table. The tension was over, and the relief of decision, even of helpless decision, held them silent in the silence for the moment. They had done their best. They had played their part in the strange play.

Then suddenly, out of the mist, a quavering, chanting voice:

"It was a woman seeking something,
Through day and night—"

"Listen!" said Dan, his face ablaze. Rose's hand went up again, suddenly, to the picture, and Lewis started to his feet. Only Gwen looked from one to the other, bewildered.

"O'er hill and dale seeking for something."

The voice grew clearer, as if the singer were toiling up the unseen path below the lilies.

"Foul play! Foul play! look down and decide."

"The mad potter," cried Dan, with wonder in his tone.

"Azîzan! it is her turn at last," cried Rose, with a hush in her voice which sent a thrill through Lewis Gordon. But he only said, prosaically:

"I'll go and see who it is."

But Dan had forestalled the thought, and, vaulting the railings, had disappeared into the mist. They could hear him hallooing down the path to the unseen singer, as they stood waiting by the lilies. Then came a quick greeting and a low reply; so, clearer and clearer—though they could see nothing—every syllable of eager questioning, till, as if from behind a veil, a strange couple stepped into sight: Dan, eager, excited, towering above the bent, deprecating figure of the old potter.

They had heard so much that Rose, without a pause, could step to meet them, and strike at the very root of the matter. "What is it? What is it that you want of me?"

The shifty light eyes settled on her face with a look of relief before the old man bent to touch her feet. "*Mâdr-mihrbân*," he said, "*Mâdr-mihrbân!* that is well."

He was still breathless from his swifter climb beside Dan's long stride, and as he straightened himself again, his supple fingers, busied already in a knotted corner in the cotton shawl folded round him, trembled visibly.

"Lo! I sent it before," he went on, in low excuse, "but it returned, as all things return at Hodinuggar. Then she was vexed and could not rest. "Send it back!" she cried, all night long. Pity of God! what a fever; but now she sleeps sound—" He paused to fumble closer at the knot.

"You mean Azîzan, your daughter?" suggested Rose, softly, while the others stood silent, listening and looking, the whole world seeming to hold nothing for them save this tall girl with her bright, eager face, and that bent old man trying to undo a knot.

"*Huzoor!* Azîzan!" came the quivering voice. "I looked for her so often till the *Mâdr-mihrbân* came. Then I found her with the pot clasped to her breast, but the bad dreams would not let her sleep. 'It is not mine! it is hers!' It kept her awake always. So when I found her again lying asleep by the river, with it still in her bosom, I said to myself, 'I will not set a writing on it, and put it in a box with a slit as I did last time, trusting it to God knows who in the new fashion. I will take it myself in the old fashion and give it to the *Mâdr-mihrbân's* own hands, and pray her to hold it fast so it return not to wake my child; for she sleeps sound at last in the dust of her fathers.'"

The knot was undone. The shaking fingers held the Ayôdhya pot for a second, the white glare of the mist shining in a broad blaze of light upon the intense glowing blue. The next, it had slipped from the potter's hand, and lay in fragments on the ground. Still fragments of sapphire color; moving fragments of milky white, rolling hither and thither like drops of dew on a leaf seeking a resting-place for their round lustre.

Pearls! The Hodinuggar pearls!

And Gwen's voice, with a triumphant ring in it, became articulate above the old man's cry of distress and the low exclamation of the others.

"So Azîzan stole them, after all!"

Rose turned on her sharply. "Who knows? This much is certain: she has brought them back, and saved George Keene's memory when we could not."

"Yes, she has saved him," assented Dan. "We have that she-devil on the hip now!"

Lewis Gordon stood silent for a moment; he had grown very pale. "You are both right, I expect," he said, quietly. "It settles everything—everything."

Gwen drew a long breath of relief, but Rose seemed lost in thought. "No, not everything," she said, absently, half to herself; "it does not tell us why George shot himself." She scarcely knew she spoke aloud; she had forgotten everything but the dead boy.

"Shot himself!" The words came back to her in a sort of cry. "Shot himself! What do you mean? What does she mean?"

Gwen stood as if petrified before those regretful faces; then as the truth struck at her, beating down her shield of self-deception, she turned, at last, forgetful of all else, to the shelter of Dan's kind arms.

"Oh, Dan! Dan! it isn't true—it can't be true! say it isn't true!"

He drew her closer to him, looking down into her agonized face with a perfect passion of tenderness and kissed it, forgetful, in his turn, of everything save that she had come to him at last.

"It is true, my darling; he did it to save me and you. Gwen! Gwen! it wasn't your fault. My God! she has fainted."

"I'm sorry," began Rose, feeling paralyzed by surprise.

But Dan's kind smile was ready, even in his distress. "Don't worry. It's best over, for I must have told her. You see, we have been engaged for years, and George knew it. If I carry her to your room, Miss Rose, she will be better there. 'Tis the shock, and she was so fond of him—dear heart!"

Left alone in the veranda while another man, before his very eyes, carried off the woman to whom he supposed himself engaged, Lewis Gordon felt that the world had broken loose from its foundations altogether. So that was the explanation! And then a low murmur of mourning from the potter arrested his attention, which, as is so often the case after a shock, had lost its balance and become vagrant. The old man, still crouched beside the fragments of the Ayôdhya pot, was rocking himself backward and forward and muttering to himself, "She will be angry; the *Mâdr-mihrbân* will be angry, and then Azîzan will not sleep."

Lewis Gordon walked up to him, and laid his hand, reassuringly, on the thin, bent shoulders. "I don't think the *Mâdr-mihrbân* will be angry. I'm almost sure she won't." His own words made him smile, until, as he looked at the old man's shifty light eyes raised to his doubtfully, he remembered the young sad face which George had painted. "And Azîzan is asleep," he said, gently; "she will not wake again." As he stooped to gather up the jewels, his eyes were dim with unwonted tears—why, he scarcely knew.

When Rose came back, ten minutes after, leaving Gwen to Dan's kind consolation, she found Lewis leaning over the railings, looking at the rain lilies through his eye-glass as if it had been a microscope. He turned to her with the air of a man who has made up his mind.

"You thought I was engaged to my cousin, Miss Tweedie," he said. "So did I. Apparently, I was mistaken. So let us set that aside, once and for all, and think over more important matters. There is no lack of other surprises, thank Heaven."

The semi-cynicism of his words did not set ill on him, and Rose recognized that he had certainly chosen the most dignified way out of the difficulty. At the same time, it left her free to consider the position as an outsider, and all involuntarily, yet naturally enough, her first thought expressed itself in words.

"I wonder what father will say?"

This was too much both for temper and dignity—fortunately also for humor; he gave her one indignant look, then relapsed into a smile. "Really, Miss Tweedie, in this comedy of errors I am only responsible for my part; and that, believe me, is rather a sorry one."

CHAPTER XXV

WHETHER Lewis Gordon spoke truth or not regarding the part he had to play, there could be no doubt that Dan found his anything but sorry. A subdued sort of radiance softened yet brightened the man as he came out to ask Rose for the loan of her *dandy*, as Mrs. Boynton was anxious to get home as soon as possible. There seemed no need for words; the situation explained itself. And even Lewis, looking at his rival's face, could not help acknowledging that Dan was more likely to give Gwen the support she really needed than he was. Besides, the sudden change in the future seemed lost sight of in that which the opportune arrival of the Ayôdhya pot had on the present and on Chândni's impudent claim. It was, of course, clear evidence against the truth of the story as far as Gwen was concerned; but whether it would prevent the woman raking up the facts of George Keene's death, out of sheer wanton malice, was another thing. Lewis felt himself rather helpless before the phenomenon of such a nature as hers, and confessed as much when Dan came racing back breathless and excited, after having seen Mrs. Boynton safely home, for a council of war. He brought a quick decision and intuition with him. The sluice had been opened by treachery, of course; now that he was free to speak of his engagement, Dan told the story of the open locket, which to him seemed proof positive that George had voluntarily taken the blame on himself when thrown off his balance by the discovery that the happiness of the man and the woman he loved best in the world depended on Dan's getting his promotion. How the sluice had been opened was another thing; Chândni said by means of a key made after an impression sent from Simla. But this was manifestly impossible, unless some servant had done it. Indeed, he had never paid much attention to this assertion, for the woman, in making it, had contradicted herself more than once, and evidently had no definite story as to how the impression had been secured. In his own mind he had determined that the key itself had been stolen from the boy while he slept heavily, and that the knowledge that this was so had had its share in bringing about the rash act. So that even if the real facts came out, nothing beyond carelessness could be laid to George's charge, now that the potter was there to prove that the girl had had the Ayôdhya pot all the time, and they were there to prove that the pearls had remained in the pot. So much for Chândni and the only possible cause of further action—a woman's wanton cruelty. For the rest, the old dewan was dead, Khushâl seemed to be out of it, and Dalel had everything to lose and nothing to gain by a scandal. These intrigues were as a house of cards: remove one support and the whole structure disappeared.

"Nevertheless," said Dan, looking across the table with a grim smile, "I'm not going to take you down as a witness to my interview with that she-devil this afternoon. You are too fine for the task, and that's a fact."

"Can I lend you anything peculiarly barbaric in the way of a knife?" asked Lewis. "I've a Malay crease in my room which fills most people with alarm, though personally I should funk at a *woorali* dart more than anything."

"Oh, you may jeer; but 'tis true. Sure, it's at the bottom of half our mistakes in this country. Even in our kindness we treat these people as we would like to be treated ourselves; it's poor philanthropy, besides, treating them as they would like to be treated. And when we come to mere justice! we might as well give a child the right to appeal against his mother when he has disobeyed her. What chance would the child have, to begin with, and then what good would it do? What good is our complicated system of procedure, save to put power into the hands of the educated few, who naturally clamor for more. But there! this has nothing to do with Chândni. She wouldn't care a tinker's dam for what you'd say to her, because you would be regulating yourself by codes and sections, instead of by the way she is made. I won't. I don't mind stooping to her level to get my will. So let me go with the old mad potter and his eyes, and see if between us we can't make a settlement. And then, please God, we will have done with the whole bad dream from beginning to end. So if you have three thousand rupees you can spare on a loan, I'll just have them handy in my pocket as a salve to her wounded feelings when I've got my own way."

What really happened at the bazaar Dan resolutely refused to say. On his return from the bazaar he asked for a whiskey-and-soda and a hot bath to take the taste of it out of his soul and body. Yet he returned triumphantly with a written declaration signed by Chândni, stating that she had stolen the key from George while he slept.

"It isn't true, of course," said Dan, with a rueful look at Lewis, "but, upon my soul, no one could tell if it were true or not. My mind seemed a vast cobweb, with lines going every way into the outside world, but all beginning in that woman. The only way was to smash through it; and she has done worse things — that's one comfort. Maybe the pearls should have gone back to Hodinuggar direct; but she will make her bargain there, never fear. And, by God, they deserve—"

He broke out, then, into curses and the tale of Azîzan's birth, which, it seems, had been his strong card—that and the potter's eyes. He had played the one against the other till he wormed the story out of his enemy, while the old man waited below, ready, if Dan failed, to be told the truth, and bring his evil glance to bear on the question. That fear had really settled it. She had acknowledged the part Azîzan had had in bringing her plans to nought, and confessed the wisdom of dancing to a different tune in the future.

"So we parted on the best of terms. She offered me cinnamon tea and fritters, and I took some as a sign of peace," finished Dan, with a final shudder. "And now I must be off to tell poor Gwen 'tis all settled forever." He lingered a minute as he rose to say, with a half-shy, half-happy smile, "Were you very much surprised, old man."

"Very," replied Lewis, with dignity. But Dan still lingered.

"I wonder what on earth the colonel will say," he remarked, after a pause, apprehensively. Then Lewis laughed; he could not help it. And actually the thought of playing second fiddle to Colonel Tweedie's disappointment in the eyes of the world helped him materially in the interview which he had with his cousin next morning. Even without this, however, he would have found it difficult to be severe, for he found her full of remorse and self-abasement—rather vague, perhaps, but still real. She would never forgive herself, she said, not so much about her indecision about Dan—she had always loved him, and Lewis was well quit of her selfish regard—no! it was about poor George! She had sided with Simla in turning the poor boy's head; she had made too much of him, and had behaved most unwisely—really, Lewis must let her say what she knew to be true; she had been over-friendly, over-confidential, and had asked him to do too much for her. All this and his foolish fancy about being the keeper of Dan's conscience, of which the latter had told her, had been too much for the dear lad's kind, sensitive heart. Then the terrible home-coming, after all the pleasure and spoiling! Was not that enough, more than enough, to upset the balance? She was so insistent on this point that Lewis had to confess his assent to it, and finally went away feeling that she had more heart than he had given her credit for in the past, and that he might be in a measure responsible for not having appealed to this better nature while he had the chance. Dan seemed to have done it successfully, for she had evidently given up all thoughts of a mercenary marriage! He understood her, she said, plaintively; he knew her faults, and yet he loved her; while Lewis—he must forgive her saying so—had always treated her as if she had no heart, no sentiment; had always committed the unpardonable mistake of making her remember that she did not love him. Of course, she had behaved abominably to everybody—far worse than they would allow, for they were all too good for her; but in the future she would have Dan, who was a tower of strength to her.

In fact, like many another woman of her type—many a man, too—Gwen Boynton had taken refuge from the greater remorse in the lesser one, if, indeed, there was a greater one; if, indeed, the real limit of her sin had not been that over-confidence to which she had confessed. Not in detail, truly; still, she had confessed it with tears to Dan, and he had forgiven her *en masse*—as, no doubt, he would forgive in detail if she had thought it right to tell him what she had told George. But what right had she to put this pain into another man's life, or speak of that vague fear which even Chândni's confession of having stolen the key would not smother utterly? It would be worse than foolish! it would be wicked; and this dreadful doubt was her cross, her punishment, which she thoroughly deserved for doing as she had done. And then, when she had got so far, her remorse was once more clear, open channel, where it could spread itself out and lose its chill under the sunshine of Dan's kind consolations.

Thus it really turned out that, after all, the person most upset by this unexpected *dénouement* of affairs was Colonel Tweedie.

"Engaged for years!" he said, angrily, in reply to his daughter's information. "Well, I am surprised! A most extraordinary proceeding, which—er—er complicates the—er— If you had said 'of late,' I might have seen some sense in it, for during the last week or so even Gordon—who is generally to be relied upon—has been absent over his work—er—not to say somewhat negligent. And, of course, being his cousin—the—er—interest—"

Rose hastened to confess that the engagement had only, as it were, been a definite one during—here she hesitated a little—the last few days. Which tribute to his perspicacity soothed the colonel's dignity, and encouraged him to further ventures in the seer's path by a suggestion that, no doubt, his daughter's improved appetite and appearance, which he had observed during the same period, was due to the proverbial interest which women took in the matrimonial affairs of their neighbors; though for his part he must say that the friendly admiration he had had for Mrs. Boynton had been very considerably impaired by—er—the lack of judgment she had displayed in engaging herself to an assistant engineer; a man whose promotion, he believed, could not possibly come before the following July—if then. He went off to discuss the departmental lists with portentous gloom, leaving his daughter defenceless before the truth. Certainly, she had been much happier since Lewis had known the truth. What is more, Mrs. Boynton's decision in favor of Dan was a great relief in one way; in another, however, it was disturbing, confusing; for, despite her theories, Rose felt that the fact of his freedom to make other ties did make a difference in her relations with Lewis Gordon. It ought not to, of course; she was angry with herself for admitting it, but she was totally unable to juggle with realities. No thought of marriage, or what she was pleased to call sentimental rubbish, had marred the self-forgetfulness of that unpremeditated appeal she had made to her belief in him. No such thought existed now, and that the fear of it should creep in was intolerable, absurd. No! she must feign the virtue of unconsciousness, even if she had it not, and by an increase of friendly confidence, combined with a strict attention to prose, prevent the awkwardness of the position from falling on innocent Lewis, and show him clearly that the altered situation had made no change in her, and was not expected to make any change in him. Only by these means could she show him—what was really the truth—that her avowal of interest was not mere sentiment.

Lewis, for his part, also tackled the position with a boldness which he had denied to himself while he was still engaged to his cousin, still smarting under the curiously mixed sensations which the knowledge of the girl's real feelings had aroused. Then he felt bound to conventional modes of thought; and, to tell the truth, had been more or less afraid lest, on inquiry, a sentimental love for Rose might pop up somewhere like a Jack-in-the-box. For her confession had affected him in a perfectly incomprehensible way; and the only other explanation of it he had been loath to admit, since it ran counter to all his pet theories. What feeling could there be between a man and a woman save the one feeling? This warmth at his heart when he thought of her praise, this pain at the thought of her blame, could only be the old, old story. And yet he had been in love before, and this was not the same experience. Well, it might be milk-food suited to babies and women. It was not strong meat for men; withal it was strangely satisfying, strangely final. So that when a return to commonplace diet became possible he found himself in two minds about it. She, however, evidently had but one; she evidently had given all she intended to give, and the only return he could make was by showing her that he did not misunderstand this, and that he did not think it necessary to salve over her wounded modesty by making love to her. Wounded modesty! The very thought seemed an insult. He could not agree with her theories altogether; but he could at least respect them.

So for the next month, while Gwen was slowly recovering from her shock, and all Simla was divided into factions over her engagement to penniless Dan Fitzgerald, a very pretty little comedy was being enacted in the big house where Rose, as hostess, treated Lewis Gordon as a friend, and he returned the compliment in kind. There was absolutely no humbug, no effort about it all. They were not in love with each other; they were not restless, or moody, or excited, but absolutely content and happy with things as they were: a state of affairs accentuated by the relief from anxiety, the improving weather, and the charming gayety and *verve* of the society in which they lived. Thus it happened that Rose Tweedie had her chance of being wooed in the only possible way in which girls of her type can be wooed. One sees dozens of them nowadays in society; one will see more and more, year by year, as the unnatural disproportion in the number of the sexes tends to intensify the seclusion of the nicest girls from the men. It is not the fault of the latter. In a bevy of several hundred young ladies, the fortunate possessor of the handkerchief throws it at some of those who press forward into individuality, or at some fair face which even a crush cannot hide.

So the choice of a wife falls on either beauty or brass. The latter may be too hard a term, yet the girls who are the most likely to make faithful wives, the most devoted mothers, are not those who are readiest to attract or assent. On the contrary, they do not fall in love easily, and men have no time to give them friendship. Friendship! They are engaged, nay married, before the mere thought of such a thing crops up.

So the younger generation of girls is rapidly dividing itself into the girls who dress and the girls who don't dress. In other words, those willing to attract men by one certain, if seamy, side of their natures, and those who are not so willing. Who does not know the opposite extremes of these two factions?—the girl who forces you instinctively to think of a looking-glass, and the girl who makes you wonder if there be such a thing in her room; the girl with not a hair out of place, and the girl with a hiatus between her skirt and blouse—between her soul and her body, as the feminine phrase runs. Rose belonged outwardly to neither faction, yet in her heart she strenuously resented the old-fashioned theory that marriage was the larger half of a man's life and the whole of a woman's. Truthfully, though she was three-and-twenty, she had never felt the slightest desire to marry anybody, not even Lewis, and she felt proportionately grateful to him for behaving, at any rate, as if he believed that fact.

Yet, even so, they sometimes found each other out, as, for instance, one day when he came back from his cousin's, full of unexpected news. Dan Fitzgerald had sent in his resignation to the department, and had accepted the offer of employment in Australia.

"I'm as glad," said Lewis, heartily, "as if I had had the chance myself; partly because I couldn't make anything of it! Brown—that is the man who has wired for him—was out here contracting one of the big railway bridges. A bloated mechanic—began life as a rivetter sort of fellow, but with a knack of making money and with a keen eye for business beyond belief. I remember his telling me that Dan was too good for us, and that if ever he came across a job in which he needed help, he would try and steal him. This is some huge irrigation scheme—private—down South. If Dan succeeds, and he will if any one can, there will be millions in it."

"I suppose your cousin is delighted," said Rose.

"Gwen? Never saw a woman so relieved in my life. For, mind you, though she is so awfully fond of Dan—fonder than I personally should have thought she could have been of any one—the idea of the poverty was telling on her. You know it *is* absurd to think of her as an assistant engineer's wife. It is really not an environment in which she was likely to shine, and, when all is said and done on the romantic side, people ought to consider surroundings in making a settlement for life. Besides, I am sure she is relieved to get away from us all and make a fresh start. She feels it more than I could have expected."

"Mr. Gordon," said Rose, suddenly, "I'm very sorry I judged her so harshly that—that time. I've wanted to say so often; then it seemed foolish—as if it could have mattered what I said or thought."

"I don't think it really did matter," he replied, frankly; "rather the other way round, I expect. Yet, if you did judge her harshly, it could hardly have been as harshly as she judges herself now; so it is far better she should leave all these associations behind. If he and she had had to go inspecting at Hodinuggar, or even if she had had to meet Dalel Beg and his wife (did I tell you that I saw her at the viceregal squash yesterday—a perfect child, in the most awful get-up?), why, then, it would revive the old affair. And if by chance—" he paused a moment. "One never knows what may crop up, and Dan is a queer chap in some ways. He works by instinct, as it were, and hitherto it has led him right. If it didn't and he found it out, I don't know what mightn't happen. He is not what I call a very safe man unless he is successful. So they are both lucky to get out of the uncongenial atmosphere which government service is to him and poverty is to her. They start in smooth water; and I must buy my wedding-present, for they are to be married next month."

"So soon!"

"He has to leave at once. The wedding is to be at Rajpore, after we all go down. No bridesmaids; and I'm best man. If you want to know the wedding-dress, ask Gwen. She is sure to have it settled long ago. Women always do."

"I haven't," protested Rose, hastily. "I shall be married in my every-day things." She tried hard to be grave while Lewis roared with laughter, but in the end she joined in the joke against herself. For they never quarrelled now. What was there to quarrel about?

It was on another of those pleasant, peaceful days that he came to lunch with the news that Dalel Beg was even now detaining her father by abject apologies for past old-style misdemeanors at Hodinuggar, and profuse promises that in the future it would be the abode of all civilized virtues. Khushâl Beg, it appeared, had died of apoplexy, brought on, no doubt, by the unrestrained orgies with which the fat man had celebrated his accession, and, in consequence, Dalel was king.

"I don't quite understand it all," he said, thoughtfully. "He is a fool, yet he is playing his cards well. Do you know that I shouldn't be at all surprised to hear that Chândni was back again as chief adviser. She is a very clever woman. It seems that there is a scheme on foot for establishing stud-farms, or grazing-paddocks, for government remounts. It is supposed to be cheaper and better in the end to buy them as yearlings and let them run loose, instead of being tethered, heels, heads, and tails, native fashion. And as the water supply is to be constant at Hodinuggar now, Dalel proposes that government should utilize some of his waste-land there, and put him in charge, or partly in charge. Of course, it will bring him in a steady income if he gets his finger in the pie."

"He ought to get nothing," interrupted Rose, hastily. "I believe he was at the bottom of all that intrigue. We shall never know what went on exactly, but there was intrigue, and that sort of thing should be punished."

"Undoubtedly. But, as I said before, Dalel is a fool—except about a horse. It was the old man and Chândni; they belong to that age. This man tries to break the Ten Commandments in two languages, and spoils the idiom of both. But he does know the points of a horse, and as government must keep up these old families and try to civilize them, it is as well to get some work out of them."

"Hodinuggar civilized! I can't imagine it," echoed Rose. "When I think of that old potter and that mirrored room on the roof, of Azîzan and the Ayôdhya pot, it seems like some old dream of life into which we nineteenth-century folk strayed by mistake."

"With disastrous results," put in Lewis, thoughtfully. "Well, with half the *dramatis personæ* of the play dead and the other half married, it should have come to an end like a decently-behaved drama. Not a very moral play, I'm afraid, Miss Tweedie, and virtue must be its own reward."

"What do you mean?" she asked.

"You and I have been left out of the prizes altogether; but then, as the potter said, we didn't belong to his world."

"I wish you had not reminded me of that scene," she interrupted, hastily. "I cannot help thinking of how Mr. Fitzgerald sat smiling at me while the old man measured him—just as George did when he measured himself, and he is dead."

"What a woman you are, when all is said and done!" he replied, smiling at her. "Still, I do think that poetic justice has not been meted out fairly all round. Gwen, for instance, has everything she wants, and I am out in the cold."

"Do you feel out in the cold?" asked Rose, quite aggressively. He hastened to assure her that, on the contrary, he was quite warm and comfortable; but, in spite of this, the conversation languished till Colonel Tweedie came in full of his intention of recommending Dalel's plan strongly to the authorities.

To say, however, that it was Dalel Beg's plan was, as Lewis Gordon had expected, to credit that gentleman with too much sense. It was Chândni's. When Dan Fitzgerald had left her, after partaking in a friendly fashion of cinnamon tea, she had put the pearls away in a safe place, and had looked after Dan as he rode away without the least malice, saying that there was a man indeed—one of the old sort, like the dewan; and if he had had her in the olden days, say, at Hodinuggar, there would just have been one order and then silence. She nodded her head and smiled over the thought. But now she had three thousand rupees and the pearls. She could not sell these, of course—could not, at present, let anybody know she had them; they were too well known, these Hodinuggar pearls, for Chândni to traffic in them without fear of being accused of theft. By-and-by, perhaps, she must trade them off on Dalel; but nothing of that sort was safe as long as Khushâl was alive. So long, too, as the palace-folk thought that the *mem* had them, they would not dare to move in the matter, now there was all this talk of a permanent water supply. For Chândni, in the wooden-balconied house at Simla, heard all the latest talk, and had quite a bevy of respectable native gentlemen, who drank sherbets at her expense. She heard also from a friend at court of this taking up of waste-land; and as she listened to all the stir of intrigue after this thing and that thing, she felt a pang of regret for that vanished dream of some day being a motive-power in Hodinuggar. This court life was as the breath of her nostrils, and if she had been in the place of that half-caste girl down in the house with the dahlias, she would not have been half-starved and beaten; for, if bazaar rumor said sooth, Dalel Beg had carried his Occidental estimate of the marriage-tie to this almost incredible length.

Then one day, after a rich Hindoo contractor roused her wrath by claiming her more or less as his especial property by reason of the money he had chosen to lavish on her, came the news of Khushâl Beg's death in the odor of court sanctity. She could imagine it all, down in the ruined palace out in the desert: the old ways, the old etiquette; poverty-stricken, maybe, yet still courtly. And why, in these pushing days, when fat pigs like that Hindoo made money, should they remain poverty-stricken? Even so, it was better to be Chândni of Hodinuggar than Chândni of a bazaar, especially as one grew older. That same afternoon a patchwork-covered *dhooli* went jolting down to the house with the dahlias—a miserable spot now, deserted, forlorn. A miserable room also, whence the indignant Parsees had reft the French clocks and the bric-à-brac. A most miserable pair of women, too, reduced to cooking their own food at the drawing-room fire, lest their overlooking neighbors might see them in the degradation of the cook-room, the deepest degradation of all in Eurasian eyes being to be servantless.

"Don't be a fool!" said Chândni to Mrs. D'Eremao's shrill abuse, as the former walked in upon them unceremoniously, and, squatting down, went on calmly chewing betel. "You have nothing to do with the business; but if she is wise, she will listen." Beatrice Norma Elfrida looked at her shrewdly and said, "Be quiet, mamma; there is no harm in hearing what she has to say."

Not much, but to the point. No doubt they had appealed to English justice, and they could force the dewan, now that he was dewan, to support his wife. But how? At Hodinuggar, under lock and key? It would not be nice, and Chândni had tales to tell which made Mrs. D'Eremao's hair stand on her head, even while she protested she was a freeborn British subject. Doubtless; but then they must give up all hopes of the position for which the girl had married such an atrocity. Here Beatrice Norma Elfrida dissolved into tears. That was not the way to treat a Mahomedan gentleman, an offshoot of the Great Moguls; but for a consideration she was quite willing to use her influence with Dalel to set things straight. She did not want him, and had flouted his proposals of peace a dozen times; but she was quite ready, for a consideration, to make herself useful. Briefly, that consideration was a free hand if she could get it, no cabals against her position, and an assignment in case of Dalel's death of a good slice of that State pension which in such case would be given to the wife. If there were children, so much the better, since the pension would be larger. The offer was a fair one; besides, to refuse it would not amend the position, since Dalel would no doubt bribe Chândni back in some way or other.

A week after this, the name of Her Highness Beatrice Norma

Elfrida, of Hodinuggar, appeared on the list of donors to a certain charitable fund, opposite to no less a sum than one thousand rupees, and she herself appeared at the next viceregal squash in full native costume. Her hair was quite straight and many shades darker in color, and she sat and talked affably to a stout English matron about her husband's great desire to assimilate the lives of Indian women more closely to those of their European sisters. So that on her return home the stout English matron mentioned to her stout English husband, who happened to be a commissioner, that the Hodinuggar creature seemed to have ideas, and should be encouraged.

And that evening Dalel said to Chândni, ere he left the little balconied room where so many grave and reverend gossip-mongers sat drinking sherbet, "Thou wilt return to Hodinuggar, as thou hast promised?"

"I will return; but not as before. I am free to come and go. And see that thou pay me back that thousand rupees out of the first batch of horses. Else Chândni goes, never to come again."

CHAPTER XXVI

It was a hot October. The rains, coming early, had stopped early, giving Lewis Gordon and Rose that charming, sunshiny month in the hills of which mention has been made—a whole month of almost idyllic happiness and content. And now, after the usual hiatus of a visit or two for Rose *en route*, and a hasty tour for her father round some outlying canals, they had settled down again for the cold-weather life at Rajpore. Perhaps it was only the rather unusual heat which made it seem less pleasing to at least two of the party than it was generally. More so, however, to Lewis Gordon than to the girl, for she had the occupation and distraction of preparing for Gwen's approaching marriage. Naturally, it was to be a great function, for if her admirers were legion, Dan's friends were many; besides, as everybody admitted, the bride and bridegroom alone would be worth going to see—worth remembering as a pattern pair of lovers. So the Tweedies were lending their house for the breakfast, which was to be a real breakfast, since the marriage was to take place so as to allow of a start by the cool morning mail, the regiment was lending its band for the wedding-march, and on this tepid October afternoon every garden in the place was sending white oleanders and tuberoses to the odd octagon church which had once been a Mahomedan tomb. Nay, more: one devoted though disappointed lover far down by some distant canal had sent, by special messenger, a great basket of belated white lotus lilies, with a request that they might be trodden on by the bride's happy feet.

Gwen, as she bent over this offering, sniffing at the faint almond scent of the huge jewelled flowers, was a gracious sight to look upon, for she had quite recovered herself, and, in sober truth, felt absolutely content. "How nice of the dear thing," she murmured, sweetly. And so it was—very nice. One might give it another epithet and say it was almost heroic; but of this Gwen Boynton had no conception, and never would have one. That side of human nature, its passion, its tears, its temptations, and its triumphs had been left out of her composition. She roused it, she played with it prettily in others, she even spoke warily and discreetly about it; yet Rose Tweedie, despite her girlish disdain, had more real sympathy with it than she.

Dan, meanwhile, in Lewis Gordon's office, disregardful of the lack of chairs, was kicking his heels as he sat on the table, declaring loudly that he would of a certainty break down in replying to the toast which was to be given at the club dinner in his honor that night. What the dickens did the fellows mean by giving him a dinner? What had he ever done for any of them? What had he ever been but a reckless, insubordinate, unsteady, loafing brute, who ought to have been kicked out of the service years ago?

"I expect they know their own minds," said Lewis, rather wearily. He had a headache; men have them as well as women, and he was telling himself it was liver, when he knew quite well it was not; a most unsatisfactory phase of depression, indeed, when even a blue-pill fails to hold out cheering hopes of recovery. Yet he spoke kindly, and patiently also, for he must have been of base clay indeed who would not have recognized that this man, transfigured on the summit of his hopes, was a worthy sight in a workaday world; that it was well to be there also. "Besides, I think I overheard Simpson saying something about a sick baby—"

"Oh, bad cess to the baby!" interrupted Dan, hastily. "Sure, it's a boy now, and one can't see a child die for the want of ice when your pony has four legs; more by token, it had but three for a month after, poor beast. But what's that to do with it? The fact is, it isn't so much that I'm too bad; it's the world that's too good, and that's the truth. When I think of all you fellows that have been so good and patient with me, my heart's broke about it entirely; and when I think of George, it's only Gwen's kind face— Oh, Gordon! what have I done that she should be going to marry me to-morrow?"

So he ran on, as many another man has run on—as most men, good and true, do run on when they are just about to marry the woman they love. And Lewis Gordon sat listening to him with a headache and a pain in his heart; for the most part thinking that if Rose could only see this man, only hear him, she might not be quite so disdainful of it all; might acknowledge that be it bad or good in its essence, it did step into a man's life for the first time and claim him body and soul, to the detriment of neither.

"And by-the-bye," said Dan, suddenly, "I've been meaning to ask you for a long time, but I wasn't sure if you'd like it. And now I'm going away for good and all, and you can't get out of being my best man, so I'll ask it: When are you going to marry Miss Tweedie?"

"Never!" replied Lewis, firmly, roused into instant resistance. "What put such a fancy into your head now?"

"Now?" Dan's face was a study in tender humor. "It's been in my head for the last year, and in yours too. I told Gwen so, I remember, before we went to Hodinuggar that time, and I could see by her manner she thought so also."

Lewis looked at him with an odd expression. "Then you were both mistaken, that's all. And, Fitzgerald, if you've quite done talking about yourself—I've a lot of work to finish, old chap—"

Dan laughed. "Well, I'll go. But it's true, Gordon, and she likes you—any one can see that."

True, absolutely true! Lewis acknowledged so much when he was left alone. The remembrance of it filled him now, as ever, with a glow of kindly emotion; and yet he was forced to acknowledge that he was not happy. The idyllic month had been charming, but the fortnight of absence had been less pleasing. What he felt now was something very different from the calm, contented confidence in their mutual friendship, though that remained as a thing apart; so that he could set the other aside, and think, with the old glow at his heart, of Rose. He had felt the other before, for other women—that restless, moody, selfish desire of appropriation. He could call it all these hard names, yet there it was, a palpable factor in his life, and he felt himself none the worse for it. And it was extremely natural; he had been thrown in the constant company of an extremely nice and rather nice-looking girl, and he had fallen in love with her. That was the plain truth. He gave a queer little grimace, and began to add up a column of figures. He would get over it, doubtless, as he had got over similar attacks in the past; at any rate, he was not going to let Rose know that, after all, he had failed to understand the absolute unconsciousness of her regard for him. Apart, even, from his pride, or from this thought of her wishes, his own seemed vaguely to resent this blending of his feeling for her with something which he had felt before for others. It seemed almost as if it would have been easier to go and tell her what had happened, if he could have kept it quite apart from their friendship; and he told himself, with a smile, that it would have been much simpler to send the barber round with proposals to her father; after all, there was an immense deal to be said for that side of the question. And then, in his careful, methodical manner, he began to add up the columns again. This time the total was different. He did it once more, and a fresh set of figures rewarded his industry. Then he threw the pen aside and faced himself resolutely. He had been doing atrocious work lately, and that was a fact! He had been thinking of Rose all day long—morning, noon, and night; and if this sort of thing was to go on, the sooner he took advantage of the many changes in the department consequent on Dan's going, and the usual cold-weather returns from furlough, in order to give up his present position, the better. There was nothing like breaking loose at once, and he was due some promotion. But if he had to do this, Rose ought to know. Why should she live in a fool's paradise? Why should she not face the facts of life as well as he? If she had been like other women, he would have made love to her and proposed, as a matter of course; but she was not like other women to him; or rather, all that he did know was that never by word or look or sign had she shown her knowledge even of the most elementary facts in life. How could you go to a girl like that and ask her to marry you straight off, especially when she had, as it were, insisted that romantic love had nothing to do with marriage? What could you do, save gloze over the question by phrases, by mixing it up with other things, and especially with that perfect, angelic, absolutely unselfish affection and regard which she had given him, and which he, apart from all this, felt for her? Still, it had to be done if he had to go away. Then, in common fairness to her and to himself, he must tell her that he was a fool, and that life was quite unendurable without her, since there was no other earthly reason why he should run away. And if all this had to be, there was no time like the present.

So, ten minutes after, he walked into the room where Rose sat making wedding-favors as for dear life, surrounded by a perfect *chevaux-de-frise* of white satin ribbons, bows, and flowers. The windows were set wide open on to the veranda, where great baskets of white flowers lay awaiting her final visit to the church. On the table lay the lotus-lily offering, with a note from Gwen to say they were too good to be trodden on, and would dear Rose see they were put on the altar, where they would look quite sweet. Wedding preparations everywhere; and Rose herself, in her white dress, her brisk hands flying about scissors, needle, and thimble, partook of the same unsympathizing connection with his purpose, making him say discontentedly, as he paused beside her to lean against the table, "I thought you didn't approve of wedding-favors." It was an opening of the siege at the very furthermost outworks of the position, which she frustrated by a laugh.

"Oh, it doesn't matter; other people seem to like them, and I've made you a beauty. There it is beside you on the table—you're almost sitting on it. Smell it—it's real orange blossom."

There was not a vacant chair, apparently, in the room. They were all occupied with white wreaths and true-lovers' knots; with a cross here and there, he was glad to see, as, still leaning against the table, he smelled perfunctorily at his own favor, and thought rather angrily of the utter inconsequence of the feminine mind. "I wish you would put that work down for a minute, Rose," he said, suddenly. "I have something I want to say to you, and it disturbs me."

Her hands paused, arrested among the white ribbons; her mind on the one word "Rose." He had never called her that before. So she sat looking at him expectantly, the light from the windows behind her edging the great coils of her hair with bronze.

"I have come to tell you that I'm a fool," he began, slowly, almost argumentatively. "At least I suppose it's foolish. I am quite ready to admit, if you like, that it is foolish; but the fact remains. I can't go on as we are—as we have been, I should say—any longer. You mustn't think it is because I don't understand your theory. I do; at least I think I do. You are a real friend, and will be that always, I hope; I don't say the best friend I ever had, or ever shall have, because that has nothing to do with the matter, and besides, there aren't any degrees in friendship; you have taught me that, at any rate. So I think you may admit I understand you in a measure—the question is if you'll understand me." He paused, and Rose's kind, shadowless eyes noted with a sudden shrinking back from the sight that his usual calm was broken by a palpable effort to steady his voice to prepare himself for what had to come! He felt, indeed, that he had not the least clew to the girl's mind, that he was absolutely taking a leap in the dark, and that what he had to say was in reality so foreign to every single word they had ever said to each other in the past that, even if she consented to marry him, he could not be sure if she meant it—if she would really understand what she was promising.

"Rose," he went on, "the fact is that I've fallen in love with—with you; and if you don't really want to marry me, I'd better go away. I would take an out-district for a time. I've had enough, perhaps too much, secretary work"—he seemed to take refuge in details from the main point, but she held him to it firmly, almost reproachfully.

"Why—why should you go away? she asked. "We were very happy, weren't we?" Her eyes had sought her hands among the white satin bows, but something in his tone brought them back to his face anxiously. Her theories were one thing, his happiness another; there could be no choice between them.

"Why?" he broke out, passionately, and as he went on his words, his voice, his manner, trembled in the fine balance between the humor of his explanation and its gravity—"ah! Rose, that's it—because I'm a fool, say you; because I'm a man, say I; because I love you, Rose; because I think of you when I ought to be thinking of other things; because I'm an idiot and have gone all to pieces; because it's torture to think you may go away and marry some one else; because I haven't even been able to add up a column of figures properly for wondering what you would say—what you will say now—now when I ask you to marry me." He had held out his hands towards her, in the growing passion of his appeal, as if deprecating her impatience, and, as he paused, hers came out to meet them and held them fast.

"Oh, Lewis!" she cried, impulsively, "what a wretch I've been. Why didn't you ask me before?"

"'Why—didn't—you—ask me before?'" he repeated, slowly, as if he could not believe his ears. The favors from her lap had fallen all round their feet, and those on the table were squashed remorselessly as he seated himself upon its edge with the air of a man who requires some physical support, and still holding her by the hands, drew her down beside him, looking at her in fond amazement. "I shall never understand you, dear, thank God!" he said, at last; then went on in a louder voice: "It is a little confusing, Rose, you must admit. All this time, ever since you told me that you—"

Her color came up then, fast and hot, and she interrupted his reminiscence sharply. "Oh! but that was a totally different thing altogether—"

"Totally different? Yes, I suppose so," he echoed, meekly; and then he paused again, his eyes on hers. "I suppose you would rather I didn't kiss you," he began, tentatively, when she again interrupted him—this time in a great hurry.

"Oh, I don't mind! it doesn't really matter—if you—you

like. Only don't talk nonsense, Lewis; please don't. I do hate it so; it makes me feel inclined to put my head in a bag."

"Then I won't; I can't afford to lose sight of your dear face just now."

"Lewis!"

"But if I am not to say that sort of thing, what are we to talk about?" he asked, but half in jest. "The weather? the news? Not very interesting topics, either of them, to a man when the girl he loves has just promised to marry him—for you have promised, haven't you, Rose?"

She took no notice of his question. "Talk about?" she echoed, her kind eyes growing a little absent. "Surely there are heaps of things to talk about besides you and me. There is the house we are going to have, Lewis; such a nice house! The prettiest drawing-room you ever saw. I will have it so; and a study for you all to yourself, sir, where you can go when you're tired of me. And then the dinners, Lewis! That's one blessing of my having kept house for father; I know all about it. There won't be any cold mutton, Lewis; but the nicest little dinners—" She paused to nod her head.

"Go on," said Lewis, falling in with her mood half-jestingly, "this is most interesting—most interesting and reassuring."

"Then the garden. I'll make you such a garden, Lewis! though I don't believe you know the difference between a carnation and a chrysanthemum. Never mind, you shall tie them up for me—I hate tying up flowers. And I'll copy your reports for you and keep the house quiet; and then—and then everybody will be so hungry, Lewis, and there will be so many bills to pay; but it won't matter, either, for every one will be happy, and the children will brag about their home, you'll see, to all the other girls and boys—"

"Go on, dear—go on." There was a little tremble in his voice now, and as she sat among the wedding-favors his right arm drew her closer to him, but she seemed not to notice it; a half-smile was on her lips, a certain sadness had come to her eyes.

"I don't know, then, dear; perhaps there will be trouble—who knows? and children die sometimes; but afterwards"—her voice took a more cheerful tone—"why then, dear, I'll grow stout—yes, I'm afraid I will—I'm the sort of girl, you know, who is apt to get stout — and you are sure to grow bald. Then I'll be cross, and you'll be cross; only it won't so much matter, for we will both be cross together; and no wonder, with the boys wanting cricket-bats, and the girls clamoring for music-lessons! So there will be more bills than ever. Then you and I will begin to get old, Lewis, and the girls will want me to sit up till three in the morning at balls, and I shall be so sleepy; but you shall stop at home and smoke, dear. And then the boys will get into scrapes—boys always do, don't they, Lewis?—they're not like girls, you know. And when they come to me to get them out of the troubles I shall say, 'No, dears, go to your father—for—for he is—the best man I ever—" Her voice ended in a little sob; he could feel it, hear it as if it were his own, for her face was hidden on his breast.

"Rose! Rose! my darling, my dear!" It was almost a cry. He would have liked to kneel before this love as he had done before the other, but with her there he could only hold her fast, and pray Heaven that in those long years to come it might be even as she had said, and that in word, thought, or deed he might never sully her pure wisdom.

So they sat silent—for, to tell truth, other words seemed to him sacrilege, and she had said her say—until, with a half-apologetic smile, she drew herself away decisively.

"I'm sure you are sitting on your favor, Lewis, and I've such a lot more to make, and I promised to go down to the church at half-past five. It must be that now, and I've wasted all this time."

"I've been here seven minutes and a half," he replied, gloomily, taking out his watch, "for I looked just before I came in."

She laughed. "Well, that was very methodical of you, and I think, on the whole, dear, that you managed very nicely.

And now, as I hear the carriage coming round, you might just help me to put in the flowers. Aren't the lotuses lovely?"

There was no help for it. She was hopelessly back in realities, and Lewis had to accept the position. After all, he acknowledged, as he watched her drive off, like a bride herself in the midst of her white flowers, she had managed to compress a great deal into those seven and a half minutes — a whole dream of life, which must, which should come true. It would be more difficult for him than for her, of course; perhaps that was one reason why he was still thinking over it long after she had forgotten everything else in the fervor of a free fight with the parson, who objected, on principle, to lotus blossoms in the chancel. They were a heathen flower, sacred to unmentionable beliefs and rites, and could not be admitted beyond the body of the church. It was but an offshoot of an old quarrel between these two, which renewed itself every Christmas and Easter; but Rose, who by instinct understood the story which these particular flowers had to tell, opened up the whole question of symbolism hotly, finally marching off with her lilies in a huff to the lectern, whence, she told herself, their message of love and sacrifice might fittingly go forth. And while she worked away under the echoing dome of the old tomb, the band in the bit of public garden close by was clashing and dashing away at "Rule Britannia" and "Ta-ra-ra, boom-de-ay," much to the delight of *ayahs* leading sallow, dark-eyed children by the hand, and a motley crowd of servants and shopkeepers from the neighboring bazaar.

Sometimes, drawn by an anatomy of a horse, a green box on wheels, with four or five specimens of Tommy Atkins and a black bottle inside, would come rattling past, and leave a shower of jokes and greetings behind it for those other green boxes on wheels driven up beside the road, while the gayly-dressed occupants chewed betel, or strolled about with clanking feet among the long shadows thrown by the flowering shrubs. Light and laughter and noise; a whole eternity of time and space between this life and the girl under the dome, decorating the Bible with lotus blossoms.

"There's going to be a big *shadi* (wedding) in the *girja ghur* (church) to-morrow morning," said a woman in tight mauve silk trousers, as she clambered back into the green box, where a figure in white lay listening lazily. "They are doing all sorts of *pooja* there to-day. It is that big long *sahib* in the canals and Boynton *sahib's* widow. *Ai*, the sorry tale! making a fuss of *shadi* about a woman who has had the misfortune to kill one man."

Chândni sat up suddenly. "*Tobah!* a sorry tale, for sure. So she is to marry him! Lo! there is a man, indeed; but I wonder what he would say if he knew what I know now?"

"Dost know aught? Dost know him?" began the other, enviously.

"I have seen him. He was down at Hodinuggar a week ago, putting up a white marble stone to the young *sahib* who died there of the sickness last rains. They were friends, see you—great friends. Lo! tell thy driver to go on, Lalu; this wearies me—the folk have no manners."

They had not far to go—only to the Badâmi bazaar, with its current of life below and its latticed balconies above. The full moon rose through the golden dust-haze, to hang like a balloon above the feathery crowns of the palm-trees, the clatter of horses' hoofs bearing their owners home to dinner died from the Mall hard by, and Rose stood at the door of the tomb, looking back into the shadowy dome, where the huge lilies showed like the ghosts of flowers. It would look very nice, she thought, in the cool light of early morning; she would have it just the same when she and Lewis were married.

But Chândni, as she paused to think of the future, thought of the past also. "He fought me fairly," she said to herself, "and for his beauty's sake I could bear more than he gave. This is our way. But she? Lo! she is even as I, and he shall know it. I will put that in the platter as the wedding-tribute, and it will help him to pay her for me. 'Tis almost as well I had not learned the tale from Dalel in those days. It comes better now."

So as the night fell she wrapped herself in the white domino of respectability, sent for another green box on wheels, and drove in the direction of the house where Dan was living. That was not difficult to discover—just a word to the general merchant who sold everything heart could desire in the shop below the balcony. And the night was warm; she would as lief sit in the moonshine, behind the hedge of white oleanders, and talk to the gardeners as stay in the stuffy bazaar, with its evening smells of fried meats and pungent smoke.

CHAPTER XXVII

"I WAS never so happy or so sorry in all my life before, and I thank Heaven that I'm enough of an Irishman still to say so without being laughed at."

He stood at one end of the table looking his best, as a gentleman always does in his evening dress — a curious fact, since there is no more cruel test for the least lack of good-breeding. But this man stood it triumphantly, and not one of those other men seated that night round the long table but carries to his grave a remembrance of Dan Fitzgerald's look when he was bidding good-bye to his friends. The eager vitality of the man — always his strongest characteristic — seemed to have reached its climax.

"I'm not going to say anything of her," he went on, the rich, round voice softening; "there isn't any need, since you all know her. Besides, though you have all come here to-night—why, I can't for the life of me tell—to wish us good-luck in the future, it isn't so much of the future I'm thinking as of the past. It has been so happy, thanks to you all; and it's over, that is the worst of it. I suppose it isn't quite what a man is expected to say on these occasions, but the ladies — God bless them — would, I'm sure, agree, if they could only be made to understand, that marriage is the end of a man's youth. It doesn't alter the case at all that it may be the end of the woman's also, or that we get something that may be as good in exchange. What has that to do with the past—the merry, careless past which I've enjoyed so much, and to which I'm now saying good-bye. Well, Heaven help those who say good-bye to it without a solid reason, or have a sneaking intention of not really saying good-bye to it at all; for their lives are in evil places. And that sounds like a sermon; and you never heard Dan Fitzgerald preach before, and you never will again. It isn't only that I'm off with the morning to the other end of the world—to a new world, if it comes to that, worth this old one, and the past, and all of you put together—if you'll excuse my saying so. It is because, even if I were stopping here, I should be out of the old life as surely as if I were dead and buried. To begin with, I shall have to think of every penny I spend, so that I may have enough to pay for Paradise! The world is full of paradoxes for me to-night, and I'm the greatest of them all myself; for I don't want to say good-bye, and yet I wouldn't miss having to say it for the world. Then it seems to me to-night as if I'd solved the great puzzle; and there's Doveton, the old bachelor, grinning as if he knew I was a fool, and that I was making the biggest mistake of my life. I don't think so—I don't think I shall ever think so; I hope not, anyhow. And so good-bye to you—good-bye! And may none of us, married or single, live to know the pain of a heart grown cold, a head grown gray—in vain!"

Down the disordered table, with its litter of glasses and flowers, its atmosphere heavy with the odors of dinner and drink, a hush lay for a second—not more. Then some one laughed, and, with a roar of applause—the general tone varying from concert pitch to normal diapason, according to the taste of the owner—struck into the old chorus: the refrain which, touching as it does the lowest and the highest ideals of humanity, has provoked more mixed sentiment and emotion than any other in the language:

"*For he's a jolly good fel-low,*
For he's a jolly good fel-low!"

Love, admiration, assent; but towards—what? That lies in the creed of the singer. And Dan, as the chorus went swaying and surging about in the discords and harmonies, was left alone—silent, as it were, on a pinnacle. Lewis Gordon, feeling responsible for his man and noting his growing excitement, inveigled him out, after a time, for a quiet cigar in the veranda, and then suggested he should go to bed. Whereat Dan laughed softly, and asked if his best man did not see that the idea was palpably absurd when life itself was a dream — a dream that only came once to a fellow; when you hadn't a wish ungratified, save, of course, that some others you wot of might have as good-luck as you had.

"If you mean me," replied Lewis, stolidly, "I'm all right. I am going to marry Rose Tweedie whenever she can spare five minutes from your wedding to arrange mine."

"You don't say so! By the powers! what a good matchmaker I am. And so it is settled. I say, Gordon, do you think there is any chance of her being up still?" put in Dan, all in one breath.

"Couldn't say; she had a lot of favors to make — and remake — when I last saw her, certainly," replied Lewis, with an inward smile at the remembrance, "but you can't go and call on her now; it's half-past ten at least."

"Can't I? There is nothing I couldn't do to-night, it seems to me. And *you* are yawning. Oh, go to bed, old man, or you will spoil the show to-morrow."

"And you?"

"I'm off, too, but not to bed. No, you needn't be afraid; I'll turn up again in time."

The glamour of the soft Indian night was on Lewis also; even on those who, one by one, drifted out from the laughter within to stand for a few minutes arrested by the peace without before going on their way. And, if this were so to men in the slack-water of life, what must it have been to Dan on the flood-tide of his threescore years and ten?—to Dan, with his vivid imagination, his soft heart, his excitable, impulsive nature? As he rode along noiselessly at a footpace through the sandy dust, which looked hard as marble in the glare of the moon, he and his shadow were the only moving things in that world of light. There was no darkness anywhere, not even in the distant arcades of trees—nothing but a soft gray mist of moonlight, blending all things into the semblance of a mirage seen from afar. A fire-fly or two flickered against the flowering shrubs in intermittent glimpses of light—here a moment, then gone; and far and near, like the beating of a heart, the soft quiver of the insistent cicadas in the air. Was not life worth living indeed, if only for such a night as this?

"*On such a night did young Lorenzo—*"

But Dan Fitzgerald had passed beyond even that flood-mark on the shore. Passion, it is true, counted for much in that elation of mind and body which was the apotheosis of both; but love counted for more, and the memory of a thousand griefs and pains with pity hidden in their hearts, came to fill the mystic cup of life which the Unseen, Unknown Hand held out to him from Heaven — the Sangreal of Humanity, the sacrament of Birth and Death. The child dying of the potter's thumb-mark in the dust; that other in loving arms, with the ice chilling even Death's cold touch; George, with the bullet piercing the devotion in his heart; Rose, with her pure wisdom fearless and unashamed — these and many another remembrance seemed to blend sorrow and joy into peace, even as the moon-mist blended the world around him into vague beauty. And there was Rose herself. He could see her, as, with the easy friendliness of India, he paced his pony through the open gates of the garden, and so past the house. She was still at work among the white flowers beside the door, which was set wide upon the warm, balmy night.

"Is that you, Mr. Fitzgerald?" she called, pausing at the faint sound of his coming to look out into the flood of moonlight, clear as noonday.

"It is I, Miss Tweedie." He had slipped from his pony, and stood beside it welcoming her with outstretched hands, as she came forth eager with some message for the morrow which he might deliver.

"Lewis has told me, and I'm so glad," he said, breaking in on her words. "It's the best wedding-present I've had yet, and I came along on the chance of seeing you. I've something to give you. I meant it for to-morrow, as a parting gift—just a remembrance of your kindness to us both. But I'd rather give it to you with our best wishes." He unfastened something from his own wrist and put it, soft and warm, into her hand.

It was a native armlet, cunningly twisted of silk thread and pearls, with a triangle of some blue stone strung in the centre. "'Tis only a glorified *râm rukhri*," he went on, half-jestingly —"the bracelets, you know, that sisters give their brothers to bring them good-luck; only it is the other way with you."

Rose looked at the blue of the triangle doubtfully, then at his kindly face.

"Yes! it's a bit of the Ayôdhya pot—the only bit that wasn't in pieces. And it has my name on the back and—and George's."

"And George's!" echoed Rose, softly.

"Aye. He would have liked it, I know; for you were kind to him — kind to us both always, *Mâdr-mihrbân*—as the old potter called you. And we two, George and I, are one part of the story. I was thinking of it as I came along just now—"

She put out her hand with a sudden gesture. "Don't think of it, Mr. Fitzgerald; forget all about it. Go away and forget."

He gave a happy laugh. "Why should I? I don't want to forget anything to-night, except my sins; the rest is all good. Let me put that on for you—so. Good-night! We'll say good-bye to-morrow."

He was out again a minute after on the deserted roads with the same happy unrest in his heart. He would go down and see the old familiar places in the garden opposite once more; even the pond where the ducks and geese had quacked and gabbled him into silence. So, through the hanging tassels of the tamarisk-trees, round the gleaming white road to the blue-tiled minarets of the old watch-tower standing causelessly upon the level plain where four ways met. Then back again, stationwards, to the stunted dome of the church. The throbbing of tom-toms proclaimed the nearness to the bazaar; but the building itself stood unassailably silent and deserted on its high white plinth. Only a string bed, set in a shadow by the door, with some one lying on it. Dan slipped from his pony again, and hitched the reins to a broken iron clamp in the stone-work of the steps. The doors he knew would be open to let in the cool night air. He would look in—go round the course—as a horsy friend of his had said when discovered doing the same thing before his marriage. The remembrance made him smile as he stepped into the dark building and paused, arrested by the strangeness of what he saw. The dome was full of fire-flies brought thither in the flowers; full of a ceaseless glimpsing of pale green fires, showing for an instant the white hearts of the fading blossoms. The air was burdened with scent, yet, distinct through it all, came a faint, deadly smell of bitter almonds; that must be from the lotus Gwen had mentioned. There they were, in the shaft of moonlight through the upper window, standing like sentinels over the lectern.

"*Om mâni padina hom!*" What did it really mean, that invocation used by so many millions of worshippers? What was the mystic jewel in the lotus? Something fair but far, no doubt, such as all religions promise; and then with a rush came the thought that Gwen would stand beside them on the morrow, fair and near!

The echo of his pony's galloping feet made that throbbing in the bazaar pause an instant as if to listen—pause and go on when he had passed. The darkened houses of his friends rose up and were left behind him, the club with its still-twinkling arches, the garden where Chândni sat gossiping, waiting for her chance to kill his faith wantonly. All these he passed, for awake or sleeping he must be near Gwen for an instant, must bid her good-night before the day came.

The chiming, echoing gong from the secretarial office rang twelve clear; then the others began, here and there from other centres of law and order, many-voiced from the massive pile of the distant city. He was too late, then, yet not too late; for there was a light still in the little front-room, now despoiled of its prettiness and littered with boxes. She was awake, busy like Rose, over the morrow.

"Gwen!" he called to her softly, for the *chick* was down, the door half closed.

"My dear Dan!" Her voice, as she opened it and came hurriedly into the veranda, was full of amused horror, half-vexed kindness. "Do go away, there's a dear! I never heard of such a thing, never! And the hotel is crammed full of people!"

"Sure, it is only to wish you many happy returns of the day, dear!" he whispered, fondly. "When I've done that I'll go away content—

"'*Ah, the jewel in the lotus, the Buddhist formula.*'

Who wouldn't be content, with you, Gwen? And yet I wouldn't spare an inch of it all—I couldn't. Gwen, do you remember the day when your bearer was cleaning the lamps out here, and we were sitting on the sofa?—Odd, isn't it, how one remembers these things all in a jumble, the one with the other; and I said to you—the very words come back to me, dear, every one of them, 'You might be bankrupt of everything, Gwen, of everything save yourself, and I'll give you credit for it all the same.' Do you remember, dear? Well I've come to take the promise back. You've spoiled me, Gwen, I can't do it."

"I—I don't understand," she said, faintly; "I wish you would go, Dan, we can talk of it to-morrow—afterwards."

"To-morrow? Sure, it's to-day already—our wedding-day! and if I can't keep the promise, am I not bound to take it back while I can? Not that I'm afraid—that is why I've come to tell you, the selfish brute that I am. That is why I want it all—every scrap of your beauty, your goodness. I'll take nothing less, dear, now, for I know it's yours, and what is yours will be mine, by right."

She had grown very pale, and a sort of terror came into her eyes. "O Dan! what is the use of talking! I give you all I can—my best. I can't do more, and it isn't kind—" She broke off almost impatiently, and yet she did not move from his clasp.

"Not kind, when I know what the best means? And yet, Gwen, it just comes upon me that I couldn't stand it—if—if it were not true! Not after this Midsummer-Night's Dream!—of madness if you will. Yes, dear, I'm going—I am indeed. But Gwen—it's an idle fancy, and yet—if there was anything it would be better to tell me now. You're not angry at the thought—it's only a thought. See, give me one kiss—just one—to be an answer for always."

One kiss! A Judas kiss! No! no! What right, she asked herself, fiercely, had she to hesitate? What possible right, standing, as she did, on the threshold of a new life, *where no one could possibly know?* She herself was back in the low levels among the ordinary considerations of convenience and safety as she kissed him, but the touch of her lips sent *his* blood surging through his heart and brain. Without another word, another look, he turned and left her—content, absolutely content. Love, friendship, pity, passion, had all combined to raise him to the uttermost limit of vitality. He might come near it, perhaps, in the future; but he was not likely ever to reach it again, not even if there had been no Chândni waiting to tell him the truth about the key, on his return to the old little house right at the other end of the station.

He was so lost, so mazed in his own happiness, that he neither knew nor cared where he was going; but his pony, feeling a free rein and tired of these incomprehensible wanderings, set its galloping hoofs on the shortest way home—that is to say, through the densely-wooded grounds of the Residency. So, dashing along a grassy ride or two, across a short cut, Dan by degrees forgot even his joy in the keen effort of steering a runaway through the trees; a runaway unheld, free to go as fast—nay, faster—than it chose, yet obedient to that grip to right or left. A mad ride—a mad rider; yet a masterful one: will wrestling imperiously with brute force, as the trees thicken and the gloom grows, bringing darkness and danger together; the dark heat of a past day imprisoned here by the dense foliage above. Dan, looking down at the pony's heaving flanks, as it paused, wearied with its short, sharp, unavailing struggle against his strong hands, felt flushed and hot; not wearied—he could not be that on such a night—but glowing, palpitating, excited—drunk, almost, as if with wine. But yonder stood a remedy in that low, long, thatched roof, supported on brick pillars, and hung round with heavy bamboo screens.

Dan laughed as he slid to the ground, thinking of the twelve feet of clear cool water running fresh and fresh into one end of the big swimming-bath, out at the other to irrigate the green levels of the garden. Fresh and fresh all through the scorching summer weather, when life held no greater pleasure than to feel that cool water close round the hot limbs. Frequented then, morning and evening; but deserted, empty, through the colder months. Only the day before, Dan's smooth, dark head had come up from its depths rejoicing, and now the thought of it was luxury itself, when the blood was beating in his temples and racing at fever-heat through his veins. More than once, coming home at night after careless, reckless enjoyment, he had stopped here, as he did now, to try the water-cure—as he had tried it in the canal at Hodinuggar.

"Sure, I need it to-night, if ever I did," he said, half aloud; "'tis the wine of life has got into my head."

Dark, almost too dark, inside. That was because the fools had put down all the screens when they should be opened by night, to let in the fresh air. He told himself that he would speak to the secretary about the caretaker's neglect, and then he smiled; how could that be, since he would never see him again? Yes, it was for the last time; and how many times had he not gone sizzling down red-hot from the spring-board, as he would do in a minute or so, to come up out of the dark water a new man, with all the evil tempers and the prickly-heat quenched out of him. Sure, as a regenerating element, fire wasn't in it with water! A leap in the dark, indeed! but that was life itself, and he was not afraid of it.

The little bars of moonlight shining through the chinks between the bamboos lay so far on the smooth white floor, and then came a soft, dark chasm, and above it Dan poised for a second.

"I come, Mother of all!" The old, oft-repeated cry rang joyously up into the roof.

Then followed a strange dull thud, and silence; dead silence. For the bath had been emptied that morning for the cold weather, and Dan Fitzgerald was lying, face downward, on the hard cement with a broken neck. Dead! Dead without a word, a sigh, or a regret. And Chândni, tired of patience, went home to the bazaar grumbling at her ill-luck, telling herself she might still write, if it were worth while.

But Dan was beyond her spite, beyond other things which, even without that spite, might have killed the best part of him. Yet, even in romance, the sixth commandment outweighs all the others. The novelist may maim and degrade, may bear false witness against his own creations, and filch from them the very characteristics which he has given them in order to make degradation happy; but he must not kill, since death, even to those who believe in another life, is the worst tragedy in this. Such, at any rate, seemed to be the verdict of most people when, in the early morning, the gardeners, coming to their work, found Dan's pony browsing, half asleep, still tethered to one of those hibiscus-bushes, whose great blossoms, in topsy-turvy fashion, show rosy-red in death and snowy-white in life.

It was terribly sad, an unredeemed tragedy, cruel! needless!—a dispensation of Providence needing much true Christian faith—one of the accidents of life, so exasperating because so causeless, so inartistic because so unnecessary. These, and many other comments, the mourners made, as, the funeral over, they returned home; and so, it being Sunday morning, they straightway went to church and sang "Jerusalem the Golden" piously.

Only Rose Tweedie lingered, her kind, soft hands laying the dead lotus blossoms like sentinels on the grave; for Gwen's prim white cross of gardenia had, at her request, been buried on the coffin.

"I can't somehow be so sorry," said the girl to Lewis, between her sobs; "he was so happy that last night. I seem to see his face still."

But the man caught his breath in hard. There was a verse which would ring in his ears and his heart; for he had helped to lift poor Dan, and it had come to him then—

"Like a potter's vessel."

Yet, what did it matter? A little sooner, a little later; that was all the difference. Yet, Rose must never know; in such things he would stand between her and needless pain.

And Gwen? She, as the phrase goes, bore up wonderfully. Not that she did not love the dead man dearly, but because she did love him. Odd as it may seem, somewhat topsy-turvy, perhaps, like the hibiscus flowers, she had the same consolation as Rose Tweedie had.

"I did not tell him," she said to herself, as she lay in her darkened room. "He was happy to the last. I did my best—I did my best."

So she cried softly; so once more she escaped from her own remorse, and was comforted.

CHAPTER XXVIII

Both for the reader's and the writer's sake, it is never fair to end a story as you would a play—in a situation; for the former tries—vainly, it may be—to present life, even in its trivialities; the latter, only in its more dramatic moments. So, though there is little more to tell, save what might easily be filled in by the reader's imagination, it would give a false impression of the real value of poor Dan Fitzgerald's tragic death were the curtain to come down on the rest of the *dramatis personæ* in the first bewilderment and sorrow which such unexpected and causeless accidents must always arouse. As a matter of fact, there is no grief that passes sooner from daily life than that caused by death, especially when a real and unselfish love has existed between the dead and the living. The mind, after the first physical sense of loss has spent itself, refuses to believe in the extinction of a feeling which, in its own experience, has survived death, and is comforted, not by forgetfulness, but by remembrance. Besides, it is false art to end any history embracing the life of more than one person with the balance in favor of pain. For were this so in reality, pain would cease to be pain, and would become pleasure, because it would then be the normal condition of life; since it is clearly to be demonstrated, physiologically and psychologically, that it is in the disintegration of reminiscent habit that the phenomena of pain arise. Indeed, in the mind pain is incredible, impossible, before we have first formed the habit of pleasure, since it consists essentially in privation.

Therefore, the novelist who wishes to give a true picture of life will always leave his puppets fairly happy. Nor does this limit his field unduly, since it is clearly as much the duty and privilege of the writer to present new forms of content to his readers, as it is for him to present them with scenes, or situations, or characters of which they have no previous knowledge. Because Jones thinks the soul of bliss is incarnate in roast beef and plum-pudding, is that any reason why the more ethereal Brown should be denied his cup of nectar, or that the philosophic Robinson, seeing that birth and death are alike inscrutable phenomena, should refuse to believe empirically that the one is joyful and the other sorrowful? "Oh, don't kill him, or her, or them," say the public, cheerfully; "let them enter into life, halt, or maimed, and blind. What does anything matter so long as they have the average number of breakfasts, luncheons, and dinners allotted to humanity, and can go down to their graves in the fulness of time with the pleasing consciousness that their funeral cortege is followed by a Noah's Ark consisting of the ghosts of the animals they have devoured?" For the world sides with Esau, who bartered his birthright for a mess of pottage. And good pottage is warming, comforting, consoling; for all that the two hundred and seventy millions of India seldom see it; and yet they are happy. But, then, to them birth and death are alike the pivot on which the wheel of life turns.

So thought the potter of Hodinuggar. So had thought his fathers who lay buried in the dust beside him, and though the old man had no son to step on to the treadles when his feet slipped from them, the wheel spun steadily, and the women of the village, as they rung the temper of the water-jars before they bought them, nodded their heads, saying: "Fuzl is a good potter. Look you, it comes with a man's birth. When he goes, we shall have to send for another. Miroo thinks he can make them because the *sirkar* taught him when he was three years in jail for cattle-thieving. But it takes more than three years to make a potter."

Still Fuzl Elâhi showed no signs of going; on the contrary, he seemed to have a firmer hold on life than ever, as if time had stood still for him. Rose Gordon remarked on it to her husband as they sat side by side on the old log. They had been married nearly a year, and he had brought her out for change of air on one of his inspection tours; for he had given up the secretaryship on his marriage, in favor of greater quiet and more freedom.

"It is so strange, Lewis," she said, "you and I being here again—and yet we have all changed—everything and every one has changed! Even the palace scarcely looks the same with that dreadful sort of Swiss chalet Dalel has built for Beatrice Norma tacked on the ruins of the old tower. And George and Dan are dead, and the water is running in the cut yonder as if there had never been any tragedy about preventing it from running there. Yet the village with the potter sitting in the topmost house is just the same."

Lewis Gordon smiled. "You never read Megasthenes' account of his travels through India in the year 300 B.C., or you wouldn't be surprised. It might have been written to-day; for these people do not change, except under pressure from without, and then they disintegrate suddenly. But the old man seems to me more sane than he was; more at rest. No doubt Azîzan's death—"

The familiar name caught the potter's ear, and he looked up from his work. "Yes; she sleeps still, *huzoor*. The breaking of the pot did not disturb her at all; she was weary, see you, after sixteen years of walking. So now when my fathers say, 'Where is Azîzan?' I can answer, 'Hush! she sleeps! she will awaken when she is refreshed.' Lo! it is well the pot broke; it was accursed—bringing ill to all."

"There, you see, Lewis!" began Rose, eagerly.

"It did not bring ill-luck to me, dear," he replied, interrupting her, "and a man can but judge from his own experience. And then, as I have told you, we really know nothing for certain—"

"Except," put in Rose, obstinately, "that poor George—"

"Don't you think we ought to be moving," said he, quietly; "remember you promised Mrs. Dalel to have tea in the chalet and inspect the son and heir. You are tired enough as it is."

"But you said you wanted to go and see some slope or another, and I'm not the least tired," she insisted, when they had left the yard and reached the road. "Lewis, you never used to fuss this way; I wish you wouldn't."

"It is only another method of showing my real views on the mental and physical calibre of women. You must have read, my dear, of the wonderful recuperative power which the lower animals have of reproducing another tail when— But, by-the-way, this is not a safe spot; I remember saying something of the same sort on purpose to annoy when we were here before—" He paused, and looked down the narrow valley of the village to where the palace was beginning to share the unreal beauty which the dust-cloud from the feet of the homing cattle gave to the whole scene. Like a golden mist it hid the dull plain, and lent distance and height to the low sand-hillocks behind which the sun was setting cloudlessly. A glorious sight; the dignity and calm majesty of which lingers long in the memory of those who have seen it in India, day after day, month after month; lingers to claim a higher place in the imagination than the more varied and complex sunsets of the West, with their stormy contrasts and passionate beauty.

"Leave me here," she said, suddenly. "I should like it. "I'll sit on that pile of old potsherds and wait till you come back. It will rest me." Peaceful enough of a certainty! Only every now and again came the tinkle of a low-toned bell from some leader of the herds below, chiming in on the musical moan of the potter's wheel heard over the low wall—

"*It was a woman seeking something.*"

The rhythm came back to her, stirring the old sense of curious interest; stirring it in others of her sex also, if one might judge by the eyes which, seeing the stranger alone, began to peer from the neighboring hovels. Deep-bosomed mothers, most of them, with a slim girl or two doing nurse-maid to other folks' babies.

Nearer and nearer they came, attracted by the great feminine quality, until, in answer to Rose's nods of welcome and encouragement, they squatted near yet far, gathered in as it were upon themselves, apart even from that other woman; even from her, with the cares of coming motherhood writ clear upon her, and making her look at those other mothers with kindly, friendly eyes.

"*Ari bahin,*" said one, with a nudge to her neighbor. "'Tis for sure she that played bat and ball last year like a boy. *Wah!* that is over; she knows her work now."

"I trow not," replied another, shrilly. "She hath been sitting with the potter's eyes upon her this half-hour past. She is bad, caring but for her pleasure."

"Mayhap she knows not," said an older voice, "and they have no mothers, these ones, nor mothers-in-law. Yea; 'tis true. My man went to dig for the *sahibs* the year there was no corn in the land, and he hath told me. They marry of themselves, and there is none to see to them that they fall not into ignorant mischief. It is fool's work."

"No mothers-in-law!" tittered a bold-faced lump. "*Ai teri!* that is no fool's work."

But the elder woman had risen, to stand a few steps nearer Rose, looking down at her with dignified wonder. "May the Lord send a son," she began, going to the very root of the matter without preamble.

"I will take whichever He chooses to send me, mother," replied Rose, smiling.

"Tra—ra—" The matron's pliant forefinger wagged sideways in that most impressive gesture of denial which is never seen out of India. "Mention not such things, my daughter," went on the grave voice, "lest He take thee at thy word; then what wouldst thou say? And see!—go no more to the potter's yard; it is not safe. Wouldst have the son come to thee with his mark on the breast? I trow not."

They had come forward one by one to cluster round the speaker, their dark, assenting eyes on Rose. "'Tis not to be helped, though," put in another. "Do I not know—I, Jewun, whose son died of it last year? Yet I remembered the old ways and my mother's counsel. Lo! it is fate; nought else. And 'tis better to crack and be done with it. Then folk know. Not like my new milk-jug this day, sound to sight and touch, yet six good quarts of milk spilled on the ground as it crumbled like sand ere a body could put a hand to it. The old man shall give me another in the place of it. It is not fair."

"Nay, Mai Jewun," put in a third, "the pots come to pieces ever. If not one, then another way, when it is tired of going to the well for water. Thou hast nought to complain about. *Ai*, sisters! hither returns the *sahib!* He will be angry that we have spoken to his *mem.*"

"He will not be angry," protested Rose; but the thought was beyond them. They were off swiftly, yet sedately, only the elder woman pausing to waggle her finger again. "Go not to the potter's. It is not well. I, Juntu, mother of seven, say so."

There were tears in Rose's eyes when Lewis came up, and, in consequence, he did look angrily at the retreating figures. She was pale and tired, he said, and must send an excuse to Mrs. Dalel. He would not have her knocking herself up with other folks' infants. So they went back quietly to the two white tents standing beyond the Mori gate, where the pigeons, as of old, circled iridescent round the dark niches. As of old, too, the clash of silver anklets came from the shadows, for Chândni was back in her old quarters and with a recognized position, Her Highness Beatrice Norma Elfrida, being a shrewd little person, knowing that she would need help to hold her own amid the intrigues of that surely coming long minority which lay in the future. For it is a recurring fraction, that long minority, in the problem of our dealings with petty principalities and powers, since civilization does not conduce to longevity with the native noblemen. Besides, Dalel, with the income from the stud-farm, was diligently burning his feeble little constitution at both ends—on the sly, however; for virtue, to all outward appearances, reigned at Hodinuggar. Only that morning Rose had inspected a female school—rows on rows of nice little girls, with very clean primers and brand-new slates; a brand-new visitors' book, too, in which Rose, with misgivings, had inscribed her name, tacked on to a trite remark about the blessings of education, for she was only just beginning to make up her bundle of opinions.

But that night, as he was carefully guiding her steps through the maze of ropes and pegs to the door of the sleeping-tent, she paused suddenly to say to her husband: "Lewis, I'm glad we came here. I thought it would be so painful, seeing George's deserted grave and reviving the old memories; but it has only seemed to make it all more natural—to make everything, somehow, more simple."

This, then, was what the years were bringing to Rose. She and Lewis were very happy; though sometimes, especially when they were out in camp together, he would enter a feeble protest against her lack of sentiment—perhaps when, after work and dinner were over, they sat beside the stove, the mingled lamplight and firelight making the tent cosey beyond belief, and he, laying down the volume from which he was reading aloud, would remark, for the hundredth time, that Rose was like one of his favorite heroines.

"If you say those stupid things, Lewis," she would reply, "I will make you read shilling shockers."

"Oh, it is all very well to scoff," he would continue, in injured tones, "but I am the victim of unrequited attachment. You are the heroine of my romance, always, and you never had a romance at all."

"Well, dear, that is better than having one with some one else, isn't it?" she would answer, placidly, and Lewis's hand would reach out to touch the one which was so busy with needle and thimble and thread—just to touch it for an instant, in a certain shamefaced, deprecating acknowledgment of her wisdom. For he knew quite well that he, like most men, had had several romances in his life, and that the possibility of several more still remained in him.

Whether the climax of Rose's dream of the future ever came about and the boys got into scrapes cannot be told, for Lewis himself is still within the torrid zone of life; but he does his best to prepare for the crisis, and he follows his wife's lead in this: that he finds life more simple and less sad as time goes on, and he faces its facts less egotistically.

Gwen Boynton, however, found it quite the reverse. She

married Colonel Tweedie two years after Dan's death, having, she said, buried all thoughts of personal happiness in the grave of the only man she had ever loved. This, as usual with Gwen's remarks, was true in itself, and yet left her free to marry for position without remorse; or, rather, accurately speaking, to utilize her regret as a motive for doing as she wanted to do without remorse. So she made Colonel Tweedie an excellent wife, much to his delight and comfort; for, as Rose acknowledged, he sorely needed some one to keep him from fussing when she had gone to perform the same kind office for Lewis. Nevertheless, Gwen Boynton, when she came back to society, after the shock of Dan's death, had lost some of her charm; and from being a fascinating woman had become elegant and interesting, as befitted one with a history. Life, she said, was so mysterious, Humanity a mere shuttlecock in the hand of Fate, beaten backward and forward by devastating passions! Altogether the world was a sad sojourning, in which a vague mysticism was the only anodyne for the sensitive. She became a half-hearted disciple of Madame Blavatsky, and reached what may be called the climax of her kindly, absolutely untrustworthy nature when, with tears in her eyes, and much gentle, mournful resignation to the mysterious Inevitable, she would tell the story she had heard from Rose, of how Dan Fitzgerald and George Keene had been measured for heroes in the potter's yard, and of their sad deaths within the year. Of course it was incredible—and yet?

Thus, none of the actors in the little drama ever knew the whole truth about it. Gwen had the best chance, so far as facts went, but she, being handicapped by her method of vision, failed to see her real part in the tragedy. For she resolutely set aside the possibilities of that hour during which her *dandy* waited outside the dress-maker's. And then she knew no more than the rest of that other key to the position which lay in Azîzan's love for George. Perhaps this remained hidden even from him, though every night, winter and summer, an odd little light, like a lost star, twinkled on the summit of the shadowy mound of Hodinuggar. It was the oil cresset which the old potter put nightly on Azîzan's grave to prevent her from having bad dreams. The branded-brick bungalow was deserted and empty, now that the sluice-gate required no guarding, so there was no one to see its feeble, persistent light. For all that, it could be seen distinctly from the little enclosure where, on a white marble stone, the legend ran that here lay

St. George Keene,

Aged Twenty-one,

Who Died at His Post of Cholera.

And between the two graves the gleaming streak of the big canal lay like a sword, splitting the world into East and West.

THE END